Whispered Moon

Book One of The Sacred Moon Series

C. Hazlewood

C Hazlewood Author LLC

This is dedicated to my amazing husband.

Prelude

"Announcing, your future king and queen of the Lycanthropy and all the realm…"

The crowd erupted into cheers, gazing upon the striking beauty that will soon be their queen. She was poised and elegant. Everything a monarch should be. No one could take their eyes away from the smiling goddess who just wed the future king of their kingdom.

Only I am staring numbly at the one beside her. The man who was once my fated mate.

His hard stare was on me, his steady topaz eyes boring into my muted blue ones.

We might be the only two in this whole hall not rejoicing at this news. Me, because I feel too numb to keep up appearances, and him, because I'm sure he can sense my presence.

He told me not to come, but I had to see for myself. I had to see the woman that was deemed good enough when I was told relentlessly for the past few months that a werewolf could never measure up to a Lycan monarch.

It wasn't just that I was a werewolf. The difference between this woman and myself was painfully obvious. She looked regal in every way, whereas I was wearing the same combat clothes I had trained in this morning.

I felt someone's presence behind me, but I didn't break my gaze away from his. I couldn't just yet.

"Don't blame him, Miss. he loves you, but he has his reasons."

Basil, his aide, managed to find me in the crowd and whispered in my ear.

I know. I know he had to do this for the good of the kingdom.

I know his father gave him no choice. It was either accept this arrangement to make another Lycan of the council's choosing his Luna, or the crown would be passed down to his incompetent brother.

I would not wish that on any subject in these lands. Lukyan was far better suited to rule than his playboy sibling. His brother himself never wanted to take on those heavy responsibilities. Casimir would rather bed every woman in the kingdom than step up to rule. The kingdom would fall apart in the matter of weeks.

I didn't blame Lukyan for any of what was happening before me. What I did blame him for are all the nights of promises and false hope, all lies to keep me by his side when he knew there was never a chance.

"I understand," I replied to the nervous aide beside me.

Basil kept fidgeting beside me.

"He asks that you return to your room and wait for him, Miss Alesta. He will come to you as soon as he can."

I nodded, tearing my eyes away from Lukyan to watch as the aide nervously retreated back, slipping through the crowd to no doubt report back to my mate... my former mate, that I agreed to wait for him.

But I had no plans to wait. I had no hope of a future here any more. Not for me, and not for....

I gently placed my hand over my lower abdomen, trying not to let my anger spill from my eyes.

If the council hears of this.... If his parents were to hear of this....

If his new Luna found out that I was carrying his child, a child that will grow and become a threat to any child she were to have for the right to the throne....

The last and only hope I had of keeping a part of Lukya' myself would be taken from me. I'd be left with nothing to he. on to.

No, I will not be going back to my room to be hidden away as a mistress until the inevitable happens. I will not suffer and put my body through the torture of feeling him consummate this marriage.

This was my last goodbye to all the dreams he once whispered to me in pretty little lies. This is my final goodbye to him before I run. Run to a better future for me and my child.

Chapter 1

Unexpected Surprise

Two days prior...

"**S**hit," Niccola stared at my hands, cut and bleeding from training. He hissed under his breath, "Prince Lukyan is not going to be happy when he sees this."

"No kidding," I laughed humorlessly, trying and failing to get the bleeding to stop by wiping my palms down the front of my pants. All I did was ruin my favorite pair of light gray leggings and cause the wounds to open more.

"Don't do that!" Niccola grabbed my hands, examining the cuts. "Why aren't they healing?"

I knew why. I knew why the second I saw Chrisley snickering on the sidelines. She was exempt from the worst of the training, thanks to the fact she was fucking one of the commanders of the purist faction. She wouldn't get punished for spreading wolf's bane pollen on the rough boulders that me and half a dozen other werewolf tributes were told to push across an open field.

She was a Lycan tribute, unlike me. Lycan tributes were treated better for the sole reason they were born a different species. Werewolves were considered less than, since we shifted into actual wolves instead of the monstrous Lycan form.

I could rip Chrisley's smug little face right off her superior Lycan body. I've proven multiple times while training.

That's one of the reasons I constantly had a target on my back. The other reason was more complicated, though when it boiled down to it, it was very simple.

"We have to get you to the medic before you go back." Niccola started to push me towards the medical tent.

"It's fine. It just has to bleed out a bit then it can start to heel," I tried to argue.

"Nuh, uh. You saw how insane the prince's beast became when you were hurt last time. We barely managed to cover that up. If your secret gets out...."

Niccola left the thought hanging in the air. I knew what he was trying to say. I knew what would happen if the purist faction found out that their future king was fated mates with a lowly werewolf. My hands wouldn't be the only thing bleeding. They would have my head by any means necessary.

The only one in this camp who knew was Niccola, and only because he was there when Lukyan and I first met. We were the last of the tributes to arrive at the castle. Both of our packs were the furthest from here.

Tributes have to swear into service directly to the Lycan royals. When I first arrived at the castle gates, I was ushered along with Niccola to the ceremonial hall to meet the king and queen themselves. King Nabian and Queen Teraphine were sitting on their thrones, their sons standing at either side of them.

As instructed, I kept my head bowed, not making eye contact until I heard the command to lift my head. I felt a piercing gaze on me though, and chanced a glance up in the royals' direction. My eyes only locked with Lukyan's for a second, and it took my breath away. I had to quickly look back down, but I wasn't able to avert my gaze for long

He didn't let me.

Nerves were already buzzing through my skin, so I didn't realize what was happening until Lukyan was upon me. He took me in his arms and snarled in my ear that one little word with such a big impact on one's life.

"Mate."

His nose was on my nape, and his tongue began to lap at that spot, the one meant for your mate to mark you as theirs. I was overwhelmed by everything, the bond flooding all my senses. I had no idea what was going on, but I also didn't care.

He would have marked me in that second if not for his father. The king ripped Lukyan back before he could sink his teeth in me. I still remember the fury on the most powerful Lycan in the kingdom's face when he sneered down at me.

"Never. Never will a werewolf be queen."

Lukyan, still overcome by the bond, didn't take those words well. As I was frozen in fear, he shifted, as did the king. The father and son would have likely brought the entire palace down in their rage, but then Queen Teraphine stepped in.

"Enough!" Her words rang out with so much authority, it brought me to my knees. The power of a Lycan Luna was already a powerful thing, but she was also a queen. Her son and her mate could not go against her order to calm the situation. Though the king stayed in his powerful beast form, Lukyan was forced to shift back.

Then she turned that powerful stare solely on her eldest son. "You know your role in this kingdom, Lukyan. Even if this," she had given me a disparaging glance, "werewolf is your mate, the council will not adhere to her becoming your mate. Not like this."

The look she and her son exchanged was so heavy. I knew they were communicating in their minds, through the mind link. Lukyan's face twisted more and more with rage by the second.

"Well," Prince Casimir came from behind me, placing an arm gingerly around my shoulders. "Even as a werewolf, it is no less marvelous, brother, that you were blessed with a fated mate. Most of our kind are not so lucky. Why not put a stop to the biting and ominous mood of it all so we can celebrate this for what it is." He squeezed my shoulder. "A blessing."

"Blessing," Queen Teraphine scoffed. Then she slowly shook her head, seeming exasperated. "Whatever you would like to see this as, one thing is certain. You can not mark her as your mate, Lukyan. Not without the council's approval."

The king's beast made a menacing cackling sound in his chest then turned into wicked laughter as he shifted back to his human form. "There will be no chance of that. You two," he snapped, looking harshly in my and Niccola's direction, "You do not speak a word of this matter to anyone outside of this room. Until it is laid to rest, it is to be kept secret."

The way the king said "laid to rest" made my skin break out in goosebumps. It was a threat. I was sure of it.

I was sure of it four months ago, and I'm sure of it now, as was Niccola, which was why keeping this a secret was so important.

Inside the medical tent, the first thing the nurse on duty did was take a sample of my blood to confirm the cause of my inability to heal.

"Wow. You don't just test for wolfsbane?" Niccola asked.

We watched as she placed drops of my blood in several separate vials, then used different solutions to test for different reactions.

"I could have," the nurse had an excited look in her eyes, "but we just received this full testing kit from the main hospital and I was eager to see how it all works. You're my first patient of the day."

Some of the tests took a few minutes for the results to be seen, so she went ahead and treated me for the poison. She knew as well as I what was in my blood.

The nurse sighed as she flushed my wounds. "These silly little tricks. It's always the same year after year. When will they learn?"

Niccola gasped sarcastically. "You mean, Lycans bullying werewolves isn't new. I thought we were the only ones privy to this treatment."

The Lycan nurse snickered. "I get it. Those of us in the working class in the capital are more familiar with working with werewolves. The isolated Lycan packs throughout the kingdom are different. The only werewolves they keep are slaves."

"That's disgusting," I muttered darkly.

The nurse nodded her head. "Aye, it is. You're going to feel a wee pinch," she pushed a needle with the antidote to the poison into my upper arm.

"I barely felt it," I looked to see if she actually poked me.

"I'm sure you didn't. Tough as nails you are. Need me to bandage your hands or are you-"

She stopped, staring at the small test vials of blood she had left on the counter. Her mouth dropped as she picked one up with a bluish tinge. She examined it in the light, then looked between Niccola and me.

"Well! This is a surprise. I'd say a congratulations is in order."

"Congratulations?" Niccola looked at her in confusion. "For what?"

The nurse chuckled. "It seems you're to be a father."

"I'm pregnant?!" Niccola looked down at his belly. If I wasn't so stunned, I would have laughed.

"Not you, crazy," the nurse grinned. "She is. I knew you two were close, but this even surprised me. It's good you brought her. The baby could have been affected if the poison wasn't controlled right away. Even a flesh wound can be fatal in these early days. So, you will need an exempt notice for the commanders, as well as a scheduled visit to the main clinic so the pregnancy can be entered on your record. Then...."

My heart froze. I couldn't hear a word she was saying after hearing the words "official report". There can't be an official report. Not.... not until I talk to Lukyan. His father... If his father gets wind of this now, being poisoned with a bit of wolfsbane would be insignificant compared to the harm the king might befall my unborn child.

"Can we not?" I spoke loudly, interrupting whatever she was currently saying. I met Niccola's eyes and he nodded, most likely coming to the same conclusion as me.

"Excuse me?" The nurse knit her brows in confusion.

Niccola spoke up before me, "The baby. We.... We weren't

exactly... Um... Well, you see." He took a breath, then said, "We need to talk, and confirm this is what we want." Niccola stared at me as he added, "We are not mates yet. It could complicate things for us later if...."

The nurse gave us a sympathetic smile. "Of course. Forgive me. We Lycans do often forget that fated mates are far more common in werewolves. If you haven't given up hope, of course an unplanned baby could come as a shock." She grabbed my hand giving it a gentle squeeze. "Take your time. I'll just send you home with the day with some supplements. I'll inform the trainers of the poisoning and use that as the reason to exempt you from training for now. Come see me when you've decided what to do."

"Thank you," I whispered.

Niccola helped me down from the table, holding my shoulders like he was helping me walk. Then he leaned in and whispered in my ear, "What are you going to do?"

I shook my head. "I don't know. I have to tell Lukyan first."

This wasn't something small, like touching wolfsbane pollen. It was a child. A combination of both of us. Lukyan has been telling me he's been trying to negotiate with the council for weeks to choose his own mate. If the news of my pregnancy gets out before then, it could ruin him.

"Man," Niccola rubbed my shoulder, giving me all the sympathy he could. "Well, congrats."

I snickered softly. "Thanks, I guess."

"Scary congratulations," he shivered. "I think as your substitute baby's father, I should do something to protect you."

I snorted, shrugging him off. "Substitute my ass. Keep your hands to yourself, baby daddy."

"Baby daddy?" a smooth, deep voice surprised both of us as we came out of the tent.

Casmir was standing there, his dark, long, waving hair cascading down around his smug, royal face. He was handsome, but in the most arrogant of ways.

"Great," I groaned, hiding my hands behind my back. "How

9

long have you been out here?"

"Long enough," he said as he examined his nails. The corners of his lips were curled. He heard everything.

"Casmir, I-"

"Eh," he reached out, silencing me with his finger. "Not here, Ally dear."

I let out a low growl. "Don't call me that."

That seemed to amuse him more. "Alesta," he purred my full name. "Come. Too many ears could be listening in."

I scoffed, "Like yours?"

"Oh, I am no threat to you, but others very well may be."

Chapter 2

Love Shed

"I'm just gonna...." Niccola tried to quietly tip toe away. "Ah," Casimir snapped his fingers at him, pushing his Alpha aura out slightly. "You're coming too, my spurious baby daddy."

Niccola's shoulders sagged forward. "Okay, fine. Can we drop the nickname though? The first prince will slaughter me. I'd like to keep my neck if you don't mind." Casimir raised a brow, making Niccola straighten and stammer, "I mean, yes Prince Casimir. Of course. Baby daddy at your command."

Casimir chuckled. "Amusing. This is why you are my favorite *little* werewolf," he tickled his finger under Niccola's chin.

"I-I'm not really little," Niccola's face showed his embarrassment.

"No?" Casimir's eyes flashed south with an arrogant smirk. "Huh."

Casimir walked towards the palace, curling his finger for us to follow. When he was a few feet ahead, Niccola leaned closer to whisper sourly, "I'm not small."

I scoffed in annoyance, "I wouldn't care if you were."

"I'm not!" He said more urgently.

"I don't care," I mimicked his tone.

He kicked the dirt, throwing a silent tantrum, but straightened up when Casimir glanced back, catching the tail end of Niccola's quiet punch to the air. Casimir raised his brows with a slight grin, his dark hair fanning around him as he looked ahead again.

"Damn it," Niccola mumbled, giving the dirt one more kick.

"Why do you let him bother you so easily?"

Niccola pouted, then mumbled, "I'm not little."

"He wasn't talking about your dick size, weirdo. Why was that the first thing that came to mind? Insecure about something?"

"No," Niccola pushed his shoulder against mine.

I shoved him back, harder. He pushed again, using his hands this time. I planted my feet firmly, shoving him back with all my force, making him fall to the ground. I burst into a fit of laughter as he began yelling insults in my direction.

"Hey, fat ass! Damn, your thunder thighs, Al! I may have a little dick, but you-"

"He admits it," Casimir stared down at Niccola as he struggled to get back on his feet. "As amusing as this is, the lunch bell is about to ring." He looked pointed at the mess hall in the distance. "Discretion is imperative given the circumstances. But feel free to yell about your bitsy bit another time."

"I don't have a bitsy anything," Niccola grumbled, wiping his dirt-covered hands down his shirt.

"Hmm," Casimir, snickered, then began walking once again.

"Come on," I grabbed Niccola's arm, dragging him along as he muttered endlessly under his breath.

"Bitsy bit. I'll show you bitsy...."

I sighed, ignoring him as he rambled. He was nervous. Niccola stammers when he's nervous. Casimir stirs him up every time they meet, all for Casimir's entertainment. Life was a playground for the young prince. Niccola was a dependable toy for the prince's enjoyment.

Casimir led us to a small back gate, only meant for royals exiting and entering the training grounds. It was manned by a single Lycan guard that opened the gate and stood straight as we walked by. The guard's eyes only moved to glance at Niccola and me. He was likely wondering why the prince had us, two lowly werewolves, tagging along behind him. I resisted the urge to stick my tongue out.

"Here we are," Casimir headed to a small outbuilding instead of the main structure. It wasn't any larger than a shed.

Walking in, the smell was so thick it made me cringe. "Smells like sex and feet in here," I muttered, pinching my nose.

"Wonderful, isn't it?" Casimir, chuckled, walking toward a wooden chair with a fur throw in the corner of the room.

"What is this place?" Niccola looked around with a measure of awe and disgust.

The rough floors were covered in all manner of animal furs, most of which were matted in large patches, like they had been laid on for long periods of time. They were rank with the stench of sex, but not nearly as bad as the bed. The black mattress covering was spotted with excrements of all kinds. I wanted to gag.

"Sorry for the mess," the corner of Casimir's lips curled as his eyes glimmered from catching our reaction. "This place... Well, it is as it seems. Since mother prohibited me from sullying the inner palace with my wanderings, I had to find other accommodations to enjoy myself." He lifted a chalice from a table, sniffing its contents before taking a sip.

I shook my head, trying not to laugh as something just dawned on me. "Did that guard think that we," I pointed my thumb at Niccola, "were to be your next victims?"

"Possibly," Casimir's shit-eating grin was infectious. "Victims is a bit insulting."

"I'm going to be sick," Niccola gagged. That seemed to please Casimir further.

"That seemed like the safer assumption for a guard to make," Casimir set the chalice back on the table. "At least until the rumor reaches my brother that I sacked the fiercest of the werewolf tributes." He looked excited by the idea. "We can speak freely here. The staff and guards know to avoid this place."

"Why when it's so charming," I took a look around the room again. "So much so, I fear touching anything for it may lose its allure."

"This is why I insist upon our friendship," Casimir tapped his fingers along the arm of his chair with a grin. "You understand me so well." He tilted his handsome face down, lifting his brow. "Friends share secrets. I shared my secret house of charms with you. Now it is time for you to fully disclose your little secret with me."

I tensed as the mood shifted in the putrid room. "It is as you overheard," Lifted my chin, crossing my arms over my chest. "With superior beastly hearing, you would be as informed as I am."

"So you had no idea?" Casimir's tapping on the arm of the chari sped up slightly.

I watched his fingers for a few seconds before I answered, "No." Casimir moved his hand to rub his chin. "Then your reason for your visit to the medic wasn't to confirm a suspicion of being with child?"

Pressing my lips together, I wondered if it would be wise to inform Casimir of the poisoning. He was less likely to go berserk, but he was still Lukyan's brother.

When I didn't answer right away, Casimir pushed his aura over us. It tickled my skin, letting me know it was there and he had the ability to command, but that was the only effect I felt.

Niccola, on the other hand, folded like a glove.

"She was poisoned!" Niccola gasped out, buckling over from the pressure.

"Pussy," I muttered under my breath.

Niccola looked at me like I was mad. "How could you-"

"Poisoned?" Before Niccola could finish whatever question he was about to ask, Casimir interrupted. Casimir looked me up and down. "By who?"

I rolled my eyes. "It wasn't severe. Just pollen on equipment. I sustained a flesh wound. Not a big deal."

"You carry my niece or nephew in your belly," Casimir's eyes narrowed. "It very well could have been a big deal. Who?"

I shrugged. When I refused to answer he looked at Niccola.

"Chrisley," Niccola blurted, then bit his lips, looking at me shamefully.

"Chrisley?" Casimir curled his fingers against the wood of the chair, the scratching audible from where I stood. Were his claws extended? "The Lycan tribute from Crimson Moon Pack?"

"We don't know if it was her for sure," I looked back at Niccola with a hard stare.

Niccola rolled his eyes and scoffed, "Right. Just like she didn't intentionally knock you into the lake last week, knowing you couldn't swim."

"I can swim," I argued. "Just not in human form."

"You had to run laps for hours for shifting without permission," Niccola added harshly. "With weights."

"It was a good workout," I retorted stubbornly, then stepped heavily on his foot, hoping he would hush.

Casimir no longer looked amused. His handsome face was hard, the smile lines missing from his eyes. "Did the commander and trainers that day not see Alesta getting pushed?" Casimir directed the question to Niccola. I went to stomp on his foot again, but Niccola moved it at the last second, avoiding my heel.

"It was Commander Silas that day," Niccola told the prince. "He noticed and even laughed, but Lycan tributes are never punished for anything."

It was common knowledge which commanders were of the purist faction, and Commander Silas was the most open with his disdain for werewolf peasants.

"Ah," Casimir's nails scratched loudly against the wood grain again. "I see."

He stared at me, studying me as the silence stretched in the nasty sex hut. Was he upset about the pregnancy, or about the occurrences all werewolves deal with during training? I could not say for sure, but I was guessing it was the latter.

After the long pause, right as restlessness was making my muscles ache, he asked, "So, my brother is unaware of the baby?"

Now I felt restless for another reason. "No. Lukyan doesn't know."

Casimir rubbed his thumb back and forth against his full bottom lip. His eyes were intense and I felt his aura push forward again. His aura tickled my skin like before, but that was the only adverse effect. Niccola groaned behind me, the effects being much more harsh on him for whatever reason.

"Tell no one. Not even my brother," Casimir said in way of a command.

My throat went dry, and I felt the tug in the back of my mind. His will was trying to overtake mine.

"Yes Alpha!" Niccola blurted out, then gasped as the pain from the command receded.

I felt no pain. Nothing overly uncomfortable to force me to submit. I never truly did when my commanders or others tried to command me. But, as I always did to keep appearances, I bowed my head and murmured, "Yes, Alpha."

Casimir's eyes narrowed. I thought he had caught on that I was submitting out of my own will and not his. Then he said, "It's imperative you keep this secret for the time being, Alesta.

It wasn't a command. Just a statement.

"Why?" I asked, my voice barely a whisper.

Prince Casimir leaned forward, resting his elbows on his knees. "You know as well as I that our honorable first prince has the weight of this entire kingdom pressing down on those noble shoulders of his." His eyes were intense, all sense of the playful Casimir I was used to seeing gone. His severity took me by surprise. "These next few days are crucial for our kingdom. I beg of you, Alesta. Do not detour Lukyan from his duty. At least for two days."

One side of me wanted to argue, tell Casimir he was being an asshole and his brother had every right to know for this new life growing inside of me. If he had left off with just his command, I might have defied him, but he was right. The weight of Lukyan's duties and obligations to all the members of this kingdom was enough to keep him away from me most nights. I'm not sure what was going on in the council that was keeping him so occupied, but I knew it was important. He wouldn't keep away if it wasn't. This pregnancy would only distract him at this time.

If the Purist faction or the council find out about a pregnancy between their crown prince and a werewolf tribute at this crucial time, it would be derailing in many ways. Lukyan was an honorable man. He was also extremely territorial, which made me nervous about being in this sex shed alone with Niccola and Casimir. If he does come to our chambers tonight and smells sex and other males on me, his beastly side will ravish me in the most brutally delish way until morning. If he were to find out I was pregnant with his child.....

I can not even imagine what Lukyan might do. I don't think a command from his mother would be enough to prevent him from revealing the connection between us.

Casimir was waiting with those intense eyes for my reply.

"I won't tell him. He's busy so often, I won't have an opportunity anyway. Two days will be easy."

Casimir sat back in his chair. "He has been rather busy as of late, hasn't he?" The amusement had returned to his eyes. Somehow, those eyes seemed to have a tinge of sadness to them as well. He looked off towards the window. "Busy, busy, busy. Always so busy."

My chest tightened. My hand involuntarily went to my belly. "It's as you said. The weight of the kingdom."

"A heavy burden to bear," Casimir sighed. He then turned those eyes back towards me. "In the meantime, if you need anything, anything at all, you come find me." There was something more in those eyes, like he was trying to tell me something else.

Before I could understand fully what the meaning behind his words were, someone knocked on the shack's door, causing Niccola to yelp.

Casimir chuckled, "Astute Prince Lukyan," he mumbled. "That didn't take long. Come in, Basil!"

The door swung inward, revealing Basil, Lukyan's aide on the other side. "Prince Casimir," he bowed his head respectfully as Casimir waved off the greeting. Then Basil turned his focus to me. "Miss Alesta. *He* is looking for you."

Chapter 3

Suffering Prince

Exiting Casimir's sex shed with Lukyan's aide was uncomfortable. Why was Lukyan looking for me at this time of day? He should assume I'd be in training.

"Um," I decided to ask instead of letting the anxiety torment me. "Why is his highness looking for me at this time of day?"

Basil glanced over his shoulder, his gaze drawing back to the shed we just left. "I'm unsure, Miss Alesta. A report came in from Commander Ivo and then His Highness, The First Prince Lukyan sent me to retrieve you." He seemed anxious as he added, "That was after he rushed back to your chambers and saw you were not there."

Commander Ivo was a loyalist, and the closest to Lukyan. He should be completely unaware of my connection to the first prince. Knowing something the commander reported to Lukyan would cause my mate to rush to find me wasn't helping me with my anxieties, or answering any questions.

One thing I did know was that I didn't want Basil thinking that I was doing what most visitors do when they enter Casimir's little sex dungeon.

"Um, back there with Prince Casimir, you know I wasn't..."

Basil actually laughed as I let my question hang in the air. "I know, Miss Alesta. Oh, I know very well." When I gave him a curious stare, he continued, "If you had done anything with anyone he wouldn't have sent me to find you. He would have felt it. None would be able to stop His Highness from finding you himself."

I shivered at the thought. I had forgotten about the pains one feels when their mate was being intimate with another. I had never felt it, but I heard it was excruciating. Cheating damages the bond between fated mates and torments the soul and our beast. Lukyan would have exploded for sure.

"How did you find me there?" I asked. Casimir and I do not make it a habit to be alone together, so surely he didn't just guess.

"Your scent. Even with the stench wafting from that shed, your scent was unmistakable. I caught it from just outside the gate."

"That's reassuring," I grunted. "That means other Lycans, like the trainers and commanders, or that bitch Chrisley may catch it if they were to walk by."

"I do not think so. Casimir's scent overpowers yours to most others. I'm just used to having to find you." He laughed softly under his breath then added, "I would have liked to see His Highness find your scent leading back to his brother. That would have been quite amusing."

"I don't even want to imagine," I groaned.

Basil waited a beat for me to fall in step with him, then leaned in to ask me quietly so no others could hear, "I would be lying to say I'm not curious as to why you were in the young prince's little house of debauchery." Basil's eyes were gleaming with anticipation for a bit of gossip.

My body tensed. I hoped Basil didn't notice my sudden tension. I laughed nervously. "Uh, I'm not really sure. I think he was messing with us, or maybe trying to show off." I couldn't tell Basil the real reason Casimir dragged Niccola and me there.

Basil seemed satisfied with that answer. "I believe the young prince may carry a special interest for your friend."

With a snort I said, "I think he might too. They spent most of the walk there talking about Niccola's *size*, if you know what I mean."

"Oh, how scandalous," Basil giggled. "Isn't it marvelous that neither of our princes seem to discriminate when it comes to their partners. It's quite the change from the precedence set by their forefathers."

"Yeah," I tried not to roll my eyes. "We should throw a parade for them both for being willing to bed those with less fortunate circumstances."

My sarcasm wasn't missed by the aid. He pushed his glasses up the bridge of his nose, then murmured, "I wouldn't go that far."

"Of course you wouldn't. Too much paperwork and planning."

He gave me an incredulous glance. "Indeed."

The rest of the walk was quiet. Basil enjoyed taking part in gossip, but didn't enjoy my smartass mouth when it was directed at him. He will giggle away when he overhears me giving others any lip, but the second I do it to him he closes up. Probably to avoid being on Lukyan's bad side in case I get carried away, like I often do.

We reached the far corner of the castle, the one closest to the barracks where the tributes are supposed to reside. The barracks were arranged so two tributes shared a two-bedroom apartment with a connecting common area. Niccola and I were housed together, despite being opposite sexes. It was Casimir who came up with the idea of claiming Niccola was attracted solely to the same sex in order to pull off the arrangement. That was the beginning of Prince Casimir's tormenting antics towards Niccola. Niccola was very bothered by the notion.

Our room was separate from the others, on the bottom floor in the drafty back corner of the building. Other tributes deduced we were being singled out for being different. Our living arrangements were thought to just be another form of bullying.

In truth, we were given a special room that only the princes were aware contained a secret passage that led into the castle. Not just any part of the castle, but the princes' wing. There were tunnels branching off to every room, but the only one I ever used was to Lukyan's. Every single night.

It was odd entering the castle the normal way, because it didn't feel normal to me. I kept looking over my shoulder, fearing being discovered.

"Is it okay entering from out in the open like this?" I whispered to Basil.

Basil looked around, as if it just occurred to him. "Oh, my. I hope it is. Let us hurry to be sure." He then mumbled under his breath," Let us hope the King does not hear of this."

"We could always claim it was Casimir I visited and not Lukyan. A guard at the East Gate could even serve as witness."

He groaned, "Oh! That would arise a bigger set of issues. Let us hurry."

We rushed into the castle, and I thought we were safe. It seemed like this part of the castle grounds were deserted, but then I felt a pair of eyes looking down at me. I gazed up the gray stone walls before taking cover inside, meeting a sharp pair of topaz eyes on an icy face.

My breath caught in my throat for that split second. Queen Teraphine caught us. I expected warriors to emerge any moment to drag me from the palace. Goosebumps had risen all over my skin. When we were almost to Lukyan's bedroom and I was still unscathed, I steadied my nerves realizing no one was coming for me. At least not right this moment.

What if she sent someone for me later?...

My hand went to my belly, and this urge that overtook my fear came over me. It was a possessiveness like I had never felt before. I wasn't going to let her or anyone hurt my child.

"Are you alright, Miss Alesta?" Basil looked back at me as his hand encircled the large brass handle of the door.

I put on a smile the best I could, dropping my hand from my stomach. "Nerves," I muttered weakly. "I... I thought we were going to get caught."

He smiled sympathetically. "All is well, Miss. No chatter in the staff's mind link. I stay tuned for the gossip at times like these. Now, hurry in. He's been waiting."

∞ ∞ ∞

"Alesta."

My body relaxed instantly at the deep rumbling of Lukyan's voice. Before Basil could close the doors, my mate was on me, his nose upon my nape as he took deep inhales of my scent. My arms enclosed his thick waist, pulling him impossibly closer.

"Luk," I rasped, shivers traveled through my veins.

"Damn it," he growled as his nose skimmed down my neck and across my collarbone.

Then he moved down my arms, his nostrils taking in all of my skin. He inspected every finger on one hand then moved to the next. The bandages from the clinic loosened and fell to the ground with his fevered inspection. His body stiffened with every deep breath. A low growl vibrated through his chest.

"You fucking reek," he murmured as his nose traveled to my hair.

Shit. I forgot about Casimir's sex shack.

"It... it's not-"

"I don't smell the poison though," he continued before I could form an excuse.

My eyes opened wide, "Poison?"

His throaty groan was like a sound of relief. "When I read the report you were excused from training, I thought I would go mad."

Commander Ivo reported I was missing training?

"How did you..." I left the question hanging in the air.

He took my hands, his eyes scanning them for any sign of injury. They were healed, but you could still see the faint pink lines from the fresh wounds.

"I read you absorbed wolfsbane pollen from wounds on your hands. You were injured enough to be excused from training for two days."

I stiffened, swallowing a lump forming in my throat. "What

23

else did the report say?"

"It doesn't matter," he planted kisses against my palms. "Damn it, I was so worried."

My heart clenched, hearing the strain in his voice. All his worry was from reading I absorbed a bit of poison in my hands. How would he react if the report contained the full details about my visit to the clinic?...

I brushed the curls from his forehead, staring up at his intense topaz eyes swimming with so much affection. "I'm fine, Luk. It wasn't serious."

He took my hand, kissing it again. "For you to miss training, my mind went wild. You're really okay?"

The earnestness in his tone caused me to smile, nodding as words failed me.

He signed deeply, resting his head on mine. "I hate not having the power to go to you myself. I thought up every dire scenario for why you weren't here when it said you went to rest in your room while recovering." He waited for a pause, then asked, "Where were you?"

I didn't want to lie to him. His worry was so deep. Casimir's warning kept ringing through my head, along with my promise to hold my tongue.

"Casimir caught Niccola as we left the clinic. He was just teasing him as he always does." I paused, then added, "I'm sorry to worry you. I wasn't aware Commander Ivo divulged my status in reports to you."

Lukyan laughed dryly. "It's not you specifically. He reports all tributes' statuses. Yours is the only one I look for."

What was in the report? I wanted to ask, but decided to let it be. My secret was not revealed, or he would have said something by now.

"My Alesta," he said my name like a prayer. "Oh, I can not wait for the day I can openly claim you as my own."

My heart quickened, hoping that day would be soon. For so many more reasons than he knew. "How are your dealings with the council?"

He tensed, and I felt his anxiety from his aura. There was something in him that wasn't there a moment ago. Some sort of wall that I could not feel past. Being unclaimed and unmarked, the bond between us had its limits. We could not use the bond to find one another. We could not heal one another when we were hurt. The most frustrating thing for me at times like this was not being able to fully feel his emotions. I could not sense his moods more than anyone else could, and I could not decipher these strange reactions when his defensive walls went up, like they were right now.

"The council is…. Difficult."

He did not elaborate more. He was so open and honest with how he felt towards me, how much he cared for me, but he would never let me in when it came to his duties as the first prince.

I knew it stressed him immensely, the things he must have to go through. When we are together, he does not want to speak of any of it.

He sighed, resting his head on mine again. I closed my eyes trying to ignore the creeping feeling in my chest. "You are my only refuge," he rasped, then kissed my head.

I smiled slightly at the familiar phrase. "As you are mine."

At times, that was all it felt we were to one another. I could not tell him of my troubles with training, for fear he would lash out, revealing what we were to one another. He would not speak of his daily dealing in the palace. He had the weight of the Kingdom on his shoulders. I suspect he did not want to yet share that weight with me.

At night, when we receded into the safe space of this bedroom, we would comfort one another the only way unmarked mates could. We would escape into the lust that was raw and overwhelming, letting it do what the unconnected bond couldn't by healing the nonexistent connection between us.

"One day," he whispered. "One day, the world will know what you are to me."

My thoughts went to my belly and what was growing inside

me as I said, "I hope that day is soon."

He tensed once again, more noticeably this time. It caused me to stare up at him curiously, but before I could voice my questions someone knocked at the door.

"Damn it," Lukyan growled. "What?!" His voice was no longer gentle and caressing. It was the voice of the fierce, bristly heir with the weight on the kingdom on his back.

"You Highness. The council demands your attention," a stern voice demanded from the other side. "The final candidate has been eliminated, and your chosen queen has been decided upon-"

"I'LL BE RIGHT THERE!" Lukyan snarled so loudly that I jumped back and gasped out of both surprise and fear. His aura was so menacing, so dangerous that it rocked me to my core.

He growled viciously, cursing under his breath. "Damn it!" Then he looked over towards me with a hardness to his eyes. "Alesta, I-"

"A chosen queen?" I whispered the words I had just heard, trying to understand what they could mean.

His irritation seemed to grow at those three words. His aura engulfed me, making it hard to breathe. "Nevermind what was said." He grabbed my chin, staring down at me with all the authority of the first prince. "It is nothing, Alesta. Nothing."

Was he trying to command me? His aura was more than just menacing now. There was some part of it that was creeping into me, like Casimir had done earlier when he tried to command me to keep my secret a secret.

"Stay in this room. You are excused from training for two days, so you have no reason to leave this room. I will return for you in two days."

This wasn't my Lukyan. This man was dominating and terrifying, but above all, he looked scared beyond belief.

Scared of what?

Like I always did, I nodded, whispering the same words I usually did in situations like these. "Yes, Alpha."

Never. Never did I think I would have to pull this stunt on this man. The creeping feeling in my chest swelled, making it feel hollow as it ached.

"Good," his shoulders relaxed slightly at my agreement.

Then his tender expression returned as he bent down and gently placed his lips on mine. "I'll be back," his voice was an aching rasp.

I nodded, the swell in my throat making it impossible to speak. His eyes lingered on my face, then he kissed me one more time. I tried not to react, but my body and the bond betrayed me. My mouth moved with his in the familiar motion.

All too soon, he groaned painfully as he tore his lips from mine, then left the room without another glance.

Chapter 4

Chosen Over Fate

I was utterly stunned after Lukyan left. I stood frozen in the center of the room, trying to comprehend what I just overheard and his reaction afterward.

What just happened? Did he try to command me to stay in this room?

.... Did that person say chosen queen?

I could still taste Lukyan's lips on mine. I could still smell his scent perforating from my body where he touched me, but the lingering tingles and sparks were not enough to override the anxiety our last interaction left deep in me.

With my hands splayed over my stomach, I prayed that I had heard wrong. My emotions were burning behind my eyes. All the nights he's spent away recently are passing through my head. All the loneliness I felt waking to an empty bed. I dismissed it all, knowing there was nothing to be done. He was the first prince, but I was a lowly werewolf sent by my pack to serve the kingdom he would one day lead.

Casimir. Did he know something? Was that why he pleaded so seriously for me not to reveal this pregnancy to his brother?

Stay in this room? Did Lukyan expect me to wait around in constant worry for him when he couldn't even explain what his servant meant? Not a fucking chance. I needed to find Casimir and find out what was going on now.

My body moved towards the door, but before my hand even

reached the doorknob, the door opened. I thought it would be Lukyan, or maybe Basil. My blood ran cold when a cold set of topaz eyes met mine, accusation clear on her arrogant face.

"Going somewhere, Alesta Raine?" Queen Teraphne raised her well-groomed brow.

My breath caught in my throat as I rasped, "My queen." I quickly bowed my head, averting my gaze to the ground. Her authority filled the room, making the air suffocating.

Her footfalls were the only sound. Each step she took as she slowly walked around me made my heart hammer harder and harder in my chest.

She stopped right in front of me, then lifted my chin with a firmly placed finger. Her eyes were sharp and piercing, even as she smiled.

"Before you go, have tea with me. There is much we must discuss."

Lukyan

Ranoldo, one of the secretaries to the council, was quiet, following me obediently out of the Princes' wing. I'm sure my anger was wafting from my every pore.

When we entered the main hall, when I was sure there was no chance of being overheard, my rage burst forth. Snarling, I grabbed his lapels and threw him roughly against the stone wall.

"WHAT HAVE I SAID ABOUT DISTURBING ME IN MY CHAMBERS?!"

My hot breath and spit flew at his frightened face. The cracks behind his head were testament to the fury he had unleashed.

"I-I'm s-s-sorry, sir. I-"

"DO YOU KNOW WHAT YOU JUST DID?!"

The confusion was evident in Ranoldo's trembling face, but that didn't subdue my violent rage. He didn't know. None in the council or those working for them knew. Very few knew of my fated mate. My father's threats were not empty. I knew what revealing her to the kingdom and the council would mean.

I have been keeping so many secrets, so many conflicting truths, that I felt they were becoming a wall stacking between me and the one I could not claim. Then she had to overhear *that* at the most pressing time, when I was already hanging on to my sanity by a thread.

The rare gift of a fated mate was the greatest treasure to any Lycan that was blessed to find theirs. That was what history said, at least. My father, along with all the current noble Lycans, never had the chance to find out for themselves. I have been the first in generations to receive this privilege.

If she had just been born a Lycan...

The council and my father would never allow an orphaned werewolf from a barbaric pack sent here as a tribute to the kingdom to be their queen. I knew there was never to be a way to change their minds.

That doesn't mean I ever planned on letting her go.

My claws extended from my fingers, pressing into his chest. The blood spreading through his shirt made the beast in me hungry for more. I wanted to bleed Ranoldo dry for causing my mate to look at me with such betrayal. I had to command her for the first time out of fear. My heart clenched thinking of the hallowed way she whispered, "Yes, Alpha."

"P-prince," Ranoldo grimaced in pain, gripping my arms with his hands, trying to loosen my hold.

I tossed him to the side, my roar filling the hall and making maids scurry for different rooms to hide from my wrath.

"NEVER ENTER THE PRINCE'S WING AGAIN!" It was a command, one he couldn't resist.

With blood still spreading from his wounds and his face twisted even more, Ranoldo struggled to his knees and bowed his head. "Y-yes, my prince."

My claws receded, but his blood remained on my hands. It dripped in a trail down the marbled floors as I stormed past the council secretary to deal with the ones who had sent him.

My future queen had been chosen? I snarled, knowing I could not put this off any longer. Father was sure to move things along now that a decision had been made.

I was taking a woman as my princess. A woman who was not my mate.

Alesta's terrified face entered my mind, and I suddenly felt sick. For the briefest moment, I thought about abandoning it all. Throwing away my crown and the future of my kingdom to run away with the only one I wanted to be with. I envied my incompetent brother. He would have done so already if he was in my place.

Then all the reasons I held on for so long came back to me and I knew I could never deviate from my plan. Not when I was so close to getting the power I needed.

"Well, look at you," a soft, bell-like voice laced with mirth greeted me from outside the council chambers. "Run into some trouble on your way here?"

Seeing Camellia helped me to relax. I knew it would be her. If I couldn't have Alesta at my side, it had to be Camellia. Father wasn't a stupid man. He knew this was the only woman I wouldn't resist.

"So, it was you," I said in relief.

Camellia giggled in the airy way she always has. Linking her arm in mine, she ignored the blood on my hands and pressed into me.

"I made sure my father gave the council an offer they couldn't refuse. Something our king was quite pleased with." She leaned in and whispered in my ear, "A certain werewolf outlining pack is being eradicated at this very moment."

A devious smile lifted my lips despite my previous mood. "Good." My plan was still in motion.

Camellia seemed quite pleased with herself as she beamed up

at me. Then she waved her hands towards the chamber doors. "Shall we enter together, my prince? Or should I call you my fiance now?"

My gut had been twisting all day. I was going to be sick.

"As the goddess, Celeste, watches over this holiest of unions, let her also watch over this kingdom with pride...."

The priest droned on, but I couldn't process anything he was saying.

Just as suspected, my father rushed the wedding, giving me only two days to prepare. For two days I've been t the mercy of the council, doing the traditional rituals and cleansing before the actual ceremony.

Camellia was doing her part. I thought this would be easy doing this without my true mate if I was doing it with my trusted friend. That didn't stop the churning feeling in my stomach or the ache in my chest.

"Are you going to make it?" Camellia asked in my head.

She knew this would be painful for me, as it was for her, but she had something I didn't; a father that truly loved her and supported her. He just wanted her happiness and knew as well as both of us that this was the only way to chaperone change in the kingdom.

"I'll be fine," I replied in a terse tone.

Camellia's worry for me was still leaking through the opened mind link. She knew where my heart was, and it wasn't here. Neither was hers, but her circumstances were different. She could be open and talk to her love.

I couldn't tell Alesta anything.

Two days. Maybe my chest was on the verge of seizing because I hadn't seen her face in two days.

"It's time! Kneel," Camellia said in my head.

I snapped out of my daze and looked at the priest, who was standing before me with a crown in his hands. He had an expectant look on his face, and that was when I realized I missed whatever instruction he had just given. Camellia gripped my elbow, and together we knelt on the ceremonial steps.

The priest raised the crown with a satisfied expression, then said, "Upon this union, I crown thy Prince, His Highness Lukyan Johann Achlyselene, and thy Princess, Camellia Amara Nova Achlyselene, thine future King and Queen of the great Erebos Kingdom. May the goddess rain her blessing upon the entirety of the Lycanthrope nation!"

After the priest and a priestess laid the crowns upon our heads, the room erupted into cheers. This was it. Camellia and I were now wed before the council and the nobles of the kingdom. It was the first major step in getting to the throne. From the beginning, this is exactly what I wanted. This was what I needed in order to protect our people, all our people. This was the start of being able to protect the one I loved.

Without the throne, Alesta would never be safe. If I were to give up the throne, being together would only burden her, as we would constantly be hunted. My father would never let us rest. My betrayal and abandonment of my duties as prince would be avenged only with her death.

I could never keep her safe. I could never make this world a place where she wouldn't be oppressed.

This was what I had always planned to do to accomplish so much. But why does it feel like I just sacrificed more than I gained?

"Look happy, dear husband," Camellia snapped.

I forced a smile on my face as we turned together to face the joyous nobles in the ceremonial hall. My father and mother were at the front of the crowd. My father had a smug grin on my face that made me grit my teeth through my straining grin. Casimir was nowhere to be seen. He was here at the beginning of the ceremony, lingering off to the side with a noble lady hanging on his side. The horehound most likely snuck off to some deserted hallway to live freely and have his fun. He could choose any partner, but I never had such freedom.

There was only one woman I wanted, and she could never be by my side while onlookers praised our union like this. Not with the kingdom the way it currently was.

The priestesses in their silver, glimmering robes led Camellia and me down the center of the room in the recessional. We were being led to the great terrace where we would be presented to the rest of the kingdom as their future king and queen.

"It's almost over," Camellia squeezed my arm.

"No, it's not," I reminded her. "After this, they will lead us back for the bedding ceremony."

She tensed, knowing that the next step would be the most difficult in our ruse. We were expected to mark each other before the council and priest, then would be left alone to consummate our new marriage.

That would never happen. We had to give the appearance of following through, even though neither act would ever happen.

Not risking to voice her thoughts out loud, she said in my head, *"They chose my father to inspect the marks. It will be alright."*

"What if the spell doesn't work?" That was my greatest fear. If I actually had to mark Camellia, what would that do to my bond with my true mate? How would that affect Alesta?

"My mate is aware of the risk. A small rejection and remarking by our true mates right after and all will be repaired."

My stomach was churning so badly at just the thought of marking anyone but Alesta. Even Camellia. Camellia and I had talked this out long ago and agreed to go that far if needed, but that was before Alesta came into my life. The only nape I wanted to sink my teeth into was my mate's.

"The damage may be too much to repair," I said glumly.

Camellia gave me an odd expression before remembering where we were and fixing her face back into a mask of elegant perfection. *"Luk...."*

"Hmm?" My head was still on Alesta. I couldn't even pretend to be happy any longer. My anxieties were too great.

"Did..." Camellia started hesitantly, then continued, *"Did you not inform your mate of the possibility of having to actually mark*

one another?"

My silence was loud in the connection of our minds. I felt Camellia's horror for me and Alesta.

Camellia's nails sank into my arm as she yelled in my head, *"Lukyan! How could you?! She will feel it. The betrayal could be inhibiting. Werewolves feel it more than we do! You know that!"* I held my tongue, then felt her mortification magnify. *"Luk... She knows about this wedding. You did... You told her the arrangement we had and our plans, did you not?"*

"No," I growled.

"Luk...."

The disapproval was thick in Camellia's voice, but I had my reasons. Everything I do, *everything*, was to protect Alesta now. If Alesta knew of my plans for the throne and my father caught on before the kingdom was handed to me....

My father was the only being that I could not protect her from. If she knew something and he commanded her to tell him, she would be forced to do so. Then he would kill her without a moment's hesitation.

No, Alesta does not know. I would sacrifice anything and everyone else, even Camellia, if I had to, but never Alesta. Her ignorance of the secrets behind the origins of this kingdom was the only thing keeping her safe.

As the towering stained glass doors opened, the trumpets sounded and confetti rained down from above. A priestess waved us to our place at the ledge, where everyone below could gaze upon the newly married future monarchs, completely unaware of the meddling Camellia and I both had to do to achieve this farce.

The subjects below roared with cheers, chanting for their future king and queen. Camellia was playing her part perfectly, looking every bit the ideal crowned princess she now was.

I stood mortified. I felt *her* before I saw her. Those eyes were unmistakable, no matter the distance. The faintest of blue, clear and stunning. They were staring up at me with such coldness; I felt my blood freeze.

Alesta. How?.... How did she remove my command and leave our chambers?

"Basil!" I snapped at my aid. *"She's here!"*

"W-who?" Basil's frantic tone quivered in my head.

"ALESTA!"

I assigned Basil to lead Camellia's fated mate through the secret passages under the castle. He would be closest to Alesta right now, and the only one who could reach her to put her back where she would be safe.

"I... I have Miss Camellia's...."

"GET ALESTA BACK TO MY ROOM, NOW!"

Fuck everything else. Camellia's mate could wait. Alesta could not. I could not even imagine what she was thinking right now.

At that moment, the great priest bellowed loudly to the masses, "Announcing, your future king and queen of the Lycanthropy and all the realm, united under the gracious eyes of the goddess, Crown Prince Lukyan Johann Achlyselene and Crown Princess Camellia Amara Nova Achlyselene!"

As the people shouted our praise, all I could hear was my heart hammering in my ears. The devastation on my mate's face was almost enough to break me. If it wasn't for Basil appearing behind her, I would have likely lept from this very balcony to get to her myself.

My nausea returned, seeing her grip her stomach like she was going to be sick. She tore her gaze from mine, then left after Basil, hopefully to follow him back to our chambers where she should have been all along.

***

"About fucking time." I tore off the ornamental links from my sleeves and tossed them to the floor.

"Father did the best he could," Camellia said as she rounded her neck. She kicked off her heels and stretched. "It was a rather long day."

"Long doesn't begin to describe it," I sneered.

It's been excruciating. The parade through the streets. The

formal introductions to the nobles. The pledging of the pack and clan leaders. Every event after the wedding should have been quick and easy, but they each seemed to drag unnecessarily longer than they should. My mother even arranged a formal dinner and receptions I was unaware of.

My mother was rather odd throughout the evening. She was unusually hyper. Her excited greetings to all the guests included dragging us to every face and holding forced conversations until she moved us along to the next introduction. Camellia and I exchanged wary glances continuously. Mother was usually one to sit stoically back on her throne and watch the celebrations from the sidelines.

My irritation grew by the second, and it was becoming harder to hide. If not for Camellia's nails embedded in my arm every time my anger began to surfaced, I would have ripped apart the reception hall long ago.

"Who will your father punish? You or her?" Camellia would whisper in my ear, reminding me why I continued on with this ruse to begin with.

Father's eyes were always on me. It was like he was expecting me to become defiant at any moment. Maybe that was why there were so many more things added to the agenda. He was waiting for me to break and give him a reason to apprehend Alesta.

Alesta. She saw everything. I could only imagine the horrible assumptions she's been making throughout the day. Maybe Camellia was right. Maybe I should have warned her beforehand. I didn't have to tell her everything. Not with father's prying eyes everywhere. I could have just told her enough to reassure her. Maybe that would have prevented the heartbreaking stare back in the courtyard.

The look in her eyes was still haunting me. Her eyes were like frigid ice, whereas before they were like the lively morning sky. She seemed so unfamiliar and distant. Seeing the way she held her stomach as if she were to be sick as she turned away still made me nauseous.

I had to explain. I couldn't tell her everything just yet, but I needed to reassure her she was my one and only. Telling her the whole truth before I was throned could put her in the greatest of danger.

I've told her every night we spent together how much she means to me. I've never lied about my intent to only have her by my side for the rest of our lives. She knows how greatly I treasure her. She is my greatest gift from the goddess herself. The rarity of a fated mate for a Lycan should be proclamation enough.

Surely, even after witnessing the wedding proclamation today, she will at least hold on to the endless sincerities I have doused over her for the past several months. She will understand. She has to…

Nevertheless, deep down, this agonizing strain tormenting my soul is just getting larger and larger. I need to get to her soon.

We didn't get to the marital chambers for the bedding ceremony until well after nightfall. Alpha Zifran, Camellia's father, had the goblets prepared for the ceremony. Instead of wine, he had the witch's brew that would give the appearance of mate marks upon both our necks, with nothing more than our lips touching the other's skin.

Thankfully, the potion worked. With so many eyes surrounding us, including my father's, simply faking sinking our teeth into one another would never have worked. Even with Alpha Zifran's confirmation. My father's eyes were sharp. The proof needed to be visible for all.

Ripping my ascot fully from my neck, I stormed to the mirror to check the temporary marking on my neck. It looked real. Too real.

Camellia grimaced, feeling her own neck. "It will take some time to fade."

"I know." I harshly began to button my collar to try to conceal it. I thought I would have some time to let it disappear, but it is already so late. I can't stand waiting a second longer.

The brick surrounding the fireplace quaked. The passage entry opened beside the crackling fire. It was a narrow opening concealed by hollowed bricks, just like the ones that led to the princes' wing from the tribute barracks. From the narrow space burst Basil and then Camellia's true mate.

Basil coughed from the dust of the rarely used doorway. "I thought they would never leave." He cleared his throat. "The coast is clear, your highnesses. The nobles retreated back to the party."

My stomach turned with anxiousness. "My father?"

Basil winced from the harshness of my tone. "H-he and her majesty retired for the evening."

"Good," I growled irritably, moving for the passageway. "Alesta?"

Basil followed me, giving Camellia and the werewolf she was fated to the privacy of our marital chamber. If anyone were to pass by, they would still hear some sort of consummation. It just wouldn't be with me.

"I have not had a moment to check on Miss Alesta personally, sir. The omega I had arranged to bring her meals confirmed she returned to the room after leaving the courtyard."

That should lower my anxiety, but the ache in my chest just throbbed more. My feet carried me quickly through the narrow passages. Basil had to quicken his steps to keep up.

Something was wrong. The closer I got to my bedroom, I felt it. Something was off. I should be able to feel my mate by now. I should be able to reach out to her, or at least feel the tether pulling me towards her in my chest.

Instead, my chest felt hollow. It was grievous, to the point I wanted to claw myself open to feel a pain more tangible. I couldn't identify what this torment was stemming from.

"You're sure she returned to my room?" I growled through my clenched teeth.

Basil was struggling to keep up in the skinny corridor. His voice strained, he said, "The omega told me as much. I see no reason for the maid to lie."

"Something is off." I felt the hair rising on my body. "What if

Alesta left again?"

"Did you not command her, sir?"

I gritted my teeth. "She wouldn't have been in that courtyard if the command had worked."

Basil seemed taken aback. "M-maybe because you are fated? We know so little about how that works. But I don't see how she could leave."

The tributes are all bound to the crown through their oaths. She couldn't leave the inner walls without explicit permission. If she wasn't in our room, she could return to the tribute quarters. Maybe that was this unease I was feeling. Maybe she returned to the barracks and not our room. That was simple enough. I just had to bring her back.

Bring her back. Bring her back. Bring her back. The thought became a chant ringing in my head.

The marital chambers were the opposite wing from where I wanted to be. The walk seemed to take far too long, but eventually I reached the narrow door that opened inside my room. The ache in my chest was intense. Her face was all I craved.

Using far too much strength, I pushed open the passage doorway and squeezed my large body through the small opening. The fireplace rattled around me. Swinging wide, the fragile brick angrily bounced off the stone wall. The metal groaning gave warning that something might have broken, but I didn't stop to see the damage.

Her scent was weak. She wasn't in the main parlor. I raced to the bedroom, leaving Basil to scramble to close the fickle door on his own.

"SHE'S NOT HERE!"

I went into each and every room, my nose flaring as my claws broke free. Alesta wasn't there. She hadn't been here for some time.

Basil was standing, staring at me like a twit. I ripped past him, rattling the bricks more. I rushed towards the only other place she could be.

Bring her back. Bring her back. Fucking bring her back.

The corridor was in danger as my body changed on its own. My beast was on the cusp of coming forth. The closer to the barracks I got, the more hollow I felt.

"Alesta!" I snarled, tearing open the more fragile, simple wood door to her and her friend's bedroom. The fire was never lit in this place, but it felt colder than it should have been. The bedrooms to either side of the fireplace were empty, their door's wide open. Not a simple light was lit. Her friend, Niccola, was absent too.

I checked the rooms over, searching for some sign of my mate. Her scent was stronger here than it was back in my room. But she was not here.

Rage and fear took out the last of my rationale. I began throwing furniture, my beast ripping out of me. As I slung the chest of drawers from her room, it splintered into pieces. Nothing was inside. Not her training clothing, or a single uniform. Not so much as a sock.

Basil came right as I was storming to Niccola's room. He gasped, seeing what I had done. "Your Highness! This isn't the place to... His majesty will-"

His words were background noise as I split Niccola's chest of drawers apart with my claws.

Nothing. They didn't leave any of their belongings in the confined space.

Turning around, I was barely human enough to roar out one last command before my beast consumed me.

"FIND HER! FIND MY MATE!"

Chapter 5

Chocolate Waffles

Alesta

Six years later....

"Alesta," a full, husky voice groaned desperately in my ear. "You're mine." His topaz eyes hooded, full of lust and wonder. "All mine."

My body was arching off the bed. Tingles shot through my chest as it pressed into his weight.

His deep groans full of passion made my breathing hitch. His touch was driving me mad. Every deep thrust sent me closer and closer to the edge.

"Alesta," he moaned. "My beautiful mate. My queen."

He was sweet, as he usually was. His touch was tender. His voice was full of love and kindness. But then, as his movements became more aggressive, more desperate, the mood suddenly changed.

"You're mine," he growled. "Mine!"

The passion was changing into violent possession. His hands, which were so gentle before, began gripping my flesh with bruising force. His eyes lost their warmth, icing into frigid gems. Their depravity rooted fear deep in my chest.

His hand gripped my throat, tightening more and more as his thrusts became more forceful.

"L-Luk..." I tried to pull his hand away, using all my strength.

But then I froze, seeing tears slipping from the corners of his gemstone eyes. His brows bowed in complete sorrow.

"Why?" *he rasped.* "Why do you leave me?..."

"Y-you lied," *I wanted to say, but his grip was too tight. He lied to me, promising I would be his and he would be mine forever....*

But then he went and married someone else.

"Why?..."

His question came in a plea. His heartbreak was clear on his face. I laid there, letting his intensity, his sadness choke me....

"MOM!"

The dream faded as my eyes fluttered open. Groggily, I reached for my neck, the pressure still looming on my skin. Sucking in deep, I inhaled some much needed air....

And that was when my son's scent wafted towards me.

"Mom! We have to go! Wake up!"

With a groan, I rolled over in bed and covered my head with a pillow.

"Mom!"

"My alarm didn't go off yet," my pillow muffled my protest.

"But it's waffle day!" Triston started tugging on my pillow. "If we don't go early, all the chocolate ones are gone!"

"Oh, no," I smirked against my pillow. "Not the chocolate waffles."

Triston let out the cutest growl, which made me laugh.

Shoving the pillow off my face, I smiled and said, "Okay, okay. Goddess forbid you not get a chocolate waffle."

Triston's eyes narrowed on me. "You've got five minutes, mom. Or I'm calling uncle Nic to take me."

"Bossy this morning, aren't we?" I playfully tossed my pillow at him. "Get out so I can change."

Triston took his pointer and middle finger, pointing them at his eyes before turning them at me. "I'm watching you."

"Okay, bossy pants."

His fierce little expression was too much for a five-year-old. Triston was sweet as could be, unless you gave him a reason not to be. Then he turned serious and stubborn. His determination was no joke.

Now that I was alone, I could collect myself from my recurring dream. It was coming more frequently again. The same dream with Lukyan, always starting out sweet, like a precious memory, but then it turns intense and painful, seeing the anger, then pain in his handsome face.

His tears still get me. Every time. I never saw Lukyan cry in real life, but I see it every time in my dream.

I wonder why those dreams are coming back to me. It's been years. I had them the first several months after leaving the kingdom and taking refuge in this remote pack at the edge of the country. They stopped after giving birth, but have been coming back to me recently.

It was probably because of the news that Lukyan was finally crowned king. When the news reached this remote pack, I didn't know how to feel. Just hearing Lukyan's name was overwhelming, but I was happy he achieved the crown.

It had been so long, and we had been together for such a short amount of time that I had almost forgotten his face. My love for Triston and the need to keep him safe overtook every craving I had for the man who helped in Triston's making. But then the dreams came again, and it took me far longer than I'd like each time to get Lukyan out of my head again. Every morning, I couldn't get his teary face out of my mind. Longing I thought was gone forever was the aftermath of the dreams.

There can't be longing. Not with him.

He's married. He has a queen. It's been six years. I'm sure he has other children. I'm sure he doesn't remember my face anymore, as I had almost forgotten his.

Those topaz eyes though..... They were too much like the stubborn little boy whose face I see first after waking up. Triston looks so much like Lukyan the older he gets. If the resemblance deepens any further, it will become undeniable who his father truly is.

I'm thankful the royals and noble Lycans never travel to werewolf packs themselves. They send the werewolf tributes instead. As long as those tributes never see me or my son, everything should be fine. It's not like they would have need to venture this far, anyway. This pack was isolated, only hearing news from the rest of the kingdom through merchants every few weeks.

After changing, I barely got my teeth cleaned and my face washed before Triston came crashing back in.

"Time's up."

Rolling my eyes, I finished drying my face, then slipped on my shoes. "Okay, bossy pants. Let's go."

Triston's pace was close to a jog as he hurried to the mess hall. He didn't give so much as a glance at any of the others wishing him a good morning. I could never be quite so rude. Not when this werewolf pack took us in when we had nowhere else to go.

After the usual chorus of hellos and good mornings, all given after my son ignored everyone's attempts to talk to him, we came upon someone Triston couldn't ignore.

Alpha Mikken Bennet looked up from talking to his Beta. "Well, good morning, little Lycan. What's the rush?"

"Waffles," Triston growled disrespectfully.

"Triston!" I snapped, tugging on his ear. "You can't talk like that to the Alpha."

"That's alright," Alpha Mikken chuckled, giving me a wink. Then he crouched to the ground to be at Triston's level. "Chocolate waffles are important for growing little Lycans. That's why I asked Maggie to put aside a few for you and your mom."

All hostility drained from Triston as a brilliant smile replaced his scowl. "Really? You did that for me?"

"Of course," Alpha Mikken ruffled Triston's hair. Then he looked up at me in that way he sometimes did. A way that made me overly conscious under his gaze. "I remembered they were your favorite. I know how grumpy you get when we run out."

I mouthed, "Thank you." Alpha Mikken nodded subtly, then went back to ruffling Triston's hair.

"Why don't you run ahead and get yours from Maggie while they're still warm."

"Thanks, Alpha!" Triston excitedly jogged for the mess hall doors.

I watched him with a relieved grin. "Thank you, Alpha Mikken. It was going to be a battle getting him to school if they ran out."

"Ken," Alpha crossed his arms over his chest with a smile on his face.

"Huh?"

"I told you to call me Ken, Alesta. You don't have to be formal with me."

There he went, making me overly conscious of everything again. Like the distance between us, which wasn't much right now, and the look on Beta Carlston's face. The Beta was watching us with unmasked amusement.

"Um, everyone should be formal with you, Alpha Mikken."

"Not my secretary. If you can't be comfortable with me, what does that say about our relationship?"

The way he said 'relationship' made me bite my lips and glance up at his grinning Beta again.

"That its professional," I muttered.

Alpha Mikken sighed, then patted my back. "One of these days, I'm going to get you to relax around me."

He didn't give me a chance to refuse before he and his Beta started walking off.

It took me a second to steady my nerves again. Alpha Mikken was generally unnerving, with his long golden hair and smoldering baby blues. Women swoon at just a glance. I was never one of those women, but since he made me his secretary three weeks ago, I've repeatedly had moments of becoming shaken by his crooked smiles and forward way of speaking.

Walking into the mess hall, I saw my son hurrying to a table where his friends were sitting with a tray full of his favorite waffles. He had far more than the other children. Four large ones, whereas the other children had two at the most.

"Hello, Miss Alesta!" Maggie, the head omega serving breakfast, said with a smile as I approached the buffet. "Chocolate waffles for you, too?" She turned for a tray sitting covered on a table behind her.

"I'm fine with the regular," I reassured her. "You gave Triston so many already."

She waved away my concern. "Oh, a growing Lycan boy needs at least that much. He usually comes to get thirds before breakfast is over."

"But still," I looked concerned back at my son. The other kids were already used to Triston's abundant appetite, but I still didn't want him to appear selfish.

Maggie passed the tray to me with firm determination. "Alpha's orders, Miss Alesta. He was adamant that you and your son get plenty of the best." She lifted the lid to reveal four more chocolate waffles, only mine were piled with bananas and whipped cream. It was exactly how I liked them.

I smiled appreciatively at the elderly werewolf woman. "Thank you. You didn't have to do that."

She laughed softly. "Thank the Alpha. It was all his doing."

"Hey, mom?" Triston looked deep in thought as we walked together to his school.

"Yes, baby?"

He wrinkled his nose, staring up at me. "I'm not a baby."

Laughing softly, I rolled my eyes. "Okay, Sir Triston. What is it the elderly Lord mayeth be think-eth about?"

He knit his brows. "You're not funny, mom."

"I think I'm pretty funny."

"Adding 'eth' to words is embarrassing. Don't do it."

"Okay-eth, Triston-eth. What be ye problem-eth?" I snickered, seeing the annoyance on my son's face.

He sighed heavily. "Jeez. Fine. Be weird, mother-eth."

"I will. Thank you for your permission."

He glared. His nose twitched as he shifted his pursed lips back and forth in agitation. Then his expression clouded over, and he looked more sad than irritated.

"Can you be a normal mom for a minute so I can ask you a question?"

His serious tone gained my attention. "What's up, bud?"

He stared at the ground as we walked, then asked, "Why aren't the other kids allowed to train with me?"

My heart beat heavily in my chest. Questions like this have come up a lot recently as he's moved up in from the pack nursery to the school where the differences between a Lycan child and werewolf are more noticeable.

"We talked about this, baby. You're just a little too strong right now."

He nodded, like he expected that answer. "Like you're too strong to train with the other moms?"

I scoffed. "Sure. Something like that." I was a top trainer and one of the elite warriors of the pack before the Alpha made me his secretary. I was the only elite warrior that was female, which is the main reason I only trained with the males.

Triston didn't seem satisfied with my answer, so I pushed further. "Is that all, Tris?"

He shrugged his little shoulders. "I don't know. I guess I'm just wondering why I'm so different. Elliot's mama told the teacher she was scared I would hurt Elliot when we were just playing in the yard. I always play with him. Why is she being a jerk now?"

I rolled my eyes. "Elliot's mom thinks drinking water from the well will make her son sick. I wouldn't put too much concern into the thought process of that worry wort."

Triston snorted. "Can I call her a wort from now on?"

"Not to her face," I ruffled his hair. "Only to me."

I could tell by the look on his face he was going to be calling her that whenever he felt like it, no matter who heard. Prissly Orval would earn the nickname 'the wort' from all of Triston's classmates before the end of the day. I should probably be more concerned about that, but I can't stand the woman either.

She's always in the Alpha's office raising a fuss over anything and everything. Yesterday, she complained about the fences around the horse yards being too tall and expressed her fear that her son would fall while trying to climb them. Last week she got pissy about the batch of sweet potatoes at the market, saying they were far too large to be considered normal. She wanted the soil to be tested for contaminants or witchcraft. Prissly was a wort in every sense.

Plus, she never missed a chance to tell people about me coming to the pack pregnant after fleeing the Lycan capital. The assumption one of the tribute commanders impregnated me came from her. Niccola and I thought it was a better assumption than the truth, so neither ever corrected the rumors. I still haven't forgiven her for running her mouth.

"Mom?" Triston pulled on my skirts as we neared the school building.

"Yes, baby?" He wrinkled his nose at the pet name, but ignored it this time.

"Is a Lycan really that different from a werewolf?"

Pressing my lips together, I thought about how to respond. "They are different, but not so much that it should matter," I eventually told him.

He nodded, then asked, "You're a werewolf, right?"

My heart quickened, knowing what his next question would be. Still, I nodded my head. "Yes. I am."

"So.... So that means my... my dad was a Lycan?"

I hesitated, then nodded again. "I've told you he was."

"Yeah," he muttered, kicking his foot while staring at the ground. "You won't tell me who he is, though."

I sighed, crouching down, so I was eye level with him. "I will one day, but not now. I told you it's... it's not safe."

He groaned. "I can keep secrets, mom. I keep them all the time."

"I know, baby, but it's still not something we can talk about just yet." I looked around at the other parents walking their kids to school. "Especially not here."

"So, you'll tell me when we're alone?"

This is about the tenth time he has asked me. I don't know what to do. I don't know if I can tell him. If his father really were just a Lycan commander, then I might have been willing to let the secret out. But him being the first son of the Lycan king would not just endanger us, but this entire pack.

"I'll think about it," was all I could say.

He growled. "That means no."

With a soft chuckle, I said, "No, it's a maybe. I... I just need to think about it some more." I need to think and maybe talk to Niccola. Niccola was the one still in communication with the one who helped us escape.

Chapter 6

Inspected

An ominous feeling pressed over me as I walked to the pack's offices. First the dream of Lukyan, and now because of my son's relentless questioning.

"Good morning, Miss Alesta," Rachel, the office clerk, smiled warmly as I made my way to my desk outside of Alpha Mikken's office.

"Good morning," I repeated back. "Anything on our agenda for the day?"

Her smile faltered. "Um, actually Alpha asked for you to see him when you got in."

"Really? I just saw him an hour ago." Her expression suddenly seemed wary. It made me anxious.

She pursed her lips, then said, "We just received a notice from the Erebos Kingdom. I'm not sure what it said, but Alpha didn't look happy."

"He never does when news comes from the capital."

After grabbing a notepad and pencil, I knocked on the Alpha's door.

"Come in," Beta Carlston was the one who answered. "Ah, Alesha's here, Alpha," he said, grinning at me.

Alpha Mikken had his head hung in his hands, sitting behind his desk. He glanced up at me, his blue eyes hooded and stressed.

"Rough morning, Alpha Mikken?"

He sighed, then sat back in his chair, crossing his arms gruffly over his chest. "Yeah. Call me Ken and make it all better for me."

Beta Carlston snickered as I smirked, shaking my head. "Sorry, Alpha Mikken."

"Figures," Alpha Mikken groaned. He started twirling a pen between his fingers. "How were your waffles?"

"Great," I smile, trying to maintain a professional air. "Rachel said you wanted to see me."

"Straight to business," he grinned while shaking his head. "Yeah. I've got a bit of a headache coming this way from the capital and am going to need you to organize accommodations and a full inspection of the warriors."

My eyes widened. "Accommodations?"

"We're being inspected," Beta Carlston told me. "Something about the new reign assessing the territories, including all the werewolf packs."

Alpha Mikken added, "Which has never happened before. The Kingdom doesn't care about werewolves as long as they get their tributes."

That may have been true for the previous reign, but I knew Lukyan wasn't like that. At least, he didn't use to be. He seemed just as concerned for his werewolf subjects and his Lycan ones. But who knows how much has changed, or if that was even his true feelings back then. He told me a lot of things that ended up just being pretty little lies.

Whatever the reason for this inspection, my concerns lie elsewhere.

"Is... is it a werewolf tribute doing the inspection?"

Alpha Mikken's gaze was steady on me. Like he was observing my reaction. "The messenger mentioned the second prince."

My shoulders noticeably relaxed at the mention of Casimir.

"Would it have been an issue if it was someone else?" Alpha Mikken asked.

I bit my lip. "I, uh, was just curious if it was going to be, the..." Instead of saying new King, I thought back to Prissy's lie. "If it was going to be any of the commanders," I smiled tightly. "So, accommodations for Prince Casimir and an inspection of the warriors?" I jotted that down in my notes with messy handwriting. "Anything else?"

When my question was met with extended silence, I looked up from my notes at Alpha Mikken expectantly. He was still studying me, tapping the pen to his lips.

"Anything else, Alpha?" I repeated.

He dropped his pen on his desk, then with total seriousness said, "I've never pushed for any details of your departure from the capital. No one detests the capital more than me, so when your friend spoke of your hardships, and how neither of you had packs to return to, we readily accepted the two, well, three of you."

I cringed when I heard the reminder that my previous pack, as well as Niccola's, had been destroyed. The details of which were not given to us as we fled, and we didn't have the resources to discover the truth about how it happened. The rumors ranged from the new queen being responsible to the old king being the one who destroyed my home pack as retribution for my existence.

I just hoped it was not Lukyan responsible. I do not know if that is a truth I could ever recover from.

Alpha Mikken continued, "I've never asked about your son's birth father, Alesta. I saw your pain as you protected and birthed him alone. I respected you for the love you showed to your pup, and never wanted to question his parentage despite his Lycan genes, but I need to know," he paused, gauging my expression, "Will you or your son be in any danger?"

Gnawing on my bottom lip, I weighed everything inside my head. That ominous feeling crept over me again, pressing into my chest. It made it hard to breathe.

Alpha Mikken, probably sensing my panic, pushed his aura over me. His eyes narrowed as he accessed me, but his commanding tone was gentle. "Do I need to protect you from this envoy from the capital?"

It was a command. Not a question.

As always, I felt the command, but it had no effect on me. Feigning compliance, I murmured, "No, Alpha. If it is Prince Casimir, all will be fine. I just... I just don't want to meet any commanders." Or the King, but no one needed to know that. Not even if he was my Alpha.

Alpha Mikken maintained his stare as his aura continued to press over me. Then he subtly nodded and let his command recede.

"Alright. If you have no concerns with the second prince, then I will trust your word."

Beta Carlston tilted his head, eyeing me skeptically. "It's not like you shouldn't trust her word, with her being under command and all."

Under his scrutiny, I nodded softly. "Right. Well, I'll get started on this right away," I waved my notepad towards them before turning for the door.

"Wait," Alpha Mikken called out to me. I slowly turned to face him again, nervous about what questions might come next.

"You know, I only ask because I'm worried about you," he said carefully. "I know you like to shoulder things yourself, but you don't have to. Especially with something of this magnitude. I'm here for you." His gaze was steady, piercing into me. "I'm going to protect you. You and Triston. I just need to know how."

I hesitated, then nodded slowly, trying to put on a grateful smile. "I understand. Thank you, Alpha."

"Ken," he sighed. "I wish you would just call me Ken."

Niccola was easy to spot as I hurried into the training fields. Female warriors, all pining to get a chance with the brave tribute who escaped the capital to save a fellow werewolf, surrounded him.

Everyone in the pack saw Niccola as my savior. When our sibling-like relationship became known, and we both made it clear there was no romance between us, he was the prime target of all the thirsty little she-wolves. Having a protective mate, willing to defy the monarchy itself, must be a prime quality females here look for in a mate.

He looked relieved when he saw me coming his way.

"Hey! Aly!" He waved enthusiastically in my direction. The she-wolves looked less than enthused at my appearance when he jogged away from them towards me. "Perfect timing."

"Is it?" I suppressed my amusement as I waved tauntingly at his fans. "You seem busy. I can come back," I joked.

"No! No, no. Not busy," he stammered, grabbing my shoulders so I wouldn't turn away. "Training's finished. Now, take me somewhere, anywhere, before they drag me off again." His eyes darted to the circle of women glaring at me.

He's lucky I needed to talk to him anyway, or I might just be tossing him to the wolves. I get enough hate for being chosen as Alpha Mikken's new secretary. I don't really want more from Nic's fan club.

"Let's go get tea," I murmured, grabbing his sleeve to drag him behind me. "They look ready to pounce."

Niccola shuddered.

"You saved me. They always try to get me to go for a run with them after training ends."

"That doesn't sound that scary."

He grimaced. "They hide my clothes, so when I shift back, I have nothing to wear. Then they wait for me near the barracks. It's embarrassing."

I chortled behind my hand. "Gets. Why are you always so easy to pick on?"

"I don't know! I've said I wasn't interested so many freaking times, but they don't listen." He pursed his lips into a pout. "I'm still waiting for my mate."

His eyes widened, alarm crossing him as it usually does when he mentions mates around me.

"I'm fine," I said softly. "You don't have to worry about me every time you mention wanting your mate."

"I know, even so," he twisted his face. "It still sucks."

"Yeah," I smiled sadly. "But I got Triston, so I'm still counting it as a blessing."

Niccola snorted. "Blessing my left butt cheek. Your little terror threatened to cut my tail off yesterday."

"Why? What did you do?"

"Nothing!" He scoffed. "I was eating *my* cookies someone so generously gave me at dinner and he wanted one."

I clicked my tongue and shook my head. "Wouldn't share your snacks with a child. Shame on you."

"Hey, they were butterscotch! Your brat wouldn't share with me either." He scoffed again. "He's got me scared to shift in front of him now."

"He wouldn't actually cut your tail off."

"He was dead serious when he said it! Your heathen is as scary as you."

"My heathen?" I raised my eyebrow.

"See!" Niccola pointed drastically at me. "You're both scary little demons when you get all pissy. You look like you want to gouge my eyes out right now."

"I just might if you keep running your mouth. Or at the very least, throw you back to those she-wolves without your clothes."

Niccola cringed. "Please don't. I'll share my cookie with your demon spawn next time."

"Good," I chuckled. "Wise choice."

"Like it was a choice," Niccola rolled his eyes. He then looked around, noticing I was leading him to the deserted part of the forest and not the pack house, like he probably expected. "Where are we going? You're not really going to throw me to the she-wolves, are you?"

I laughed softly. "No. Not yet anyway. We'll see how this conversation goes first."

"What conversation?" Niccola eyed me warily. "What's going

on?"

I looked around, biting my lips. When I was sure no one was around or listening, I asked, "Have you heard from Prince Casimir lately?"

Niccola shrugged. "Not of anything remarkable. Just his general nonsense. Why? What happened?"

As I hesitated and looked around again, I felt my nervousness mingling with that ominous feeling that had been creeping over me all day. "Because. I just got news that Prince Casimir is going to be inspecting the pack on behalf of the new king."

Chapter 7

Little Lycan

Triston

"**A**re you sure my son will be okay?" That wort woman, Elliot's mama, started to nag the instructors again while we warmed up for training. She's not even supposed to be here, but she keeps showing up, anyway. "He's not built like the rest of us. They're beasts!"

I mistakenly let out a low growling noise of irritation as I bent over to touch my toes. I didn't mean to, but she was being a big wort. My little, innocent growl caused her to yelp, then point her bony finger at me.

"See! He's rabid, I tell you! What can you expect when he was created through violence!"

"Created through violence?" I scoffed loudly. "Do you hear yourself when you talk, lady?! If my mama heard you say that, she'd show you real violence."

"AH! Did you hear him?! He just threatened me!"

Instructor Zaden rolled his eyes. "He's got a point, Mrs. Orval. Secretary Alesta would get violent if she heard the way you are carrying on about her son. The kid's never done anything wrong. He's given no one any reason to worry, so if you have complaints, I suggest you take them to Alpha Mikken or-"

"What about Alpha Mikken?" The Alpha himself sudden;y appeared at the entrance to the training field. He had his hands in his pockets, looking relaxed, but I could see a vein pulsing in his neck. His aura was filled with the same feelings I had right now, too. He felt annoyed.

"She is being a wort!" I told him honestly.

The wort huffed and choked on her words loudly, pressing her hand to her chest. "Alpha! I... I would.... Do you hear the way he is speaking to me!"

"Don't be a wort and I won't talk to you like you're being one!"

Instructor Zaden was trying and failing to not laugh. He had to walk off as his amusement spilled out of him in snorts and chortles. Even Alpha cracked a smile.

Alpha held his hand out to Elliot's mom when she started to be whiney again. "How's she being a wort, Triston?" He squatted down, so he was staring right into my eyes.

"She keeps saying Elliot can't train or play with me. She's a wort because she's mean and says things my mama wouldn't like!" I then let out another involuntary growl as I glared at her. "She better watch out or I'll start telling mama everything she's saying."

Alpha was quiet, watching me for a second, then asked, "What all is she saying, Triston?"

I pressed my lips together, not wanting to tell him. It was embarrassing, and I know it would make mama mad. I also didn't know if it was true, and didn't want Alpha to know what Elliot's mom thinks about me.

"Triston?" Alpha raised his eyebrows, his tone a little more forceful.

I sighed, shagging my shoulders. "Fine. She called me a beast and said I'm a brutal bastard because of where I came from. She says bad things about mama. Like mama got hurt by someone when she had me."

This time, it was Alpha that growled. He looked really, really mad as he turned his angry face at Elliot's mom. She looked scared for once and had nothing to say.

"Is this true?" Alpha asked her.

"W-well…. I…."

"IS THIS TRUE!" He stood and pushed his aura over her so harshly that I even felt it. It itched my skin.

"Yes!" The wort fell to her knees, the aura from the Alpha hurting her. "I… I'm sorry, Alpha! B-but she… He is a b-b-bastard, so to speak-"

"ENOUGH!" He bellowed. "You are banned from the training grounds. Report to Beta Carlston in the morning for disciplinary action. Someone get her out of here before I deal with her myself."

"Can I deal with her?" I asked, glaring at her as two of the female instructors began dragging her away from the field. Elliot was watching, looking all kinds of embarrassed. "I want to punish her for being mean about mama."

"How would you punish her, little Lycan?" Alpha raised his eyebrow.

"Change her name to 'The Wort' on all official papers. Maybe write it on her forehead to warn others she's a big one."

INstructor Zaden, who had just walked back now that the wort was gone, started bursting into laughter again. "I can't with this kid, Alpha," Instructor Zaden wiped tears from his eyes. "There's never any filter. It's fantastic."

"He's just like his mother," Alpha smirked down at me. The way his eyes looked and his aura felt, I could tell he wasn't mad much anymore. He almost felt proud. "She doesn't put up with that ignorant crap, either. That's why I made the woman my secretary."

"Is that the only reason, Alpha?" Instructor Zaden elbowed the Alpha with a snicker.

Alpha smiled crookedly, his aura changing to feel like mom's when she's being shy. "Who are you to ask me that?" Alpha elbowed Instructor Zaden back.

"Your curious friend."

Alpha covered his face with his hand. "Be less curious and pay more attention to the kids. That one over there is throwing mud balls at the wort's kid." Alpha pointed to Elliot and Ryan, who were tossing mud at each other while Instructor Zaden was distracted.

"Boy!" Instructor Zaden walked off to get on to them.

Alpha crossed his arms, looking amused at my friends. "Boys will be boys. Isn't that right, Triston?"

I shrugged. "I don't know. I don't like throwing mud like they do. It feels gross in my hands."

"Really. I like the feeling of dirt and mud under my nails." Alpha examined his fingers.

"I don't. Mama doesn't like it either. She doesn't do the prissy stuff to her nails like some of the other moms, but she does clean under them for a long time when she gets done with runs."

"Really?" Alpha frowned at his nails, then closed them into fists like he was hiding them.

"Yeah. She doesn't like long nails either. The wort's nails are super long, but mom's are short. She makes me cut mine short a lot too. Says it looks better."

The Alpha's frown deepened. "Hmm. Guess mine are getting a little long." He held his hand out again.

"Yeah," I looked at his fingers. "She would make me cut those."

He nodded, pursing his lips. "Good to know." He sighed, then put his hands in his pockets. "Hey, Triston. How about you train with me today? Maybe you can tell me more about all the things your mom doesn't like."

I looked him up and down, wondering if I wanted to train with the Alpha instead of my friends. Now that Elliot's mom was gone, I could have fun with him, but the Alpha looked more sturdy. I wouldn't have to be careful like I had to with the other kids.

With a shrug, I said, "Okay. But only if you don't tell mom about calling Elliot's mom a wort. She told me not to."

Alpha chuckled. "You got a deal, little Lycan."

∞ ∞ ∞

Alesta

"Did you ready the rooms?" I double-checked with one of the omegas as we did a final walk-through of the living quarters Casimir and his people will be using.

"Yes, Miss Alesta. We brought in the last of the drapes early this morning and we are hanging them in all the windows right now. They have been laundered, as were the bedding and table linens."

"Great. Everything looks good here." I smiled at one of the bouquets of wildflowers that were brought in to set in the hallway table. It wasn't grand and overdone like the arrangements would be at the palace, but I found wildflowers to be far more charming.

"Miss Alesta! The kitchen is calling for you!"

"Coming," I said, dismissing the omega and following the aid to the kitchen.

The pack house was still in a frenzy trying to get last-minute preparations finished, but it was all coming together. There was not a speck of dirt or dust on any surface. I could see myself on the polished floors. The air smelled fresh, like lemons and herbs.

While walking through the main corridor, I saw more crude vases filled with the same wildflowers that were in the guest quarters upstairs.

"The flowers are a nice touch," I thought out loud.

Sam, the aide, chuckled under his breath. "It was worth the effort then. The Alpha will be pleased to hear that."

I furrowed my brows in confusion. "What do you mean?"

Sam's smile just grew. "The Alpha heard that you liked wildflowers is all, Miss Alesta. Alpha Mikken organized the children to pick them all day yesterday, excusing them from school and training so we would have enough for the entire pack house."

"Alpha Mikken did that?!"

"Yep," Sam chuckled. "He even went out there for a few hours to pick them himself."

I wondered where he had disappeared all day yesterday while I was organizing the warrior's presentations. Gamma Kender was the one with me instead.

"W-why would Alpha Mikken go through so much trouble at such a pressing time just because he heard I liked wildflowers?"

"I wonder." There was a twinkle in Sam's eyes that had my face growing warm all of a sudden. He chuckled again, then went on to explain more about the issues that arose in the kitchen. I was only half paying attention as I thought about the wildflowers and our Alpha.

Alpha Mikken had been making me far more flustered than normal the past few days. I thought it was just because I've been a little frantic trying to get everything completed before the Lycans came onto our territory. He would always distract me from my own chaos with flirtatious gestures or light teasing.

Random snacks also have been appearing on my desk quite often too. When I got back from warrior training yesterday, there was a place of peanut butter cookies waiting for me. I thought that maybe Nic had left them, seeing how stressed I was during formations. He was one of the few people that knew my favorite treat.

When I thanked Nic for the cookies this morning, he gave me a dumbfounded look and said he did not know what I was talking about. His pressing and teasing afterward made me drop the whole thing, but now I'm wondering if Alpha Mikken somehow heard I like peanut butter cookies too. Maybe from the same individual who told him I liked wildflowers.

I had a hunch about who that individual might be.

The kitchen was in an uproar as the two main chefs were

arguing over what the main course should be served at the welcome dinner. One wanted cod and the other venison. It was an easy enough argument to settle. Though Lukyan would have preferred the venison, his brother liked his courses light. Fish would be his preference.

With that sorted, both chefs gruffly going back to their own stations to prep. I snuck over to the spread of sample plates to try out the different options the cooks had been preparing all day. They were likely left out for Alpha Mikken to try, but I'm sure he wouldn't mind if I snuck a few small bites. The scents were so mouthwatering that it was hard to resist.

With the first taste of a sugar-glazed sweet potato, my eyes rolled to the back of my head and a satisfied moan escaped my sugary lips.

"That good, huh?" A deep, smooth voice startled me as my Alpha chuckled.

I turned to see Alpha Mikken smirking. His crooked grin was disarming, as it usually was. I quickly swallowed, then turned around to hunt for a napkin to wipe the embarrassment off my lips.

"Need one of these?" Alpha Mikken held a handkerchief he pulled from his pocket up in the air.

I nodded, trying to hide my shame from my gluttony shadowed by my hair. I reached for the cloth, but he lifted his arm, putting it just out of my reach.

"Hey," I grumbled.

His throaty laughter made me growl in frustration. "Here. Let me help you."

He gently rested a hand on my face, tilting my face up to make it accessible to him. My eyes widened in surprise as he took the handkerchief and began gingerly wiping the sugar glaze from my lips.

His intentions may have been just a friendly gesture, but it felt awkwardly intimate. The kitchen staff were whispering excitedly and giggling among themselves, so I know I wasn't the only one that thought so.

I reached to take the cloth napkin from his hands. "Alpha, I can-"

"Almost done." He didn't let me take it.

He moved his elbow to block me as he wiped the last of the sugar from the corner of my lips. His bare finger barely brushed against my sticky skin. When he looked down at the sugar residue that passed for me to him, his blue eyes were fluid, like the movement of the ocean on a sunny day.

Everyone gasped, no one louder than me, when he lifted his finger to his lips and licked the sugar off. I was sputtering, fully unnerved once again. That just made his laugh more.

"Mmm. It is good."

Chapter 8

Unwelcome Teasing

I was too stunned to move. I couldn't believe he just did that. He was taking his teasing too far, and this time it was in front of the entire kitchen staff.

After a deep breath, I finally found my voice. "Alpha, that was entirely inappropriate."

"Ken," he smirked. "You forgot to call me Ken again."

My shock was being taken away by the irritation I felt. So many eyes were on us. The rumors his teasing and comment would cause would make my job so much harder.

"Alpha Mikken, I already told you that I-"

"Shh," he took the fork from my hand, then filled it with something from another plate before pressing it to my mouth. "We have plenty more dishes to try."

I couldn't even taste what I was eating. The tightening in my chest was different from usual. It was weighed down by that recurring ominous feeling creeping over me at the most random of times. This time, it felt triggered by my Alpha's close proximity, and the many eyes watching us as he repeatedly tried to feed me bites of different foods.

I wanted to refuse, and even thought of lashing out, but he was the Alpha and I couldn't disrespect him in front of the staff. He may have the power to disregard the audience observing his behavior, but I did not have that luxury. I would just have to discuss this with him later to ensure he knows my boundaries as his secretary. He is crossing all of them rather forcefully right now.

Eventually, I wrestled my fork away from him, and provided him with a new one so we wouldn't continue sharing. I wanted to trade mine out for a new one too, feeling slightly nauseous thinking about his mouth having touched this one. Before I could, he reached for a napkin and accidentally knocked all the spare forks to the ground. I was stuck with the overused one.

That nausea worsened the more food we sampled together, and the pressure in my chest grew. He placed his hand on the small of my back at one point, and I thought I was going to truly be sick.

What was wrong with me? Did I overwork myself too much in the past few days?

"Are you okay, Alesta?" Alpha Mikken caught on to my sudden distress, pressing closer to me. He rested a hand on my forehead, making my chest tighten to the point I groaned out in pain. "What? What hurts? Did you eat something bad?" His eyes scanned the plates of food we had gone through.

"No," I stepped away from him. The pain in my chest eased up a bit with the distance. "I don't think it's the food. Maybe I haven't been getting enough sleep."

He came closer again, his expression almost desperate, like he was searching for a way to help me. "You should rest then. I'll help you to my-"

"Alpha!" Beta Carlston rushed into the kitchen at that moment, giving me the distraction I needed to put space between me and the Alpha again. "Alpha! We have a problem! A hu-uuuge fucking problem!"

Alpha Mikken's lips twisted, like he was annoyed at the interruption. He may have been annoyed, but I was grateful. Grateful for the opportunity for the attention to move to something else while I tried to better hide the discomfort I was feeling.

"What kind of huge fucking problem?" Alpha growled.

Beta Carlston grimaced at Alpha Mikken's harsh tone. "Um, the kind I think you should see in person."

Alpha's lips curled in irritation. "Just tell me!"

His outburst sent a chill of fear through the room. The kitchen staff were standing completely motionless, watching with caution as their Alpha snapped at the Beta. Even the Beta was hesitating to irritate the Alpha more.

This was the real reason why I was promoted above everyone else native to this pack as his secretary. On the rare occasions our Alpha lost his temper, it never affected me. His Alpha aura, like all Alpha auras, didn't immobilize me or cause me panic. If we were in training and someone royally messed up, he would, on very rare occasions, unconsciously push his aura over those around them. While others fought to keep their dignity in the face of an angry Alpha, I could always remain calm.

I'd never seen him irrationally irritated like he was now. Seeing the unease on the staff's faces, I ignored the tightness in my chest and decided to step in.

"Alpha," I gently placed my hand on his arm. He didn't even flinch, not responding in any way. "Ken," I whispered. His glare moved from his Beta and his eyes softened before he looked down at me.

With a heavy sigh, his aura receded. "Sorry. I guess I haven't been getting enough sleep either."

"Grumpy-ass," Beta Carlston mumbled under his breath.

I braced myself, thinking the Alpha might lash out at his Beta for that comment, but he surprised me by chuckling instead. His fluid blue eyes crinkled in the corners as he gently reached for my hand. The tightness in my chest returned in full force, but I internalized the pain given the situation.

"I guess we should go see what the problem is. Huh, Alesta?"

I felt everyone's eyes, as painfully as I felt the undeniable pressure. The Beta was smirking as others were murmuring to each other.

"Did you see that? She calmed him with a single touch."

"Maybe the rumors are true."

"Look at how he's staring at her. They're still holding hands, too."

I quickly pulled my hand from his, looking at the ground to hide my annoyance. Another boundary of mine had been crossed, and this time it was a big one.

"Let's go," I mumbled, moving past him to the door.

"She must be shy," Beta Carlston said as Alpha and he followed behind me.

I rolled my eyes, looking ahead so they couldn't see.

"I don't think it's her being shy," Alpha Mikken replied.

We were out in the hall, no others in earshot. Just the Alpha and Beta. I stopped on my heels and turned to glare at both of them.

"I'm not shy. I'm upset." I held my head, trying to find the words without being outright disrespectful. "I understand your teasing when we are in the office, but that was way over the line just now. People are going to think that there... that there is something between us!"

The corner of the Alpha's lips curled up. "You did call me Ken."

"Because!" I stopped myself before I exploded, pinching the bridge of my nose. He was trying to provoke me. After exhaling deeply, and when I was sure I could speak calmly, I continued, "Okay. Let's measure this up to you being exhausted. I am as well. But your teasing needs to stop. Especially in front of others, Alpha. I don't want more false rumors to spread about me, especially concerning the leader of our pack."

Alpha Mikken pursed his lips, seemingly unpleased with what I had just said. "Would it be so bad to have rumors about you and me?"

"Yes!" I exclaimed. "I'm not some single young she-wolf open to such gossip on the off-chance it might one day be true! I'm a mother, and rumors impact my son as well."

Alpha Mikken's expression turned guilty, then he nodded his head. "You're right, Alesta. I was being inconsiderate. It won't happen again." His eyes held my gaze as he took a step forward. "But I'm not just teasing. Not with you."

My chest tightened again. That unnerving feeling crawled over my skin. He was an attractive man. Extremely attractive. If it wasn't for the pain in my chest, I'd be more shaken.

But the pain in my chest as he placed his hand on my shoulder overshadowed everything. It made our close proximity feel wrong.

The silence stretched, the tension building as his blue gaze never left mine. It suddenly snapped when Gamma Kender started yelling from down the hall.

"They're here! They're here!"

After I jerked away, being the first to lower my gaze, I heard Alpha Mikken let out a small groan before he turned his attention to his Gamma.

"Who?!"

Beta Carlston rolled his eyes. "The tooth fairy. Who do you think? That's why I was coming to get you, genius."

Alpha Mikken let out another sound of annoyance. Before we had any more delays or awkward conversions, I pushed past him to hurry down the hall.

"We shouldn't keep them waiting."

Beta Carlston snickered behind me. "Of course not. Not when royalty comes all this way."

I wouldn't make a big fuss over Casimir or roll out the royal carpet for a man that had a sex shack behind the kingdom's palace. Maybe instead of preparing the guest quite, I should have tidied up the broken down garden hutch behind the pack house.

"They're coming early," Gamma Kender whispered loudly as we passed a group of maids hovering around a window. "You said they wouldn't be here until tomorrow."

I craned my neck to see out too, but there were too many heads in the way. I couldn't see anything.

"They weren't supposed to be," Alpha growled low and deep. "It's like they are trying to catch me off guard."

"Maybe they're just in a hurry to visit our lovely territory," Beta Carlston mused.

Gamma Kender quickened his pace to catch up with me. "You're from the capital, Alesta. Do the royals have a curiosity about how the poor werewolf folk live out here in the boonies?"

"I do not know," I murmured.

"None? Have you ever met the royals before?"

I hesitated, then nodded subtly. "Tributes have to pledge themselves to the royals upon arrival." I swallowed. "I've met them."

The memories of that first meeting made my chest ache again, but in a different way. There was a longing in the pain, but that longing would never be fulfilled. Not anymore.

"So, you know what Prince Casimir is like?"

I snorted at Gamma Kender's question. "Everyone knew what the philandering prince was like. The guy had a damn sex shack on the palace grounds."

"A sex shack?!" Gamma Kender exclaimed, like he was appalled.

"A sex shack, huh?" Beta Carlston was smirking. "And how would *you* know he had a sex shack? Pay any visits to it during your time there?"

Laughing, I looked back at my Beta and said, "I had, actually."

"What?" Alpha Mikken's expression hardened.

Beta Carlston looked like he was ready to bounce on his feet with glee. "You spent *time* with Prince Carlston? Oh, my. Could he be...."

"No," I stopped that thought before he fully voiced it. "*I* was not on the young prince's radar, but Niccola sure was," I chuckled to myself. "The only time I visited his love hut was with Nic for a *very* short period of time. I was just passing through."

I tried not to notice how relieved Alpha looked.

The front doors were opened, the guards assigned there standing tall but visibly nervous.

"Fuck," Alpha Mikken mumbled under his breath. "I'm not fucking ready for this."

"Aw, you look nice," Beta Carlston patted his back.

Alpha Mikken shoved his hand away. "I'm not talking about my outfit, idiot."

He meant he was not mentally prepared yet to act friendly or respectful to the Lycans he despised.

Turning around, I stopped him with my hands on his chest. "You two go ahead and greet them first. We will be right out," I told the Beta and Gamma.

Beta Carlston snickered. "Okay, *Luna*."

I growled. Beta Carlston was pushing his luck with me, too. He just laughed to himself and wrapped his arm around Gamma Kender's tense shoulders, chuckling all the way out the door. I heard the carriage pull up and had to focus back on Alpha before he had to face Prince Casimir.

"I'm going to end up kicking his or your ass before the day ends," I mumbled under my breath, focusing on fixing Alpha Mikken's skewed shirt.

He had a napkin shoved in his front pants pocket from the kitchen still. I hurriedly took it out and waved an omega over to take it for me to the trash.

"I know you hate Lycans and the royals, but Prince Casimir is truly not that bad. Your biggest worry will be keeping him out of the she-wolf rooms, but I've already warned all the warriors to give him a firm no, if he should ask. He's a man whore, but he doesn't cause trouble."

Alpha was silent for several seconds until I looked up to meet his grinning gaze. "You couldn't kick my ass."

I raised my eyebrow. "I could if you keep pushing me. I don't like being teased."

"Hmm, that's too bad, because I happen to really like teasing you." He pinched my nose, making me growl and swat at his hand.

"I noticed," I growled.

All of a sudden, my chest grew tight, far tighter than before. I groaned, pressing my hand against it. Alpha Mikken reached out to support me before I buckled over.

"What's wrong?! What happened, Alesta?"

I couldn't form words as Alpha held me in his arms. The pain was unbearable. All I could do was grit my teeth until I heard a fierce snarling coming from the pack house doors.

I recognized that snarl. The aura pressing over me with sudden imposing force was all too familiar as well. It wasn't Prince Casimir's scent wafting towards me, making the pain in my chest ease with every breath.

No. It was not the royal we were expecting.

Clenching the front of Alpha Mikken's shirt, I rasped, "Lukyan...."

Chapter 9

Lost Mate

Lukyan

Earlier...

"I t's rather quaint out here," Casimir said, uncharacteristically commenting on the terrain for the tenth time in the past hour. "This Alpha must take great pride in his pack. His pack members must be well taken care of."

"Indeed." Ruth, my wife's true mate, smiled, staring out the window while absentmindedly rubbing Camellia's bare feet.

His crimson eyes were assessing the landscape in a way I always find unsettling. The hybrid werewolf, his blood mixed because of his witch mother, saw the world differently than the rest of us. He saw the underlying currents of mana passing between living things, reading their vitality.

Those invasive crimson eyes of his have helped me significantly in my rise to power. As much as they creep me out, I am thankful for their ability.

"What do you suppose the main building, their pack house, will be like?" Casimir's lips curled in that way they did when he was entertained by his own thoughts.

Camellia opened one of her eyes to gaze at my brother. "Why are you so enthused about this inspection? You even insisted on us accompanying you. Is there something special about the Hallowed Moon Pack we are unaware of?"

"Oh, I don't know," Casimir snickered. "I've seen so many of these hinterland packs, but never have I so anticipated a first meeting like this." He waved his hands towards the window. "Because of the quaintness of the terrain, of course."

It was strange that Casimir insisted upon my company. This pack was not on the council's radar, seeing as it was too far from our capital to be of much consequence. We hadn't even taken a tribute from the Hallowed Moon Pack in nearly twenty years.

My focus has been on the werewolf packs where our prime tributes our sourced from. Now that power was mine, my goal hasn't changed. I need to change everything before the past repeats itself.

I've lost far too much to give up now.

Casimir's insistence wasn't the only reason Camellia, and I came to this inspection. Something my mother said also influenced my decision. After hearing her words, I knew the nagging feelings she and my brother stirred within me wouldn't subside until I saw for myself what was so special about this pack.

"They're scrambling," Camellia mused while staring out the window. Her soft smile displayed her sympathy. "We're early. They must be frantic."

"The prince urged that we keep ahead of schedule," Ruth reminded her.

Casimir waved his hand in the air. "I so love surprises. I live for them."

"They don't seem to share your sentiments," Ruth smirked.

There was this painful throbbing in my chest. It's been hollow for so many years, but ever since Casimir urged me to join him, the hollowed void began to throb around its edges at the strangest of times.

Right now, the pain was beating like a hammer in my chest. I knew it couldn't have been my heart, because my heart left me six years ago.

"What is the Alpha's name?" I asked.

Casimir stared at me with his fingers pressed to his mouth. There was a smirk playing on his lips. "Are you suddenly curious about this pack, brother?"

I growled, my mood darkening visibly at his teasing.

He chuckled, seemingly unaffected. "Alpha Mikken Bennet. He's a fair and honest man from the reports I've seen. You can relax, brother." He looked out the window as he said, "I wouldn't want you to have another episode."

My lips curled, and a warning tone shook the carriage. The draft horses, as large and powerful as they were, were extremely calm creatures. They were not easily startled, but whined loudly because of my snarl.

Camellia smacked Casimir with the back of her hand against his chest, giving him a warning look of her own. We may not be truly mated, despite the fabricated marks on our necks, but she still was the one who took to calming my *episodes*, as my little brother called them.

As hard as I tried, I sometimes couldn't stop myself. My beast has become more and more unstable over the years. Ever since *she* left.

I need to finish what we started before my rabid nature consumes me. I took to focusing on what I needed to accomplish to make the aggression coursing through my body subside enough that the threat was gone.

Camellia smiled sadly at me, then turned those same eyes up to her mate. He seemed to know what he was thinking and kissed her head before resting his cheek on her. She would have become as miserable as me if her mate had left her as mine did. Maybe this was why Lycans did not receive the blessing of a fated mate as often as the werewolves did. Our beastly side could not recover from the loss if things went awry.

The sounds of the werewolves hustling in a panic grew louder. We must be nearing the pack house now. I sat alone on the seat facing backward as my wife and her mate sat opposite of me with my brother. They were watching out the window at the chaos outside as I closed my eyes and tried to focus on the void in my chest. It was paining me again, and I feared my beast would unleash himself if I did not quickly overcome the pain.

I felt Camellia's presence shift to right beside me. To keep up appearances, we would need to carry on the image of a united king and queen. Her mate would be our werewolf advisor, and my brother had the simple task of just being himself.

The pain in my chest just seemed to intensify the longer I tried to fight it. It was as if it got worse the closer we got to our destination. My beast was more on edge than before, which confused me further. Usually it was only... only the things that reminded me strongly of *her*, the one whose name I haven't spoken since giving up on her search.

Minutes later, much sooner than I would have liked, I felt Camellia's hands pressing into my leg. She was gently helping me break free from my failed meditation. "We're here, Lukyan. Are you going to be alright?"

Opening my eyes, I was met with the concern of Camellia, Ruth's invasive stare, and my brother's arrogant smirk.

My frown deepened. "I will have to be, won't I?"

Her smile tightened as she patted my leg. "We'll make the introductions quick, then you can retire for the evening. Maybe a night's rest out of this carriage will help to settle you."

"I doubt that," Casimir murmured, being the first to descend from the carriage upon the coachman opening the doors.

He helped Camellia down, then I waved to Ruth to go ahead. There was something about the air in this place that was making the painful void inside of me so much more excruciating.

I gritted my teeth, barely containing my menacing aura as I was the last to descend from the stuffy carriage to the open air of the Hallowed Moon Pack. I tried to hold my breath, which I'm sure turned my expression into something unsettling. I could taste the fear of the werewolves lined up on either side of us. I felt their apprehension.

That stirred my beast in a different way. The corner of my lips lifted, and I inhaled to chuckle... but then a painfully sweet fragrance filled my lungs and I froze in place instead.

"Honey?" Camellia came up beside me and began to link her arm in mine.

Before she fully could, I tore through the progression line, right past my brother and Ruth, as they were speaking with two burly werewolf men standing in front of the open doors.

"That didn't take long," Casimir snickered.

"Lukyan!" Camellia called for me, but my beast was focused on that scent and the direction it was coming from.

Upon stepping into the pack house, all hope that had gathered in the void in my chest dissipated into a vicious snarl when my eyes landed on her.... in someone else's arms.

The pain in her eyes stunned me, then she spoke my name, just above a whisper. "Lukyan..."

It was her. My lost mate. In the arms of another man.

Alesta

"*No....*"

I didn't know if I spoke out loud or in my head, but then I heard my Alpha's voice, even though his lips never moved. I must have spoken my one word of protest in my mind.

"*No what, Alesta? What's happening to you?*"

Alpha Mikken was cradling me in his arms, all my weight being supported by him. I balled my hand into a tight fist, twisting his shirt and dragging him closer to me.

The ache in my chest had warped into this deep feeling of regret mixed with so much heartache. I was wishing for the previous pain to return.

Seeing the fierce look of betrayal on Lukyan's face, a face I hadn't seen in six years.... It made everything inside of me feel like it was breaking. Worse than the night I left. His pain shone through those beautiful topaz eyes. It was too much for me to take.

Then that woman appeared. The one I saw at his side the last time those eyes had met mine. It was his wife. His queen.

"Lukyan! What is the matter with you?!" She came to his side, resting her hand firmly in the crook of his arm. "There are formalities."

Lukyan never looked away. It was like he didn't notice she was there. He was still staring at me with a look of mixed anger and betrayal. His aura was vengeful, coming off of him in waves.

His wife's knit brows studied his face a second longer, then she turned to gaze to follow his line of sight. As her eyes rested on me, her confusion clear, I realized how dangerous of a situation I was in.

"*Please get me out of here,*" I begged my Alpha while turning my face away. "*Please...*"

Alpha Mikken looked down at me for a long time, his concern etched into every one of his handsome features. Then he scowled, looking up to meet the eyes of the Lycan king.

"Pardon my rudeness, your Majesty. I will return to greet you properly in just a moment."

Alpha Mikken stooped down to lift me fully, so I was strung across both of his arms while I still clung to his shirt. My body was still in shock. I didn't know how to loosen my hold.

"Oh, my. Is she alright?" The regal woman offered Alpha Mikken a concerned smile. When those shining eyes met mine, I cringed into Alpha's chest.

I'm not a cowering person. Very few things scare me. The thought of what this woman wearing my fated mate's mark on her neck could do if she discovered my son's lineage frightened me to my core. My body began to break out in a cold sweat.

"Excuse me, your majesties," was Alpha Mikken's only response. As he carried me away, he barked orders at the staff watching silently nearby. "Get the doctor to my office. Now!

You, go get the blanket from my bed, and all the peanut butter from the kitchen."

Peanut butter? If I wasn't so fearful of meeting the queen's gaze again, I might have looked at Alpha Mikken and laughed.

The further we got from the doors, the more my chest ached. I couldn't resist one last glance toward the ones putting my mind and body and such duress.

Those topaz eyes were so intense it caused me to squeeze tighter to the one who carried me. As a result, Alpha kissed the top of my head and whispered, "It will all be okay."

I was stunned. Not only because of Alpha Mikken's affection, but because of Lukyan's reaction to it. Lukyan snarled fiercely, his beast ripping out of him. But before he was fully shifted, a single tear escaped the corner of his eyes and rolled down his rough cheek.

It ripped my heart in two. I felt pain like never before seeing him tear himself apart, then run outside in a raging fury. I could hear his agony in every roar.

Then there was his wife, staring with knit brows and an expression full of confusion. When she looked my way, I hurried my face into Alpha Mikken's shoulder again.

"Feral beast," Alpha muttered under his breath, hurriedly heading towards the offices and away from the royal Lycans. We could still hear Lukyan's howls deep within the pack house. That look on Lukyan's face.... What right did he have to stare at me like I had betrayed him? While he stood there with his wife. Surely she had to suspect something now, if she hadn't figured it out already.

Triston. I needed to hide Triston. I needed to take him and run before Lukyan's queen discovered everything.

I began to hyperventilate.

"Hey. Hey!" Alpha Mikken laid me across his couch, then grabbed my face. "I got you. I got you, Alesta."

"Triston!" I rasped. "I... we need to go. We need to run..."

"Alesta!" Mikken shook me, but it did little to calm my panic.

With a frustrated growl, he grabbed my face and kissed me. His lips crashed to mine in desperation.

I gasped, and he used the sudden opening to deepen the kiss. Pain ripped through me as I heard a deep howl of pain in the distance.

Rearing my hand back, it struck Alpha Mikken's cheek with a resounding slap.

Striking your Alpha was not done. Instant death came to most who showed such disrespect. Even in my current circumstances. That was why when he burst into laughter while rubbing his cheek, I could do nothing but stare in confusion.

"There she is. There's my fighter."

Anger coursed through me. "You kissed me."

He shrugged. "And you slapped me. I think we're even."

I scoffed. "I would have preferred you slap me than kiss me."

His smile faltered. "That's too bad, because I would never strike you. Now," he leaned forward. "Mind telling me what's going on between you and the Lycan king?"

I turned my face away stubbornly. "I would mind, actually."

Alpha Mikken huffed dramatically. "That's too damn bad, Alesta, because you're going to tell me."

"Nothing is going on," I lied rather badly.

"Bull," he snorted. He was kneeling so close to me I could feel his breath. "It sure as hell wasn't me he was looking at like that."

"Like what?" I continued to play dumb.

Alpha Mikken was quiet long enough that it caused me to look his way again. He had an unidentifiable emotion hooding his sky-blue eyes. "He looked at you like he'd just found his entire world in the arms of another man."

Chapter 10

Secrets

My heart hammered in my chest. Is that the way he looked? I saw nothing but anger and betrayal. If Alpha Mikken saw that, what did Lukyan's queen see?

"He's married," I whispered roughly.

Alpha Mikken laughed dryly. "That doesn't always matter, does it?"

"What do you mean?"

Alpha pursed his lips, then said, "You looked at him the same way."

I shook my head, full of denial. "No. I didn't."

With a sigh, Alpha Mikken sat back on his heels. "Fine. Explain it then."

"I can't!"

"You can and you will," he lifted his chin. "Even if I have to command you."

I snorted. "Yeah. Go ahead and try." That probably wasn't a smart comment to make, but my emotions were still high and I wasn't thinking clearly.

Alpha Mikken looked at me with narrowed eyes. "If you were anyone else, Alesta...." He growled and leaned in, barely an inch away from my face. "You're lucky my desire to protect you is far greater than my desire to make you submit."

I didn't know if that was a threat... or something else.

Right then, the doctor showed up, knocking softly on the Alpha's door. Alpha groaned at the interruption before he called for the doctor to come in, along with an omega who had a blanket and a jar full of peanut butter in her hands.

Alpha directed the blanket and peanut butter to be placed on his desk as the doctor checked my chest. I insisted I was fine, but the doctor was thorough. He left shortly after, confirming I was telling the truth.

"What's the peanut butter for?" I eyed it as Alpha Mikken took the blanket and laid it on my lap as he knelt on the ground before me again.

"A reward for after you tell me your secret," he said tauntingly with a smirk.

I raised a brow. "I don't want it that bad."

He rolled his eyes, resting his arms against my knees while leaning in. "How am I to protect you if you don't?"

"You can't protect me," I whispered. "Not from him."

"Not if you don't tell me what's going on."

The silence stretched between us. Our breaths mingled. Mine stubborn huffs of frustration and his patient and steady. Neither looked away. Not until his eyes flashed down to my lips again, and I quickly leaned away before he could act on his constant need to tease me.

He would not let this go. That was becoming increasingly clear. "Fine. If this puts you in danger too, that's now on you. You're forcing me."

His eyes darkened. "Danger from what?"

I still couldn't form an explanation in my head. Alpha Mikken said he wanted to protect me, but what if he punished me himself when he learned the truth? What if he punished Niccola?

His expression softened as I struggled to find the right words to say.

"Alesta," he cupped my face, holding it tenderly in both of his large hands. "Is...." He pressed his lips together, like he was considering his words. "Is... Is Triston's father a part of the inspection party from the capital?..."

I waited a beat, assessing Alpha Mikken's features before slowly nodding.

He closed his eyes, taking a long and deep breath. When he opened them again, they were molten, like blue fury. I sensed fear in him and knew what question would be next.

"Is he among the visiting royals?"

Grimacing at the truth being known, all I could do was nod, then look away out of shame. He didn't let me look away for long. He gently slid his fingers to the back of my neck, then turned my face to his. His thumbs rubbed tenderly down my cheeks.

"Is... Is it the king? Was he the one that hurt you?"

"No," gasped. The mere idea of Lukyan committing such despicable acts was ridiculous and made me mad. "He never hurt me. Not like that."

Alpha Mikken's eyes widened. "Then you willingly...."

"He was my mate!" I burst out before more shame could fall upon me. A ragged breath tore through my chest. I folded in on myself, all the pain and heartache hitting me once again. "He was my mate," I rasped shakily. "But I am not a Lycan."

A feral growl escaped Alpha Mikken. "So you were good enough for his bed, but not to become his mate? Is that what happened?"

Tears burned through my clenched eyes as I gritted my teeth to prevent my sobs from escaping. Alpha Mikken had spoken nothing but the truth. I was never more than the werewolf Lukyan used to warm his bed. It still hurt to hear out loud.

Another growl left my Alpha, and seconds later, my body was being lifted by him again. He sat upon the couch and nestled my crumbling form across his lap. Strong arms engulfed me as I let my sorrow break free.

I never thought I would see Lukyan again. Seeing him here... with her....

The pain was unimaginable.

Keeping strong for my child as I ran for my life and started anew had built a dam around my heart. I felt like it burst completely the moment the woman, the queen, touched his arm and said the name of my fated mate with so much concern. He chose her. He had to. I knew he was backed into a corner and left with no other choice. It didn't make it hurt any less.

My tears eventually receded into hiccups. Alpha Mikken chuckled softly and gently patted my back. I cried for what seemed like hours, but when I glanced at the clock, it had only been about twenty minutes.

That was still too long.

I sat up, belatedly realizing whose lap I had settled on. After hurriedly scooting off to the cushion beside my patient Alpha, I noticed the stain of snot and tears I had left on his shirt.

"I'm so sorry," I mumbled, wiping at my messy face as I started to get up. "I'll get a new shirt right away-"

"Sit, Alesta," Alpha Mikken reached to grab my hand, anchoring me in place.

"You... you told them you would be right back. The formalities are-"

"It doesn't matter. The.... the queen went after the *king*," Alpha Mikken sneered at the title like it disgusted him. "Carlston already led the rest of their party to their quarters. He told me while you were getting looked at."

I tried not to show any discomfort at the mention of the king and queen, but it was difficult. Then a thought came to mind that drained the blood from my face.

"Triston... What if they-"

"They won't," Alpha Mikken stopped me before I could go into a full panic. "Zander took him from class and is keeping him in the bunkers under the guise of cleaning duty until we can figure out a better solution."

"A better solution?" I mumbled under my breath. There was only one. "We have to leave."

Alpha Mikken gave me a disapproving look. "You're not leaving. I told you I would protect you."

"You can't protect me from this, Alpha."

"Ken," he interjected stubbornly.

I rolled my eyes. "Not now. You've pushed the limits of tolerable teasing for the day."

"It's not teasing, you maddening woman," Alpha Mikken looked down at his hand holding mine. He sighed deeply when I pulled away. Then he looked up to meet my eyes with a serious expression. "Why did you challenge my ability to command you earlier?"

I bit my lip nervously. I already told him my biggest secret. What was one more on the list? "Commands do not work on me."

Alpha Mikken's eyes widened in surprise. "Any commands? Even Mine?"

I shook my head.

He rubbed the back of his neck. "What of *his*? The kings?"

I hesitated before answering. "None he had ever given me before ever did." He's king now. That may have changed, but somehow I don't feel it has.

"So no one's command has ever affected you?" Alpha Mikken looked for deeper clarification.

I smiled sadly as I remembered one command that stuck. It was one I didn't truly need because I would have followed it, nonetheless.

"Only one. The previous queen's."

"Going somewhere, Alesta Raine?" Queen Teraphine raised her well-groomed brow.

My breath caught in my throat as I rasped, "My queen." I quickly bowed my head, averting my gaze to the ground. Her authority filled the room, making the air suffocating.

Her footfalls were the only sound. Each step she took as she slowly walked around me made my heart hammer harder and harder in my chest.

She stopped right in front of me, then lifted my chin with a firmly placed finger. Her eyes were sharp and piercing, even as she smiled. "Before you go, have tea with me. There is much we must discuss."

Never. Never in a million years would I have guessed I'd be in Lukyan's sitting room having tea with his mother. My movements were stiff as I followed her to the small table. One of her maids, the one usually by her side, was her only companion.

After the maid finished setting up the tea, Queen Teraphine gave her a strict order. "Leave us, Letty. Do not let anyone enter this room."

Letty bowed her head and followed the command. By the time I heard the door click closed, I thought I might truly be sick.

The silence stretched as Queen Teraphine took a graceful first sip from her elegant tea cup. Then she hummed in appreciation.

"This rooibos blend is delicious. It is quite good for delicate women, such as yourself."

I couldn't help but to frown at the word 'delicate'. I was far from delicate, even if I didn't quite feel so strong sitting before the queen.

Her smile stretched. Then she nodded to my cup. "Drink, Alesta. It's good for the baby growing in your womb."

My heart stopped. My mouth went dry. How? How did she know?

Instinctively, my hands went to my belly, as if to shield it. My fear of the Queen did not stop me from letting out a low growl of warning.

"Calm yourself," Queen Teraphine sat back in her chair. "I wish no harm upon you or my grandchild."

Then what did she want? Was this some other form of threat? "What do you want from me?" I eventually asked with clenched teeth.

Her smile was sad, but her eyes were fierce. I suddenly felt a chill roll down my spine as her aura crashed over me. The impact of her authority was so much stronger than Lukyan's.

She was the queen. The only one who could stand against the king of this kingdom and all his commands. The queen was the only being who had the power to suppress any creature under the goddess as long as it was within the moon goddess's will.

Her topaz eyes shimmered like glass as she commanded me, "Protect my grandchild. Over everything else."

∞∞∞

"I felt her command take hold of me," I whispered to Alpha Mikken. "I would have protected my child despite her words, but that cemented my resolve to put Triston before everything. Even my fated mate."

I went silent as emotions filled me, remembering how reverent I felt towards Lukyan's mother. It was the first time we had spoken, and the moment seemed so intimate now. At the time, I was so filled with fear that I never reflected on just how powerful that teatime was.

Alpha Mikken interrupted my solemn remembrance by brushing the back of his hand across my cheek, moving my hair that had been shadowing my eyes.

"She was the one that told you to run away?"

With a timid shake of my head, I said, "No. She simply told me to protect Triston. The one who organized our escape was someone else."

He looked at me with confusion.

I laughed dryly, remembering what happened after that meeting with the Queen. "It was Casimir. Prince Casimir organized our escape."

His lips pressed together, and I could see him working it all out in his head. He had so many questions. They were burning in his blue eyes. The one he asked first wasn't about Casimir, or even Lukyan, like I was expecting.

"So, the only person with the ability to command you is the Queen?"

"It seems so," I hesitantly answered.

Alpha's expression turned serious as his eyes swept towards

the door, then back at me.

"The only person," he said in a low whisper, "in the entire kingdom whose command affects you is the queen."

It wasn't a question this time. It was a statement.

"Yes, but I just told you she only wanted to protect Triston."

His blue eyes darkened, and a frustrated rumble vibrated his chest. He leaned in, just inches from my face. "Alesta. The *only* person who can command you is the queen."

"I know! I told you that."

He gave me a dumbfounded look, then growled, "The *queen* of the Lycan kingdom. Who is that right now?"

Then it hit me. The queen that once commanded me to protect my son was no longer the one holding that title. That position now belongs to someone else.

"But... but we don't... Shit..." My mind raced as panic caused my heart to race. I raked my hands through my hair, pulling it so the slight pain helped to clear my mind. "I have to run, Alpha. I have to. That's the only way I can-"

Alpha pushed his finger to my lips to silence me. "That won't work, Alesta. He knows you're here. He will hunt you."

"He won't." I shook my head. "He... He can't. He's married and marked. With *her*. He-"

"He will," Alpha Mikken said. "That was not the stare of a man willing to let his fated mate go. Not again. He will hunt you. I'm sure of it."

"Then what do you suggest I do?! *HE* is not my biggest worry. *She* is right now! Running away is my only chance to save my son from her."

"That's not the only way." Alpha folded his hands together, his fingertips white from his tight grip. He was anxious too. "We just have to make it clear you are no threat. That your son is not a threat."

"How?!" I stressed.

Alpha Mikken stared into my eyes, then reached for my hands. "Do you trust me?"

Chapter 11

Weirdo

Triston

The spider, the one I had been teasing with the lint at the end of my broom, crawled out of my reach onto the ceiling. The wooden beams covered in cobwebs were Instructor Zaden's job, but he was too busy acting weird in the corner to clean.

"Crap," I heard him whisper to himself.

I stopped looking around the dust basement for a chair to climb on and decided it was time to complain.

"Mom is going to be getting me soon." I crossed my arms over my chest right in front of my blurry eyed teacher.

His eyes went back to normal as he stammered. "Uh, no. She's still working."

Instructor Zaden shook his head, then gave me another one of those smiles that made me think this was more than just a special errand for the Alpha. He looked guilty. My teacher was acting weird and looked guilty.

"I want my mom."

"What? I just told you she was-"

"I don't care. I want my mom now."

"Why?" Instructor Zaden scoffed, like my demand surprised him.

I crossed my arms over my chest. "Because mom said not to be alone with weirdos and you're acting weird."

Instructor Zaden made a snorting sound like a laugh. "How am I acting weird?"

"Saying how you're not acting weird would be a shorter list," I mutter under my breath. I walked towards the door. "I cleaned everything I could reach while you were being a weirdo in the corner. I'm going to get my mom."

"Wait!" Instructor Zaden hurried to block my path. "You can't go up there yet!"

A low growl made my chest feel all ticklish. "I can if you get your weird butt out of my way."

Instructor Zaden's eyes got all squinty, like he was mad. "You've got a lot of lip on you today."

"I have the same lips as every day, you weirdo."

"Watch it, kid."

I was about to stomp on his foot and make him move, but right then the spider I had chased up the wall started to drop from the ceiling on a single thread. Its inky body and wiry legs were reflecting the light from above.

A naughty smile spread across my face. "Look up."

Instructor Zaden looked up in confusion, then his eyes went big and he screamed like a girl when the spider dropped just inches above his big, weird head. He dropped to the ground and crawled backward to get away from it.

With a carefree laugh, I caught the spider on the end of my broom, then waved it toward my teacher. He screamed louder than before as he furiously crawled further away.

"GET RID OF THAT THING!"

"It's only a spider. It's not even poisonous."

"You don't know that!"

I rolled my eyes. "I do know that. Mom told me."

"Well, get rid of it!"

I snickered as I walked towards the stairs. "Fine. I'll let it go outside on my way to get mom."

"No!" Instructor Zaden started to get up off the floor, but then hunkered back down when I turned around with the broom so the spider was between us. "Damn it, kid. You're going to get me in trouble!"

"Good! You should have been helping me clean instead of being a weirdo."

He pursed his lips, eyes still on the spider. Mom would get mad at me if she knew I was threatening my teacher with a spider. I needed to be careful or I might be in trouble, too.

I sighed, then turned the broom away from him. "I'll see you tomorrow, Instructor Zaden."

"Wait. Wait!" He got up from the ground and hesitantly walked closer to me without getting too close. His eyes kept flickering to my broom. "Come on, kid. You're putting me between a rock and a hard place here."

"Is the spider the rock or the hard place?" I asked stubbornly.

"I don't know! As much as that thing freaks me the fuck out, Alpha scares me just as much when he's pissed."

My mouth dropped. "Teachers aren't supposed to use those words."

"Yeah, well, students aren't supposed to call their teachers weirdos."

I wrinkled my nose, thinking about what he said before. "Why would Alpha scare you more than a spider? Because you weren't cleaning like he told you to?"

The way his face got all scrunchy, I knew there was something else he wasn't telling me. It made my chest itching as I growled again.

"Fine, weirdo. I'd be more scared of my mom than Alpha, though." Mom will not like that I was missing school to clean a yucky basement alone with my weirdo instructor. She's scarier than Alpha when she's mad.

"Your mom knows you're here!" Instructor Zaden burst out as I stepped on the first stair. "That's why Alpha said to bring you down. It was because of your mom."

"Because of mom?" That didn't make sense. "Why?"

"I don't know, kid. I was given an order and I'm following it. All

I know is what I'm hearing from the chatter on the pack mind link."

I thought about my mom and how she had been acting the past few days. I guess mom was being weird too. She was worried about something at work. She would stare off into space for long periods of time at home, always looking like she was tired. Uncle Nic was acting weird, too.

Everyone was a weirdo. I'm surrounded by them right now.

"Is mom in trouble?"

Instructor Zaden's expression twisted, and he didn't answer right away. It wasn't until I turned the broom towards him again that he sputtered a response.

"Fine! Geez! No! Well, maybe... I don't know. She is with Alpha though, so she will be okay. I just know that I have to keep you down here until your mom or Alpha comes to get you."

"Not good enough," I waved the broom towards him, making him scream again.

"STOP! AH! IT'S MOVING!"

"Then tell me what's wrong with mom!"

"I DON'T KNOW!" Instructor Zaden had tears in his eyes as he hid behind a table. The man was a big warrior and was getting bested by a little boy with a spider. I smiled to myself with pride. "All I know is that she didn't react well to the King showing up unexpectedly. She got sick and Alpha took her. That's all I know!"

I narrowed my eyes until I was sure he was telling the truth, then lowered the broom. I turned it so the spider was facing the stairs again.

"Why would mom get sick because of the King?" I didn't know much about the king. Just what I heard from school and other adults. Mom never talked about the Lycan royals.

"Who wouldn't get sick because of the royals?" Instructor Zaden scoffed. "I don't know, Triston. Just... please... Please cooperate. And get rid of the spider."

I stared at him, deciding what I wanted to do. I *wanted* to go see my mom, especially if she was sick, but I also knew that if she wanted me down here, it must be for a reason. Alpha even ordered it.

Maybe because I'm the only Lycan kid in the pack. If the royals saw me, maybe it would be bad. I don't know.

"Fine. I'll just put the spider outside, then come back down. Is that alright with you, weirdo?"

Instructor Zaden let out a heavy breath, then nodded. "Yeah, but come right back."

With another eye roll, I took my broom and went up. Right before I reached the door, I stopped. I felt a tremor beneath my feet. There was a strange feeling building in my chest, too.

Then a powerful roar made the doors and walls shake. It wasn't a normal beastly cry from a werewolf. No werewolf here had a roar that loud or strong. Not even Alpha.

No. That was a Lycan. I was sure of it. A very powerful, very angry Lycan.

Lukyan

A deep vibrating sound of contentment rumbled through my chest as I finished off another boar. The dirt under my claws was turning into a sticky clay as the fluids of my latest kill dripped down my arms.

"I'm going to be sick," Camellia groaned, covering her mouth several yards away. "Fine. You want to kill every last animal in this pack's hunting grounds? Go ahead." She walked away muttering, "All reason leaves him when he's like this. I'm done trying."

I heard her words and knew their meaning, but that didn't stop the bloodlust from taking over. I felt compelled by my every instinct to kill or destroy until the bloodlust was satisfied. When this would happen at the palace, she was the only one that could approach me, thanks to a charm of protection placed on her by her mate. Others mistake her effect on my feral beast as the influence of the mate bond, not knowing we don't truly have one.

Camellia has been following me since I left Hallowed Moon Pack's pack house, and almost had the beastly side of me seeing reason. That was until I felt a tearing inside of my chest, like my heart was being ripped from my body. Instinctively, I knew. I knew what the pain was.

Alesta. It had to be Alesta.

Just thinking her name made my beast rampage once again. I tossed the grotesque body of the wild boar I had just been mutilating to the side in search of fresh blood. My anger had to be quenched with blood. I was rational enough still to know I couldn't take the blood of the bastard that carried my mate away, so the wild game littering his pack lands would have to suffice.

The forest here was thin. The trees weren't like the great oaks and pines back home. The vegetation was fitting of the hot climate, with palms and skinny cedars that would break with a powerful gust of wind. Wildlife was harder to find, but it felt so much more satisfying when I caught the trail of something. My sharp beastly eyes focused on a set of tracks that fit some sort of large cat. A thrill ran up my spine in anticipation of a fight. I prowled through the sparse vegetation, following the tracks. My footfalls were as silent as my breathing now that I had locked in on my prey.

It didn't take long. There was a rushing stream with larger trees all around its banks. Perched on the thick branch of the tallest tree was a mountain lioness. She focused on licking the feathers off a large bird she must have just killed.

My monstrous body coiled, ready to attack. Right before I could spring out from behind the large leafy fern I was taking cover behind, two small growls caused me to freeze. A pair of cubs stumbled from a den I hadn't noticed before. It was tucked away behind a shrub.

That would have done little to stop me before, but the way the lioness looked down upon her babies triggered something in me. Then, she must have sensed something, because her gaze swept over the landscape until it hovered over me. Those eyes of the lioness reminded me too much of someone else. I couldn't do it. Not to a mother raising two cubs on her own.

When she jumped down from the branch with the large half-plucked bird in her jaws, she nudged the two small cubs back into their den and followed them in. That was when I finally moved from my place. They were wild beasts. I should have still been able to take the kill, but just considering it made my skin crawl.

Whatever the reason for my hesitation, it snapped my rational back into place. I was no longer deep in bloodlust, my mind disconnected from my body. I was simply a Lycan roaming the forest now. A disgruntled, heartbroken Lycan, but a Lycan nonetheless. The untamable beast I had momentarily become was gone.

That didn't make the brokenness in me any less painful.

Alesta. She was standing right there. Her scent was driving me mad. Her beautiful eyes, so full of fear and surprise, were upon me once more. I had imagined what seeing her again would be like, but I never thought I would have to see my lost mate in the arms of another man.

What's more, I was in no position to interfere. That reality was what had caused me to run instead of tearing their meager pack house into splinters like I wanted to. I was here as the king, accompanied by my queen and an entourage of inspectors and staff from the palace. As much as I wanted to rip the arms from the Alpha holding my mate, I couldn't.

Then there was that pain I felt not long after. Fated mates may be mythical to most Lycans, but we still understand the pains that come from a bond being tampered with. Chosen mates felt pain too when there was a betrayal. I had witnessed it enough times to understand what that pain in my chest had meant.

I found my mate. My Alesta. But she was with the Alpha of this pack. Fate was cruel and heartless.

"There you are," an aggravating voice called from ahead. Casimir smiled arrogantly, holding a stack of clothing in his hands. "When you weren't where Camellia said she left you, I got worried."

Now that I was calm, shifting back was easy. I was in my Lycan form one step, then human the next.

My eyes narrowed on my smug-faced brother. "You knew."

He shrugged. "Perhaps. Surprise, brother." He chuckled under his breath. "I forgot to get you something for your last birthday. Better late than never, they say."

"Enough!" I snatched the pants from his hands. "How did you find her?! And why... why didn't you tell me?"

His smile lost a bit of its arrogance. "I couldn't tell you."

"Why not?" I snarled through clenched teeth.

"Because," he looked down at the ground, moving the dirt with the point of his shoe. "I was given an order."

"An order to hide the fact that you found my mate?" I scoffed and shook my head. "That makes little sense." I'm the only one with the ability to command my brother now. I would never give such a command.

Casimir sighed, leaning back against a large palm as I kicked on the pants in an angry huff. When I stood there gruffly afterward with my arms crossed tensely over my chest, Casimir finally spoke.

With a roll of his eyes, he said, "The command was given long ago, brother. And it wasn't quite that."

"Long ago by who?" I sneered. Then my eyes went wide as something dawned on me. "No. She couldn't."

Casimir shrugged, a smile still playing on his lips. "I couldn't say if *she* did. You know how the royal orders work."

I did know. That was why I had to wait so long to take action against the twisted system the council and nobles had in place. My father, who very much liked the system we lived in, would have prevented me from continuing towards my goal no matter the costs. I needed the throne and the power behind it before I could act.

There was only one way to get my brother to tell me the truth now. One way to overturn whatever command he had previously been given.

As if he could read my mind, Casimir began to uncuff the sleeve of his shirt, then offered me up his bare wrist.

There was only one way to overturn the command given by a previous royal. A blood oath to the newly reigning monarch. He had to freely offer his blood to me. Royals doing so was something unheard of and would be discouraged by the council, but the council isn't here. And I am desperate to understand.

With a firm grasp on his wrist, I plunged my teeth into his flesh. As his blood poured down my throat, my venom seeped into him. It would cleanse any influence on his will other than mine. He would now be forever loyal to me.

When the exchange was done, he groaned, sinking down to the grassy ground. His eyes were tense with the suppression of the blood oath.

My blood-stained lips curled with hostility. "Now tell me. Everything."

Chapter 12

Mother's Command

"There is a pack of werewolves totally detached from the rest of the kingdom," Queen Teraphine told Alesta and Niccola. Casimir and Niccola appeared from the secret passage in the wall shortly after holding Alesta back for tea. "The pack is so neglected that the king and council haven't attempted to collect a tribute from them for the duration of his reign."

"Why?" Alesta asked cautiously. "Is there something wrong with the pack or the Alpha?"

Queen Teraphine looked slightly uncomfortable with Alesta's question. Still, she answered as diplomatically as she could. "Not at all. I have been secretly keeping tabs on the outlining packs without my husband's knowledge for years."

Casimir looked forlorn before diverting his gaze to the ground.

There were so many questions scrambling in Alesta and Niccola's minds, but Niccola was the next to voice one crucial one out loud.

"Why can we not just return to our former packs?" Niccola looked at Alesta then calmly reassured her, "My Alpha is a kind man and will gladly take you in."

"No." Queen Teraphine's voice was firm. "I'm afraid that is not an option."

"Why not?" Alesta asked warily.

The queen pressed her lips together, a sadness resting in her eyes. "Because there will be no pack for either of you to return to."

Alesta and Niccola looked confused. Alesta's mouth was open, as if she was about to speak, but words were failing to come to her.

"I'm sure you have heard murmurings of the council's search for the next queen of this kingdom?" Queen Teraphine directed the question at Alesta.

Alesta's eyes filled with pain as she nodded softly.

"They have chosen," Queen Teraphine said directly, not sugar coating what was to happen. "In doing so, an offering was made." The queen held up her chin with an icy demeanor as she revealed the evilness of the council and their king. "Your packs have been eliminated to appease the elders."

Alesta stood suddenly, anger vibrating through her limbs. "Lukyan wouldn't-"

"He had no say in the matter," Queen Teraphine cut off her denial. "He is not yet king. He may say that he can protect you, but when it comes to his father and the council, he is powerless."

Tears were burning in Alesta's furious eyes. Niccola sat in stunned silence, his face as white as a sheet.

"Which brings us to the current situation," Casimir said calmly. "My brother will be forced to marry. Soon. Within two days, I expect him to be wed, and once that happens, my father will not let something as trivial as a fated mate interfere with the security of the throne."

Alesta wiped away her tears of fury. "So you want us to run away to some distant pack because I'm a threat to Lukyan's new marriage?"

The queen and second prince remained silent, but that silence was heavy. It was confirmation that she was in danger, more so than ever once Lukyan was forcibly mated to someone else.

Queen Teraphine kept her arrogant air, the impeccable image of a Lycan queen, but there was a kindness in her sad eyes as she stared at Alesta. "You know you are, Alesta. More so now than ever before."

Casimir rested a hand firmly on Niccola's shoulder. "And you are the only other tribute that knows the nature of their relationship. My father will not hesitate to eliminate you to bury the secret the royal family has been keeping since your arrival."

Niccola tried to swallow down his sorrow, but his voice still cracked as he spoke. "So we are to run away?"

Casimir's lips lifted, though his smile did not reach his eyes. "Yes."

Alesta shook her head fervently. "No. It's not that simple. We... We are tributes. We are sworn to the Kingdom. To the royals."

"Not anymore." Queen Teraphine stood from her chair, then walked gracefully before the two grieving werewolves. The air in the room thickened with the weight of her authority. "I, Teraphine Achlyselene, Queen of the Lycan Empire and Erebos Kingdom, relieve you, Alesta Raine and Niccola Steel of your duties to the monarch and dissolve your allegiance to the Erebos Kingdom."

Alesta and Niccola both fell to their knees, the lifting of their oaths causing their bodies to bend. Alesta gritted her teeth and Niccola gasped at the sharp pain that came before the relief of freedom.

"With this, you are both free. Casimir will aid your escape."

"When?" Niccola asked as he helped Alesta to her feet.

Queen Teraphine held Alesta's gaze. "During Lukyan's wedding festivities. The palace will be distracted with celebration."

All eyes were on Alesta as her face twisted in pain. She looked at the ground, hiding her face in the shadow of her hair. She couldn't hide the tear drops dripping to the floor.

"Maybe he won't do it," Niccola whispered to his friend. He gently rubbed her back. "He could protest-"

"He won't," Casimir stated firmly. "He knows better than anyone that only he can rule. To get the throne, this marriage will have to be seen to completion."

Alesta buried her face in her hands. Her body shuddered with a heavy breath. "I knew it was impossible." She wiped her hands down her face, then looked up at the ceiling with blotchy eyes. "I knew we could never truly be together. I just...." She bit her lips to keep from crying as she gained control of the moisture filling her eyes. "I just hoped he would find a way."

Casimir sank down to kneel before her. Alesta watched him warily. "You can have a new life. A new beginning. Years from now, this pain will be gone and all that will be left are the memories of the

hope you and my brother shared."
She smiled sadly, all wariness leaving her. "You know as well as I that will be impossible."
Casimir patted her knee. "Nothing is impossible, Alesta."
"No," Queen Teraphine said calmly, letting her sympathy show through her usual queenly facade. "A new life is what you will have. To save both yourself and my son." She then shut her eyes, squaring her shoulders, and the weight of her authority filtered through the air again.
When she opened them, they fixed on her youngest son as she said, "You, Casimir, will ensure it. After they've safely escaped, you are to watch over them, but never reveal anything to anyone other than me. This is not a command as your mother, but your queen."

∞∞∞

The anger coursing through me was equal to the questions piling up in my mind.

"You and mother took my mate from me."

"To save her," Casimir said, staring at the ground. Then he looked up at me with a somber expression. "You know as well as I that father would have killed her."

"I would have protected her!" I snarled.

"No," he laughed dryly, shaking his head. "You would have been as helpless as her. You were not yet king."

"Still," I twisted my fist in the front of my brother's shirt. His hand in my mate's disappearance was not the only fuel to my rage. "You knew! You knew the arrangement between Camellia and I!" My heart ached just imagining what Alesta thought watching us declared the future king and queen before escaping the capital.

Casimir's eyes filled with pity. "Mother did not know, but even if she did, would that have mattered?" He shook his head, answering his own question. "Father would have killed her, just the same."

"No." I tossed him back against a tree. "I could have hidden her away."

Casimir's arrogance returned as he righted himself and shook his head. "No, you couldn't have. You and I both know from just the few months Alesta was in the capital that she never would have accepted being your mistress. Even if your marriage was only political."

No. I scoffed, knowing what he said was true. It was a large part of why I didn't want to tell her about the engagement. I knew she wouldn't wear the label of mistress.

I tried so hard to protect Alesta from my father. From the vile eyes of the council. Protecting her was what I deluded myself into believing I was doing by keeping her in the dark, and in a large part, it was true. My father would have killed her if he learned the truth of what I was doing as his heir. But I also knew Alesta wouldn't have accepted being with a married man.

My brother and mother weren't just saving Alesta in aiding her escape. They were saving me from my own feeble attempt to maintain control over my claim to the throne and my claim over her.

Still... I felt there was more to this than what my brother was telling me. There was an itch crawling over my skin that I was missing something important.

"You're king now," Casimir continued on, ignorant of my internal struggle. "Father can no longer threaten your coming into power. And the council will soon be in your hands. You finally have the power to protect what is yours."

I scoffed. "You saw her," I hissed under my breath. "You saw the way she looked at me."

Casimir waved his hand dismissively. "The distance between love and hate is not far. I'd only be concerned if she seemed indifferent."

"She crumbled at the sight of me!"

"You made her swoon," my brother chuckled to himself.

I let out a low growl. "She swooned into the arms of another man."

"Oh. That." He smirked while crossing his arms, leaning casually against the tree. "So your tantrum was not from finding your mate, but from seeing her with another man."

A threatening snarl echoed between us. "You were keeping tabs on her all this time and thought it would be a good idea to bring me here to find her mated with someone else?"

"Mated?" Casimir gave me a curious look. "I did not see a mate mark upon her neck. Did you?"

I stood frozen, retracing the memory of her frightening form in that foyer. "No," hissed, my brows knotting together. "No, I did not."

"Me neither," Casimir snickered.

My answering snarl wiped all the amusement from his expression. "Is it funny to you? Seeing an Alpha playing around with my mate?"

"Well, I wouldn't say he was playing around with her. He was-"

"He's touching what is mine and doesn't have the audacity to even mark her!" I seethed, remembering the pain in my chest.

"Geez, brother," Casimir shook his head. "Most would be glad to hear the one they love was still unmarked and available."

"HE'S FUCKING MY MATE BUT WON'T HONOR HER WITH A BOND!" My anger reached new heights. "THE BASTARD IS-"

"Fucking?" Casimir scoffed. "How crude, Lukyan. Alpha Mikken and Alesta are not fucking."

Gritting my teeth, I spit out, "Whatever you want to call it, touching my woman but not doing the respectable thing of-"

"Touching your woman? No, brother. I think you misinterpreted what you saw," Casimir interrupted me. "The Alpha of this pack and your mate are not together."

Involuntarily, I started to rub my chest. "I felt it," I said in a hushed whisper. Phantom pain caused my chest to tighten.

"Felt what?" Casimir looked at me with confusion.

"Them!" I hissed. "The pain was unmistakable."

He had the audacity to smirk. "But was it unbearable? Seeing as the blood on your hands is from an animal and not the Alpha's,

I doubt it was anything serious. Probably just a small peck on the cheek. A blow job at most."

I snarled viciously at his crude attempt at a joke. "You find it funny?!"

"Yes," he huffed out a laugh. "The simple fact you felt anything at all means you are still connected. The bond is there."

"Why wouldn't it be?!" My anger was rising at the suggestion mine and Alesta's bond could sever.

His smile left his eyes. "Mother and I had wondered if she anger might have rejected you." He grew quiet for a moment, then added, "Your spells have gotten more savage. We were worried you were losing your sanity due to your bond being lost."

My anger settled as I understood what he was saying. I saw the reason behind why mother and Casimir were so adamant that I come on this trip. Why my brother would risk my wrath by revealing this betrayal.

Casimir rested his hand on my shoulder. "I was going to wait until you accomplished your goal before bringing Alesta to you. I still don't think it's entirely safe enough for her to return to the capital. But then I received a report that the Alpha of Hallowed Moon Pack was setting his sights on Alesta. The severity of his affection even caused him to take her from his warrior force and make her his secretary. She works alongside him every day. If he managed to take her as his chosen mate..."

The pain I felt at the mere suggestion was like my heart was being constricted from the inside of my chest. "Never," I sneered.

"I know," he laughed dryly. "The sins of the father, right? Mother and I both agreed we could never allow that to happen."

Realization dawned on me, quelling the hostility in my chest. "No," I whispered. "That would be the end of everything."

"That's right," he said gently, squeezing my shoulder. "So, let's make a plan to get your family back."

"Family?" I furrowed my brow at his choice of words.

He chuckled, then went to say something more, but before he

could, we heard someone shout in the distance.

"STOP!" a male voice screamed. "YOU SAID YOU SET IT FREE!"

A higher-pitched voice laughed excitedly. "Yeah! That one is free right now!"

"YOU HAVE IT ON A STICK!"

"No-ooo," a young boy snickered. "This is a different spider. I guess his friend told him how much you liked playing with them."

"TRISTON!" the grown man screamed.

They were just coming into view over a pair of tall bushes. The pair were quite a distance away, but I could still see their features with my Lycan eyes. One was a gruff-looking man, built like a werewolf warrior. His eyes were wide with fear as he hurried ahead. The other was a young boy with dark hair, his back turned to us as he was waving a stick in the air.

"You scream like a girl, weirdo," the boy laughed heartily.

His laughter made me chuckle. It was contagious, despite my previous bad mood.

"I'M TELLING YOUR MOM!" The burly man ran away as the boy chased him with the stick. "YOU KNOW I HATE SPIDERS!"

Casimir and I watched as they disappeared in the distance. The boy was laughing and tormenting the man the entire way. I couldn't take my eyes off them, or keep myself from smiling at the boy's antics.

"That dad's got his hands full," Casimir chortled. His eyes then swept in a different direction. "Seems we are no longer alone in the wilderness."

I followed his line of sight, then caught the movement of a warrior several hundred yards away, running along the stream. This one was completely naked, probably just shifting back to human form. When his frantic face swept in our direction, we both recognized who it was right away.

Casimir rubbed his hands together, chuckling gleefully under his breath. "Oh, how the goddess must love me."

Chapter 13

Catching Up

"It's confirmed, mother," Casimir mind linked Queen Teraphine the moment he heard the nurse reveal to Alesta her condition.

The queen knew this time would come. She had hoped it wouldn't, but she also knew it was inevitable given the fated mate bond between her oldest son and the werewolf tribute. The myth of fated mates was said to be a blessing, but it seemed more of a curse. Given that Lycan's rarely found a mate predestined just for them, the queen knew the future king finding his in the ignorant she-wolf sent from a remote, meaningless pack would only bring her son misfortune.

Misfortune for her son and the pitiable girl he was fated to love.

She knew she had to take matters into her own hands to prevent both her son and the girl from breaking entirely, dooming the kingdom to the same tragedies of the past. Her husband's sins were great, but no greater than those of the generations before him. Her son was fated for more than just a predestined love. He was fated to change everything, saving their corrupt empire from total deprivation.

Deprivation was also the key in making her plans succeed. In order for the queen to ensure her grandchild's safety, she needed a way to keep constant tabs on the woman doomed by fate to her eldest son. To achieve that, she would have to allow her youngest son the sinful task of forcing his mark on another.

"You know what to do," the queen told her youngest son.
Prince Casimir chuckled gleefully in reply. "Oh, gladly. The goddess shines down upon me."
The goddess had no part in the tangling of their fates, but it needed to be done. For the good of the kingdom.

Niccola

Those stinking women. I should have taken precautions. I didn't think they would steal my clothes during an ordered border run.

"Get back here, Steel!" Alpha growled at me through the mind link. He's been telling me to get back for a while now.

I've had to keep the pack mind link shut out to ensure the channel was only open to him. There was so much gossip rambling on in the pack link, and I was scared I'd miss some important order from my Alpha. When he called me out of guard duty, he sounded pretty tame, but his orders have been more demanding since.

"I'm trying, Alpha! I'm sorry. They took my clothes again."

"Your clothes?" He paused, then laughed darkly. *"The female warriors giving you a hard time again, Steel?"*

"It's not funny, Alpha!"

He sputtered in laughter through the link. Then he sighed, *"Oh, fine. Find your clothes then. Zaden should be fine bringing the pup back on his own."*

"The pup?" I was confused for about half a second, then asked, *"Triston?! Is everything alright with Triston?!"*

"Triston's fine," Alpha stopped me before I panicked. *"We just had... a minor irritation with our visitors from the capital."*

A minor irritation? The second prince's face came to mind, and I had a guess as to what that irritation may be. Prince Casimir should have 'irritation' added to his official title. Casimir, Prince of all irritation. That's all he ever is to me.

My hand went to the scar on the inside of my thigh, so close to my scrotum that none could ever see. Even in wolf form, it was hidden fully by my fur and tail. No one knows the true reason I avoid all the she-wolves chasing me continuously who always manage to steal my clothes. Not even Alesta knows how I've kept in constant communication with the second prince, with no one knowing.

This was a secret only three people were aware of. The second prince, myself, and the one who ordered it all the day she told my pregnant friend and me to leave.

"Damn it," I groaned, feeling a shiver up my leg. I always got this strange sensation whenever that blasted prince was about to pleasure himself. I didn't need this right now. Now when I was naked and running through the forest, hiding from whoever it was this time that confiscated my clothing.

It could be worse. The damned playboy prince could be causing me actual pain. I had my doubts, but he kept his word and has shielded me from that all these years. Whether it be with a bond numbing potion or whatever, I am just grateful I didn't have to experience that agony.

"Now that she is gone…." Casimir smiled slyly after Basil took Alesta away.

I knew something bad was about to happen. That look in his eyes was far too telling. Prince Casimir liked to fool around with me, for good reason, but I somehow knew his teasing would be reaching new heights.

"I, uh, should go after her." I tried to excuse myself to follow after my friend.

"Uh, uh, uh," Prince Casimir was out of his crusty, fur-lined chair, moving across his sex cabin to block the door before I could reach it.

"Not so fast, my little pet."

My eyes narrowed. "I'm not little. You know that. If you keep calling me that, I'll show it to you again myself."

I instantly regretted those words.

Prince Casimir's lips curled up. "Show me, then."

I gaped in surprise. "I... I was joking."

"Well, I'm not. Show me this 'not little' part of you, since you're so boastful about."

He was serious. His voice was playful, but it was the force behind it that made it impossible to object.

"P-please," I whispered. "I... I told you I wouldn't do that again. Not with you."

He lifted his brow, seeming hurt by my words. "Why not? Did you not enjoy our night together?"

My eyes narrowed. "You know that is not the case."

"Then what is?" Prince Casimir stepped closer, his authority wafting over me, seeking the truth. "Because I am a prince?"

I tried to resist, but I had no choice but to tell him. "You are not my fated mate."

A growl vibrated between us. He hated that excuse. That was the excuse I told him when he asked for me to become his the first night we met. My damned libido caused me to bed the wrong partner, and I have been suffering the consequences since.

It was before I knew he was the prince. I had been delaying my arrival as much as possible, and spent the night at a tavern in the capital that was tailored to werewolves and the less desirable citizens of the city. I never expected the Lycan I drunkenly hooked up with that night to be the second prince. Not until I saw him in the chaos of the throne room the next day.

He was not my mate, and I wouldn't commit to someone exclusively unless they were. No matter how great the chemistry was. Once I discovered who he was, I was more reluctant than ever about his advances, but he never pushed me like he was doing now. He toyed with me, but didn't cross that line.

I guess this was his limit. His morality must have twisted even more.

Casimir stepped up, so he was only a breath away. He seemed taller than me now, but I knew his secret. He was the same height as me without his boots. Even his body was on par with mine. A mere werewolf warrior. He inherited the queen's grace, while his older brother inherited their father's ruthlessness.

"Fated or not," his eyes were hard as gems, "this is what must be. For the kingdom, and for your friend's safety."

My brows furrowed. "What do you mean?"

The saddest smile lifted the corner of his lips. "You will find out soon enough. Now, we don't have much time. Strip, Niccola Steel. You shall not refuse me again."

That memory from his sex cabin made my legs tense. All the blood flowed south without my approval, but there was little I could do. Whether or not I wanted it, Prince Casimir was my mate. He was the object of my desires and the only one now who could get me to react like this. Until the day we meet again and I can reject him face to face.

Hopefully that day will be soon. He was on his way here to the pack. It's already been six years. I didn't want to be in this limbo any longer.

Hope filled my chest as I continued to run along the stream to the pack house where, hopefully, another male could bring me clothes. If a female saw me in my current state, I'd end up breaking my unwilling loyalty to *him*. We didn't need an angry Lycan loose in the pack going mad because of betrayal pains.

Suddenly, I stopped running and froze in place. The tingling in my legs made it hard to focus, but I instinctively knew I was being watched. There was rustling in a shrub up ahead. I braced myself for the unwanted attention of a female, but when the person came through the clearing, I was faced with something more alarming.

"Hello, *mate*," Casimir drawled with one of his sultry grins. His eyes raked down my naked body, causing me to yelp and cover my erection as best I could with my hands. He smirked at my attempt. "It's good to see you, *all* of you, even the not so little parts, once again."

How come, despite my previous thoughts of rejection, I still felt a thrill and a longing I couldn't describe while staring at the one who forcibly marked me once again?

"Casimir," I rasped, taking a step back.

His eyes narrowed on my movements. "Don't run, pet. We have *so* much to catch up on."

Alesta

"This isn't going to work," I groaned, looking at my reflection in the mirror. "I told you pink wasn't my color."

"Pink is every girl's color," Gamma Kender sat back on my bed with a smirk. He brought me a dress for the welcome dinner this evening and insisted on staying to see if it would work.

It doesn't. I hate pink.

"Doesn't your sister have a dress in a better color?"

"Define 'better'."

"Black," I grumbled.

Gamma Kender snickered, trying to hide his amusement behind his hand. "Not a girly girl, huh?"

"Gee. I wonder what gave that away."

"Not having a dress," he didn't miss a beat in answering. "What kind of she-wolf doesn't own a single dress? How are you supposed to attract the opposite sex?"

"I'm not."

He rolled his eyes as he leaned back on his hands. "I guess you manage without dresses."

"What's that supposed to mean?"

His smile turned mischievous. "I don't know, *future Luna.* Whatever could I mean?"

I growled in warning. My limit for being teased had been reached long ago. "It's all a farce. You know that, so shut the hell up."

"Whoa. That's no way to speak to your loyal Gamma, *Luna.*"

"I swear, I'm going to snap your fucking neck before the night is through."

He was barely stifling his laughter. Watching him in the reflection made me growl again.

"Hey, I got a question," Gamma Kinder tilted his head to the side curiously.

"The answer's no."

"The answer is never no for me," he declared smugly.

"It's no right now."

"Well, I wasn't about to ask a yes or no question."

"The answer is still no."

He ignored me and asked anyway. "Why are you so chill and normal with me, but get all up tight around Alpha and Beta Carl?"

"What do you mean?" I adjusted the bust on the strapless gown, shimmying it from side to side to shove more of my breasts in the constricting fabric. I felt too exposed like this.

"I mean, you feel no reservations around me. You threaten to kick my ass or critically hurt me all the time, but as soon as Alpha or Beta are nearby, you get all uptight and formal."

I shrugged my shoulders, regretting the action instantly when it caused my cleavage to return. "I don't know. I trained with you for years. I guess I just got used to working with you."

"So when you get used to working with Alpha, are you going to threaten to snap his neck too?" He raised an eyebrow.

I narrowed my eyes. "You know I can't do that."

"Why not?" That mischievous look returned to his face. "You are his future Luna, after all."

"That's it," I snarled, lunging for him.

Gamma Kinder screamed, rolling backward off the bed before

my fist could connect with his face. The skin-tight dress tore up the side as we continued the chase around my bedroom. I didn't care. I'd reimburse his sister for it later. I wasn't eager to wear it, anyway.

"I'm sorry!" Gamma Kender begged, giving up with his hands in the air. "I won't call you Luna again."

"You better not." I faked a punch, then kicked him in the shin instead.

"Ow, damn it," I jumped around on one foot, holding his other. I chuckled devilishly. "You earned that."

"No, I didn't, you hussy!"

My bedroom door suddenly opened, and in came Triston with a fierce look on his little face. He marched over to Gamma Kender and kicked his other shin.

"OW!" Gamma Kender fell to the ground, rocking back and forth as he held both his ankles. "What was that for?!"

"Don't call my mom names, you wort!"

"Shit. Sorry! Sorry, Gamma. Alesta." Zaden raced into the room, buckling his belt. "I slipped to the bathroom. I thought he was busy with his homework."

"I told you I don't need a babysitter, you weirdo," Triston looked back at his instructor with a look of disgust.

"Triston," I said his name in warning.

"What?! He is a weirdo! He's scared of spiders."

"And you're scared of broccoli," I retorted. "Can I call you a weirdo for that?"

Triston shrugged. "Sure. Call me whatever you want, as long as I don't have to eat it."

My son chose the most stressful times to be exasperating. I was hoping Nic would be able to come help with him, but apparently he got held up with border patrol. Alpha wouldn't tell me what, but by Alpha's amused grin, I knew it wasn't for any dire reason. I had worried he came into trouble with the royals or something.

"What's going on in here?" Alpha Mikken walked into my bedroom, taking a look around at everyone in different ranges of stress or irritation. "Are we having a party?"

"Pre-party, Alpha," Gamma Kender said smartly. "I love a good ass kicking before a night of engaging with royals. It gets me ready for the ever-long sensation of constantly getting kicked in the balls."

"Watch your language around the pup," Alpha said harshly, though hilarity filled his sky-blue eyes.

Triston wrinkled his face. "Does being around royals really feel as painful as being kicked in the balls?"

Alpha let himself chuckle at my son. "Very much so." He then ruffled Triston's hair.

Triston looked at me with concern. "Then I don't want my mama going. She doesn't have balls, so she doesn't know how bad that hurts. Why can't she just stay home with me and you put the weirdo in a pink dress?"

Alpha Mikken looked at my ripped dress up and down. His pressing lips told me he was holding back his laughter. "I don't think the weirdo would look nearly as good in it."

My face grew warm as he stared. Self-consciously, I cover the rip going all the way up my thigh.

"I ruined the dress, anyway. Maybe I should just stay home."

"Oh, Alesta," Alpha Mikken sighed. "We both know you can't do that."

I do know that. We discussed it in detail earlier. Our "plans" were solidified when Alpha received news that King Lukyan had returned to the pack house and insisted on a conversation with me. Beta Carlston had to give the excuse of me still being unwell and assure Lukyan that I would be in attendance for tonight's dinner for him to relent.

Not going tonight would cause Lukyan seeking me out himself, no matter what Alpha or Beta Carlston said. That could be catastrophic. I had to go to him if I wanted to avoid Triston being discovered. Lukyan can never lay eyes on my son. He would know just looking upon his face who his father was.

With a frustrated groan, I looked towards my wardrobe. "Can

I just wear my uniform then? I really don't own a single dress. This was from Gamma Kender's sister."

Alpha smirked, his blue eyes glinting with mirth. "I've gotten you something better. Consider it a uniform if you must."

Chapter 14

Another Man

Nerves were eating away at my insides as I took a last look at my outfit in the mirror of my bedroom. I didn't know if this dress was better or worse. The dark navy of the fabric underneath was more my color, but there was a shimmering layer over everything that made the dress resemble the midnight sky.

I might as well be in the bright pink dress. I would stand out even more in this.

Knock Knock

"Alesta. We need to go."

I groaned, resisting the urge to stomp my feet and throw a tantrum. I really didn't want to do this. Not just because I was going as Alpha Mikken's date. I didn't want to face Lukyan again. Especially while wearing this dress.

Knock Knock Knock

"I'm coming!"

Alpha Mikken's laughter was soft on the other side of the door. The dress wasn't the only surprise Alpha had for me. It came with an outlandish pair of shoes that added several inches to my height. I slid them on my feet, then attempted to bend down to fasten them, but the dress made it hard to do so.

"Damn it," I grumbled, sitting back on my bed to try and fasten them that way.

"Everything okay in there?"

"No!" I huffed. "These shoes are ridiculous. I can't even get them on."

There was a pause, then Alpha said, "I'm coming in."

I didn't have time to protest. He opened the door before I could. His eyes widened upon seeing me. I suddenly felt self-conscious. "I know. I look weird in this, don't I?"

He averted his gaze, rubbing his chin nervously. "N-no. Not at all."

That response didn't help my nerves. "It's not too late to take someone else. I can just hide in the bunker with Triston and the spiders until the inspection is over. Or until the world ends. Whichever comes first."

He let out a half-hearted chuckle. "You'd get bored with the spiders in an hour. No. You're going with me."

"Not if I can't get these shoes on." I lifted the hem of the dress and waved an exasperated hand towards my feet.

Alpha Mikken eyed my legs, then rubbed his chin more aggressively. "I, uh, can help you with that."

He dropped to one knee, lifting my right foot into his lap. I grew more aware of his closeness as his hands gingerly touched my skin. This ticklish sensation traveled up my leg as he carefully hooked the straps into place. After he was done with my left foot, he hesitated for a second before setting it back on the ground.

Alpha Mikken's blue eyes stared up into mine. I became insanely aware that my Alpha was kneeling before me in a very intimate setting. Under any other circumstances, this would be considered indecent. All the rumors Prissly the Wort would spread if she were to see this scene would label me as shameless.

"You look beautiful, Alesta." Alpha Mikken's voice filled the limited space between us. "Really beautiful."

His compliment made my face heat up. "Um, thank you. Y-you look nice as well, Alpha. Thank you for the dress."

He scowled, then said, "Ken. You are to call me Ken from now on, Alesta, or this will not work."

I gulped nervously. "Alright... Ken."

His warm smile unnerved me once again. If not for the slight pain building in my chest, I might have even gotten butterflies. He helped me up, then took a moment to look me over once again now that I was standing.

"Truly beautiful. You are the epitome of a Luna in this dress."

"Thanks, but don't get used to it. I can't wait for the inspection to be over."

"I don't know," he gave me an impish grin. "I may just decide to promote you again. The salary as my Luna would be most rewarding."

I rolled my eyes. "I told you to quit the teasing."

"Oh, I never tease," Alpha Mikken said as he held his elbow out to escort me. "Not with you, Alesta."

The tightening in my chest returned the moment I took his arm. It got worse as he kissed the back of my hand before tucking it tightly in the crook of his arm.

"Ready?"

"No," I shook my head. "But we can go, anyway."

Zaden was sitting on the ground with Triston, arguing over the rules of the game they were currently playing. Both stopped mid-argument and looked up at us as we came out of my room.

"Whoa," Zaden's eyes went wide. "You clean up nice, Alesta. You almost look like a royal yourself."

"Don't even joke like that," I grumbled. The image of Lukyan's wife standing upon the balcony after their wedding came to mind. I could never look that regal. She was a goddess compared to my humble appearance. It made me sick to even think of the comparison.

"You look cooler in your warrior clothes," Triston said sourly. "You look too much like a girl right now."

Zaden and Alpha Mikken both chuckled as I rolled my eyes towards the ceiling.

"She is a girl," Zaden corrected my son.

Triston growled at him. "Shut up, weirdo. That's my mom, not a girl."

"Thanks," I huffed, sick of the attention already. "Don't tell your teacher to shut up. You better behave, Triston. Or I'm going to force-feed you broccoli for breakfast tomorrow."

Triston made a horrified expression. "But he locked me in a basement!"

"Triston," I groaned.

"Alright," he hung his little shoulders. "Can I have chocolate waffles for breakfast in the morning if I behave?"

"I'll do you one better," Alpha smiled crookedly. "I'll ensure that a chocolate cake is brought to you tonight before bed if Zaden tells me you've behaved."

Triston excitedly licked his lips. "Okay. Deal!"

"Thank you," Zaden sighed heavily, looking relieved.

Triston looked over at him like he was about to say something smart, but caught himself before he did. I still had my apprehensions about leaving my child with Zaden, seeing as Zaden couldn't handle him well on his own like Nic could have, but I had little choice. We had to go. We would be the last to arrive to dinner as it was thanks to my shoe debacle.

As Alpha and I made our way to the banquet hall, I grew increasingly uneasy. This plan sounded fine at the time we conceived it, but now I was having my doubts. With every step forward, my stomach twisted even more.

"What if this doesn't work?" I whispered.

Alpha squeezed my hand. "Why wouldn't it?"

"He's not stupid, Alph-... I mean, Ken. What if he doesn't believe you're really taking me as your Luna and starts asking questions? What if he discovers the truth?"

Alpha Mikken was quiet for a long moment before he answered. "I know you already said no once, but I'm going to ask again. Do you want me to mark you? Really mark you, Alesta? There would be no doubt then."

I hurriedly shook my head. "No. I'm not your mate."

His expression turned uncharacteristically stoic. "That doesn't matter. Not with you."

"I know you want to help keep me safe, Alpha, but no. I will not damage your chance at finding your fated mate. I'd rather take Triston and run."

His brows pulled downward, shadowing his blue eyes to make them look like stormy seas. "Then we will make this work." His eyes lightened as he lightly tapped the end of my nose. "And remember to call me Ken."

Lukyan

"Thank you once again, your majesty," the Beta bowed to me with a stoic expression. "Our pack is most grateful for the game you personally hunted in our lands."

It was a backhanded comment. Camellia was the one who ordered our people to retrieve the animals I slaughtered and offer them to the pack as atonement for my behavior. I could hear the Beta's true meaning behind his words.

How dare you slaughter our game to vent your anger...

I wonder if Alesta told them what I was to her. I wonder if that was why this Beta has been so reserved in providing me any I formation about my mate, or why the Alpha has been elusive since my arrival.

"Thank you, Beta Carlston, for the gracious welcoming feast you have provided for us," Camellia spoke on my behalf as she placed a steadying hand on my arm. "Our early arrival must have been most surprising, but you've been most accommodating."

Beta Carlston gave Camellia a more genuine smile. "Not at all, my Queen. Our Alpha and future Luna worked tirelessly over the past few days to ensure everything was ready. I'll pass along your regards to them both."

"Where is the Alpha?" I asked with nearly contained irritation.

"Shouldn't he be the one offering his gratitude and hosting our company?"

Camellia's hand tightens its grip.

The Beta's expression turned stony once again as he addressed me. "Alpha Mikken will be here soon. I believe he had to allow extra time for his date to get ready."

My eyes darted around the room, searching for the person I truly wanted to see; the woman this Beta promised would be in attendance for tonight's feast.

"And where is Alesta?"

The Beta's expression showed pretension as the corner of his lips lifted into a smirk. "As I said, our Alpha's *date* needed more time to get ready."

My nostrils flared at what he was insinuating. If it wasn't for Camellia's nails sinking into my skin, my beast may have broken free.

"Thank you, Beta. We will anxiously be waiting for their arrival," Camellia said in her most honeyed tone.

The Beta's tight smile was his only response before walking away. My eyes trailed after him to the end of the hall, where he began speaking in inaudible whispers to one of the werewolf warriors standing guard. Using all my focus, I caught just a few words, but they were enough to help me calm my inner beast.

"Alesta and the Alpha are on their way."

The fact my mate was with the Alpha was infuriating, but she didn't have a mark on her neck. She wasn't his yet. I would do all I could to ensure she never would be.

"What is wrong with you?" Camellia had the uncanny ability to keep a benevolent expression while speaking in furious whispers to me. "If you do not start communicating with me, I will not know how to help you. Why have you been so animalistic? More so than usual?"

Ruth was sitting on her other side, and I noticed his curious glance my way. Casimir was off at another table, bullying Alesta's friend as he used to. Casimir must not have spoken to them yet about the true reasons he insisted Camellia and I join the inspection of Hallowed Moon Pack. I had half expected him to.

"She's my mate," I grumbled roughly in the lowest tone I could muster.

Camellia's eyes went wide. "Who? The sickly girl from the foyer?"

"I doubt she was truly sick." Seeing me again after escaping the capital most likely caused her to panic. I saw the fear in her eyes.

"So, it was her?" Camellia had a huge expectant grin on her face.

I nodded tersely.

"That's magnificent! Who would have thought that-"

"Cami," Ruth discreetly squeezed her leg to curb her enthusiasm. "Magnificent would not be how I'd describe discovering my fated mate in the arms of another man."

Camellia let her regal facade drop for a moment as she gasped. "That's why?! I thought... I don't know. I didn't realize that was why you lost control suddenly."

The phantom pains of betrayal in my chest resurfaced. "That wasn't the only reason."

Camellia looked at me in confusion. "Why else?"

I looked around the room and shook my head. "This isn't the place for this discussion."

"I'm sure none can hear what we are discussing," Camellia whispered. "Werewolf hearing is not as sharp as ours."

"Their ability to hear isn't the only issue with openly talking about fated mates. Mine especially."

All eyes were glancing at us, the Lycan royals in attendance, every so often. I could feel their anxiety pulsating around the room. Lycans already didn't have a reputable notoriety among werewolf packs. Especially ones such as this who had experienced the harshest cruelties dealt out personally by a prominent Lycan figure.

If Alesta was truly the chosen Luna to this pack, I had to be extremely careful with how I persuaded her to come back to me. I'm sure the older generations and the Alpha himself have not forgiven us for the tragedies of the past. The Alpha especially....

Camellia, not possessing the full knowledge of why this pack had been left alone for so many years, seemed confused. Ruth was looking at me with his eerie, knowing gaze.

Then he sat back and lifted his glass. Looking straight ahead as he lifted the chalice to his lips, he murmured, "This pack has been desperate for a Luna for far too long."

He knew. I don't know how, since it was the best kept secret in our recent history, but Ruth knew.

In a shared link, I said, "*Openly speaking about their Luna prospect being my mate would be most unwise. This has to be kept quiet among us.*"

"*Obviously,*" Camellia huffed. "*I'm not ignorant of the fact we need to keep up appearances. I think I'm doing my part far better than you.*"

It wasn't just for appearances. I don't know what Alesta told this Alpha. This was a delicate situation when considering our history with Hallowed Moon. Why my mother would send her here of all places, I do not know. It seemed like an extremely precarious decision made of desperation. Maybe mother did not intend for Alesta to ever return. That was the only explanation I could conjure up.

Now that I found her again, the reasons would have to be revealed later. All my energy needed to be in getting my mate to return to the capital with me of her own free will.

That seemed like an impossible task. If her mind was made up to leave me six years ago, my sudden reappearance would not change anything. She believed I abandoned her to marry Camellia. Casimir told me as much. My mother didn't have to persuade her to leave. She just had to tell her the truth. The truth I had obtusely kept from her after trying to confine her to my room.

If that was the only reason she left me, simply showing her the truth would hopefully be enough to persuade her. Ruth and his eerie eye being here with us could solidify the evidence that Camellia and I were never truly together. I never abandoned Alesta. I could never…

"They're here." Casimir suddenly appeared at my side. We've not been here a full day, and he already reeked of debauchery. His eyes were swimming in delight.

"Who?" I stupidly asked, right before I caught her scent.

My nostrils flared, trying to catch as much of her as I could breathe in. Automatically, my head turned towards the doors, wanting more of her delicious scent. Then, as I caught sight of the flawless beauty on the arm of the aloof Alpha, a burning need tore through my chest.

"Seems pack life suits our little Alesta," my brother murmured tauntingly in my ear. "She's glowing."

She was. I had never seen her dressed up like this. She was fucking perfect, and all for a man that wasn't me.

Chapter 15

Dinner Date

Alesta

"You ready?" Alpha Mikken placed his hand protectively over mine linked to his arm.

After a deep, steadying breath, I nodded. "As ready as I'll ever be."

"I've got you." Alpha gave me one of his unnerving, boyish smiles. "Just stay by my side."

"I will." I had no plans to leave my Alpha's side. I was basically using him as a shield, but he freely offered to be one. I feel no shame. Not when it pertains to my son's safety.

I avoided looking around as we passed through the opened doors. I felt eyes on us coming from everywhere, but I refused to return a single gaze. Thankfully, Beta Carlston was waiting for us.

"Finally," Beta Carlston said in exasperation. "You know, when I agreed to be your Beta, I never agreed to take on an angry Lycan King in your stead."

"Ah, but you've been handling yourself so admirably," Alpha Mikken snickered.

"Admirably," Beta Carlston huffed sarcastically. "I would have died admirably if not for the queen. She's the only reasonable one among the Lycans. She even tried to cover for the good king's massacre by offering the mutilated corpses to us, labeling it as game."

I stiffened hearing about the woman by my fated mate's side. Alpha Mikken maintained his playful air but firmly squeezed my hand in comfort. I ignored the pain in my chest and the eyes burning into my skin and tried to focus on just Alpha Mikken's touch.

"Serve it to them for tomorrow's dinner," Alpha Mikken replied. "Say it was far more than our pack house residents could consume. Lycan's have greater hunger," he snorted. "They believe they have greater everything, so it's a feasible solution."

That comment didn't sit well with me. I understood their frustration, but my son was a Lycan and he very much had a greater hunger than his peers.

"You sound like a wort," I muttered without thinking, then quickly covered my mouth, realizing I said that out loud.

Both men gawked at me. Alpha Mikken's astonished slow grin made my face burn in shame.

"Oh, my," Beta Carlston looked beyond amused. "Did our professional little Alesta just call her Alpha a wort?"

"I think she was calling both of us worts."

I wanted to hide my face and run from the room.

"What an adorably creative pet name."

Alpha Mikken snorted. "Like mother like son."

I furrowed my brows. "What do you mean?"

Alpha shrugged his shoulders. "That's a secret between me and my little Lycan friend."

What did Triston tell the Alpha? Geez.

"What's going on?" Gamma Kender asked as he walked over.

"Alesta called us worts." Beta filled him in with a smirk.

Gamma Kender's eyes glimmered impishly. "Did she, now? Did she threaten to slit your throat yet?"

Alpha Mikken and Beta Carlston exchanged looks, then shook their heads, almost in unison.

"No. Was she supposed to?" Beta asked.

Gamma Kender stretched his arms wide, then carefully set one around my shoulders. "She only does that to her closest friends."

"Or total idiots," I scoffed.

"See," Gamma Kender looked smug. "She only gets mean to those she likes."

Alpha Mikken pushed his Gamma's arm off me. "Get off her, *idiot*."

"Yeah, *idiot*," Beta Carlston sneered.

"You two are just jealous that you aren't as close to Alesta as I am yet."

Rolling my eyes, I turned my head so Alpha wouldn't see my blatant disrespect. That was a mistake, because the second I looked away, my gaze caught a fierce pair of burning topaz eyes, blazing into me.

Lukyan was sitting at the table elevated at the head of the room. His dark clothes accentuated the ominous mood around him. His shirt was unbuttoned around the neck, revealing his tanned skin underneath. Memories of running my fingers over that firm patch of skin made something inside me clench. I unconsciously licked my lips, and that was when his fierce expression changed.

The corner of his lips curled tauntingly as his eyes burned against my skin. I became overly conscious of every exposed inch of my body, feeling the searing itch of his gaze. I couldn't look away, though in the back of my mind, I knew I had to.

"Alesta?"

I gasped, snapping back to the present as Alpha Mikken called my name. I started to turn back to the man posing as my date, but before I could, my eyes met *hers*. Lukyan's wife. His queen.

She was staring at me with blatant curiosity. I felt like a bug under inspection at the regal woman's observation. Her shining smile made guilt chew away at me. Her composed presence was the total opposite of how I felt right now.

How impossibly stupid could I have been to let myself get lost like that?

"Hey. Little Alesta?" Gamma Kender waved his hands in front of my face. "Are you just blatantly ignoring us now?"

"No," I answered breathlessly. "No. Not at all. Sorry. I was just.... Distracted."

"Hmm," Gamma Kender tilted his face to the side as he examined mine.

"Hey." Alpha Mikken gently turned my face to look at him. "Are you alright? Is this too much for you?"

Swallowing down my panic, I shook my head. "No. No, I'm fine." I tried to search for some excuse for my behavior. "It's just... these shoes..."

"Ah," Alpha Mikken gave me a knowing grin. "The troublesome shoes. Should we take our seats, then?"

I forced a smile as I nodded again. Despite the tightness in my chest, I was starting to feel normal again. Even with Lukyan and his queen sitting in the same room. It wasn't until Alpha Mikken started leading me to the head table that I felt my anxiety rise once again.

We were sitting with them. Of course we were. Alpha Mikken was, well, the Alpha. He always sat where the royals were sitting now when we had any pack functions.

And I was acting as his future Luna. I couldn't sneak away or find an excuse to sit somewhere else. I'd have to endure it.

More eyes than before were on us, and the room steadily grew quiet as we approached the Lycans. The muted murmurings of the pack members seeing Alpha Mikken and his secretary together were tickling my ears. I could not even imagine the rumors that would go around by the time this dinner was through.

"What the hell is going on?" Niccola's voice filtered through my head.

I looked around just enough until I found him sitting at a table with other warriors and trainers near the front of the room. He was in his formal attire, with a vacant seat beside him. No doubt that seat was intentionally left open for me.

"I didn't have time to tell you-"

"Tell me what?!" Niccola interrupted me. *"Lukyan is right fucking there, Al. I thought you were going to hide away until the royals left."*

"There was a change of plans," I grimaced. *"He saw me already. I couldn't just hide anymore."*

"What about Triston?...."

This was for Triston. To keep my son hidden, I needed to stay out in the open, pretending I had nothing to hide.

"He's safe."

There was a pause of relief, then Niccola asked, *"But why are you with the Alpha?"*

I didn't respond. Niccola would know in just a few more seconds.

Alpha Mikken placed a hand on the small of my back, cradling my side in his. My chest throbbed thunderously from the intimate contact, but I had to bear with it. Just for tonight.

The scent that still haunts me began invading my lungs. I felt those fiery eyes searing into me again. I knew if I looked up, I wouldn't be able to look away. I'd be caught in his topaz spell.

"King Lukyan. Queen Camellia," Alpha Mikken said to Lukyan and his queen. His voice dropped to a stoic tone, all the usual merriment gone. "My apologies for the late greeting. I am Mikken Bennet, Alpha of the Hallowed Moon Pack." He tightened his hand around my waist. "And this is my future Luna."

Lukyan

"...this is my future Luna."

The Alpha's tone as he introduced my mate as his was abundantly arrogant. The way he looked at her made my beast push to come forth. What made it worse was that she wouldn't look at me. I knew she could feel my stare, but she was purposely avoiding my gaze.

"A fine Luna she will be, I'm sure," Casimir lifted his glass with a smirk. "Does this future Luna of yours have a name?"

Her eyes tensed in their corners, the action so slight I would have missed it if I hadn't seen it before. She was masking her annoyance. Even after seven years, I still could recognize her smallest emotions.

That would have made me happy if not for the fact she was on the arm of another man.

"Alesta," the Alpha spoke right as she was getting ready to speak. "Her name is Alesta." The bastard smiled warmly down at her.

I deep rumbling vibrated my chest as she gave him a grateful smile in return. He prevented me from hearing her voice. I was coiled too tightly inside in anticipation of her every single motion. She was drowning all my other senses. I just needed to hear her speak.

"What a beautiful name," Camellia said, leaning forward with one of her coyly stunning smiles. "It's very nice to meet you, Alesta. I hear it is your praise we must sing for such wonderful accommodations. Our rooms were absolutely lovely."

Alesta bowed her head as she murmured, "I'm pleased you found everything to your liking. Please let me know if there's anything more you need."

"I most certainly will. I especially loved the flower arrangements. Did you gather the flowers nearby?"

Alesta glanced up at the Alpha and the two shared a secretive smile.

"Actually, Ken gathered them himself."

The way my mate stared at the damned Alpha made my blood boil.

"Not just me," Alpha corrected her. "I barely helped."

Alesta shook her head with amusement dancing in her beautiful eyes. "You organized all the children and gathered the flowers with them. I would hardly call that barely helping."

The Alpha shrugged, his eyes only for Alesta. "The kids wanted to help." He then pulled her close. My chest burned as he gently kissed her on the head. "Plus, wildflowers are Alesta's favorite." The pain tearing through me may have been enough to cause my shift, but I noticed my mate's expression. For just a second, her face wasn't that of a woman being adored by her lover. She was in pain, too. I saw it in her eyes that were clenching in their corners. Her entire body went rigid in the span of a second until his lips left her skin.

She was feeling this pain, too. All from his intimate touch.

"How charming," Camellia said, her tone a little edgy. She was probably anticipating my beast to break free and rampage through this dining hall at any second. Her hand slid over the table to grasp my wrist, her nails digging into my skin. "You two must be deeply enamored with one another."

Alesta's eyes followed the movement of Camellia's hand. The narrowing blues flashed with aggression.

"We very much are," the bastard Alpha said confidently, but his face changed when he looked down to see Alesta's gaze on where Camellia was touching me.

A deep feeling of satisfaction consumed me. She was deeply bothered by another woman touching me. The bond was fully there. Even for her after even years apart.

Her reaction was missed by no one. Camellia slowly released me, no longer fearing my beast would come forth, but wary of Alesta's.

"Alesta?" Alpha Mikken called gently.

Alesta jerked her head up, then a look of shock painted her lovely skin the most delicious shade of pink. Her shame was my glory. My effect on her was greater than her soon-to-be mate's. That was evident.

"Are you not feeling well again?" Alpha Mikken tried to play her behavior off.

Alesta smiled weakly. "I'm fine. I'm sorry Alph-, I mean, Ken."

She looked apologetic for a moment. It wasn't an expression I had seen. The Alesta from my memories didn't apologize to anyone. Not even me. Not that she ever had reason to. I was the one that needed to apologize for so many things.

What I was entirely unapologetic for was the fact I was going to get my mate back. By her reactions, I was fairly certain it would be easier than I originally anticipated.

$$\infty\infty\infty$$

Alesta

"Here, love," Alpha Mikken pulled back a seat for me. Thankfully, it was three spaces down from Lukyan.

"Thank you," I whispered as he helped to push me in.

"Of course." He pecked my head again, just as he did earlier.

I tried to contain the pain radiating through my chest. It was aggravating to keep experiencing the tightness in my chest. I was curious about where it was coming from. It seemed to only happen when Alpha Mikken touched me.

If I didn't know any better, I would suspect the discomfort was being caused by a betrayal to my fated bond. That couldn't be the case, though. No, I didn't outright reject Lukyan before leaving seven years ago. I couldn't without alerting him I was leaving.

The bond would have been voided anyway the second he marked his new bride. Seeing as they both have marks on their necks, I know the pain couldn't be from our broken bond.

"Some wine, *Alesta love*?" Casimir asked mockingly from the other side of my Alpha.

I mustered up a smile and nodded my head. "Please." Maybe the wine would help me calm down. I needed to compose myself better, so a blight like what had just happened in front of Lukyan and his wife wouldn't happen again.

Casimir slid a freshly filled chalice towards me. Alpha Mikken eyed the exchange warily as he took the seat between Casimir and me.

"Thank you," I murmured. Bringing the wine to my lips, I caught a whiff of its fragrance. It had a floral note to it. This was not the wine I had the kitchen prepare.

"A gift from the capital," Casimir raised his glass. "We brought along several cases."

"Since you were indisposed, I asked your staff to prepare a few bottles for our table," Queen Camellia smiled brightly at me. "I do hope you are feeling better now."

"Much better. Thank you." I didn't feel better at all. Not with those topaz eyes still searing into me.

"Sick, huh?" Casimir had that devilish look on his face. It had been seven years, but I knew it all too well. I tensed in reflex, anticipating what he may say next.

"The doctor cleared her to be here tonight," Alpha Mikken said as he rubbed my back. "But I don't believe the strong premium wine of the capital would be good for her disposition right now."

He lifted the chalice from my hands before I could even have a sip. I was pouting internally, really wishing for the help of alcohol at this moment.

"Her disposition?" Casimir raised an eyebrow. "Why, you make it sound like her ailment wasn't an ailment at all." His smile darkened with mischief. "Is *Alesta love* carrying some *good news* for us to celebrate this evening?"

My eyes widened in shock. What the hell was he saying?

Before I could deny his accusations, or carve that damned smile from Casimir's face, Lukyan stood abruptly, his eyes like fire and his expression deadly.

"You're pregnant?"

Chapter 16

The Queen

"**W**hat?! No!"

I should have punched Casimir right in his mouth before he could open it. Why the hell would he ask that in front of his brother?

"What? She's pregnant?..."

"She and Alpha have been really close recently...."

"He suddenly made her his secretary. I thought something might be...."

The murmurings of our own pack members angered me more. Casimir and his damned mouth.

"I'm not fucking pregnant!" I snarled loud enough for everyone to hear. "And quite frankly, it's rather damn rude for you to ask such an inappropriate question upon our *first* meeting."

Casimir, not affected by my energy, raised one of his groomed brows. "Oh? I could have sworn you and I had met before."

Was our game of ignorance over? I guess it had to be, seeing as Lukyan had yet to take his seat. I've been actively avoiding his topaz eyes, but I still know they are blazing towards me. No one would be able to miss the tension between us.

When a whisper from a member of our pack reached my ears, an icy dread made my body freeze.

"By 'met before', you don't think the second prince could be the boy's...."

Alpha Mikken's plan didn't factor in Casimir's smart mouth. He just declared me his chosen Luna, and now the pack was under the impression my son might be Casimir's. That will reflect on Alpha Mikken.

Casimir was the one that helped me escape, knowing I was pregnant. I'm not sure if he didn't mention my son to his brother yet. What was his goal in goading me like this?

Without knowing what else to say and fear for my son gripping me, I stood up from the table. I mechanically dropped my napkin on the table and focused on the minor task to try to distract myself from the war going on in my head.

"Excuse me," I murmured.

Lukyan was still standing, his searing eyes burning into my face. I couldn't stop myself from stealing a glance at the man who, even after seven years, was affecting every cell in my body.

Those topaz eyes…. I expected anger or some level of accusation. Instead, they held so much guilt. There was so much pain in his gaze that I felt tears prickling behind mine as I forced myself to look away.

Hurrying through the now silent hall, I didn't lift my burning eyes from the ground. I didn't want to meet my pack members' eyes. I didn't want to feel the shame or embarrassment from their interpretation of Casimir's questions or Lukyan's reaction. I couldn't process my emotions as it was.

Then, like the final blow to my chest, I heard Queen Camellia's coaxing voice.

"Luk, sit with me, my dear. Let the Alpha convey your brother's apologies." There was a loud thump and rattling of dishes. "I know you don't tolerate disrespect towards our kingdom's Alpha's and their partners. Rest your anger at your brother for now."

She was placing all this on Casimir, speaking as if Lukyan's reaction was caused by the young prince's behavior.

This was a bad idea. I should have just taken my chances of running away.

"I'll be right there, Alesta," Alpha Mikken's calming tone echoed

in my head. *"I'll be right after you."*

He must have predicted my thoughts. He was telling me not to run away. As much as I wanted to, I knew I couldn't. Not right now. I could end up leading Lukyan right to my son.

Instead, I turned for the front doors, going the opposite direction of home.

"Alesta!" Niccola's voice called from behind me. "Wait! I'm coming!"

I didn't slow my pace.

"I'm coming too!" It was Gamma Kender this time.

"Can I not be fucking alone?" I hissed under my breath. I wanted to fall apart without an audience.

"Nope. No can do," Gamma Kender said. "Alpha's orders. Plus, we're best friends."

"Um," Nic eyed our Gamma from the corner of his eyes. "I don't think so."

"Why? You think it's you?!" Gamma Kender scoffed. "Uh, has expressed her desire to touch you? I don't think so. She does it to me all the time."

"I believe you've misinterpreted things she truly said," Nic said warily.

If this damned dress wasn't so tight, I would have gone into a full sprint to get away from their banter. If this dress had been a handed down one from the Gamma's sister, I would have ripped through it and shifted to my wolf.

"So, where are we going?" Gamma Kender asked cheerfully.

My lip curled in aggression. "To act on my desire to touch you."

Lukyan

I wanted to go after her. I saw the fear in her eyes. Fear aimed at me.

That fear broke my heart all over again.

The only thing keeping me from chasing her down was Camellia's nails embedded in my leg. She was furious. She may not be showing it on the outside, but there had been an endless stream of curses from her flowing through my mind since I stood abruptly.

I couldn't stop myself. Imagining my mate growing round with the Alpha's child had my beast growing feral. That was not something I could survive. It wasn't something my beast would allow the Alpha to survive.

"Oh, my," Casimir said as he ran his finger around the edge of his wineglass. "I was simply trying to be friendly."

His voice had the same arrogance it always carried, but his eyes were narrowing on Alesta's friend as he followed her out. The werewolf ex-tribute's stench was still cloaking my brother. It seems there is still more about Casimir's involvement that I was not informed of yet.

"Friendly, you say," the Alpha said with a deadly calm, bringing my attention back to him. "Not a second of this visit so far has seemed *friendly*."

"Careful," I growled with clenched teeth. "Did you forget who you are speaking to?"

His mouth twisted. "I know exactly who I am speaking to." He lowered his voice to barely a whisper. "I know a lot more than even you."

He knew... He knew...

"Good," I said coldly, leaning over to take the wineglass in front of him. The one that Alesta's lips had touched. I brought it to mine, not moving my stare from his. "There will be no surprises for you later."

As I drank, Casimir scoffed softly to himself. "Surprises, surprises."

Alpha Mikken's eyes darted to my brother, a brief look of panic flashing behind them.

What was he hiding? And what more did my brother not tell me?....

∞ ∞ ∞

Camellia

"What are you thinking, my love?" Ruth discreetly ran a hand down my spine while leaning forward to get the wine.

I'd been deep in thought, wondering what to do about Lukyan and his.... Situation. As things stood, this pack would be in ruins and Lukyan would go irrevocably feral by the end of the week. Then the kingdom would revert back to its wicked ways, undoing all we had sacrificed to work towards for the past seven years.

"We have to do something," I told my mate. *"We can't let this get any more complicated."*

"Or..." Ruth smiled deviously behind his wineglass. His hypnotic eyes were swirling with mirth. *"We could always complicate things just a bit more..."*

I narrowed my eyes at him. *"What are you thinking?..."*

"Oh, nothing much." His smile made my heart flutter and my legs press together. *"It's such a lovely night for a stroll, don't you think, my love?"*

Alesta

"Okay! Okay!" Gamma Kender crawled backward on the ground away from me. "That's enough touching!"

I smirked sinisterly. "I thought you wanted to be touched by your best friend?"

"He can be your best friend!" He pointed an accusatory finger

Niccola smirking on the sidelines of the field while holding my dress.

"He's more like my brother."

"Then why didn't you borrow your *brother's* clothes?!"

I chuckled under my breath. I would have been fine sparring naked as the elite warriors often did while shifting back and forth while training, but Gamma Kender was the one who was adamantly against it. I wasn't ruining the dress Alpha lent me, so I demanded Gamma Kender's if he didn't want me to spar in the nude. As I wore his pants and undershirt, he was left in just his underwear.

I ran my finger under his chin. "You may not have won, but at least you can say you got me out of that dress and into your pants."

A shiver wracked his body. "Yeah. I'm definitely not repeating that to anyone."

"Repeating what?" Alpha Mikken asked, coming from around the warrior's building.

"Nuh-nothing, Alpha!" Gamma Kender scurried back, away from where I was crouched in front of him.

Alpha Mikken looked me over as I stood to my feet, amusement playing in his eyes. "Did you find your Gamma's clothes more to your liking?"

I rolled my neck, loosening my muscles. "I'd hold a lot less guilt ruining his clothes than the dress you loaned me."

"Loaned? I gave that dress to you, Alesta," Alpha Mikken said in a disapproving tone.

"I'll have no use for it once the royals leave." Or when I take my son and run away, which I am still very much considering doing.

"You think I have use for a formal dress?" Alpha lifted a brow towards me. "I would never look nearly as good as you in it."

"I'd clash with your eyes," Gamma Kender snickered, then tightened his lips when Alpha gave him a look.

After expelling so much pent up energy and frustration on Gamma Kender, my mind felt clearer. I stared at Alpha as he looked back at me. The silence stretched until I finally said, "The pack thinks Prince Casimir and I had *relations*. Openly calling me your chosen Luna is no longer going to work."

Niccola coughed loudly, then waved his hands dismissively when we turned to look at his coughing fit. "Sorry," he muttered, bending over and rubbing his hand down his thigh. It was a weird motion, especially considering he was coughing. You'd think he'd cover his mouth or something instead.

Alpha Mikken's eyes tightened ever so slightly. "That won't be an issue. I told you I'd handle it."

I shook my head. "You shouldn't have to handle that. Especially since it involves rumors with royals. The pack will never accept me, even as a farce. I think your plan is going to do more damage than help."

His blue eyes flashed with untampered exasperation. He closed the distance between us, speaking low. "It doesn't have to be a farce, Alesta. I already told you. And I would never allow anyone in this pack to treat you with anything other than the respect you deserve."

My chest throbbed thinking about his offer again. Even though I had adamantly refused before, it was tempting now. If not for every cell in my body screaming that it would be wrong,I might have given in. One mark on my neck would conclude everything. Lukyan would be forced to treat me as the official Luna of Hallowed Moon Pack. Hiding Triston would be much simpler without worrying about my unmarked nape.

But then Queen Camellia's slim neck, marred forever by her own chosen mate's mark, came to my mind. The mental image brought tension to my limbs and my chest clenched.

"No. I told you, I am not your fated mate." More than ever, I know I can never hurt another woman by taking her mate from her. Even if Alpha Mikken hadn't met her yet.

Alpha Mikken sighed, dropping his shoulders like he was exhausted. Then he ran his hand through his hair. "You're aggravatingly stubborn."

"Or just aggravating," Gamma grumbled. When I glanced his

way, he blew a kiss at me, then looked away guiltily as Alpha looked back.

"I should go back home," I mumbled, knowing any more discussion here wouldn't be wise.

Alpha held my gaze for several seconds, then sighed again. "Alright. I'd like Zaden and Niccola to remain with you for the time being, if that is alright?"

"Why Zaden?"

He leaned in and whispered in my ear, "Since I can not command you, I'd like some reassurance you won't take my little Lycan friend and escape during the night. Unless you think moving to the Alpha wing would be better?"

"Nope. Zaden can have the couch," I quickly said, shutting that down before it could gain traction.

"Um," Gamma Kender mumbled cautiously. Brushing the dirt and grime from his bare flesh as he asked, "Could I possibly get my clothes back?"

Alpha Mikken raised his eyebrows. "Are you telling Alesta to undress?"

"No! No... I was just... You know what? Keep the clothes. They look better on you, anyway."

I smirked. "I know. I should get in your pants more often."

"And I out of your dress," he added, then gasped when he realized he had played along. He sent a nervous glance to Alpha Mikken. "I was joking."

"Hmm. Stay back and tell me more of your *jokes*, Kender. I'd love to hear more."

I laughed as Niccola and I started walking back towards the pack house. Gamma Kender was screaming playfully, running from Alpha towards the building.

"I think I see the appeal in stealing other's clothes," I snickered to Niccola. "It's somewhat satisfying."

"How about I steal yours next time you go for a run?" Nic scoffed. "We'll see how satisfying it is for you, then."

I was about to retort without another smartass remark about being in the nude when we heard muffled noises coming from the path ahead. Both of us stiffened, then cautiously continued forward, hiding behind the thick shrubs and bushes as the noises got louder.

Then, several feet off the trail, we saw a couple in a passionate embrace against a thick oak. A man's back was to us. His clothes were in the process of being peeled away and a woman's bare legs were wrapped around his waist.

It wasn't anything too alarming. Couples were known to get carried away in the woods at night after a run in the moonlight. Niccola and I exchanged an amused look, then started for the pack house again. Before I fully looked away from the couple, the woman's face fell back as the man kissed down her neck.

I knew that woman. Her regal face beaming next to my fated mate after their marriage had haunted my dreams so many nights. Her wanton appearance replaced the queenly air. The man she was entangled with was not her husband. Lukyan's scent wasn't among the lusty others hitting my nose.

For just a moment, she opened her eyes. She met my shocked gaze and had the audacity to smile. Then she hung her head back as the man she was with rocked his hip in rhythm with her airy moans.

Niccola grabbed my hand and ran with me in tow. What the hell did we just witness? Why was Lukyan's wife embracing another man? And why wasn't his Lycan raising hell at the pain of her betrayal?

Chapter 17

Uncle Casimir

Niccola

"Come out, come out, wherever you are...."

Damn it. I rolled over where I lay on the floor to see Triston sleeping soundly in his bed. Zander was snoring from the sofa and Alesta was silent in her room. She was quite shaken after stumbling upon our new queen on the path back home.

I wasn't. Not after my run-in with Casimir....

"Oh, my ornery little wolf. Don't make me come find you."

I growled back through the link at the second prince. *"I'm coming! And I'm not little."*

"Hmm. Aren't you?..."

His cackling irritated me to no end. *"I'll show you. Again."*

"Ooh, promises. Promises." He chuckled darkly. *"I'll be waiting, mate."*

A chill traveled down my legs. My rationale was going to snap the second I saw him. He's been nothing but a nuisance since his arrival.

Creeping out of Triston's room, I cautiously listened for any movement in Alesta's room. There was none. Just soft breathing when I gently rested my ear against the door. Zaden was snoring like a bullhorn so I knew he was out for the count.

With the rest of the house dead asleep, I slipped out the door, ready to find the young prince who turned the dinner party earlier into chaos.

"There's my *little* mate," Casimir said, leaning leisurely against a tree.

"Shut up," I snarled, quickening my strides until he was within my reach.

Our teeth clashed, his smirk interrupted by my growling lips. In seconds his body was molding to mine, the thin layers of clothes separating ups being ripped apart as the sparks stirred us on.

"You piss me off," I said as my teeth scraped across his neck. I could feel the pulsing of his vein. My tongue ventured to taste its warmth. "You couldn't just let her be for one night."

"Of course I couldn't," Casimir answered breathlessly. "Not when my dear nephew was on the verge of calling that arrogant Alpha 'daddy' instead of my brother. It would have been an injustice to allow them to have a peaceful dinner."

I tore my lips away from his delicious taste, angling my head back to look at him. "So, King Lukyan knows of his son?"

Casimir's demeanor changed, his eyes cast down. "Not yet. But I made a blood oath."

I sucked in a breath, knowing fully what that meant. He wouldn't be able to keep Triston a secret from his brother much longer. The command from his mother would mean nothing now. If King Lukyan willed it, Casimir would have to obey with full candor.

"Does he know about us?"

Casimir's smirk returned, his eyes filled with sensual hunger. "You mean, does my brother know how you prove to me how not little you truly are?" He pressed into me, his bare chest making mine tingle in pleasure. His hand trailed down to my waist, then dipped into my pants. I let out a guttural groan as he stroked the *little* part of me. "Would it please you if I told him how this makes my hole twitch and spasm, driving into me relentlessly, even though I'm not your *fated mate*?" My head sank back as he stroked it more aggressively.

"There's only one way you can please me right now," I hissed, grabbing a handful of his beautiful hair and yanking him back as I pressed him into the tree.

With sharpened claws, I raked my hand up his thigh, ripping his pants at the seams. They sank to the ground around his feet, leaving him exposed to me.

His eyes danced, watching me sink to my knees. I lifted his legs over my shoulder, exposing the mate mark which matched my own. I stared back, delighting in the tremor that traveled through him as I ran my tongue over the scarred flesh. His hole was still soft around my fingers from our earlier rendezvous.

Seven years of pent up frustration. My body was ready to take it out on the man who forced me into the years of celibacy.

"You will need more fingers than that if you want to prep me for your *little* pecker."

My answering growl was feral. "Your tight ass could never fully prepare for what's to come."

Alesta

Sitting at the small table in my kitchen, I watched Triston eat left-over cake across from me. He was swinging his legs, humming gleefully with chocolate frosting all over his lips.

"We should have cake for breakfast every day!"

I had to cover my mouth to keep from laughing.

"Can I have a bite?" Niccola asked, coming up from behind Triston while rubbing a towel over his wet head.

I narrowed my eyes at my friend. He came in early this morning, reeking of a certain young prince. I didn't ask any questions. Not after what happened last night. I wanted to, but in this small apartment with Zander and my son within earshot, I knew this wasn't the place.

This also wasn't the place to dive into the scene we stumbled upon on the trail home. So many questions were still racing through my mind, but I couldn't speak a single one with Triston and his intuitive brain and curious ears anywhere near. Triston discovering his father was nearby would be just as back as Lukyan discovering I fled with his child. My son would waste no time in escaping the confinement of our home to hunt down his father himself.

"Go away," Triston growled at Nic. "This is mine. Be thankful I let you have a bite last night."

"You're really not going to share?!" Niccola's mouth dropped into a pout.

Triston lifted an eyebrow, watching his *uncle* warily. When Nic deepened his pout, Triston sighed, then scooped the smallest bite into his spoon.

"Fine. Be thankful I'm so nice."

Zaden lifted his head from the couch. "Can I have a bite?"

"No, you weirdo. You don't deserve cake."

"Triston," I said disapprovingly.

"What?! He won't let me go to the dining hall! It's cinnamon bun day!"

Rolling my eyes, I told him, "I'm the one that said you had to stay home. Remember. We discussed this."

Triston's mouth twisted in irritation. "So what if the stupid royals are here? I don't see why I have to avoid the king and queen."

I leaned forward and rubbed the chocolate from the corner of his lips. "I know you don't understand, baby. One day you will."

His scowl turned into a pout. "Would it really be bad if they learned a Lycan boy was living in Hallowed Moon Pack? Would they take me?"

I pursed my lips, unsure how to answer. Nic spoke before I could.

"It's just a precaution, Tris. We talked about this."

"I know." Triston's shoulders sank. "I'm just going to be bored with the weirdo all day, though."

"Hey!" Zaden grumbled. "I'm fun."

"You're a weirdo," Triston grumbled back.

Nic ruffled Triston's hair. "Well, your mom has to work, but I can stay and play for a little while." Then Nic met my eyes, his gaze full of unspoken concerns. "I have a friend that would like to meet you, too."

"No way!" I hissed at Niccola in my bedroom after dragging him out of the kitchen. "Are you fucking insane?!"

"Come on, Alesta." Nic rolled his eyes. "Casimir already knows about Triston."

"But his brother obviously doesn't!"

My chest heaved as I tried to rein in my anger. Triston was no doubt eavesdropping. I wanted to skin Nic for putting me on the spot like he did.

Nic's lips twisted, his expression becoming more hesitant. My guard was up before he opened his mouth.

"Maybe the king should know…. Know that he has an heir."

I clapped my hands over his mouth, looking worriedly at the door.

"Are you crazy," I hissed. *"Triston is probably listening in."*

"He won't know what we're talking about."

"Oh, please. My son is not as stupid as you are."

Niccola laughed softly. "No. He didn't inherit his mother's ignorant trait. Just her anger issues."

"What the hell is that supposed to mean?" I growled.

"Nothing," Nic sighed. "I guess I should be grateful you walk around with your blinders half on most of the time."

"Blinders? What is it you think I'm blind to?" My gut twisted as I asked, "Are you talking about what we saw last night?"

He laughed, shaking his head. "No, but we can start with that. Did the shock factor wear off now?"

"No!" I looked back at my door, realizing I had just raised my voice. *"That shock will never fade."*

"I imagine not. You just witnessed the woman who stole your mate fucking another man. A werewolf by the scent of him."

Nic's words stung. I winced at the reference of her stealing Lukyan. *"We were never mated. Nothing was exchanged but empty promises. What goes on in their relationship is none of my business."*

"Isn't it?" Nic gave me a pitying look. *"Al, the king obviously still loves you."*

I scoffed at the idea. *"I don't think he ever loved me, Nic."*

"That's not true. He went fucking mad seeing you."

"That's not a good thing!"

I started pacing, anxiety filling my chest. *"If he went crazy seeing his ex-mate, how do you think he'll react learning I gave birth to his son? How do you think the queen will react finding out I gave birth to his first son?! The matter of her affair will mean nothing when a threat to her position is revealed."*

"You don't think King Lukyan would protect you and Triston?" Nic stepped close behind me, placing a warm hand on my back. *"He still loves you, Alesta."*

"He doesn't," I said firmly, not letting his words give me any form of hope. *"Love doesn't lie. Love doesn't run off and marry someone else."*

"It was for the kingdom. You know the council."

I nodded. *"I do know. That was why I left silently. I gave his a clear path to follow through with his choices. I'm not going to be a stumbling block for him now, and I sure as hell am not putting my son in that situation."* I turned and stared up at Nic, pouring the severity of this situation into every muscle in my face. *"Lukyan can not find out."*

Nic looked down at me, a war raging in his eyes. He bit his lip, then slowly nodded. *"Fine, but Casimir wants to meet his nephew. You and I both know if the second prince wants something, it's better to not fight him."*

After last night, I don't feel I owe that asshole prince a thing, but I knew what Nic was saying was true. Casimir might announce Triston's existence at the next formal dinner if I refused.

"Fine," I sneered. *"But you better make sure he doesn't say shit*

about his brother."

Niccola's smile was full of relief. *"Thanks, Alesta."*

"I'm serious, Nic. I don't care if he's a fucking Prince. I'll castrate him if he says anything. The last thing I need is Triston going to find his father himself."

"I'll make sure he's careful with his words," Nic chuckled as he hugged me.

"You're not understanding how serious I am. That prick will lose his pecker and never use his sex shack again."

"Even without a pecker, I'm sure he still would," Nic laughed harder. Then he sighed and squeezed me tightly around my shoulders. "Thank you, Alesta."

"Why are you thanking me?" I gave his relief a confused look. "Did he threaten you?"

"No." He shook his head, chuckling. "No threats. He just expressed his desire."

There was some emotion under the surface of Niccola's expression. There was even a hint of affection in his tone that caught me off guard.

"I'm serious, Nic."

"I know. I know." Nic ruffled my hair before letting me go. "We'll be careful."

Niccola

"So, I can't mention my brother, Camellia, my family in general, or make any references to the lad being my nephew?" Casimir rubbed his hands roughly over his stubbled chin. "It feels like a crime not to let the boy know a stunning specimen such as myself is his kin. What if he incurs an inferiority complex due to my dashing good looks?"

My eyes almost reached the back of my head. "Triston would

never let himself feel inferior to anyone. We're safe."

"Ah," Casimir nodded. "He must have gotten that from his dashingly handsome uncle."

"Sure he did."

The closer we got to Alesta's apartment, the more nervous I felt about this. I was confident it was the right thing to do when I brought it up, but I didn't factor in Triston's attitude. He definitely didn't possess Casimir's flippancy. In fact, I truly believe he has his father's naturally resigned demeanor, along with his mother's short fuse for bullshit.

When we reached the door, I took a deep breath, ignoring Casimir's frolicsome glimmer in his eyes.

"Just... please watch what you say around Triston," I urged once again.

Casimir's smile slipped. "Do you truly believe I would say something to jeopardize my own nephew's well-being?"

"No." I shook my head. "Not intentionally. I just know Triston."

Casimir wrinkled his nose. "Is that some jab for not knowing my nephew?"

"No! Not that. I just... I know Tris. I don't know how he will handle, uh... you."

Casimir scoffed. "With wonder and amazement. How else?"

Before I could express my exasperation at his lighthearted attitude, the door burst open.

"Uncle Nic? I thought that was you. What are you doing out in the hall?"

"TRISTON! I TOLD YOU NOT TO OPEN THAT DOOR!" Zaden screamed, coming out of the bathroom with his pants around his knees. He was barely hanging onto his underwear. The man was always pooping at the worst of times.

"I told you to quit being a weirdo, you weirdo," Triston sneered. He turned his focus to us, scrutinizing Casimir openly. "Who are you, *Lycan*?"

Before I could answer, or think to stop Casimir from answering, Casimir crouched down to eye-level with Triston.

"Well, hello there, Triston. My name is Casimir. Prince

Casimir." He paused, as if he was waiting for a standing ovation. All Triston did was stare stoically, unimpressed.

Triston's lack of reaction must have triggered something in Casimir. His shoulders squared like he was stepping up to a challenge.

"And…."

"Casimir. Don't-" I tried to stop him.

"I'm a friend of your father."

Damn it. Alesta was going to kill me.

Chapter 18

Topaz Eyes

Alesta

"**L**una, can you look this over?" The head chef handed me a menu for the rest of the week.

I tried not to recoil at being called Luna for the hundredth time today. "It looks fine to me, but Alpha gives the final approval for these things."

Her face softened into a coy grin. "He gave the staff explicit instructions to treat you as his Luna, and menus are the Luna's duty. If this looks good to you, that's all I need. Thank you, Luna."

I smiled tightly as she walked back towards the kitchen. Gamma Kender was snickering behind me, making it hard to not snap his neck in front of the staff.

Through clenched teeth and a forced smile, I muttered, "Laugh again and I'll shove my fist down your throat and rip your voice box out."

"Ah," he chuckled. "There you go, expressing your desire to touch me again. Sadly, Alpha's threats were worse, so I'll have to decline."

"It wasn't an invitation. I'm telling you to quit hacking like a goat."

"Yes, *Luna,*" he snorted.

I growled low in my chest, but knew I was fighting a losing battle. After last night, I couldn't avoid the "Luna" title. To tell people otherwise would be a direct contrast to Alpha Mikken's word. I was stuck with being his future "Luna" for now.

Even Gamma Kender was following me around as he would if I were the actual Luna. I suspected it was more to be a pain in my ass than because he was following his role.

"*Alesta, can you come to my office for a moment?*" Alpha Mikken spoke through the link.

"*Yes, Alpha. I'll be right there.*"

"*Ken,*" he corrected me for the millionth time.

"*Ken. I'm on my way.*" Arguing with him was a waste of time.

"*Thank you, my Luna.*"

Gritting my teeth, I made my way to his office.

"Where are we going now, Luna?"

"Up your ass."

Gamma Kender snickered. "Line me up first, please."

"Nope."

He nodded. "You're right. That's not your style. Raw and aggressive. That sounds more like you."

He wasn't wrong. Topaz eyes flashed in my head, along with nights of lots of raw and aggressive everything. My face flushed at the sudden memories. Gamma Kender wasn't wrong.

My thoughts must have been a beacon. Those hauntingly beautiful topaz eyes suddenly startled me as I turned down the hall that led to the offices.

Lukyan was like a statue; a glorious, monstrous statue taking up residence in a prime spot on the usually busy hallway wall. The surrounding air was stifling. His aura was dripping from every pore on his brooding body. His dark clothing added to his intimidating air.

Then, he looked over at me, his stony expression transforming into radiance, like the sun was shining on his blooming smile.

"Alesta. I was waiting for you."

I swallowed, feeling the effects of being near him. Without

the tension brought by the eyes of an over observant crowd, I allowed myself to take Lukyan in.

No one could be as handsome as the mm smiling before me. In a perfect world, I'd be waking up to this handsome face every day.

But this isn't a perfect world. It's a cruel and heartless bitch sometimes.

"Hello, King Lukyan," Gamma Kender said, coming to stand between Lukyan and me. "I beg your pardon, but the Luna has urgent matters to attend to with my Alpha. So, if you could excuse us-"

"Go," Lukyan said firmly to Gamma Kender.

"Um, excuse me, your majesty, but I-"

"If you have urgent matters with your Alpha, then leave." Those topaz eyes burned my skin, traveling over my face. "I have urgent business to discuss with Alesta."

Gamma Kender's face twisted. "I guess I can wait then."

"No. Go," Lukyan said more forcefully. "I'd like to speak with her alone."

"Um, your majesty. I'm her Gamma. It's my job to-"

Lukyan cut off Gamma Kender's words with a fierce growl. "Don't make me repeat myself."

Gamma Kender flinched at the weight of Lukyan's words. He wasn't even using a command.

"It's okay," I said, softly touching Gamma Kender's arm.

He hesitated, but then nodded. "I'll get Alpha and be right back."

Steam was practically coming from Lukyan's flared nostrils. Gamma Kender didn't meet Lukyan's stare as he walked off. Lukyan's topaz eyes followed Gamma Kender's every movement like a predator watching his prey. His look was so intense, it sent shivers down my spine.

"Excuse his impertinence, your majesty," I quickly said to turn his attention away from Gamma Kender. "He's diligent in his duties. I'm afraid he offended you out of loyalty to Alpha Mikken."

"Alpha Mikken," Lukyan huffed. "Is it common to call your betrothed so formally in this pack?"

Damn it. Alpha just corrected me to call him Ken too.

"It is common to speak formally to Lycan royalty, especially the king, your majesty."

He leaned close, his sweet breath causing me to blink. "You were never formal with me, Alesta. Why start now?"

My lips curled in irritation. "Things have changed.... Your majesty. You are my king, and I am sure your *queen* wouldn't appreciate me being familiar with you."

Lukyan chuckled, the sound doing things to my insides. "She wouldn't mind."

"Yeah," I scoffed. "I guess she wouldn't."

Lukyan's eyes narrowed. "What do you mean by that?"

I would not be the one to tell him of his wife's affair. He couldn't be ignorant of the fact. He would have felt the pains. Maybe they just had some sort of arrangement. An arrangement I would not be a part of.

"Nothing, your majesty. Is this all you wish to discuss? The way I address my betrothed? If it is, I must wish you a good day and-"

"Drop the act, Alesta," Lukyan husked, pressing even closer to me. I could feel his heat. Tingles were making the hairs raise on my arms. "You do not really care for that *Alpha*."

My mouth dropped, and I sputtered before I said, "You do not know that."

"I do," he breathed, making me blink rapidly.

He lifted his hand, resting it on my cheek. I gasped, feeling the explosion of sparks on my skin.

"H-how?!..."

"I think you know." Lukyan's topaz eyes were intense. "You have to know, Alesta. Just as I know that you aren't truly with *him*."

My eyes flickered to the mark on his neck. That was when I noticed no scent other than his was coming from his skin. If he was mated, he should share his mate's scent. That was what happened when you marked one another. You polluted one another's blood with your essence, declaring in every one you belong to one another.

Lukyan carried the same scent as seven years ago. He was completely untainted by another.

My eyes widened, looking back into his shining topaz jewels. His smile was all-knowing. Smug. His chuckle as he trailed his knuckles down my cheek to my nape darkened when I shuddered.

"You're still mine, Alesta. You always will be."

He had enraptured me... until he said that. I stepped back, away from his touch. I didn't belong to him any longer. Only one Lycan with dazzling topaz eyes could command my heart now. No matter the arrangement between Lukyan and his queen, Triston would still be a threat. The same council that refused to allow their future king to take a werewolf mate would revolt to learn that werewolf bore his first heir.

"I no longer belong to you, Lukyan," I whispered. "That ended the day you got married."

"My marriage is not as it seems," Lukyan snarled, but there was a vulnerability in his topaz eyes I didn't recognize.

I pushed my own desires aside. He was still married, and Queen Camellia, despite her faults, seemed like a capable partner for a king. It would only hurt Triston to fall into this trap of emotions.

"But you are still married. That will not change."

Lukyan took a step forward, his hand lifted like he was scared I was going to run away. "Alesta..."

"Alesta!" Alpha Mikken suddenly came running down the hall from his office. Gamma Kender was following closely behind.

Lukyan growled low and deep, his topaz eyes burning like flames. As his lips curled to show his protruding canines and his muscles coiled like they were about to explode, I reached out to him. It was like a basic instinct. I didn't even think about doing it.

I touched Lukyan and whispered, "Please don't."

His entire body instantly relaxed. His burning eyes looked back at me, the vulnerability back in the blazing jewels. His breath caught in his throat. There was something so deep and pained in his gaze it stunned me. I didn't see my king who hurt me. I saw my son's eyes pleading with me. For what, I did not know, but at the same time, I did. I knew. I was choosing ignorance.

Before I could decipher anything more, Lukyan bit down hard on his full bottom lip, blood spilling from where his canines pierced through his skin. Then he rushed off, hurrying down the hallways with his cape billowing behind him, like a storm cloud on a thunderous night.

"Alesta." Mikken cupped my face in his hands, forcing my attention away from the direction Lukyan had disappeared in. "Alesta, are you alright?"

I bit my lip, avoiding Alpha Mikken's sunny blue eyes. My heart clenched at Alpha Mikken's touch. I now knew why.

Twisting my face away, I took a moment to collect my thoughts before answering my Alpha. If I opened my mouth now, I may cry, and that was the last thing I wanted to do.

"Alesta?..."

"I'm fine," I rasped. Then I took a couple more breaths before putting on a forced professional smile. "I'm fine, Alpha. I was just caught off guard."

He was staring at me with worry. Gamma Kender too.

"I'm really fine," I said more calmly. "What was it you needed to see me for, Alpha?"

Alpha Mikken stared at me with those clear blue eyes for a few more seconds. Their vibrancy unnerved me.

"Geez," he sighed, rubbing the back of his neck as his eyes averted to the ground. "I'm just wasting my breath."

I was wondering what he was talking about, then I realized I had just called him Alpha again. I didn't see how that mattered when Lukyan wasn't nearby. The ruse was up anyway.

"Alpha, I-"

"Ken, Alesta. I get you aren't comfortable with it yet, but you've got to be more casual with me. Especially right now."

I furrowed my brows in confusion. "Why right now?"

"Because," he groaned, swiping a hand down his face. "I've got the werewolf ambassador to the Lycan council sitting in my office, and he's asking to speak with my future Luna."

Chapter 19

Son

Lukyan

"Casimir!" I snarled, ripping through the confusing hallways of this ancient pack house. "Where are you?!"

"Someone sounds extra cheery this morning."

I growled, low and deep. I didn't need his lip today. *"Where are you? I need you to find that friend of Alesha's."*

"Niccola?" Casimir's voice sounded much more careful. *"What do you need him for, if you don't mind me asking?"*

"DO I NEED TO EXPLAIN MYSELF TO YOU?!"

"No! Jeez. Okay... Well, I'm with Niccola now...."

Fuck. I could scent Alesta's friend all over my brother yesterday. I know exactly what Casimir was so excited about in the forest when we stumbled upon the naked werewolf.

"When you two are done, *come find me. I have some questions for him."*

"Sure thing, oh mighty king. I'll, uh.... Let you know when we are finished."

As frustrated as I currently was to find out exactly what Alesta's life was like here in this pack; to hear more about how they came to live here and... and why she is so resistant to our bond.... I didn't want to be near my brother and one of his playthings after their intimate encounter. It would just piss me off more. Alesta barely settled me in time to prevent my shift; to prevent me from tearing this pack apart from the inside out.

If she hadn't touched me, I would have murdered the presumptuous Alpha where he stood, staring at me like I was the enemy of my mate. I knew all about this Alpha, and I knew more about this pack than he probably even did. I understood why he chose Alesta. He chose a powerful warrior in place of what should have been his fated mate. Alesta would be a prize for any man. Her bond with me probably only solidified his resolve.

I understand what he is trying to do. Knowing this pack's history, and the transgressions my father committed against it, I understand why he wasn't giving me an inch to get close to her. Any fondness he holds for her aside, he'd still be protecting her from me, even if he had no interest in making her his Luna. But he clearly had a great interest in Alesta. Alpha Mikken Bennet wasn't just staking his claim to save her from me. I recognized that look in his eyes as he watched her. I saw the pride on his face when he introduced her, proclaiming her his chosen mate.

But I would not let that happen. I would not allow my mate to be marked by anyone but me.

I just needed to figure out what to do. She felt the sparks. She knows the bond between us is still there. She has to know what that means. Camellia and I are nothing. She would have felt it if we weren't. Just as I felt it when that damned Alpha touched her.

There has to be a bigger reason why she wouldn't accept me. The bond is still searing in my veins, demanding I go back to her. It couldn't be much different for her. What was holding her back?

Turning the corner, I almost sighed with relief to see I was at the front doors. The foyer was busier than I would have liked. Warriors were standing by the open front doors, blocking some sort of commotion on the other side.

"I need to speak with Alpha Mikken!" A shrill woman's voice pierced my ears. "He can not truly be considering taking that…. that Lycan-bedder as the Luna! He can't!"

My chest heaved as I turned to see who it was insulting my mate.

"Mrs. Orval," one warrior growled. "You have been warned repeatedly about your disrespect towards the Luna."

I could see the mousy woman's pinched face. "Alesta Raine is not my Luna! I will never accept a Lycan whore or her half-bred brat as the Luna and future Alpha of this pack! Her son is a menace! The Lycan-spawn should be reason enough she shouldn't be-"

"WHAT DID YOU SAY!?"

My body moved on its own. Pushing past the guards, I towered over the vindictive shrew. Her spiteful expression fell into one laced with fear as she felt the full-weight of my fury. I didn't let up even as she dropped to her knees, her body tensing until she turned bright red.

"REPEAT WHAT YOU JUST SAID!" My steaming spit flew into her face. My beast that Alesta just tamed was pushing to be released again. The only thing holding me back was my need for answers. "Whose Lycan spawn?! TELL ME!"

"Secretary Alesta." The woman cowered backward, stumbling down the stairs. I followed, not letting up my aura. "I-I-I was… I mean…. She… She has a child…."

"PRISSLY ORVAL!" one guard shouted fiercely. "Alpha Mikken said-"

"SILENCE!" I sneered his way. The doors shuddered on their hinges. "LET HER SPEAK!"

"My… My King," the guard bowed, wincing from the weight of my words.

I turned my gaze back towards the woman. I needed answers. "How old is this child?"

She looked at the guards, her eyes red and strained in their corners.

"Don't look at them. Look at me!" I commanded. She whimpered, flinching away as I crouched over her crumpled body. "How old is this child?"

"N-n-nearly seven, y-your majesty. He's i-i-in his f-f-first year of t-t-training. Like my son. He's a brute of bast-"

My sinister snarl cut off whatever insult she was about to spew. "I-I'm sorry, my king!" The sniveling woman had snot dripping from her nose. Her blotchy skin and tears made me sick. "I m-m-meant no insult to-"

"You're sure Alesta has a seven-year-old child?" She flinched, closing her eyes as I got closer. "YOU'RE SURE?!"

"Yes!" she heaved, then sobbed uncontrollably. "I-I'm sure!"

My lip curled, a low growl vibrating in the air. I slowly stood and turned for the guards. "Is this true? Does Alesta have a child?"

The guards exchanged a hesitant look.

"I ASKED YOU A QUESTION!"

"Yes, my king!" They answered in unison. Then the older of the two continued, "Our Luna has a child."

She left me seven years ago. I felt no pain, and no signs of betrayal in all that time.

"She has a son?" The sniveling woman said 'he'. She said *he* was in his first year of training.

The older guard tensed, his jaw set stubbornly. I pushed my aura over him, causing his front to break. He burst out, "A SON!", then began to pant to catch his breath. "Miss Alesta has a son."

Alesta has a son. A half-Lycan, nearly seven-year-old son.....

I have a son.

"What's his name?...."

Alesta

I didn't know what to expect when I walked into Alpha Mikken's office. I was still in my head about what had just happened with Lukyan, so when the man seated across from my Alpha's desk turned around, I was visibly shaken.

It was him. The man who was with Lukyan's queen last night in the woods.

"I brought her, Sir Ruth Frost," Alpha Mikken said with barely contained agitation. "I'm sure you heard my introduction last night, but let me introduce my future Luna again. This is Alesta Raine."

"Alesta." Sir Ruth stood with a genuine smile. His eyes disarmed me as they met mine. "I have much anticipated speaking with you. I do hope you are alright after our dismal Prince Casimir made such careless remarks."

Dismal prince? The man before me was clearly a werewolf. Would he be alright speaking so flippantly about a royal Lycan?

"I'm alright," I muttered. "Forgive me for having to leave before the meal was even served."

He laughed softly. "I would have left too if I were in your position, Miss Raine. Not before leaving a well-deserved imprint of my hand on his face."

I bit back my smile. "I could never..." I started to say, but my expression was telling. If I hadn't left when I did, I likely would have struck the young prince.

Sir Ruth's face transformed with his boisterous laughter. It was infectious.

"Ah, Miss Raine. I think you and I could become good friends."

I smiled politely, unsure of how to respond.

"So, Sir Ruth." Alpha grabbed my hand and led me around his desk. I had to grit my teeth to hide the tightness forming in my chest from his touch. "What was it you wanted to speak with my Luna about?"

"Ah." Sir Ruth's fluid eyes were bewitching. "Just the

typical query. Every ranked member is required to undergo questioning during our inspection."

"You make it sound like we are being interrogated," I murmured.

"Not at all." His smile widened. "Just the standard procedure. The council requires the new reign to do a royal inspection upon the passing of the crown. I've done this enough times now that it should be quick and painless."

Alpha Mikken sat at his desk, waving a hand at the seat that Sir Ruth was just in. "Let's get this over with, then."

"Actually..." Sir Ruth looked apologetic. "It's customary for the interviews to be one-on-one. I was hoping Miss Alesta could show me around the pack as we talked. You wouldn't mind? Right, Alpha Mikken?"

Alpha Mikken looked ready to refuse, but I placed my hands on his shoulders to stop him.

With a professional smile fit for my secretary duties, I asked, "What would you like to see first?"

∞ ∞ ∞

We walked throughout the pack house, Sir Ruth observing the way the staff and omegas addressed me. I felt this was some sort of test, but had no choice but to play along.

Those eyes of his were piercing. I could feel them looking through me. My nerves were already on edge being alone with him after what I had witnessed last night.

The queen had seen me. Was Sir Ruth unaware?

As we made our way outside, I became aware that Sir Ruth's eyes weren't the only ones on me. Gamma Kender had been following at a distance since we left the office. It wasn't obvious in the confines of the pack house.

"Oh, my," Sir Ruth sighed. "I had hoped we could talk more privately with no walls closing us in. It seems the Alpha is very protective of you, Miss Alesta."

"Seems so." I glanced back at my Gamma.

Gamma Kender gave me a little wave, but when Sir Ruth turned to look at him, Gamma Kender's face turned to stone.

"Quite a friendly pack you chose to join."

I flinched at his words. "Chose to join?"

His eyes danced with mirth, hypnotizing me. His lips turned up in a crooked grin. "There couldn't have been a further pack from the capital to run to. I'm quite impressed you made it this far without detection."

I stopped walking, too stunned to move. "Did... Did Casimir?....."

"The young prince? Ahh!..." He nodded, understanding passing over his face. "So it was Prince Casimir who helped you leave the Tribute Guard, was it?"

I couldn't speak. This man was sleeping with the queen. One wrong word... One slip of the tongue or mention of Triston and....

"Or perhaps it was the queen? She seemed eager to have King Lukyan visit the Hallowed Moon Pack."

I gulped nervously. "H-how do you know all this?"

"I know quite a few things that would surprise you," he chuckled. He glanced back at Gamma Kender, watching attentively a few dozen yards behind us. "I know that man, that Gamma, is mind linking our every move to his Alpha. Even right now, he is telling your Alpha that you look uncomfortable, so if you could do me the favor of continuing to walk as you hide your shock so we can continue this discussion in peace, I would appreciate it."

It took me a moment to force my face to comply, but I managed to put back on a professional demeanor and led Sir Ruth towards the warrior building where the Beta was currently leading the training of the elite warriors.

"There," Sir Ruth grinned. "That should save us some more time. I wasn't quite ready for your overbearing Alpha to join us again."

I murmured low, but coldly, "Speaking ill of Alpha Mikken is not something I will tolerate."

"Speaking as someone he took in, or as his future mate."

I gritted my teeth. "Both."

"Hmm." He rubbed his chin. "Even though your fated mate has appeared?"

I stopped again, unable to hold the facade any longer. "How do you know that? Did Casimir tell you that too?"

"Oh, Miss Alesta." SIr Ruth shook his head. "Some things don't need to be spoken to be uncovered. Our good king's behavior was very telling when he caught your scent."

"So? That means nothing."

"Oh, I think it does. I think it means quite a lot. Not just for you, my lovely Alesta, but for our king. You see, King Lukyan is our kind's," he waved his hands between us, "only hope."

"What do you mean, *our kind*? Werewolves?"

His smile stretched. "Werewolves. The goddess's original children. Why do you think the previous monarchs have suppressed our kind so aggressively for so long? Change is coming, and it all rides on the shoulders of your fated mate."

"I do not know what you are talking about, but that has nothing to do with me."

"It has everything to do with you, because our king has slowly been degrading since you left. He needs you, Alesta."

"No," I shook my head. "He made his choice. He married someone else."

"Ah, but Camellia and he are not truly one." Sir Ruth leaned close and pulled the collar of his shirt, showing a mate mark where his neck and shoulder meet. "Not everything is as it seems, lovely Alesta. Including you."

I stared at the mark on his neck until he fixed his shirt back in place, then I slowly swept my eyes back to his, trying to not show how uncomfortable his eyes made me.

"Not everything is as it seems," he repeated.

Chapter 20

Prince's Command

Casimir

"So, you're telling me you are a close friend of my dad?" The little prince was still staring at me with untrusting eyes. "How would you know who my dad is? You don't even know me."

"Of course I know you," I smiled. "Why would I come to see you if I didn't know you?"

"Because you're a creep." Triston scoffed, looking me up and down. "You look like a creep. Like that old man who's never had a mate that isn't allowed near my school."

Niccola choked on a laugh, turning away to hide his amused face. At least he's laughing now. He's been glaring at me since I had my slip of tongue.

"Never had a school banned me from their premises."

"Because you're a royal?" Triston crossed his arms and lift one of his tiny brows. "No one can command a royal but the king."

"How do you know that?"

Triston lifted his chin. "Mom told me."

I chuckled. "Your mom is a wise woman, but that is not entirely true."

"Yes, it is," he argued stubbornly. "Everything mom says is true. Mom doesn't lie."

"She doesn't, does she? What has she told you about your parentage, then?"

"Huh?"

I couldn't resist my grin. "Your father. What has she told you about your father?"

"Oh." He averted his glare to the ground. "Stuff."

"What sort of stuff?" I pushed him further.

"Young Prince." Niccola grabbed my arm, then looked pointed at the warrior watching us nervously from the kitchen. "Maybe this line of questioning isn't wise."

"Why? Because of him?" An idea suddenly came to me. A painful grin split my face. Chuckling softly under my breath, I took slow strides towards the warrior. "Instead of questions, how about a lesson for our young student?"

"What are you doing?" Niccola asked cautiously. "Zander hasn't called Alpha yet, just as you ordered. Leave him alone."

The warrior had wide eyes. Fear polluted from his pores. My sadist side was awakening more and more at the scent.

"Oh, relax." I dragged my finger under the man's chin, subtly letting my claw extend. "It's a lesson on commands and who can give them. You're young Triston's instructor, correct? It's your job to help guide him."

The man shivered as my nail flicked out from under his chin, creating a satisfying white line in its wake.

"Correct?" I leaned closer.

He furiously nodded his head. Triston was chuckling darkly behind me. A sense of pride bloomed in me hearing my nephew's laughter.

"Correct!" The man hurriedly nodded, with a frantic look in his eyes.

A deep rumbling laugh bubbled out of me. "See, Triston. No one can go against a royal Lycan's command. Even the noble families of the capital have to have a blood bond to refuse a royal's order."

I slowly circled around the jerky warrior, running my nails across his chest and back. Niccola was pinching the bridge of his nose, shaking his head.

"Being a prince, there are perks. A few words from me and I can have this strong, capable, werewolf warrior on all four, purring like a kitten."

"Casimir…."

I smiled coyly at my mate. "Like a cute little baby cat."

"That's not what you meant, and you know it."

My grin was deepening. Jealousy looked good on Niccola.

"I won't, love." I scratched under the warrior's chin. "This is all hypothetical, for the sake of learning."

Triton came beside me, jumping up and down excitedly. "Can you command him to eat a spider?! Like, a really, really big spider?! The kind with hair on its legs?"

"Triston!" Niccola snapped. "Do you want your mom to find out that you're still antagonizing your teacher?"

The warrior's fear thickened the air. Triston's nostrils flared, as if he could smell it. His excitement grew.

"Fine," Triston murmured as his eyes gleamed. "What about just making him hold one?"

"Ah, come on, Tris," the warrior begged.

Triston's devious grin made me proud.

"I'm trying to help you, you weirdo. What kind of warrior is scared of bugs?"

"I dislike creepy crawlers, though I would go so far as to say I'm scared of them," I said thoughtfully, holding the warrior's scared gaze. "Don't fear, my friend. Today's lesson does not involve *bugs*. Not even spiders."

"Aw, man." Triston stomped his foot in a pout.

"Now, don't feel dejected just yet, little one. Instead of spiders, how about I teach you to use your Lycan ability to command your teacher right now?"

The warrior's mouth dropped, and his eyes nearly bugged out of his head. Triston looked thrilled at the idea. I could see the gears turning in his head.

"Absolutely not," Niccola snarled.

"Aw, come on, Uncle Nic. I'm gonna learn, eventually."

"No! Your mom will murder all of us."

He was right. I had already pushed Alesta too far yesterday. If I taught Triston his royal ability to use commands, she might actually kill me. She'd get away with it too, knowing my brother's devotion.

With a low chuckle, I said, "Your uncle Nic is right. Maybe today isn't the best day for a thorough explanation. Instead, I'll just demonstrate."

Grabbing the warrior's face, I let my aura wash over him. His eyes focused on mine as his body went rigid.

"I command you to keep the discussions and today's meeting a secret from your Alpha. Can you do that for me?"

His neck strained, then he blurted, "Yes! My prince!"

"Ha ha! You look like you have to poop, Instructor Zaden." Triston skipped in place.

"Shit," the warrior gasped. He bent over to catch his breath as I pulled away. Poor thing. He was a classic case of being in the wrong place at the wrong time.

"Let's do Niccola now!" Triston said excitedly.

I stilled, meeting my mate's angry gaze. "Um, that would be rather hard for me."

"Why?" Triston cocked his head to the side. "He's a werewolf too."

"He is, but his mate isn't."

Triston's eyes widened. Both he and the warrior looked at Niccola in surprise.

"You have a mate, Uncle Nic?! Why didn't you tell me?"

Niccola was glaring at me. "Things are going too far, Casimir." His tone was bitter. I would pay for this later.

"But wait," Triston said, looking back at me. "You said that a royal Lycan can command anyone. Why wouldn't you still be able to command Uncle Nic?"

Intuitive kid. I see why Niccola instructed me to speak carefully now.

"Because his mate is powerful," the warrior whispered roughly. "More powerful than the prince. Is that why you came here with Miss Alesta?"

Through clenched teeth, Niccola said, "I came because my *mate* told me to, but I would have come, anyway. Alesta is a sister to me."

"What a good brother you are," I said kindly, trying to soften his anger. My words held little effect. His scowl deepened.

"Wow! Your mate is more powerful than the second prince?! Who is it?"

"No one of importance," Niccola seethed.

Triston went deep into thought. Then asked me, "So, his mate commanded him to come with my mom to this pack? Why?"

I slipped up more than I realized.

"Mates can not command one another, Triston," Niccola answered instead. "Not after they mark one another. They can use their bond if it's strong enough to subjugate, but not command."

"Hm," Triston sighed, resting his hand on his chin. "You said my mom was wrong; that someone other than the king can command royals. Who can do that?"

My mistakes keep piling high.

"The Queen," Niccola said. "The rightful Queen of the Kingdom can not be commanded, and has the ability to take charge of any individual under the goddess's moon."

"So the Queen is the most powerful person in the kingdom?" Triston tilted his head in the other direction.

"Yes. No one commands the queen without a blood oath, which is impossible for most to achieve."

"So only the Queen is un-commandable?"

I smiled down at my nephew and his made up word, placing my hand on his small shoulder. "Only the queen and the goddess's direct descendants are above the King's command. Remember that, young Triston."

There were so many more questions spilling from the boy's lips, but before I could answer any of them, a powerful voice shouted in my head.

"MEET ME NOW!"

Oh, boy. *That* was a command.

∞ ∞ ∞

Lukyan

I was pacing the bedroom floor, wearing a path in the patterned carpet.

The guards from the front door and the mousy woman had been commanded to silence for now. There were too many eyes to interrogate them further.

Everyone in this pack knew of Alesta's child. They didn't know who his father was. They knew he was Lycan and were commanded to secrecy. That was the extent of what I learned.

His name is Triston. I have a son, and his name is Triston....

If I hadn't found the strength to hold back my beast, I would have caused such a scene that his paternity would no longer be in question. I wanted to tear apart this pack until I found the boy. I wanted to hunt for Alesta and demand the truth. I wanted to sink my fangs into her sweet little neck and place my mark where it should have been for the past seven years.

Before I did anything, I needed answers.

"What has you all riled up already this morning?" Camellia asked, coming into the room from the lounge with a book in her hands. "Did you not find Alesta?"

"Oh, I found her," I snarled. "I found more than that."

Camellia looked at me curiously. "Was she embracing the Alpha again?"

My fiercest growl escaped me at the mere thought.

Camellia gave me an exasperated look. "It was a jest. Your dear mate is on a stroll with mine right now. Undoubtedly talking about you."

I stopped mid-step. "Why is this the first I'm hearing of this?"

Camellia smirked slyly. "Because I took matters into my own

hands. I'd like this farce of a marriage to be dissolved quickly too, you know. Now that you are king, it can be done."

I took long strides until I was towering over her. She was completely unaffected by my close proximity, simply looking annoyed.

"What is Ruth telling her?"

Camellia scoffed. "The truth. What you should have told her before she ran away?"

"Damn it, Camellia!" I snarled, then returned to my frantic pace. My hands tore down my face as additional worries stacked on the old.

"What?! I'm helping you!"

"You're meddling! Things have become more complicated now!"

"Complicated how?"

Just then, Casimir pushed open the doors, taking a careful look between Camellia and me.

"I came as you commanded, but if you two are busy arguing, I can-"

"STOP!" I commanded as he turned to leave. I prowled closer, letting my anger flow forward.

"Brother, I really must insist on-"

"Did you know?" My jaw tensed. "Did you fucking know?!"

"Know what?" Casimir looked taken aback.

"You had to," I seethed, pinning him against the wall. "You knew!" I punched the space beside him, making a vase full of wildflowers rattle on a nearby table before falling to the floor. Glass exploded all over the carpet.

"You're going to have to tell me what I did or didn't know before I confirm or deny anything."

"Lukyan," Camellia said in warning. "You need to calm down!"

"Calm Down!?" I snarled. My beast was pushing forward. I was barely holding myself at bay. Leaning in, I growled in my brother's face. "You knew I had a son."

Camellia gasped and Casimir's eyes went wide. His head banged against the wall as he looked up at me in surprise. "Did

Alesta tell you?"

So Casimir really did know all along. I had my doubts, but he just confirmed it. Did my mother know too?

I grabbed Casimir by the collar of his shirt, jerking him forward. "You.... Tell me everything. From the beginning. And you better not leave a damn thing out."

Chapter 21

Stolen Time

"So, that's about it," Casimir said while staring at the ground, avoiding my fierce gaze. "Mother had me keeping tabs on Alesta's health. She was scared what would happen if she had a child before you were crowned."

"Wow." Camellia had her fingers pressed to her lips. Her eyes were wide with shock. "How could you? How could you keep this from Lukyan all this time?"

"I had no choice." Casimir lifted his head, genuine remorse on his features. "Mother wanted to make sure her grandchild was safe. That Alesta remained safe and out of father or the council's reach."

I gritted my teeth, then slammed my fist on the table. "I could have kept her safe."

"No," Casimir smiled sadly. "You couldn't even tell her about Camellia."

My lip curled in anger. "That was-"

"Because you were scared she would reject you," Casimir interjected. "I know. Mother knew. And she agreed." His uncharacteristically serious expression caught me by surprise as his eyes bore into mine. "This kingdom would be doomed if what happened to father happened to you in the capital. There would have been no way to cover it up. Alesta rejecting you would have killed us all."

He was right. My fear of becoming like my father has been

undeniable my entire life. Ever since I learned the truth about the Lycan lineage, a king like him was something I aspired to never be. Having a werewolf mate I couldn't yet make my queen.... That was a fact that haunted me.

Things are different now. My greatest fears have changed. The only thing that I fear is Alesta never accepting me. I fear she will never give me a chance to have her.... or our son.

"What's he like?" Camellia asked softly. "The boy?"

Casimir's answering smile was too genuine. It suddenly filled me with longing.

"He's my lovely nephew, with every trait to make the fact undeniable."

"You mean he's handsome?" Camellia asked, invested in his answer.

"Handsome, clever, brilliant; he is everything my nephew should be."

"Does he look like her?" I asked, my voice barely above a mumble. "I hope he does."

"No," Casimir laughed merrily. "Not at all. He looks exactly like you, brother. It's no wonder they're keeping him hidden in her home."

"That's too bad," I whispered, but I couldn't stop a smile from infecting my cheeks. "I would have liked our children to resemble their mother."

"You act like you have more," Camellia giggled. "Does your mate have more of your children hidden somewhere in this pack?"

"He's speaking of the future," Casimir chuckled with a glimmer in his eyes. "If he had his way, I'd be crawling with little nieces and nephews."

More children with Alesta would be like a dream, but I wish I hadn't missed experiencing the one we already have. Picturing my mate round with new life made everything insides of me ache. How I would have loved nurturing her as she nurtured my child.

I missed everything. Everything was stolen from me; His

birth, first words, first steps. If not for my father and the council, and the endless sins of the monarchs before him, I would have been there for it all.

I will not miss another second. Everything that was taken, I'll get it all back. Then I'll put Alesta where she belongs; on the throne beside mine.

"Where is the boy now?" I asked my brother.

"At home." Casimir waved his hands flippantly in the air. "The Alpha commanded a warrior to guard him. They're imprisoning the boy until you leave."

"Why?" Camellia gasped.

Casimir lifted his brows, giving her a pointed look.

"What? Because of me?!"

Casimir shrugged. "You are the queen."

Camellia's forehead knotted. "But I'm no threat to the boy."

"She doesn't know that. All she knows is that you married her mate and you're the official queen. If you were anyone else, the boy would be a threat to your position."

"That's silly. We can easily rectify the misunderstanding."

"Can we?" Casimir sat back and crossed his arms. "Have you ever tried to reason with a scorned woman? It's not an easy feat."

"I don't make a habit of bedding everything with a pulse and tossing them aside when I'm done."

"My, Camellia. I wasn't aware that you were in the habit of bedding women at all. Though, I suppose Ruth is very beautiful for a man. If I had known-"

"Your mouth is about to get you into trouble again," Camellia cut him off with a warning tone.

"Oh, my mouth is capable of getting me in and out of all sorts of trouble."

"Sounds like a disease," Camellia said with a baleful smile. "Maybe we should sow your mouth shut to prevent more filth from spilling out?"

"Pardon me," Casimir scoffed. "Is that any way a lady should speak? A queen, nonetheless."

"I'm merely concerned about the safety of our kingdom. I wouldn't want your diseases to turn the world into mayhem."

"How kind of you to think my skills would affect the entire world."

"Enough," I snarled, done with their needless bickering. "Ruth. Is he still with my mate?"

Camellia's eyes unfocused as she reached out to her mate. When she focused back on me a minute later, her expression turned grim.

"I'm afraid not. He's with their Beta now, asking questions about the way they train their warriors." She hesitated before adding, "The Alpha came to get her some time ago."

"Of course he did," Casimir chuckled. "That man isn't giving anyone an inch to get too close to her."

"For now," I growled.

Camellia looked concerned. "Do you suppose he truly loves her, or is he just trying to get back at you for what your father did?"

Casimir shook his head. "He wasn't aware of Alesta's connection to the royals before yesterday. Niccola alerted me months ago that the Alpha was interested in her. He only recently began to act on his feelings."

"Then how did they think her child came to be?"

Casimir grimaced at Camellia's question. "The assumption had been that she was... assaulted. By one of our commanders..."

My fierce snarl shook the pictures on the wall. I knew it wasn't true, but just the idea filled me with putrid anger.

"That's unfortunate," Camellia sighed. "She never spoke out against the rumors?"

"Neither of them did. The rumors seemed safer than the truth to her. Her lack of denial, along with her disinterest in finding a mate, or members of the opposite sex in general, solidified the assumption."

"Hmm," Camellia tapped her fingers to her lips. "She seems ignorant of her Alpha's affections too."

Casimir laughed softly. "It's as if her heart has been reserved for another. She can't even fathom the idea of being with anyone else." Casimir pulled something out from his inside pocket.

Camellia grinned. "That's good news. If you hold her heart, it shouldn't be too difficult to win her affections, too."

Casimir reached out to hand me whatever it was he withdrew from his pocket. I hesitantly took it, unsure of what it might be. As my eyes swept over the small canvas, my heart leapt.

"Swiped that from a shelf on my way out of her apartment. I thought it might come in hand if you had another one of your fits."

It was a picture of Alesta with a young boy sitting on her lap. She was wildly gorgeous, as she had always been. The boy looked like every young portrait of me. Seeing them both in my hands made my chest feel swollen.

"You know everything now, brother," Casimir said, leaning forward to rest his elbows on his knees. "What are you going to do now?"

Mikken

"They've emerged, Alpha," my guard posted at the end of the guest wing informed me.

My eyes flickered to Alesta sitting at her desk. Her concentration as she worked through a stack of paper made me smile involuntarily. She was so diligent in her duties. She would make an amazing Luna.

If only she was even the least bit receptive to my advances.

I understand her. Especially now, knowing what I do about her fated mate. Werewolves rarely took chosen mates, especially Alphas. And once a she-wolf found her mate, no other man was a man in her eyes. Just a fellow beast.

Not only did Alesta have a fated mate sniffing around my pack, she birthed his child. My gentle approach would no longer work. I saw that now.

Not that it was working, anyway. Alesta was strangely obtuse.

"*Alesta and I are not to be disturbed,*" I told the two guards stationed outside my office. "*If the royals appear, inform your Beta.*"

"*Yes, Alpha.*"

That Lycan bastard already disturbed Alesta enough for one day.

"Alesta?" I called for her.

She lifted her head, her eyes landing on me. I watched in fascination as her pupils adjusted from staring at her papers for so long.

"Yes, Alpha?"

A sigh left me as she continued to forget to call me by my name. "I was wondering if you'd like to have dinner with just me tonight?"

Alesta tilted her head to the side. "Just you? What about the royals? Aren't you required to dine with them?"

I pursed my lips. She wasn't wrong. It was my duty, but it wasn't yet hers.

"Actually," she said, standing as she checked the time. "I need to do the last checks in the kitchen."

"I can do that!" I hurried to my feet.

Alesta gave me an odd look. "You have a pile of inspection documents to review and sign. I don't think-"

"I'm needing a break," I said, stopping her irrefutable logic from spilling out any more. "A walk to the kitchen and back sounds like the perfect opportunity to stretch my muscles. You just continue with your work here. I'll have an omega bring you tea and peanut butter cookies."

Her face lit up at the mention of the cookies. She was so dazzling, even more so because her charm was never intentional.

"Well, if you insist. Thank you, Alpha."

"Ken," I couldn't stop myself from correcting her.

"Ken," she smiled tightly.

"It will catch on one of these times."

She chuckled, averting her eyes back to her work.

Making sure the door was closed completely, I ordered the guards to say no one was here if anyone asked for Alesta. With enough luck, she would remain undisturbed.

Luck wasn't on my side today, for when I turned the corner, I encountered the person I wanted to avoid most.

"King Lukyan." I bowed my head as I tried to hide my disdain. "Were you perhaps looking for me?"

His lip curled in disgust as his sharp eyes moved to the door to my office behind me. "I suppose so," he muttered. Then his nostrils flared like he was hunting for a scent.

"Well, I was on my way to the kitchens. If you'd like, we could talk while walking."

He kept his eyes fixed on my door. "It would be much more comfortable to sit down for a discussion, would it not?"

I laughed dryly. "Perhaps, but unfortunately, I have work to do."

"I don't mind waiting for you to finish." His gaze suddenly turned fierce. "Or is there some reason you don't want me to be here?"

My hands balled into fists. "Is there a reason for you to be here if I'm not here?"

He laughed dryly, then leaned in closer. "I know she is in there, *Alpha*. You can not keep her from me."

So we were being frank now.

"She may be in there, but you have no business with Alesta." I whispered fiercely, "You made your choice, and she's made hers." I huffed arrogantly, "*King* Lukyan."

He raised a brow at me. "You do not want to make me your enemy."

"Ha. Does the capital no longer keep its promises? The former king sent a decree of protection."

"Protection from the tribute system and nothing else." There was pity in his eyes as he said, "I'm aware of the pain my father had caused you and your pack, but that does not excuse you for keeping my mate from me."

My eyes narrowed, and teeth clenched at the mention of the past. "What does your *queen* think of your little pursuit?"

"My true queen is sitting in your office."

"You mean the werewolf woman you betrayed and now scheme to make your consort?"

"I never betrayed her," King Lukyan said confidently, standing tall and unwavering. "I am not my father."

"No? Then why does this cycle continue?" I hissed under my breath, "I won't let you do to her what your father did to my mother."

His eyes narrowed. "Again, I am not my father."

I scoffed, "Then leave Alesta alone."

Holding out my hand, I motioned for him to leave. He sneered, but didn't object. It was strange that he didn't. The king had the authority to force his way into my office. I would have been powerless to stop him, no matter how much venom was in my threat.

Just as my father was powerless to defend my mother....

"Oh, by the way," King Lukyan murmured as we headed towards the main corridor. "I heard a strange rumor today."

"Oh, yeah?" My tone was flat and cold. "What rumor would that be?"

His eyes felt penetrating as he stared at me. I felt an icy wave of dread travel over my body.

"Is it true there is a young Lycan boy living among your pack?"

I stopped dead in my tracks. "W-what did you-"

"A Lycan pup living in a pack of werewolves," he mused, running his hand over his chin. "There must be quite a story there."

His gaze was unwavering, taking in my every reaction. My stomach dropped, not knowing what to do. If he knew about Triston....

That changed so much. I was already playing a dangerous game, but if he knew Alesta had a child, *his* child....

"I'd very much like to meet this Lycan boy." He grabbed my shoulder, squeezing hard enough where I felt it in my bones. "Do you think that would be something you could arrange?" Nervously, I swallowed, my mouth suddenly feeling parched. King Lukyan let out a dangerous chuckle, then roughly patted my back. "I'll see you at dinner. *Alpha.*"

 His confident gait as he walked away shook me even more. "Shit."

Chapter 22

The Queen

Alesta

"Mama! Mama! Mama!" Triston brought me another book. "Read me this one now!"

"That's a big one," I chuckled, eyeing the thicker children's book.

"You've got time. Alpha said you had the day off today."

That he did. It was strange how insistent Alpha was about me staying home today. He even brought us breakfast to deliver the news.

"Consider this your day off. Sit this one out," Alpha Mikken told me early this morning. *"Just.... Stay out of sight. You deserve the break."*

He was acting off at dinner last night too. Alpha and I sat at the seats furthest from the royals, though he should have sat right next to them.

I didn't mind keeping my distance from Lukyan. Perhaps Alpha was just being considerate of me because of what happened yesterday in the hall. That was also probably why he excused us the second the meal was finished.

Lukyan watched me the entire time we ate, but he never said a word. I tried to avoid his attention entirely. Especially with his queen watching me just as closely, though she didn't seem angry to any degree. Just observant.

I didn't need a break from work, but I appreciate having a day off from interacting with the royals in any capacity. Plus, I missed spending time with my son.

Seeing how hyperactive Triston was, I feel Zaden was the one who needed a break. Nic would have been more than capable of watching Triston, if that were the case. Instead of me staying home, it would have made more sense to assign Nic to babysit my son instead.

Now that I think about it, Nic had been pretty absent since yesterday morning. He left shortly after I arrived home yesterday and came back right as we were going to bed. Then he left again after our Alpha finished dropping off chocolate waffles from the dining hall.

Nic was probably stressed as well. I heard from others that Prince Casimir has been excessively hanging around Nic since his arrival.

He didn't mention Casimir meeting Triston, and when I asked Triston about it, he just shrugged and said, "Yeah. He was funny." Nothing more was said. Maybe I was worried for nothing. Triston would have surely had questions if Casimir said anything he shouldn't have.

As I sat and began reading the short novel about a Lycan Prince defeating a demon king, I started to wonder where Triston had gotten this book. It wasn't one I had given him.

"Hey, Tris?"

"Yeah, mama?" He wrinkled his nose, like he was annoyed I had stopped in the middle of his story.

"Where did this book come from? Did you get it from school?"

His school wasn't likely to carry children's books on Lycans, but perhaps a teacher got it specifically for him.

Triston averted his eyes, looking guilty all of a sudden. "I don't know," he shrugged. "Maybe that weirdo left it here."

"Triston...."

"I meant Instructor Zaden," he scoffed, rolling his eyes. "The *werewolf* who's scared of baby spiders."

Zaden didn't seem like the type to give books away. He didn't seem like the type to read books, either.

But if Casimir was here yesterday....

"Are you sure Instructor Zaden gave you this?" I asked, flipping through the pages to the back of the book. The book looked expensive to boot. The pages were thick with gold leafing. It would be a hard book to obtain in our outlining pack.

And it was a book about a Lycan prince.... Not a regular Lycan boy, but a prince.

Triston made this small squeaking noise that drew my attention. He had this tense look of guilt shadowing his little features.

Maybe there was more to Casimir's visit than Triston was letting on. I suddenly got the feeling he and Niccola were hiding something from me.

"Triston....."

He kicked out his legs, tossing his head back on the cushion.

"Fine! I'll tell you. I got it from-"

KNOCK KNOCK KNOCK

"Whew! Saved!" Triston relaxed.

I narrowed my eyes at him. "We'll continue this in a minute."

That worried look crossed Triston's face again.

Opening the door, I found two nervous warriors on the other side.

"Yes?"

"Um, L-Luna. We.... Uh... I know you were to be undisturbed today, but...."

"What? Spit it out," I demanded, annoyed at being called Luna in my own home.

The warriors exchanged a look. "Um, the Queen, Queen Camellia.... She's asking for you...."

Triston

I crossed my arms angrily, giving the two stupid warriors sitting across from me dirty looks.

"Alpha said mama had the day off," I growled at them.

One warrior gave out an aggravating sigh, throwing his head back against mom's couch. "Quiet, squirt."

The other elbowed him. "Hey! Alpha said-"

"Alpha didn't say shit about this half breed. His dirty mother might have the Alpha's favor, but there's no way our Alpha would care about a Lycan brat."

A low growl left my chest. The silent warrior looked worried, glancing back at me, but the mean one just chuckled.

"What an animal. Why don't you go take a nap or something, you mutt?"

I kicked off the chair, stomping towards my room.

"Are you crazy!? Alesta will have your head if she hears how you've talking to her son."

"What can she do while the royals are here, huh? Alpha ordered everyone to keep the brat a secret. She can't do anything during an inspection."

That's what he thought. If mama couldn't do anything, I'd just have to get Uncle Nic's friend to help. He was a Lycan. Not even Alpha could stop Mr. Casimir from teaching that warrior wort a lesson.

Plus, I had some questions. Uncle Nic told me not to tell mama too much about his friend, and to go to him or Mr. Casimir if I wanted to know more about the things he said. Mr. Casimir said he could tell me all about my real dad later, but only if I didn't tell on him to my mom. He said mom would stop him from coming.

I liked Mr. Casimir the more he talked and showed me stuff. I didn't want mama to tell him he couldn't come anymore. But he and Uncle Nic weren't here right now. I'd have to find them myself if I couldn't tell mama anything.

I chuckled to myself, wondering if Mr. Casimir would command the wort warrior to eat a spider. It'd like that a lot.

Grabbing my desk chair, I dragged it to my window to figure out how mama opened it. The little lock thingy was hard to twist, but I eventually got it.

The lever let out a loud groaning noise, which made me wince. Just as I was hurrying to get the window open, the wort warrior opened my door with a mean look on his face.

"What the hell do you think you're doing, you brat?"

Anger made my chest vibrate. "I'm not a brat! You're a brat!"

"Get down here, you little shit."

He reached for my arm, but just as he touched me, a strong feeling started at my toes and moved up my body to my face.

"Stop!" I yelled, feeling weird, like when I run for too long and my body burns.

The warrior listened, stopping mid-step. His eyes went wide like he was scared.

That made me laugh. I liked that he was scared. I could smell his fear, and it tickled my nose.

My eyes were tingling, just like my chest. There was something pushing out from my body that I could see, like smoke or fog. It wrapped around the warrior, but I don't think he could see it too because he was still looking at me.

"Don't talk about my mama, you wort! And I'm not a mutt. You are!" The fog around him got really thick, making his body tense. "Why don't you act like one until I get back!"

A glimmer shone in his eyes, then he dropped to the ground. He let out a funny barking noise, making me laugh louder and louder. He was acting like a dog. I actually commanded the wort, and he was doing what I said!

The other warrior walked in, looking surprised. "What the-"

"Attack!" I pointed my finger at him, then the wort warrior ran at him on his hands and knees before snarling and tackling him to the ground. It was so funny and I wanted to watch, but I got to get away before the not-wort warrior got me.

I hurried out the window, then ran as fast as I could before they could catch me. I was going to find Uncle Nic's friend, then I was going to have him help me force spiders down that jerk's throat.

Alesta

So much for staying out of sight and enjoying my day off.

There was a knot in my stomach as I made my way to the formal sitting room where the guards told me the queen was waiting for me. Sitting to tea with my formal mate's queen was something I never expected having to do. I did not know what to expect.

She noticed the connection between Lukyan and me. There was no way she wouldn't. Anyone at dinner would have noticed.

If that was the reason she called for me, then what did she plan on doing?

I'm suddenly grateful for Casimir. He knew of Triston and surely wouldn't allow the Queen to harm him. The lengths he and his mother went to ensure he was safe wouldn't be for not. If I'm confident in nothing else concerning Casimir, it's his devotion to his mother and her will. I'm willing to bet that book was even a gift from the queen, given through her youngest son.

"Uh, Luna?!" Gamma Kender saw me from across the great room as I walked through. He looked around anxiously. "Aren't you supposed to be home?"

I gave his anxious face an odd look. "Supposed to be."

"Then what are you doing out here?"

"Oh? You know. Just taking a leisurely stroll."

He fell in beside me and hissed, "You think that's a good idea?"

I rolled my eyes. "I was summoned, genius. Do you really

believe I enjoy walking through the pack house and being called Luna relentlessly?"

"Ah," he murmured. "So, Alpha summoned you?"

Pressing my lips together, I hesitated before I answered, "No. it was the queen."

"The queen!" He shouted. I had to hurry to cover his mouth as staff and pack members turned to stare.

"Hush! What are you yelling for, idiot?!"

"Does Alpha know?"

"I have no idea."

"Well, don't you think you should check with him first?"

"Why? Can he refuse the queen?"

Gamma Kender cringed, knowing our Alpha couldn't. "He's not going to like this."

I muttered, "I'm not going to like this much either."

Gamma Kender's eyes glossed over and I knew he was mind linking our Alpha, anyway. When he was finished, he said, "I'm coming with you."

"Alpha's orders?" I raised an eyebrow.

Gamma Kender lifted his chin. "Maybe. Even if he didn't, I'd be tagging along, anyway."

"Oh yeah? Why is that?"

He gave me a huffy look. "Because I'm your Gamma. It's my job to protect my Luna."

"I'm not your Luna," I grumbled.

Gama Kender just chuckled under his breath, following obediently behind me. I'd never admit it to him, but I felt some relief that I wasn't walking into the lion's den alone.

That relief didn't last long.

We both entered the sitting room, bowing respectfully as we lowered our gaze.

"You summoned me, my queen?"

Her lighthearted laughter caused me to look up. She was staring at Gamma Kender.

"I did ask to see you, Alesta dear, but I don't remember inviting anyone else. I was hoping it could be just us." She stepped forward, catching me by surprise by grabbing my hands and squeezing them tightly. "Just us girls." Her smile was radiant, taking me back.

She looked pointedly at Gamma Kender.

"I, uh...." He looked at me like he didn't know what to do.

I smiled tightly at him. "Thank you for walking me, Gamma. I think I'll be fine without you for a little bit."

His eyes seared into mine. *"I'll be right outside the door. Call me if you need me."*

I wanted to roll my eyes, but couldn't in my present company. Gamma Kender would be useless if the Lycan queen had any ill-intent towards me.

Once the door was closed, Queen Camellia was the one that ushered me to take a seat.

"Sit, sit! I had my chambermaid prepare rooibos tea. I do hope you like it!"

I froze, watching as the omega poured the steamy liquid in both our cups. The familiar fragrance brought back memories and so many emotions tied with them.

As Queen Camellia dismissed the omega, so it was only the two of us in the room, I managed to find my voice.

"Rooibos tea?" I asked in a barely audible whisper.

"Yes! It's one of my favorites. Are you familiar with the blend?"

"I've had it once before." Seven years ago.... With the previous queen.

"Well, now you've had it twice," the queen said brightly.

After forcing a smile, I lifted the cup, studying the amber liquid before taking a hesitant sip.

"It's very beneficial to one's health. Queen mother gifted me some for our journey." She took a long sip, holding my gaze. I squirmed in my seat, feeling a wave of unease passing through me. "I heard the Queen Mother also shared a cup with you before your journey to this pack."

The porcelain cup tumbled from my hands, crashing to the floor. Hot liquid spilled all over my legs and feet, but I barely felt the pain. The burning heat didn't warm the icy dread rushing over me.

"Goodness!" Queen Camellia dropped to her knees, dabbing at my scalded skin with her napkin. "I didn't mean to startle you. Cold water! We need-"

"You know, don't you," I rasped. "That's why you called me here. You know."

Queen Camellia looked up at me with so much sympathy in her eyes. He gently grasped my hand in hers. "Yes. Yes, Alesta. I know you are Lukyan's mate. But we need to treat your leg or he will-"

"What are you going to do to me?"

"Pardon?" She looked taken aback.

I swallowed down the knot that was choking me. "Are... are you going to kill me?"

Triston... Casimir, or at least Nic, would protect him without me. They had to.

"Kill you!" Queen Camellia looked shocked. "Heavens, no! Why would you..." Then understanding crossed her face. "It was the tea, wasn't it? I thought it would be a good opening for what I wished to discuss, but I guess I didn't think things through. I should have considered your perspective."

Queen Camellia sighed, looking at the broken teacup and the stain from the tea. As she started to pick up the broken pieces of glass, I gained the ability to move. I slid onto the floor from my chair and began to help.

"I... I can get it," I whispered, grabbing my napkin and putting the pieces in the fabric so the sharp edges wouldn't cup my hand. Queen Camellia watched me for a moment, then followed suit. She had little knicks on her palms from holding the glass bare.

Queen Camellia glanced at my legs. "We really should get you medical attention."

"You as well." I nodded towards her cuts.

She smiled softly. "These will heal on their own. I'm more concerned about you. If Lukyan finds out you were burned because of me..." She shivered.

I bit my lip, hesitating before I asked, "Did he tell you, or did you figure it out?"

Her expression dripped with compassion. "I knew of you long, long ago, Alesta. Long before you knew about me." She pursed her lips, gaining an air of caution. "If Lukyan had done what I said, you should have been fully aware of our arrangement before the wedding. My mate knew and understood. I'd like to think you would have, too."

My brows knit together. "You... You have a mate?"

Her smile brightened. "I do. You can probably guess who it is. You caught us in the woods."

So she did see me that night. I thought maybe she hadn't clearly seen my face, or I had just imagined our eyes met.

"Sir Ruth," I murmured. "He's your mate?"

Queen Camellia ran her fingers over the mark on her nape. "He's my one and only."

"But.... Lukyan has a mark on his neck too."

"Magic," she giggled. "It's not real. There has never been anything between Lukyan and me other than a sibling-like friendship." She grasped my hand again in a tender manner. "I called you here to explain, and to maybe answer any questions you may have. Can I pour you another cup of tea, and tell you just how much your mate needs you right now?"

Chapter 23

Runaway And Rogues

Mikken

"Any word?"

"*Not a single one, Alpha,*" Kender replied. "*I think I heard a cup break, but she hasn't called for me.*"

I frowned deeply, my worry for Alesta burning my chest. "*Go check.*"

"*Me?! Alpha…. It's the fucking queen.*"

A growl of frustration left me. It would be one thing if I barged in there to check on her, but Kender could be reprimanded severely.

I should have just brought Alesta with me. She would have been more than helpful at the moment. When I received word the king and his brother left for the forest to train, all I'd wanted was to keep a distance between the king and Alesta. I hadn't expected the queen to be the one to look for her.

"*Stay close to her,*" I growled at Kender. "*As close as possible.*"

"*Already doing that, Alpha. You know it'd be easier for me to shadow her as her Gamma if you'd just hurry up and make her your Luna already.*"

"*Not yet,*" I muttered. "*I won't force her.*"

"*No, but you could try actually telling her how you feel.*"

She probably still wouldn't get it. I kissed her, and she simply thought it was a jest.

"Maybe I should just head back," I thought out loud.

"What?!" Carl hissed, turning to look back at me. "We haven't found them yet. You can't be serious."

"Of course I'm not serious," I snapped.

Early this morning we got a link from the border patrol that they came across a rogue trail leading into the pack. The rotten stench ended at the river. My Beta and I, along with two other elite teams, have been going up and down the rushing water all morning looking for any signs of the rogue invaders. We haven't found them yet.

Having rogues is bad enough, but it's a common occurrence for our outlining pack. Alesta had helped many times to exterminate the demented beings that were once werewolves, but had lost the goddess's blessing.

Rogues were crazed beasts, like rabid dogs on the loose. They lost all sense of humanity, leaving just a feral outer shell that won't think twice about taking the life of one of ours.

The timing couldn't be worse with this inspection under way. With royals in our territory, it could be trouble if we don't handle the issue before someone else finds the rogues and gets hurt.

King Lukyan would find any excuse to extend his stay. I want to prevent that at all costs.

"*Alpha!*" A warrior suddenly linked me, pulling desperately on the pack mind to reach me. "*Alpha!*"

"*What?! Did you find the trail?*"

"*No! It's not that!.... Ahh!!*"

"*Then what?!*"

It's the boy.... The Lycan boy!"

My stomach dropped. "*What happened to Triston?*"

"*What happened.... Hold on....*" There was a brief pause, though I could still feel his frenzied panic. "*I'm locked in a closet now. Can you send help?! Gunther went insane!*"

"*Gunther?! What about Triston?*"

"*Triston did it!*" The warrior rasped. "*I don't know how, but the boy commanded Gunther to attack me and he did…. Like a fucking dog!"*

He wasn't making sense. Triston was just a kid.

"Where is Triston now?"

"I don't know! He yelled attack and then jump out of his window! Gunther bit me twice before I could call you! I told that idiot not to goad the kid."

I snarled, trying to imagine what Gunther might have said to make Triston run away from home. Triston was a good kid, unless you gave him reason not to be.

This was the worst fucking time for someone to anger the little Lycan. I would have never allowed Gunther to watch the boy. He's always been open with his hatred of Lycans, including the boy. He was the brother of the woman who was always complaining about Triston at his school.

"I'm sending a team to you now." I hesitated before adding, *"and I'll alert Gamma Kender. He will need to enlist Alesta to help find her boy."*

I'd wished to give her a day of peace with her son. How could things have gone so horribly wrong?

"I'm heading back," I told my Beta.

"What?! Fuck, Alpha. Alesta can handle her own with that queen. Seriously. If we don't find these rogues quickly and the royals find out-"

"Triston is missing," I said curtly, cutting into his nagging. "How will the royals react to finding him?"

My Beta looked stunned, the horror of the situation all over his face. None of us wanted to lose Alesta to the royals. I was sure King Lukyan already knew, but if the Queen or their aides discovered the boy….

"Let's go," Carl growled, shifting quickly and sprinting towards the pack house.

Triston

"Gosh, dang it." I walked around a big bush, hoping the pack house would be on the other side, but it wasn't. "This is annoying."

After kicking the dirt a few times, I turned around to see if I could follow my trail back to where I came from. I ran so fast that I wasn't paying attention to where I was going. I was just trying to avoid more wort warriors from seeing me.

The woods are confusing. Everything looks the same. I've never been in them alone, so I don't know how to find my way out.

A growl shook me as I bent over to study lots of footprints on the ground. The dirt was soft, and I could see the marks from lots of claws at the end of all the different sized footprints.

There were other people out here, probably warriors. So much for staying out of sight.

I started stomping on all the different prints, angry that they were keeping me from finding the marks from my shoes. How was I going to get back home now? Mama was going to be mad if I didn't find her soon.

Then I had an idea. If these were warrior footprints, couldn't I just follow them back home? Even if they led me back to the warrior building, I knew I could find my way to mama from there.

I crouched to look at the footprints closer again, trying to figure out which way they were going. My nose burned from the stinky smell all over the ground next to them.

"These worts need to shower." I pinched my nose and stood back up. I laughed as a fun idea came into my head. "I'll ask Mr. Casimir to toss them in the river."

Luckily, the river was close by. I could hear it. Hopefully, I found Mr. Casimir or Uncle Nic before mom found me. I'd get to ask Mr. Casimir to punish the wort warrior back home, then I could finally ask him about my dad.

Suddenly, a deep snarling came from behind me. It made me jump and turn around, looking everywhere for where it came from.

The smell was way worse. It made me gag.

"Gross!" I coughed. "Who's there?! You need a bath!"

The snarls got louder, then a dirty old man with scabs all over stepped out from a group of trees. He had long, thin hair growing in just a few places on his head. I think it was supposed to be white, but it was too dirty to tell.

His eyes made me gasp. They were the eyes of a wolf, but he was in human form. Then I saw his bare feet and his hands. I saw a weird cat at my friend's house once that didn't have any hair. His hands and feet reminded me of that cat. They just didn't look right, and his claws were out.

"Look what I found," his yucky, throaty voice hissed. "A Lycan pup, all alone in the wilderness-sss. My friends would *love* to meet you..."

Lukyan

"Tell me again about the spiders," I laughed, sitting in the dirt across from my brother and Alesta's friend. "He truly chased his teacher with a spider on a stick?!"

"Yes, my king," Niccola smiled softly. "He called Instructor Zaden a weirdo for fearing them."

Casimir chuckled. "He asked if I could command the warrior to eat the crawling bugs. Ah," he sighed blissfully. "The palace will be so lively when the new prince arrives."

"There's never a dull moment with Tris," Niccola agreed.

"I think I'll gift my nephew a crawling pet next."

"Please don't," Niccola groaned. "I'm scared of what Alesta will do when she finds that book."

"What book?" I asked.

"From our mother. She sent the *Lycan Prince Defeats the Dragon* for her grandson."

"I remember that story," I smiled reminiscently. It was my favorite when I was a boy.

"Mother was surely thinking of you when she gave it to me." Casimir looked at Niccola. "Why would our werewolf mama be wary of an innocent book?"

"Because she'll know it came from you." Niccola narrowed his eyes at my brother.

"Why is that an issue? I thought she allowed Casimir to meet him?" I asked with envy.

Niccola stared coldly at Casimir. "Because that wasn't the only thing your brother left Triston with."

Casimir looked away guiltily.

I asked firmly, "What did you do?"

"I… may have said a few things…."

"He told Triston he was a friend of his father." Niccola's face grew grim. "Alesta was firm about Casimir not saying anything about you."

"I told the boy not to tell his mother," Casimir said in defense of himself.

"Triston can't keep things from his mother. She will know he's hiding something, especially when she questions him about the book."

My heart sank hearing what I already knew. Alesta was determined to hide my existence from my son, just as she was trying to hide him from me. I wanted to confront her, but didn't want her to resist me more.

"What was he like as a baby?" I asked softly, trying not to spiral into self-pity concerning my son's mother.

Niccola smiled gently. "He was lovely. Beautiful. His charm quickly bewitched even the nurses who had been reluctant to care for a Lycan pup." He laughed softly to himself. "And he loved his mother. There wasn't a moment from the time he was born until he started school that he didn't want to be by Alesta's side. The warriors quickly grew fond of Tris. Well..." His lips twisted. "Most of them. There were a few who remained cold simply because he was a Lycan."

My thoughts went to the shrill woman who unknowingly revealed my son's existence to me. "With the history of this pack, the majority accepting him seems like a miracle."

Niccola seemed confused. "History?"

Casimir chuckled dryly. "I forget you don't know. Father forbade the entire Hallowed Moon Pack from speaking of the incident."

"Mother didn't tell them before sending them here?" I raised my eyebrows.

Casimir shook his head. "She didn't want to give Alesta reason to resist joining the pack."

That explains why she remains ignorant of the Alpha's advances. She's probably unaware that the Alphas of the Hallowed Moon Pack never found their fated mates. They have to take chosen mates to continue their lineage.

The current Alpha's mother was unlucky in finding her fated mate after being chosen as the previous Alpha's Luna. She had already been marked and had a child, which made her completely resistant to her fated mate bond.

How father knew she was his fated mate, though both he and the Hallowed Moon Luna were marked and fully mated to another, has remained a mystery to me.... But the fact he killed her remains. My father murdered the former Luna of this pack, leaving a scar so deep they've been relieved of all their obligations to the kingdom since then.

"I can fill you in later," Casimir told Niccola. "I think my brother would rather hear more stories about his son than a retelling of our father's misdeeds. Tell him about Triston's toddler years. I'm sure he was quite the terror," he chuckled.

"Oh yeah," Niccola laughed. "He'd always be off looking for trouble. If Alesta took her eyes off him for any amount of time, he'd be trying to face off with grown men for their snacks. I don't think the boys ever been full a day in his life. He's always loved to eat."

"He's a growing Lycan pup," I chuckled. "We tend to eat more than normal children to fuel our dormant beasts. We gain our ability to shift much younger than werewolves."

"You shifted for the first time at eight if I remember correctly," Casimir commented.

"So early?!" Niccola's eyes went wide. "Werewolves don't shift until their fifteenth birthday."

"Our King was early, even for a Lycan." Casimir looked at me from the corner of his eye. "Our ruler was just built differently."

It had nothing to do with my anatomy. Shock and fear brought on my first shift. Nothing else. Seeing the truth behind the tribute system would be a shock for any individual, but as a child....

Now more than ever, I need to create a better future for our kind; for my son, and any future siblings he may have.

"Um, King Lukyan?" Niccola's tone was cautious, and I could suddenly feel his unease, with a touch of bitterness behind it. "Can I possibly ask a, uh.... A delicate question. It's something Alesta and I have been wondering about since we left the capital."

My brows knit together. There were a number of sensitive subjects that came to mind. My body grew cold, wondering which one had created this tension around my mate's friend. "Of course. You can ask me anything."

He looked to the ground, and then at Casimir. Casimir nodded at him subtly, and that was when Niccola took a deep breath and finally asked, "I heard that my birth pack and Alesta's were destroyed. Was... was that your father's doing?"

I swallowed past the lump in my throat. I had put that incident out of my mind. How would I tell him about what truly happened without explaining the vile things this kingdom, and the entire Lycan race for that matter, were built on?

"It was mine and Camellia's doing, but it is not how it sounds." Casimir wrapped an arm around the werewolf warrior and said, "Your pack and hers are safe. They're just not where they once were."

"W-what does that mean? We were told our entire packs were destroyed."

"They were destroyed," I said calmly, "but none of the people in them were harmed."

Niccola shook his head. "I... I don't understand what you're-"

His eyes suddenly glazed over. His mouth dropped open, and his expression turned to one of horror. When his eyes gained their focus, he looked around urgently, like he was searching the woods for something.

"What? What is it?" Casimir urged him.

"Triston," he whispered hoarsely. "Shit!" He got to his feet, then hurriedly stripped from his clothes. "Triston ran away."

"Well," Casimir chuckled nervously, eyeing the werewolf as he undressed. "Isn't that common with children locked in a cage?"

"No, you don't understand," Niccola shook his head. "Rogues entered the lands. Alpha hasn't found them yet, and now Triston is missing."

A growl ripped through my body as the urge to shift pressed painfully into my joints and bones.

Then we heard a high-pitched snarling in the distance, followed by a collection of haunted howls.

My beast ripped out of me.

Chapter 24

First Shift

Alesta

"So, you see, we aren't and never will be mates. We simply came together to work towards a common goal." Camellia, seated across from me, offered a beaming smile like she was proud of her explanation. Before this tea, I thought the queen was the epitome of royal grace with noble decorum. The more she speaks, the more I see a uniqueness that made her almost seem normal, if that made any sense. She seemed so unreachable before, like a star in the night sky.

Now, with her grinning proudly from ear to ear, I couldn't help but to smile with her. She wasn't as unapproachable as she first seemed.

"So, the mark on his neck... Sir Ruth put that there?"

She waved her hands towards me. "Oh, just call him Ruth. Luk simply bestowed a title upon him for appearances. But, yes. Ruth gained magic through his ancestry. Fabricating a mate mark was easy for him."

My eyes flashed to her neck again. Her mark was real, given to her by Ruth.

It was hard to wrap my mind around all these truths, but the more she explained, the clearer the situation was becoming.

"You say that Lukyan hasn't been the same since I left? That his beast would overtake him and he wouldn't be able to calm himself down?" I swallowed nervously before asking my real question. "That's happening because of me?"

Her smile turned sympathetic. "Lycans can't handle rejection well, or any amount of distance from their mates. I suppose that is why the goddess doesn't grant many of us with fated mates. The Kingdom would turn into chaos."

That would explain his behavior upon their arrival. Finding me in Alpha Mikken's arms surely triggered his shift.

Then a thought struck me. What about when the Alpha kissed me to calm me down? How did Lukyan react to that?

I received so many answers, but that just caused more questions to spin around inside me, making me grow dizzy as I tried to figure them all out. Queen Camellia wouldn't have the answers to most of them. Only Lukyan would. There was still one question she should know, though.

"Lukyan," I whispered softly, dragging my eyes from the ground that I'd been staring at in a daze to look her straight in the eyes. "Does he know? Does he know about my son?"

Queen Camellia pressed her lips together as her shoulders dropped. I could guess the answer to my question by her expression alone.

Before she could voice a response, the door suddenly burst open and Gamma Kender came frantically into the room.

"Alesta!" He hurried to my side. "We…" He glanced nervously at Queen Camellia, then whispered, "We have to go."

He took my hand and dragged me from the chair.

"Go? Go where?"

"Just… Just come on." He tugged against me until we were out in the hall.

I looked back at the queen, who was looking after us worriedly. Soon, she was out of eyesight as Gamma Kender continued to pull me behind him like there was a fire or something.

"What is wrong with you?! You can't behave that way in front of the queen!"

"I had to!" Gamma Kender snapped. "We need to hurry. Now!"

"Hurry where?"

My confusion deepened seeing the chaos in the great room, bleeding out into the foyer and front doors. Warriors were everywhere, barking orders like they were searching for something or someone. There was a nervous energy in the air that made my heart hammer in my chest.

"What's going on? Why are the warriors mobilized?" My eyes widened as I recalling the last few times we had been mobilized to this extent. "Rogues?"

Gamma Kender nodded, then looked around grimly. He was never this serious. Even when we were on missions together, he never looked this desperate.

Then Gamma Kender said the worst thing he could say possibly to a mother.

"We have to find Triston," he hissed. "Your son went missing."

Triston

"Let me go, you smelly baldy!" I snarled, swinging to hit the wort in his stinky chest. He was dangling me in front of him by my foot. My head was hurting from being upside down, and my nose burned from the way he smelled.

"If you don't quit squirming," the smelly freak sneered in a voice that sounded like a dying frog, "I'll rip that flapping tongue right from your mouth."

I pressed my lips tightly together, but that didn't stop a growl from escaping me.

The freak laughed. It sounded like a dying frog, too.

I didn't know where he was carrying me. I was already lost before he grabbed me, but I didn't recognize anything anymore. Mama never brought me here. Ever. There wasn't even a trail. He was walking through tall grass and bushes that slapped my face and hands.

My tummy was getting tight. The smell was making me want to throw up. Then I got nervous as the forest got really quiet. The birds weren't making any noises in the trees and I hadn't seen a squirrel in a long time. The leaves didn't even seem to be moving.

Then, all of a sudden, three more smelly freaks leaped down in front of us. They fell from the trees. Were they hiding up there the whole time?

They were snarling in a way that was much scarier than the one holding my ankle. They had yucky goo dripping from their sharp teeth, black bits and blood caught in the mouth slime.

I was scared. Not like before, but really, really scared. They looked more like demons than people. They moved like animals. The crazy kind of animals that would attack for no reason.

I was suddenly dropped. I let out a scream as I fell to the ground. My head hit a thorny bush. I felt warmth running down my head. The smell of trash was mixed with the scent of blood.

Everything was dizzy. There was a pounding in my head as it was spinning around. The forest and monsters were blurring together.

"Feast," the first freak growled in his dying croak.

At that one word, the pressure in my head exploded. My body burned until it felt like it was being ripped apart.

The next monster growl didn't come from any of them.

It came from me.

Lukyan

The smell of blood mixed with the unmistakable rogue stench hit me. The sounds of flesh tearing and screaming snarls pierced my nose. Everything blurred past as my beastly legs pushed forward, faster than I'd ever run before.

That was my son. I knew deep down that my son, the child I had never met, was at the center of the horrendous noises perpetrating the forest. Fear like I had never felt before forced my body to push beyond its limits to get to him.

Triston... Just hold on.

"There!" Casimir's voice blasted through my mind. He and Niccola were right behind me, their desperation almost matching my own.

Up ahead, in the thickest part of the brush, chaos was ensuing from its center. Blood covered the tree branches above. Ear shattering screams were piercing the air.

My heart stopped, seeing the reason behind the deathly screams. A small Lycan pup was viciously tearing into four rogue werewolves. Even with his small stature, his strength was massive. They didn't stand a chance.

I passed just for a second, just long enough for my beastly eyes to take it all in. Then I moved, ripping the first two rogues away from my pup.

They were already a mangled mess, screeching for their lives. Seeing me, those screams intensified until I silenced them for good.

Their skulls crushed in my giant beastly palms, like squeezing a ripe apple. Tossing them to the side, I saw Casimir handling the other two while Niccola attempted to calm the boy.

Triston's beastly ears were tucked back, and his small Lycan eyes were crazed with genuine fear. Niccola was in his human form, arms wide, showing he wasn't a threat.

"Tris, please. It's me. You're safe now."

Triston snarled, and the hair on his dense skin was standing on end. Blood was dripping from his claw and fangs. He wasn't a boy at the moment. He wasn't Triston. Fear made his beast take control.

When Niccola took a step forward, I recognized the look in Triston's eyes. Before he could lunge for his mother's friend, leaving a scar that would never heal in his heart, I put myself between them, catching my son, so his teeth and claws sank into me.

"TRISTON!"

Alpha Mikken appeared with his Beta and a group of warriors. They looked stunned. Some were even showing disgust.

"He's gone feral," one of the warrior's voice was dipping in fear. "The boy's gone mad!"

"He's just scared!" Niccola snapped, blocking mine and Triston's bodies with his small human one.

I tuned out their murmurings, trying to focus on my son. Their comments would just make me angry, but what Triston needed now was for me to remain calm.

Gently, I grasped his small face with one of mine, squeezing his cheeks just enough for him to loosen his fangs embedded in my skin. My aura washed over him as I stared into his eyes.

"You're safe," I whispered in his head, watching as his eyes slowly regained their humanity. *"You're safe, my son. I've got you now."*

Alesta

"Triston!" I screamed until I felt like my lungs would burst. Tears were streaming down my face. We've been looking for him for what felt like hours, but had really only been ten or fifteen minutes.

"Alesta!" Queen Camellia called to me. I turned to see her and Ruth on the trail nearby. "Follow us!"

I shook my head frantically, tears flying from my cheeks. "I can't... my son..."

"He has him! Come on!" She waved me along, and when I didn't move fast enough, she rushed to my side and grabbed my hand, disregarding Gamma Kender and the warriors with us.

My heart pounded in my chest. "H-he has him?... Lukyan?"

Camellia squeezed my hand, a look of concern passing over her face. Ruth looked back at Gamma Kender and the warriors with worry before looking at me.

"We need to hurry."

"Why? Oh, goddess. Is he hurt? Is Triston-"

"He's fine physically," Camellia whispered in an aching voice. "But he needs his mother right now."

What happened? What happened to my boy?

Ruth and Camellia were leading me far off the trail, deep into the untamed part of the forest. The grass was waist high, and the shrubs were unforgiving with their wild thorns.

My son didn't belong in a place like this, far from the safety and comfort of home. He should have been at home with me, reading books and trying to hold on to some resemblance of normal. I was supposed to give him that today; a reprieve from the chaos that has been happening since the arrival of the royals.

This ominous feeling that everything is about to change settled upon me, stirring with the fear I felt for my son. Triston was with Lukyan. Our normal would never be the same. I knew that in my soul.

There was a crowd of warriors up ahead. Frantic murmurings reached us even from afar.

"The boy is dangerous...."

"Our children won't be safe...."

"He fought four of them and doesn't have a scratch...."

"Did you hear what he did to Gunther?...."

"He could do it to any of us...."

At the head of the pack, the Alpha stood, his Beta right at his side. Beta Carlston was whispering something to Alpha Mikken with a grim expression, their eyes cautious as they stared ahead.

Then I saw them; Lukyan and my son. Triston was draped over Lukyan's shoulder. His limp body was covered in blood. There were bite marks and scrapes along Lukyan's neck and shoulders, but Triston didn't have any noticeable wounds anywhere I could see.

Casimir was carefully wrapping my boy in a cloak much too fancy to be anyone else's but his own. Niccola was between them and the pack, his arms crossed with a fierce look on his face. He was staring the others down with distrust.

"Deal with the Alpha," Camellia told Ruth, pulling me ahead with her towards Lukyan and my son.

"Triston," I rasped, letting her go to run ahead.

Alpha Mikken's head snapped in my direction, hearing my voice. "Alesta! I was-"

"Leave her be," Ruth said in a firm tone, leaving no room for discussion. "Your people have done enough."

I did not know what he was talking about, and any explanation would have to wait for later. My mind could only focus on Triston for now.

"Triston," I cried, trying to take my boy from Lukyan's arms.

Lukyan stared at me, his expression hard as stone. I pleaded with my eyes. I'd deal with whatever may come with Lukyan later, but right now, I just wanted to hold my baby.

He relented, passing Triston down to me.

"My baby," I cried, tucking Triston's limp body against my chest. He was so warm and his heart was beating steadily. The blood covering him was clearly not his own. The stench was too potent to be anything other than rogue.

Lukyan watched us as he pulled on pants his brother offered him. Then, without warning, he bent down and lifted both me and Triston, pulling us tightly against his chest.

"Tell our physicians to meet us in my chambers," Lukyan told Camellia. Then his topaz eyes seared into me. "Alesta and I have many things to discuss concerning our son."

Chapter 25

Mine

Mikken

"He's the king's son?"

"That's not what he said, right?"

"I knew the boy was a freak."

"He attacked the king. We're fucked."

"She fucked the king…. Alpha can't really make her Luna now… can he?"

Gritting my teeth, I felt my anger escalating as I heard what my own warriors were saying. I couldn't blame them for their reaction. I was stunned seeing my little Lycan friend in such an out-of-control state. I still didn't want to hear what they were saying, but couldn't punish them given the reason and setting. The boy shifted. He was not yet seven, but he shifted into his beast. Not only that, but he took on four rogues on his own.

My warriors were justified in their fears, but it didn't stop my irritation from showing.

"What do you want me to do?" Carl whispered urgently.

"I can follow them," Kender offered. His eyes were trailing after King Lukyan as he carried Alesta towards the pack house.

"They are to be left alone," Sir Ruth said again. His eyes were spinning like stormy skies. "I suggest dealing with your own people first." He then looked at Gamma Kender. "You as well."

Kender's lip curled aggressively. "She's my Luna."

"No," Sir Ruth scoffed. "She is not. Your services as Gamma will not be needed any longer."

With that final warning, he followed the rest of the royal party, leaving us here to deal with the carnage they left behind.

Kender started pacing around aggressively, his anger spilling over. "She can't really leave with them," he seethed. "She's... she's one of us!"

"Calm down. Nothing has been decided yet," Carl snapped at him.

"Alpha," a young warrior, barely of age, crept ahead of the rest. His expression was uneasy as he stared at the broken rogue bodies, then at me. "You... you aren't going to keep the boy here too, are you?"

The pure fear in his eyes shook me. As I looked around, I saw the pure fear reflected in all my warriors. Old, young, experienced and not; all my bravest men were afraid of a six-year-old pup.

"Let's get this mess cleaned up," I said, not able to give him any sort of answer. If it were simply up to me, Triston would be staying. He was a part of Alesta, and I could no longer see anyone as my Luna but her. But it was out of my hands. I couldn't contend with his father. Especially with my pack scared of his son.

Alesta

"I'm sorry, mama," Triston whimpered, rubbing his eyes with the backs of his hands. "I know I shouldn't have run away."

"Shhh." I pushed his freshly washed hair from his forehead. "I'm not mad, baby. I'm just happy you're safe now. You're going to be okay."

He looked around the massive guest bedroom occupied by Lukyan. His red-rimmed eyes matched those of the man watching us from the doorway. When Triston saw him, he sat up on the bed.

"Mister King!"

Triston had been calling Lukyan *Mister King* since he woke up. While the royal omegas were preparing his bath, he kept asking me who the man who saved him was. I didn't know what else to tell him. I simply said he was the Lycan King.

Lukyan's lips twitched like he was trying not to smile. He pushed off the door frame and took slow strides towards the bed. His topaz eyes flashed to mine, but I averted my gaze. I didn't know how to face him. Not after all the truths between us had been disclosed in such drastic ways.

Lukyan crouched beside the bed, becoming eye level with Triston. "How are you feeling?"

Triston put on a brave face, only ruined by the tears still sticking to his rosy cheeks. "I... I'm sore. My whole body feels like my legs do when I run too much."

Lukyan's soft chuckle caused my insides to flutter against my wishes.

"That's to be expected. You're holding up better than most after their first shift."

Triston wrinkled his nose. "I really shifted? For real?"

Lukyan looked perturbed. "Of course you did. What else do you think had happened?"

Triston shrugged his shoulders, playing with the fringe on the blanket. "I don't know. I guess I was hoping it was just a bad dream. Like the ones mama gets sometimes."

I gasped. "How... I mean, what do you mean?" I'd never told Triston about my dreams.

"You know. The ones that make you cry sometimes. You cry in your sleep and say stuff like "you lied" or you just cry "Luk" over and over again."

My face felt like it was heating to the point my brain should be boiling.

"Does she, now?" Lukyan muttered. Then, as he stood, he said, "Triston. I'm going to have my physician look you over while I talk to your mother. Would that be alright?"

"Of course it would!" Casimir said cheerily, walking into the room with Niccola and a familiar woman. "We'll keep our little warrior prince company."

I glared at Casimir, and he pressed his lips together, realizing his slip up.

"Like in the book you gave me?" Triston's face lit up, but then he held his hands over his mouth, looking at me with a guilty expression. "Oops. I forgot I wasn't supposed to tell."

Good to know Casimir was already becoming a *great* influence on my son.

The woman with him was staring at me with knit brows. It took me a moment to realize it was the clinical nurse that had diagnosed my pregnancy seven years ago. She seemed to recognize me about the same time I remembered her.

She looked back at Niccola, then at Triston. After studying Triston's features, and probably seeing the lack of similarities to the man she originally thought was my child's father, her mouth dropped open. She gaped at Lukyan and me, her expression almost comical given the situation.

Lukyan didn't look pleased by her reaction. No doubt he was going to have enough questions for me as it was.

With a sigh, I bent to kiss my son's head. "Be good for your uncle," I whispered, meaning Nic, but not missing the smile that appeared on Casimir's face. "I'll be right back."

Triston settled into the bed, hiding half his face with the blanket. "I'll be good. Just don't let that mean warrior come back. He called me a mutt."

I let out a mix between a groan and a growl, knowing I'd have to deal with the reason Triston ran away soon too.

But first I had to deal with his father.

"Follow me," I murmured without meeting the fiery topaz eyes I could feel singeing my skin.

∞ ∞ ∞

Walking through the sitting area, Sir Ruth and Queen Camellia stood upon seeing us.

"Is the lad okay?" Ruth asked.

I smiled tightly. "He's going to be fine."

Camellia gave us a curious look. "Where are you two going?"

"Your room," Lukyan said, grabbing my hand and walking ahead.

The sparks that shit up my arm made me gasp involuntarily. I didn't expect him to grab me so suddenly.

Glancing at his expression, unease stirred inside me. He had a crazed look in his topaz eyes that I hadn't noticed in the room with Triston. Anxiety mixed with anticipation of what Lukyan would do now that he knew.... Knew of our son.

Lukyan pulled against my hand, pushing me into the room before him as he slammed the door behind me. I stood there panting, unable to control the panic within me.

"L-Lukyan, I'm-"

"Shut up," he snarled, looming over me.

The room was dim, but his eyes seemed to glow through the shadows covering his rugged face. I felt like a child before his massive frame.

It took about three seconds before anger replaced my fear. How dare he try to intimidate me?

"I see your manners are as refined as ever," I scoffed. Then I pointed a sharp finger in his chest before I snarled, "You don't get to tell me what to do."

"Shut up, Alesta," he said in a deathly whisper. His jaw tensed to the point the dimples on his cheeks were twitching. His aura started pulling down on me. "I'd be careful if I were-"

"No," I snapped, shoving my finger harder to his chest. "You don't get to do that. You think you can command me to comply with you now? Well, I got news for you. You can't, MMHM!...."

His mouth suddenly came down on mine. Electric bolts traveled through my veins like lightning strikes, immobilizing me completely.

All thoughts left my mind as his lips moved forcefully against mine. Soon, no force was necessary.

My fist clenched his shirt, pulling him closer when his taste was no longer enough. The tingles erased everything but this feral need for him. The bond I once thought was dead erupted into new life, more powerful than before.

A gravelly growl vibrated between us as he lifted my body and slammed me against the wall. His movements were rough and frantic, mirroring the Lukyan in my dreams. Only now the aching feeling of despair was gone in me, leaving only the overwhelming pleasure of being entwined with my fated mate.

Deep down, I knew this was wrong, but there was a larger part of me that knew this was so right. He was my mate. Mine.

But he was married to someone else.

My head couldn't come out of the fog of lust enough to grasp the situation.

"Mine," he rasped as his lips moved down from the corner of my lips. My eyes rolled back, soaking in the sparks shooting through my skin. It wasn't until I felt his canines scrape against my neck that reality came rushing back to me.

My eyes shot open. I slammed my palms into his firm chest, pushing against him. "Wait! Lukyan..." I struggled for his attention, my groans only exciting him further.

"LUKYAN!" I snapped, slapping my hands harder against him.

He growled, looking up at me with sultry eyes without taking his lips from my skin. "I thought I told you to shut up."

Anger coursed with the sparks traveling through me. "I thought I told you not to tell me what to do."

His dark chuckles made my insides clench. A fact I'm sure he was aware of. His hardened eyes glanced down at my heat pressed against his hard stomach.

"Your body betrays you."

"Don't flatter yourself." I shoved against him. "Anyone would react in this situation."

"Anyone?" He raised an eyebrow, then started kissing my collarbone, laughter shaking his chest when the sparks made me shudder. "Would you like me to do this with anyone?"

My eyes narrowed. "Would your wife?" I asked arrogantly, even though I knew the answer.

His laughter just deepened. He pressed his lips to my ears and whispered roughly, "I'm about to fuck you in my wife's bed, with her right outside listening. What do you think about that, little mate?"

My heat leaked abundantly at the prospect. He had to have felt it, if not at least smelled my body's betrayal.

"You're a pig," I hissed.

"Maybe," he murmured, then ran his tongue down my nape with a smile as my body shuddered from the sparks. "But you gave birth to this *pig's* heir. There was little chance of me letting you go as it was. Now...." A deep, thunderous rumble echoed in his chest. "You're mine, Alesta. I'll never let you escape again."

Triston

"All looks well," the pretty doctor lady smiled at me. She was a Lycan too. She didn't look at me the way the pack doctor did when I had to go get a checkup. She was really nice. "You're a healthy boy! An early shift won't cause any harm."

Uncle Nic didn't look convinced. "What about the rogues? Did they get any bites in? Their venom can-"

"There wasn't any venom in him," Mister Casimir grabbed Uncle Nic's shoulder. "My brother checked."

"Your brother?" My eyes got really big, and I sat up quickly.

"You mean Mister King?!"

"Mister King." Mister Casimir snorted. "I love that. Maybe I can persuade the guards to address Luk like that."

"Luk?" I tilted my head, feeling confused. "Is that Mister King's name?" It was the same name mama says when she's sleeping sometimes.

Uncle Nic and Mister Casimir looked at each other, then back at me.

"It's just a nickname," Uncle Nic muttered, glancing at the doctor lady as she giggled. Then he asked, "So, are you ready to tell me why you decided to take a walk alone in the woods by yourself?"

"That was a very naughty idea," Mister Casimir chuckled.

I know Uncle Nic was trying to distract me. Mama acted the same way when I asked about Mister King. I wanted to ask more questions, but Mister Casimir saying I was naughty made me too angry to go back to asking about Mister King.

"I had to!" I crossed my arms over my chest. "That wort warrior called me a mutt! He said mama was dirty too." My chest made a growly noise thinking about that jerk. "I was going to find Mister Casimir so you could make him eat a spider."

Uncle Nic groaned, putting his hand over his face like he does when he's upset. Mister Casimir even looked angry, and the pretty doctor too.

"Well, little Tris. I think I can do you one better than a spider." Mister Casimir snapped his fingers and a man in a funny coat walked in. "Larson, I'm going to need a bucket and a leash. A pretty red leash with a collar to match."

Excitement bubbled inside of me. "Hehe. What are you gonna do, Mister Casimir?"

"Call me uncle, love. This uncle of yours is going to give this warrior the treatment he deserves."

Chapter 26

Like A Dog

Alesta

It took some convincing to get Lukyan to put me down. He still had me pinned against the wall, his arms like an iron prison.

He meant what he said. He wasn't going to let me get away again.

Despite Lukyan's intense presence, I wasn't intimidated like before. Not now that I knew where that intensity was coming from.

"You wanted to talk. Then talk," he husked, his nose inhaling my scent from my hair.

My eyes flashed to the chair beside the window, and then the bed. "Can't we talk while sitting down?"

A dark grin spread across his face. "Would you like to move this to the bed?"

"No!" I huffed. "I'd just like some space to think." The sparks from the bond were mind-numbing, and being this close still made it hard to think with a clear head.

"This is all the space you're getting," Lukyan mumbled. His fingers skimmed my side to my hip.

I glared as the sparks made me shudder. He laughed, the deep rolling of his voice making my body react in other ways.

"You're still an arrogant prick."

He squeezed my hip tightly. "And you're still as stubborn as it gets."

"Stubborn because I won't gravel at your feet and obey your every command?"

"I don't need you to grovel. Seeing you on your knees would be nice, though."

"Fuck off." I shoved with all my force against his chest.

He didn't budge.

Instead, he pressed into my hands, forcing me to feel the vibrations of his deep growl. "I'm holding on by a thread, Alesta. Don't push me, or I might forcibly mark you right here."

"You wouldn't dare. You wouldn't take that choice from me."

"Oh, you test me." His dark chuckles were laced with anger. "You didn't give me a choice when you left, or when you stole my son from me without giving me the choice to even know he existed."

"Because I didn't have a choice!" My breaths came out in heaves. "You were married!"

"My marriage wasn't a choice!" He seethed, his face just inches from mine. His eyes were fiery, boring into mine. "Have you any idea what father would have done to you had I not married Camellia?!"

I swallowed the lump that had formed in my throat and said hoarsely, "Probably the same that he would have done if he found out I was pregnant."

His labored breathing fanned my face, washing me in his sweet scent. It made everything from the past so much more painful.

"I understand that," he rasped, grabbing my face in his rough hands. "I know, Alesta. I know about my mother, and about her command. I know, Alesta!" He shook his head in exasperating defeat. "I know! So, why can't you understand me?"

I did understand him now. Queen Camellia settled the only fears I had. Triston wouldn't be a danger to her position since she wasn't truly Lukyan's mate.

"You should have told me," I whispered brokenly. "I asked you.

That day you left me in your room, I asked what was going on. You chose to command me to stay without any explanation. *That* was your choice." I pressed my lips together to suppress the sadness from breaking out in ugly sobs. "*You* chose to keep me in the dark. You can't fault me for not trusting you now."

He hung his head, burying his nose into my neck as he took a ragged breath. "That was the greatest mistake of my life."

We stood there, the tension building until something inside me snapped. Tears spilled from my eyes as my arms wrapped around his neck, holding him to me. His arms encircled my waist, squeezing me with such desperation.

"You're still an arrogant prick," I rasped between my sobs.

His shuddering chest was a mixture of lather and sadness. "And you're still my stubborn little wolf."

He lifted his head, wiping the tears from my cheeks with his thumbs. My heart ached seeing the glistening moisture running down to the dense hair outlining his handsome face.

His lip started to move towards mine, but when they were just a breath away, someone knocked urgently on the door.

"Luk! Uh, you better get out here!"

Lukyan snarled, hearing Camellia's frantic voice.

Then vicious growling broke out in the next room, along with raised voices speaking all at once.

"Shit," Lukyan groaned, wiping a hand down his face. He took my hand and pulled me with him as he opened the door.

I gasped, seeing one of the pack warriors being forced to kneel in front of Prince Casimir as a collar was strapped to his neck. The collar was bright red, with spiked studs decorating its length.

I knew the warrior. He was not an elite, so we didn't train together often, but I recognized him as being one of the guards who came to inform me the Queen was asking for me. He and the other guard were supposed to be watching Triston during the time he ran away.

Triston was watching smugly, standing next to a sour-faced Niccola. The protest and growling were all coming from the door, where a group of pack warriors were being held back by the royal guards.

Sir Ruth was beside Casimir, hissing in his ear, "What in the goddess's name do you think you are doing?"

"I'm just playing a little game with my newest friend," Casimir chuckled.

"What is going on here?!" Alpha Mikken bellowed, coming up the hallway. "Let me through!"

The warriors parted so he could get through, but the royal guard stopped his entry. His eyes flashed to me, falling to where my hand was still tightly gripped in Lukyan's. He tore his gaze away like it pained him, then looked at the scene playing out in the center of the room.

"What is he doing?" I asked Camellia.

She shook her head. "I'm not sure. All I know is he sent his aid for the leash and a bucket and the guards for this man." She waved her hand towards the humiliated warrior on the ground. "He wouldn't answer either of us seriously when we asked. That was why I called for him." She shoved her thumb in Lukyan's direction.

Lukyan's eyes narrowed on his brother. "What is the meaning of this?"

"Oh, my dear brother," Casimir sighed, holding his face in his hand. "You've appeared just in the knick of time. Did either of you perhaps hear the reason *why* my dear nephew ran away from his babysitters?"

My body tensed. I pulled free of Lukyan's grip and stepped around him to better see the warrior kneeling on the ground. "What did you do to my son?"

"Alesta!" Alpha Mikken shouted at me from the door. "This is a pack issue. The royals should not be handling-"

"I ASKED!..." I cut his words off with a deathly glare before turning my attention back to the warrior. "What did you do to my son?"

"Well?" Casimir raised an eyebrow, looking down on the man. "Are you going to tell the woman, or would you prefer she asked you again?"

The man met my stare, then cringed, locking his lips together like a vice. He wasn't going to say a word to damn himself further.

I looked at Triston, then asked, "What did he do to you?"

Triston huffed. "He was being a giant wort."

Nic nudged him. "Tell her what he said."

Triston looked hesitant, but meeting my eyes again, he sighed and slumped forward. "Fine! He called me a mutt, mama."

"And what else?" Casimir urged my son to say more.

Triston's eyes iced over as he glared at the warrior. He looked so much like Lukyan when he made that expression.

"He called you dirty, mama. So, I was going to find Mis-, I mean, Uncle Casimir to make him eat spiders." Triston's little body shook, and a growl escaped from his chest. Niccola put a steadying hand on Triston's shoulder until he calmed down and wasn't at risk of shifting anymore because of his anger.

I couldn't care less about the things being said about me, but calling my son a mutt....

"Alesta," Alpha Mikken groaned from the doorway, pushing against the steel arms of the Lycan warriors. "I was going to deal with him after we finished disposing of the rogues. I just-"

"Silence!" Lukyan's voice carried a heavy weight to it. "Alesta can deal with this injustice herself."

I prowled forward, predatory eyes fixed on my target as the rage built up inside of me. "My son encountered four rogues on his own because of you." I crouched down, getting eye-level with the bastard. "If he wasn't a *mutt*, and didn't have Lycan blood in him, he would have died. *Died*." I grabbed his chin, forcing him to look at me as my nails pierced into his skin. "You not only owe my son an apology, but you should *thank him*. For, if he wasn't a *mutt*.... You would be facing a much more painful death than him." I scraped my nails down his neck, leaving a trail of blood. Then I squeezed my hand around his throat right above the collar, making him choke.

"P-please... Luna... I-"

"I am not your Luna," I sneered. "And I told you the only words I want to hear from you." I grabbed the collar, jerking his head to the side to look at my son. "Say it."

"I... I'm sorry!" He cried, his face contorting into an ugly expression of fear. "I'm sorry, and.... And thank you...."

"Good," I sneered as I stood. With little consideration of the consequences, I swung my leg, kicking the bastard in the stomach, causing him to buckle over and choke on the air that was leaving him.

The warriors and everyone in the room went silent as I bent over him, grabbing his hair as he struggled to breathe. "If I ever hear of you saying anything derogatory to or about my son again, I won't be this forgiving." I leaned in and whispered in his ear, "This *dirty* mother will kill you in the most painful way imaginable."

Jerking my hand roughly from his head, I turned to wipe where we touched down Casimir's shirt, intentionally making a point to rid my skin from the true filth in this room.

"My turn?" Casimir smirked, raising an eyebrow in question.

"Have at him," I muttered, turning to look at the offender one last time.

As my eyes lifted from the quivering warrior, who was still struggling to breathe, I noticed the expression on every warrior's face. There was anger and resentment, maybe even a little fear. Alpha Mikken was staring at me in a way that startled me for a moment. There was sadness in his sky-blue eyes, and his face was lined with tension.

Maybe I took things a little too far, but I don't regret my actions. The man could have caused my son to be killed. I thought I showed great mercy, given what could have happened.

Tearing my eyes from Alpha Mikken's, I looked back at Lukyan. There was pride shining in his topaz eyes, and a small smile playing on his lips.

Triston started to giggle. "You should have listened to your friend. He said my mama was going to kick your butt. Stupid wort."

"Oh, your mama is just the tip of the iceberg, little prince," Casimir said with a glimmer in his eyes.

He then took a tin bucket and a leash for dogs from a royal omega and crouched on the ground. The warrior watched with fearful eyes as Casimir fastened the leash to the bright red collar on his neck.

"Say ah," Casimir gleamed, holding the bucket by the handle.

The warrior hesitated, but knew he had no choice but to comply.

"A-aahhh- *omph....*"

Casimir shoved the wooden handle into the man's mouth, then slammed his mouth closed with a forceful hand under his chin.

"We're going to play a game called... *The mutt and his filth.*" Casimir ruffled his hair like one would do to a dog. "Triston and I are going to walk you all over the same woods you caused him to be lost in, and you are going to personally clean up any animal *filth* we find."

The warrior's eyes went wide as Casimir's words sank in. Clenching the pail between his teeth, he groaned weakly as he began to stand on shaking legs.

"Oh, no," Casimir drawled, pushing the man back down to the ground. "Where do you think the *mutt* comes into our little game?"

The man's shock was clear. The humiliation he felt had to be astronomical, greater than any pain I had caused him.

"This is going too far," Alpha Mikken said through clenched teeth.

"Oh?" Casimir cocked his head to the side. "Maybe we can first sit around and discuss the incident of the rogues, or the immense prejudice your pack members seem to have towards my nephew?"

"Nephew?"

"So it's true?..."

"She with the King?..."

...."No wonder the boy's a monster..."

"Shh, or you could be next...."

The warrior's murmurings about me were to be expected, but I didn't expect the hostility aimed at my son and the look of fear in their eyes.

Alpha Mikken's gaze flashed to mine as new worry lines formed on his face. "I'd like to speak with Alesta. As her Alpha, I think I have that right."

"You think you have a right to speak alone with my mate?" Lukyan spoke up, coming to place a possessive hand on my waist.

Triston gasped, covering his mouth with his hands. He looked from Lukyan to Alpha Mikken, then back at me, over and over again.

"Lukyan," I hissed.

"What?" His voice was like stone. "I thought we were past the deceits?"

I closed my eyes briefly, trying to ignore the sparks from the bond and settle my racing heart. This wasn't how I wanted my son to find out.

When I opened my eyes, there was a defeated look that settled over Alpha Mikken's features.

Things were changing way too quickly. This morning, I expected to have a normal day off with my son. It now felt like normal was a concept I'd never know again.

My resolve to do what was best for my son was the only thing that hadn't changed.

"We should talk," I said softly to my Alpha.

Lukyan growled, low and menacing until I rested my hand over his chest and shook my head. Then he quieted, but still had a hard set to his jaw.

I implored him with my eyes. "*All* of us need to have a discussion. Together."

Chapter 27

What To Do

Triston

My mama had a mate...

I heard right. I know I did. It just didn't make sense to me.

Mister King was my mama's mate. He said it himself. But.... He was married. Wasn't he? To the pretty blonde woman. But then why did the blonde lady not seem bothered when Mister King said that?

That wasn't the only thing I didn't get. Mister, or rather, Uncle Casimir, said he knew who my father was. He was the brother of Mister King, though.

Everything was getting more and more confusing.

Mama told me she would explain everything when she was done talking to the Alpha. I wanted to ask Uncle Nic and Uncle Casimir questions, but she asked me to wait for her and told them not to say anything more. She even said some curse words and really scary threats to Uncle Casimir.

I kicked the dirt as Uncle Nic and Uncle Casimir argued in front of me over something stupid again.

"Full means to the top," Uncle Casimir said, pointing at the bucket of poop the wort warrior was dragging with his mouth. "There are clearly still several inches of empty space to fill."

"I think it's full enough," Uncle Nic hissed. He glanced back at the guards from the pack trailing behind us. Beta Carlston was standing all grumpy in the middle of them with evil eyes aimed at Uncle Casimir.

"What about you, Triston?" Uncle Casimir looked back at me. "Do *you* think the bucket is full?"

I shrugged my shoulders. "I don't really care about the bucket." I looked over my shoulder, right at the warriors.

"You don't? Why not?"

"Because," I grumbled.

Mister Uncle Casimir looked where I was looking, then back at me. "Is it because of them? Do you want me to send them away?"

I shrugged my shoulders, staring at the dirty wort warrior with animal poop all over his hands. He didn't look like he felt bad at all for what he said about my mama. He had angry eyes too and would make mean faces at me when the others weren't looking. I'd make him do this for a month, but....

Uncle Nic bent down in front of me. "Are you worried about what Beta and the others are thinking of you?"

I shrugged again.

Uncle Nic sighed. "This guy had it coming. You did nothing wrong, Tris."

"I know," I mumbled.

"Then what's wrong?"

I waited, looking back one more time before I confessed, "I don't want anyone else being mean to mama."

"Ah," uncle Casimir nodded. "I see the predicament, but I truly do not believe you need to worry over the matter too greatly, dear nephew."

"Why?" I tilted my head up to look at him.

He smiled big. "Because pretty soon, no one will be able to harass your mother in any capacity. You too, for that matter." He looked back at the Beta and two warriors, then said, "Things are changing. No one will go against Alesta when this is all finished. She was fated to a destiny far greater than this."

It didn't feel like he was talking to me. He was saying the words, but it was like when Uncle Nic and mama had coded conversation where they thought I wouldn't understand they were really insulting one another.

Was Uncle Casimir being mean to our Beta? Or was he just mad at our pack all together?

He looked down at me again, his smile coming back as he handed me the red leash. "Do you truly not want to try?"

The wort warrior glared at me, like he was daring me not to take it.

Yeah, he wasn't finished picking up poop yet.

"Sure," I took the leash. After pulling it hard, yanking wort warrior to follow me, I said, "Come on, mutt. I see more poop over there."

Alesta

Queen Camellia, Ruth, Lukyan, Alpha Mikken and I were all sitting, or standing in Lukyan's case, around Alpha Mikken's office.

When we got here, I started falling into my secretarial habits and began gathering more chairs. Lukyan stopped me, pulling me to sit in one, then hovering behind me with his hands on my shoulders.

"If more seating is required, I'm sure the Alpha can arrange it." Alpha Mikken just growled aggressively, then stormed out before dragging in the two chairs from the other offices. To say he was in a bad mood would be an understatement.

I wasn't much happier. Not only because of the way my son had been treated, and the fact he almost died. I felt the dynamics of the pack changing. There was a division that I'd never experienced before.

The pack house was tense as we walked through it earlier. The whispers and glares were chilling. Even the staff I'd grown close to over the years who were eagerly calling me Luna just this morning were looking at me differently.

I felt so fucking blind. I knew my son was different and that would come with some challenges. I never expected him to be ostracized the moment his Lycan abilities bloomed.

What pissed me off more than anything was the reasons why he shifted early. I expected more understanding and compassion from adults, or at least from the warriors. This sort of treatment was beyond comprehension to me.

Alpha Mikken began tapping his fingers on his desk, his stare fixed on me and Lukyan standing behind me. Lukyan tightened his grip on my shoulders, sending fresh waves of pleasurable tingles down my body.

That made Alpha Mikken's face slip into a deep scowl.

"Pardon my rudeness, but wouldn't it be more appropriate for you to be standing with *your wife*, King Lukyan?"

I pinched the bridge of my nose when Lukyan squeezed me tighter while letting out a snarl. "Your rudeness is not pardoned."

Alpha Mikken pointed his hand at Camellia. "What of the rudeness you are showing your queen?"

Queen Camellia smirked, reaching for Ruth's hand. "I don't mind. Really."

Alpha Mikken seemed surprised. His mouth dropped, but he quickly recovered, instead looking angry. "Is this the way the capital is run now? Is our kingdom still governed by greed and debauchery? If so, we are all doomed. You're no better ruler than your father."

Lukyan snarled, moving around my chair like he was about to attack. Alpha Mikken stood, his eyes darkened with defiance.

"Enough!" I shouted, grabbing hold of Lukyan's arm. I stood abruptly, tugging on Lukyan's sleeve until he groaned and gave in, sitting in the chair I just vacated. Then I focused my glare on Alpha Mikken. "Before your pissing contest continues, I'd like to know more about why some warrior thought it was okay to degrade my son."

Alpha Mikken's lips pressed into a thin line, his tension deepening on his usually glowing expression.

"That never should have happened. I should have taken measures to prevent those who hold the strongest grudge against Lycans from interacting with your son."

Lukyan snorted. "Would that not also include you?"

Alpha Mikken fixed his gaze angrily on his king.

"Do you not agree? No one should hold a stronger grudge against our kind than yourself."

Alpha snarled, his claws extending from his nail beds. "I would *never* convict a pup for the crimes of- *GAH...*" He made a strangling noise, like we were being choked trying to finish his sentence. His face turned a bright crimson as he panted to catch his breath. Then he said, "I'd never blame Triston for *that.*"

"You expect me to believe that?" Lukyan asked, grabbing my waist and pulling me into his lap. I didn't fight him. I felt somehow this wasn't possession, but him trying to calm his anger. "Were you not targeting Alesta and hiding my son as revenge against my father? Can you honestly tell me that wasn't a motivating factor at all?"

Alpha Mikken slammed his claws on his desk. "It wasn't!"

"Truly?" Lukyan scoffed. "Given the extent you were willing to go by declaring Alesta your Luna upon our arrival, I'd say your intentions were clear."

"What are you talking about?" I asked Lukyan, then looked at Alpha Mikken. "What revenge? You were using me?"

"No! Never! Even before I knew... I knew who Triston's.... Fuck!" He slammed his hands down again. His eyes tore up at me, pain outlining the tension in their blue hues. "I'd never choose my Luna based on revenge. Never." He softly shook his head.

"I know that," I murmured. My eyes swept awkwardly around the room, and I suddenly became very aware of the tingle traveling up my spine from sitting on Lukyan's lap. "It... I know it was a farce to protect me. Being Luna wasn't what I was asking. I wasn't questioning your integrity."

Lukyan scoffed while Ruth and Camellia exchanged a look that had me feeling like I was left out of something. Alpha Mikken was even averting his gaze.

"My, she is quite naive when it comes to matters of the heart," Ruth murmured.

"What?" My brows knit as an awkwardness settled in the air.

"Oh, my," Camellia whispered.

Lukyan encircled my waist with his arm, pulling me back to his chest as a disgruntled noise came from his throat.

Alpha Mikken softly shook his head, looking entirely defeated. "It was never a farce for me." His blue eyes were drawing as they swept up to meet mine. "I would have made you Luna, Alesta. I still would, but I know that is impossible now."

My mouth opened slightly in shock. "B-but... I'm not your fated mate."

He laughed humorlessly. "No. No, you are not, but fated mates mean little to the Alpha's of Hallowed Moon Pack." He sank back down in his seat, then said, "Because of a curse, my lineage isn't granted a fated mate. We choose ours. Our goddess took the blessing of a fated pairing from the Alphas of this pack long, long ago."

So all those times he tried convincing me; they weren't for the sake of keeping Triston and me safe. Not solely. Alpha Mikken truly wanted me. *Me*. Why?

"But I have a child," I whispered. "I couldn't...." I left the thought suspended unfinished. Lukyan was tensing more and more behind me.

"I care for the boy," Alpha Mikken said with a sad smile. "I truly do. And watching you be a mother was one of the reasons I chose you."

"But she never even considered you," Lukyan huffed darkly, his arm tightening around me.

"Luk..." Camellia said disapprovingly.

He shrugged. "It's the truth."

Ruth spoke up, "Antagonizing the Alpha isn't what we came here to do."

"No? I came to put an end to this little game and take my family back from the Alpha trying to claim them."

Camellia chided, "Given his history, you, of all people, should be more understanding."

"I understand his men almost had my son killed," Lukyan snarled.

I still understood nothing. Cutting into their tirades, I asked, "If you were to take me as Luna, Triston would have been... been a candidate for Alpha."

Alpha Mikken nodded once. "He would have."

"But... the pack. They wouldn't have... I mean, they are so scared of him now as a little boy. That never would have worked."

"With enough work, it might have," Alpha Mikken stated. His sadness bled into his words. "The curse haunting the leaders of this pack could have been broken with him."

"Then find another single mother," Lukyan spat. "Alesta and Triston are going back to the capital with me."

Alpha Mikken glared at him. "You think that wise? As a married king, how will your subject react to a sudden heir from a werewolf mistress?"

I cringed at the word 'mistress'. Lukyan seemed to notice, grabbing my hand and holding it like he would never let it go.

"Alesta has always been my queen," his voice held such conviction. With a gentle hold of my chin, he turned my face towards his and said, "Since the moment the bond fell into place, she's reigned over my every thought, every emotion, and every desire. Each and every one of my breaths belongs to her and no one else." His topaz eyes burned with fire and his thumb glided over my stunned lips. "You were never a mistress. You are my queen."

His empty promises of the past... Now that I understood him, they didn't seem so empty any longer. I wanted to believe him, not because I wanted the useless title. Because I never truly stopped wanting *him*.

"Then what of your current queen?" Alpha Mikken asked sourly. "I doubt the council or your *father* would grant a divorce."

Camellia and Ruth's eyes gleamed at one another, a quiet understanding passing between them.

"A divorce between Lycan's is a gruesome process of cutting one's mark off the other. Luckily," Ruth pulled down the collar of his shirt, "*these* marks are the true ones while our King's are merely a spell used to trick the nobles."

Camellia had a mischievous glint in her eyes. "We'll handle the rest, paving the way for their return as true mates."

Alpha Mikken looked at Ruth and Camellia, seeing their relationship for what it was. The surprise played across his features, as I'm sure it did mine when I found out. Then he looked at Lukyan and me.

"Your bond was still in place?"

I nodded softly. "That was why I was unwell the day they came."

Lukyan growled. "And I, as well."

Understanding dawned on Alpha Mikken's face, but not an ounce of remorse. I still didn't know what revenge they were speaking of earlier, but I no longer felt asking Alpha Mikken to be wise. He seemed unable to tell me, anyway. The way he started to choke on his words, almost like he was commanded not to speak them...

I so desired to ask, but knowing my Alpha's true feelings and why he was trying so hard to protect me stopped me. I felt like a fool for missing so many signs and righting them off as having a protective Alpha. Niave was an understatement. My ignorance caused Alpha Mikken enough grief.

"Alesta," Alpha Mikken said, bringing me from my wandering thoughts. "Have *you* decided then? Or are these people deciding for you?"

"Decided what?"

"To go back with them?" His expression was hard as stone. "Have *you* decided that you want to go back to the capital? You and Triston?"

My stomach knotted at the thought of returning to that awful place. The factions and politics, and the awful treatment werewolves received from the noble Lycan houses.

But would it be any better staying here? My son was being shunned; feared for things out of his control. He was almost killed by rogues when he should have been protected by the ones that drove him away.

Would things be better in the capital?

What in the goddess's name should I do?

Chapter 28

Dirty Desk

I had no answer for Alpha Mikken. The longer I sat, mind racing on what to do, the more tense Lukyan became. His hands went rigid, squeezing into my flesh.

Alpha Mikken just stared, his eyes hard as glass as he lifted his chin indignantly.

Before the silence could stretch for too long, there was a knock at the door.

Alpha Mikken growled in annoyance. "We'll have to continue this later," he said before ripping open the door.

Gamma Kender was on the other side. "They're ready for you, Alpha."

"Let's go," he replied, his tone deeply grave.

Gamma Kender looked my way, his expression like he wanted to say something, but Alpha snapped at him to hurry up. Gammer Kender just frowned before walking away.

"Well," Camellia clapped her hands together after a few seconds. "That was fun."

I scoffed. "Yeah. Fun." I was just as confused as before, with the added burden of what to do now.

Ruth looked around the room, his eyes glowing in the dim lighting. His irises were moving, like swirling storm clouds in their purple hues.

When they landed on me, he smiled tightly, as if he knew what worries were raging in my mind.

"You seem more frustrated than before, Alesta."

"Nothing was clarified," I grumbled.

Camellia chuckled. "Some things were."

Lukyan let out a low growl, causing me to roll my eyes. I stood from his lap, now that Alpha was gone and I knew Lukyan wasn't in danger of tearing into him.

Leaning against the desk, I muttered, "I had no idea he felt that way."

"His intentions were clear," Ruth said softly. "I knew upon seeing him for the first time."

My face reddened. "I guess I was just blind then."

Camellia smiled sympathetically. "We become blind when we find our fated mates. You trusted him as your Alpha. He had a fine line to walk in his position of power. I can see how his actions could have come across as your leader's protection and goodwill."

A heavy sadness pressed against me. Alpha Mikken was a great Alpha. I respected him deeply. He took us in when we had nowhere to go. Any woman in my position would be lucky to have him as a chosen mate.

It just couldn't be me. Being near Lukyan again, I knew it could never be me.

"You truly did not know the bastard wanted you?" Lukyan snarled, glowering at me.

I frowned. "He's my Alpha. I thought he was just protecting me."

Lukyan's eyes darkened. "Being Lycan, this may be an ignorant question, but do Alphas usually go around kissing their pack members in the name of protecting them? Is that not abusing his position of power?"

Camellia gasped as Ruth shook his head at Lukyan like he was urging him to stop. Lukyan focused his attention on me. His mood darkened like my own.

"Does that bother you? The *married* man is bothered that an unmarried man kissed me; an unmated shewolf?"

"Unmated? Then what am I?"

"My *King*," I said, exaggerating the title. "A king who uses his *position of power* and our bond to force his kiss on me."

There wasn't much force involved, but the angry side of me didn't care.

Lukyan sneered, "Don't test me, Alesta."

"No, you don't test me," I growled. "*I* did nothing wrong."

He leaned forward, his elbows resting on his knees. "You're saying it wasn't wrong? Did you enjoy his lips? Is that why you defend him so and convict me, even after all that has occurred in *his* pack?" His expression grew dangerous, daring me to say more. Camellia and Ruth were watching anxiously. Lukyan's anger was fearsome.

He could scare anyone else, but not me.

"I defend him because he's my Alpha! He may have made a judgment error, but that doesn't change who he is."

"An opportunist? A defiant bastard who tried to take my mate and my child?!"

I angrily shook my head. "I'm not yours to take. Where you saw me inferior, at least he thought I was worthy of openly standing by his side! You should check your own past actions before coming after him *or* me!"

My temper was speaking. The past insecurities and resentment I held were coming out unfiltered. I didn't want Alpha Mikken. The thought never crossed my mind, but endless thoughts fueled by my rage at Lukyan were running through my head for years. His temper was the reason they were breaking free like this.

Lukyan slowly stood to his feet, prowling forward. His sweet breath fanned over my face. "It wasn't like that. You know that now."

Scoffing, I muttered, "Now. *Now* being the key word there. For seven fucking years I thought the worst of you, Lukyan. And through all that time, my Alpha supported me. There were seven years of trust built here. That was more than we," I pointed my finger into his chest, "ever had." I shook my head softly.

"*We* have a bond," he hissed.

I shook my head. He wasn't getting what I was saying. "Maybe because you're Lycan, you don't understand the *bond* between an Alpha and their pack."

The trust and devotion a pack holds for their Alpha is the foundation on which the pack stands. In return, the Alpha protects us, leads us, with our best interest in mind. I've witnessed the leadership of Alpha Mikken in my time here. He may have made mistakes recently with me, but he was a good man.

The same can not be said for the way the Lycan kingdom was run. There was little to no trust in the monarchy. Whereas werewolf leaders are selfless for their pack, Lycans had a history of selfish motives.

Lukyan was not his father. King Nabian was notorious for his barbaric ways. Such rumors had not yet spread about Lukyan, and I knew him well enough to know there was no reason there would be. But with the history between Lukyan and me, he had no right to belittle Alpha Mikken like he was.

Lukyan, as if to prove my point, ran his nose along my nape, sending waves of tingles through me. He was trying to calm me, like I had calmed him earlier by using our bond. He was trying to make me give in.

I refused, holding my stance. Growling through the shudders, I kept my temper in place.

Camellia slowly stood to her feet. "I think we should go…"

I glowered at Lukyan, pushing against his chest. "Maybe you should all go. I've got some work to do."

"Work?" Lukyan snarled in question, shadows casting over his fearsomely handsome face.

"I'm still the secretary of this pack."

Ruth coughed, then said, "Let's go, Cammy. We should do some damage control, anyway."

Camellia looked worried, but with a touch of urging from Ruth, they left together. She kept glancing back at us until she was out of view.

"You should leave too," I snapped at Lukyan. "I wouldn't want you to spend another moment in the office of a man you hate so severely, despite how much he's done for your child and his mother."

"I'm not going anywhere. You're not leaving my sight."

I scoffed loudly. "Fine. Stand there and watch the show. It will be thrilling to see the humble job of the woman not good enough for you to wed."

"Alesta!"

"Just leave!" I screamed, putting all my emotions into my trembling voice. My chest heaved as the rush subsided, and I felt nothing but exhaustion. I didn't want to argue anymore. I was tired of being angry. "Please. I just need to be alone."

He calmed visibly in the matter of seconds. With a much softer tone, he asked, "Can't you be alone in our room?"

"Our room?" I repeated in disbelief.

"Yes, *our* room. The room prepared for the *king* and *queen*."

I shook my head in disbelief. *I* prepared that room for the king and queen, and never once considered using it myself. "I'm not your queen, Lukyan."

"You are!" he hissed urgently. Both his hands cradled my face. "*You* are my queen, Alesta. Only you."

"No," I whispered, my voice sounding as tired as I felt. "I'm just the secretary of this humble pack, and I've got work to do."

Alpha Mikken made a mess in his anger. Papers were scattered about and his pens and such were overturned. The secretary part of me couldn't leave his office as it was. Or maybe it was because my mind was desperate for some kind of busy work to help process the worries jumbled up inside my head.

Lukyan's topaz eyes followed me as I walked around the desk. He made no motions to leave. His aura and scent perforated the air, not helping my thoughts untangle from him.

I straightened the correspondence with the other packs first, making sure they were organized the way Alpha Mikken liked them. Then, as I was picking up all the pens, Lukyan snarled and swept his large hands across the desk, tossing everything onto the floor.

"What the hell!"

He stalked around the desk, zeroing in on me. I took a step back, but he caught me before I could get far.

"I'm not going to stand back and watch you play Luna to that bastard!"

"I'm not playing his Luna! I'm his fucking secretary, you asshole!"

Lukyan's hand closed around my neck, pulling me towards him. His mouth was just a breath away from mine. "You wanna play secretary so badly? Fine." He grabbed my ass roughly, lifting me to sit on the desk. "Pretend I'm the Alpha you trust so much."

"What the hell are you- hmph..."

He aggressively covered my lips with his. Sparks shot through me, but the pleasure didn't stop me from fighting against him. He snarled as I bit down on his bottom lip hard enough I could taste the coppery tang of blood.

His fist knotted in my hair, pulling me back. Droplets of blood slipped down my chin. I ran my tongue over it, furious for so many reasons.

I swung my fist towards his face, but he caught it easily. Then the other. He had both my wrists in his hands as he pushed his body against mine, forcing me back against the hard oak surface.

His weight was like a prison. I knew I couldn't escape. I wasn't fully sure I wanted to escape. My entire body felt alive, an energy buzzing right under the surface of my skin.

"Get off me," I hissed.

"Oh, I'll get you off," he snickered darkly. "Thanks for the invitation."

"Fuck you!" I sneered.

His dark chuckles made my core heat in a maddening way.

"Not yet, my little mate. Soon. But not yet."

His hand glided down my side, leaving a trail of pleasure in its wake. When he got to my skirt, he bunched it in one hand, bringing it up over my thigh.

"What the hell are you doing?"

"Doing what you told me to." He inhaled deeply. His eyes darkened with lust. "Trust me, little wolf."

"Trust what?! This isn't a fucking game."

"Oh, but it is." His fingers trailed to my inner thigh, making me whimper as they skimmed my sensitive flesh. "This is all just a game, remember? I said to pretend I'm your trusted Alpha. You can be my dutiful secretary."

I flailed in anger, trying and failing to get free. "If you want to play my Alpha, then get the fuck off me!"

"Why?" he groaned, kissing along my tense jaw. My quivering reaction made his deep laughter spill out again. "Your body seems to enjoy it. You're reacting beautifully."

"I'm not reacting to my Alpha! I'm reacting to you!" I heaved, then growled in defeat. "As fucking aggravating as it is, I only react to you!"

Lifting his head, his topaz eyes glimmered into mine. A smug grin lifted his handsome features. I wanted to punch his beautiful lips... or kiss them. It was infuriating how mixed my emotions were.

"Good," he huffed, nuzzling into my neck. His fingers found my entrance, making me gasp. "Let's make sure he knows that."

Swiftly, two thick fingers slipped into me, pressing against my walls. My back arched off the hard surface, absorbing the shock of ecstasy blasting through my center.

"Fuck," I hissed. My hips automatically bucked against the friction of his palm.

"That's it, little wolf," Lukyan purred in my ear. "Feel me."

His fingers stretched me, working their magic in the roughest way. It had been seven years since a man touched me; seven years since *he* touched me. My body didn't forget. It reacted as if we were in the past.

"You're becoming so wet for me, little wolf," Lukyan husked. His breath tickled my skin. "This sweet cunt remembers, doesn't it? It remembers who it belongs to."

"Fuck you," I snarled, grinding into his touch.

The pleasure was explosive. Wave after wave of aching sweetness crashed relentlessly into me, washing away the years of depravity.

"Imagine," Lukyan whispered against my ear. "Imagine how fucking me would feel. Not my fingers, but my aching member pounding into this sweet cunt all through the night." His nose nuzzled my nape, making it hard to think of anything. "I'm going to stretch you nicely, molding your insides to the shape of me. My dick will be the last thing you feel every night, and the first thing you feel every morning."

"Lukyan...." I moaned, my build-up getting ready to explode.

"Cum for me, little wolf," he purred. "Give in to it, baby."

That was it. At his command, my legs shook as I screamed out my orgasm. His fingers pumped harder... faster.... He was pushing my climax as far as it could go.

When it was over, and the quivering in my legs subsided, he slowly pumped his fingers in and out of me a few more times. Circling them once, then twice, he then pulled them from under my skirt.

Moving the glistening digits between us, he held my gaze as he slowly inserted them into his mouth. I shuddered, hearing him moan as he sucked them clean.

"As delicious as I remember," he declared in smug satisfaction.

I narrowed my eyes at him as I tried to catch my breath. "Why would you do that?"

He lifted a brow incredulously.

"No. Why here, of all places?"

His dark chuckle was answer enough. "*My* mate is no longer his secretary. Now you both know."

Then he lifted me off the desk, ignoring my protest as he carried me away from the mess we made. Seeing the slickness left behind by his actions, I felt mortified. I never should have tried to clean.

Chapter 29

Blunt Son

Lukyan

"Let me go, you ass!" Alesta continued to twist and jerk, fighting my grip on her lithe body.

I couldn't let her go. Not after that. She'd hit me and run. Or worse.

When we got out to the busier hallways leading to the staircase, she stopped fighting me as much and resorted to hiding her face against my chest. Her groans of frustration were cute, but I couldn't enjoy them. Not when I was so worried about what she'd do when I eventually had to put her down.

I acted irrationally. I let myself snap. Hearing my mate being confessed to like that, and seeing the guilt on her expression, fear, an unfamiliar emotion reserved only for Alesta, just took over.

She didn't reject him. Not like I wanted her to. A fact that irked me more and more as she defended him while condemning me.

My rage tipped over the edge when she started touching his shit. The bastard in his tantrum wrecked his own desk. She had no reason to clean up his mess. Seeing the care she took in organizing his things, all while covering the Alpha's private space with her scent, broke my rationale completely.

The momentary satisfaction I felt making my woman cum all over the bastard's desk disintegrated as soon as my rational thought returned to me.

I was supposed to be winning her heart. Winning her trust. That wasn't the way to do it.

Her taste was still coating my lips from my fingers. My tongue still tingled with her decadent flavor.

I wanted more. I wanted all of her.

Now, I was scared that she would further distance herself from me. I was scared that she would reject me, ruining me completely.

Alesta

Humiliation clouded my mind with Lukyan's possessive display. I felt every set of eyes on us as he stormed to the guest wing of the pack house.

My relief when we arrived was short-lived as he walked angrily right to his room; the room Triston had laid in just hours ago.

Lukyan kicked open the door, not waiting for the omega tending the quarters to scurry for it.

"Hey! You're replacing that!" I screeched, hearing the crunching of wood. "You're a rude fucking bastard, just doing whatever the hell you want all the damn to- AHH!"

Lukyan growled after dropping me roughly on his bed. "Don't even think of leaving this room."

"Are you crazy! I'm not staying here!"

He snarled, leaning over my body while smothering me with his aura. "You wanted to be alone. This is your only chance." He ran his nose down my neck, caressing my nape. "Unless you want me to continue where we left off."

I kicked him hard in the gut, making him groan and buckle. Shock filled his eyes, and that was when I realized my mistake. He was trying to force me to submit. His aura would have been enough to make a normal werewolf cower helplessly, but it didn't affect me at all.

"How…"

"Get off," I hissed, rolling out from beneath him now that I had the opening. I glowered at him as I got to my feet. "Get out."

He stood to his full height, eyes fiery as he continued clutching the spot I'd kicked him.

"You don't leave. You don't go anywhere without me by your side."

I scoffed. "You don't own me."

A dark grin appeared on his face. He lifted his fingers to his nose, inhaling deeply. My face burned, realizing where those fingers had been.

With a snarl, I said, "Just because you got me a little wet doesn't mean you own me."

"A little?" Lukyan huffed. "Let's see if your beloved Alpha thinks it's *a little* when he sees what I left for him on his desk."

"You!…." I stabbed my finger towards him, stomping my foot in silent rage. "You ass! Goddess, you're fucking infuriating!"

"As are you."

I stomped around, looking for something to throw. Not finding anything satisfying enough, I resorted to tossing a pillow right for his head. He caught it with a clawed fist, tearing the thin fabric. Feathers flew everywhere, coming down like rain.

Throwing another pillow, the result was the same. White feathers clouded my view of him. When the air cleared, he was closer, clenching the torn pillowcases in his fist. He tossed both pillows to his side, sending the remaining feathers flying. He stalked towards me, the same look in his eyes as when he caught me in Alpha Mikken's office.

"Don't." I lifted my hands. "Stop, Lukyan! Stop!"

"Why should I?"

"Because!" I screamed. "You're just going to make me hate you more!"

That halted his steps. His expression changed from fierce to stunned. "You hate me?"

No. "Yes," I lied. "You're doing the same as before. Only doing what's best for you. You have no consideration for me. No respect or interest in even considering what I want. Why wouldn't I hate you?!"

He looked horrified, fear igniting his topaz eyes. Guilt took the breath from me. I didn't truly mean half of what I said.

"Lukyan, I..."

"I'll go," he whispered, cutting me off. "Don't say it. Please. I'll go."

Say what? What did he not want me to say?

He backed away, moving slowly, like he was trying to prevent me from getting spooked. As he rushed to close the doors, it suddenly dawned on me what he feared.

He thought I was going to reject him. The bond was throbbing in my chest, reflecting his emotions.

I've never seen Lukyan afraid. It shook me.

I had no intention of submitting to him. I wasn't going to stay in this room... But I suddenly couldn't find it in me to do anything to make the fear return in his eyes.

Nic was with Triston. I'd do as Lukyan said for now and stay here until Nic brought my son back. For now, I'd use this time alone to reflect and decide on what to do.

"Mama! Mama!" Triston came skipping into the bedroom some hours later. "Mama! Do you know what we did?!"

I smiled at his enthusiasm, but my smile faltered when I saw Lukyan looking in from the sitting room.

"Mama!"

Tearing my eyes from Lukyan's, I forced my smile in place while turning my attention back to my son. "What did you do?"

"I walked him like a dog! That wort warrior! He had to carry the pail and pick poop up with his hands! It was so much fun!"

I cringed, my idea of fun not involving poop at all. I wasn't sure how I felt about Casimir's choice of punishment for the one that insulted my child.

"You know what else?! Uncle Casimir said he'd get me a real dog! One that I can walk whenever I want!"

"Did he, now?" I narrowed my eyes at the dark-haired prince looking in beside Lukyan. Lukyan frowned at his brother too.

"Yeah! A big dog! He said real dogs can't pick up poop though. But that's okay. That part was stinky anyway." Triston wrinkled his nose.

"I bet," I muttered, glaring at Casimir again. I didn't appreciate him promising Triston a living creature to care for without consulting me.

"Mama?" Triston tapped my face.

I smiled at his touch. A lot of my anxiety from the last few hours thinking alone in this room was leaving me by the power of his little hands.

"Yes, baby?" I placed my hand over his.

He frowned, then looked back at the door before looking back at me. "Um, you said... you said you'd...." He glanced back at the door again, then leaned in and whispered in my ear, "You said you'd tell me stuff when I got back. Can you tell me now?"

He wanted to know what was going on with Lukyan and me. I knew he was confused after hearing that I had a fated mate, and it was none other than our king. I wonder if Nic kept Casimir in line so he didn't say more to Triston.

"Did Uncle Niccola or Mr. Casimir say anything more to you?"

Triston tapped his finger on his chin. "Uncle Casimir told me to call him uncle. And he promised me a dog."

"Nothing else? He didn't give you any more picture books or anything like that?"

Triston looked guilty and quickly shook his head.

I nodded, then glanced up at the two men standing in the

doorway, wondering how to explain who they were to my boy. It seems as if Casimir already went ahead and declared himself Triston's uncle. Did he also tell Triston, in his roundabout ways, that Lukyan was his father?

Lukyan locked his gaze with mine; his topaz irises imploring me. There was such longing in his expression. My heart ached for so many reasons.

"Mom?" Triston murmured, then his eyes followed mine. A little frown formed as he stared at Lukyan. Lukyan seemed to be holding his breath.

"Do your questions have to do with King Lukyan?" I whispered softly.

Triston hesitated, then nodded firmly twice.

Pressing my lips together, I looked at his father again. Then I asked, "Do you want him to be here so you can ask him yourself?"

Triston watched Lukyan for another few seconds, tilting his head as he studied him. "Is... Is it okay to ask mister king stuff like that?"

I laughed softly. "You can ask him anything you want, baby. I don't think he'll mind."

"I won't." Lukyan took a careful step forward. "Ask me anything."

Lukyan's desperate enthusiasm almost made me smile. He pissed me off plenty, but I could see how much he wanted to be close to his son. I didn't want to deprive either of them of the relationship I know they both want so desperately.

"Okay," I whispered roughly, running my fingers through my son's hair. Looking back at Lukyan, I nodded. "Come in."

His relief was palpable.

"No fair," Casimir grumbled as Lukyan started to close the crooked-hanging door in his face.

"Wait," Triston hurried to say. He looked nervous for a moment, then set his shoulders and turned to me. I thought he was about to ask Casimir to stay here too, but instead he asked, "Can I talk to mister king on my own?"

My mouth opened in surprise. "Without me?"

Triston nodded. His mind was made up. I knew that stubborn look in his eyes.

"Ha!" Casimir chided from outside the room. "Join me in the reject room, Alesta! I'll pour the tea!"

My gaze locked with Lukyan's. Anxiety of leaving my baby alone with him flooded me, but I could see the anxiousness in him, too.

He wouldn't hurt our son. Not physically. I was more worried about the damage he would do if the two became close, and then the kingdom tore them apart. Like what happened between Lukyan and me.

***

Lukyan

This was unexpected. More unexpected than sitting alone in a room with my son was that Alesta allowed it.

I could see the struggle on her face as she left with my brother. She lingered her eyes on Triston, as if she was hoping he would change his mind, but his jaw was set in that stubborn way that hers often did.

Triston directed me to sit on the bed, then went to grab the chair to move over beside it. I felt the roles were reversed here. I was feeling like a child who was about to be interrogated for some wrongdoing. Despite that, I would only do what Triston directed me to do.

Triston was sitting in front of me with a stoic expression and his arms crossed over his chest. I felt like I was being scrutinized. Nerves had my breathing coming unevenly as my hands grew damp.

I was the fucking Lycan king. My presence would make children quake and hide under their mother's skirts on the best of days.

Not my son. He wasn't showing any discomfort. He was making it clear he was running this show.

Pride bloomed inside of me. Alesta raised him well. That was plain to see. I suddenly realized what that bastard Alpha meant when he said watching Alesta be a mom was one reason he chose her. She raised a leader. There was no doubt about that.

"So," Triston said, sitting up straighter. "You're my mama's mate?"

I smiled at his straightforwardness. "Yes. I very much am."

"Hmm…" He tapped his fingers on his arm and lifted his chin. "Are you sure?"

His expression made me more nervous than before. "Yes… Yes, I'm sure."

Triston shook his head, tightening his lips into a thin line. "I don't know, mister king. I don't know if I believe you."

My brows knit together. Every muscle in my body grew tight as my stomach turned. "Why wouldn't you believe me? I'd never lie about that."

"Because," he leaned forward, almost aggressively. "You're married, mister king. I don't know how you can be my mama's mate if you already have one."

Chapter 30

Night Visit

Mouth agape, I stared at my son, stunned by his words. Triston sat there, face stoic and unwavering. His presence was commanding, even at his young age. Personal shame mixed with paternal pride in me.

"Triston, I... there are things that you can't possibly understand. Adult problems a boy of six couldn't possibly-"

"Please," Triston groaned, rolling his eyes. "I may be a kid, but I'm not stupid. Uncle Casimir told me enough for me to understand."

I swallowed the knot lodged in my throat. "What did Casimir say?"

Triston shrugged. "That he knows my father. He's really close to him. And he kept calling me nephew. I don't think he was saying it like Uncle Nic does either. He meant I was his nephew, and as far as I know, he only has one brother. Isn't that right, *King* Lukyan?"

So he knew. This wasn't a matter of Triston getting an understanding of the situation with my marriage and my mate bond with his mother. He already came to his own conclusions.

He was confronting me. He was accusing me to my face of his suspicions with a line clearly drawn in the sand.

"What are you asking me, son?"

Triston cringe at the term. For a split second, he looked his age again; vulnerable and anxious. Then his stoic facade slipped back into place.

"I think you know."

I remained quiet, letting my aura leak just enough to make him uncomfortable so he would continue. It wasn't enough to cause him pain. I wanted to hear him say it. If he was accusing me of something, he needed to voice it with his own words.

He winced, then squirmed a bit in his chair. When the facade was gone and back was the anxious little boy, I pulled my aura back, waiting patiently for him to continue.

Triston let out a frustrated growl, then blurted out, "Are you my father?!"

I couldn't help a satisfied smirk from lifting the corner of my lips. I had no issue answering this question.

With a voice dripping with pride, I declared, "Yes. Yes, Triston. I am."

His next question made all the momentary gratification fade to dust.

Crossing his arms, he sat back and asked, "Then, who did you betray? Your queen, or my mother?"

Alesta

Sitting in the next room, I couldn't help but stare anxiously at the door. My fingers drummed restlessly on the bench of the settee.

Casimir sat across from me, chuckling to himself. "Nervous, are we?"

"Shut up," I muttered. I wasn't in the mood for his mouth right now.

My dark mood just made Casimir all the more delighted. "Ah, I missed you, Alesta. I really did."

"Why don't we go outside and get reacquainted a bit better than?" I'd love nothing more than to beat the arrogance right out of this prince.

"Don't tempt me with a good time." His eyes shimmered over his teacup.

"Don't you have *princely* things you should be off doing? Skirts to get under and stuff like that? The pack has a storage shed behind the warrior building. I'm sure you could have all sorts of *good times* in there."

He sighed. "Sadly, sheds no longer hold my interest. I haven't set foot in mine since the day you were last there."

My eyes widened in shock. "That was seven years ago."

"Indeed, it was," he sighed reminiscently. "It's been a long, dry seven years."

"Why? Did it rot off? Did one of your partners cut it off in a rage?"

"How rude. My body is a national treasure. It's very much in working order. I just remained abstinent... For personal reasons."

My face must have shown my shock, because he chuckled as he studied me.

"Your surprise is nearly insulting."

"Nearly?" I raised an eyebrow.

"Eh," he shrugged, downing the last of his drink, which I was starting to suspect was not tea. "Insulting, but not surprising."

He tapped his finger on the empty teacup, staring absently into space. Then he asked, "Were you ever curious *how* Niccola and I kept a line of communication over the years?"

I shrugged. "You're a prince. I was sure you had spies or whatnot at your disposal."

"Ah, that would be troublesome, considering any spy *I* enlisted would ultimately be under the command of my father."

I furrowed my brows, unsure what other method they could have used. The only other thing I could think of was.... No. No. I would have seen a mark on Niccola if they had done *that*. There's no way....

Casimir chuckled softly. "I can see your mind working, Alesta. Don't hurt yourself. If you have suspicions, just ask."

"You want me to *ask* the *insulting* questions spinning in my mind?"

He smirked. "When have you ever held yourself back?"

I scoffed. "I hold myself back quite a bit."

"Are you holding yourself back right now?"

Glancing at the door to Lachlan's guest room again, I sighed. "Very much so."

"Hmm. Maybe I should allow you to take me outside after all. Maybe then I could get a glimpse of Niccola since your Alpha called him away."

Staring ahead, I weighed my next words carefully before I asked, "You like Nic, don't you?"

Casimir scoffed. "That's an understatement. I find Niccola to be the most amusing being I have ever encountered."

"That doesn't answer my question."

He returned my gaze, his expression uncharacteristically serious for once. "Of course I *like* him. Deeply. What man wouldn't hold affection for their mate?"

My mouth dropped. "You're joking."

Casimir scoffed. "I'm most definitely not. I wouldn't remain abstinent for no reason."

"But... How?" I still couldn't believe it. "You... you didn't react in the throne room, and he doesn't have a mark. Neither do you."

"I never said we were fated mates," Casimir said carefully. "And there is not a limit on where a mark can be held."

I was confused about what he meant until he started to rub his inner thigh while giving me a pointed look. I'll be damned. No wonder Niccola hated being naked around anyone.

I just couldn't believe Niccola *let* Casimir mark him. He's always been so adamant about finding his fated mate.

Dozens of other questions popped into my head, but before I could voice any of them, the door suddenly burst open and Triston came storming out.

"Tris? Are you okay-"

"Let's go, mama," he sneered, throwing a deadly look over his shoulder. "I wanna go home."

"Why?" I stared over his head at Lukyan, who was sitting on the bed with his head hung in his hands. "What happened?"

"Nothing," Triston spat. "I don't just don't want to be here anymore. I don't want you here either."

Lukyan looked so dejected; so broken that it struck me deeply. It was like I could feel whatever pain he was feeling, but I did not know what that pain was coming from. I rubbed at my chest as it got uncomfortably tight.

"Let's go," Triston commanded, grabbing my hand and pulling me towards the exit.

Casimir looked just as shocked as I felt. Lukyan didn't lift his head. Even as we left.

When we were in the hall all alone, I asked, "What happened? Did he say something you didn't like?"

"Oh, yeah," Triston growled.

When he didn't elaborate more, I asked, "Did he hurt you?" I knew Lukyan wouldn't physically, but if he said something....

"No, but he..." He paused, then growled under his breath, "I just want to go home."

"Okay, baby," I whispered, resting my hand on his stiff little shoulders. "Let's go home."

Lukyan

"Holy, goddess. What happened in here?" Casimir came striding into the bedroom, his hands tucked into his pockets. "My little nephew left in quite the rage."

My fingers dug into my temple punishingly. "He's smart," I muttered. "Too damn smart."

"He's got quite the temper as well." Casimir chuckled, "I'd wonder where he inherited that from, but both his parents are quite hot-headed."

Growling, I sneered, "I'm not in the mood for your nonsense right now."

He sighed. "No. I imagine you're not. Instead of winning over the mother, now you must win the trust of the mother and son."

I groaned, the task seeming impossible.

"Cheer up, brother. You did save the boy. That has to count for something towards Alesta. And I didn't miss the scent wafting from you both earlier."

I automatically smelled my fingers, remembering what I did to her in the Alpha's office. Her scent still lingered, as did the shame.

"So," Casimir murmured, staring at his nail beds. "What happened with your son?"

Huffing, I shook my head. "He's too intelligent, is what happened. And he's fiercely protective of his mother."

"Like father, like son. But, really, now. An actual answer..."

He left his question hanging in the air, looking at me expectantly.

Relenting, I confessed, "He asked who I betrayed; Alesta or Camellia."

"Ah," he nodded, then pursed his lips.

I recognized his pride, because I felt it too for Triston until it came back to bite me in the ass. Honestly, I still felt pride in how strongly Triston cares for Alesta. I just wish I knew how to convey the reasons for the choices I made that affected his mother to a boy of six years old.

"You know," Casimir mused, sitting in the chair Triston had used. He crossed his legs as he rested his finger on his chin. "Alesta didn't seem opposed to you as much as you may suspect. Niccola told me on many occasions that it was Camellia she was worried about."

"What are you saying?"

He shrugged. "Winning Alesta may not be as difficult as we originally thought. Considering you two have already... been intimate, I'd say you're doing alright."

I cringed internally. Maybe a little externally too.

"What? Why are you making that face?"

I shook my head. "You don't need to know." I got up and started moving towards the door.

"Where are you going?" Casimir asked.

I paused, realizing I didn't know. "Come," I commanded. "Show me where their home is."

Alesta

"You truly don't want to tell me what happened?" I asked for the hundredth time tonight as I tucked Triston into bed.

He vehemently shook his head. "I just don't like him. He's not a good mate."

A million thoughts ran through my mind, but I voiced none. Instead, I brushed my fingers through my son's hair, wondering if letting him leave on such a grim note with Lukyan was the right choice.

"Mama?" Triston brought my attention back to him.

"Yes, baby?"

He hesitated, then asked, "We're staying here in the pack, right? We're not going to leave with... with the king, are we?"

I answered honestly, "I don't know, baby. Why? Would you want to leave?"

He looked conflicted, then said, "No. I don't want to leave."

Now I felt conflicted. I saw the way the pack looked at my son. The fear in the warriors' expressions after Triston shifted scared me. I didn't get anywhere talking with Alpha Mikken about it. I left that office more confused than ever... for many reasons.

"You've had a long day," I whispered, fixing a smile on my face. I kissed his forehead and said, "Get some sleep. We can talk more about this in the morning."

He nodded, snuggling deeper into his covers. As I was about to close his door, he spoke through the darkness, asking one more heavy question.

"Mama. Do you hate my dad?"

I paused, but only briefly, due to surprise.

"No," I said truthfully. "How could I ever hate him? He gave me you."

Triston, seeming satisfied with that answer, smiled and said, "Okay, mama. Good night."

After closing his door, I pressed my head against the frame, wondering what to do now.

The apartment was a wreck. When we first got home, there were omegas that had just begun to clean on Alpha Mikken's orders. I didn't like the looks they kept giving my son, so I firmly sent them away.

Triston may not want to leave this place, but I don't know how we are going to stay. Not with things as they were.

I started to clean, tidying the sitting room first, then moving to the kitchen that had been overturned by that asshole warrior while he was acting like a dog.

As I passed the door carrying a pile of ripped linen, I heard a rustling on the other side. It was probably someone just passing by, but something inside me told me to check.

Carefully, I opened the door just a crack and looked out, only to throw it open in surprise at seeing who was on the other side.

"Lukyan?" I hissed, taking a careful glance over my shoulder towards Triston's room. "What are you doing here?"

His giant frame was leaning against the wall across from me. The dark shadows cast by the dimly lit hall made his topaz eyes shine in contrast. He looked exhausted, but still as handsome as ever. Maybe even more so since he wasn't wearing the stiff outfits befitting a king. He was dressed comfortably, as I remembered he used to when we were alone.

His nose flared as he took a deep breath, then he visibly relaxed. "I'm just standing here, Alesta." His low, gravely tone made my heartbeat quicken. He glanced at the bundle of torn linen in my hands, the remnants of what used to be my curtains. Lifting a brow, he asked, "Doing laundry? At this time of night?"

"No," I huffed, tossing the pile to the side and out of sight. "I was just cleaning before bed. Now, what are you really doing outside of my home *at this time of night?*" I asked again, mockingly.

He shrugged his giant shoulders. "I told you, I'm just standing here."

"Standing there? Outside my door?"

"You're very inquisitive this evening."

I scoffed, finding his arrogance irritating.... And also a little provocative. It was like the moment in Alpha's office when I wanted to be enraged, but found my body betraying me instead. I bit my lip and resisted the urge to press my thighs together at the memory.

Damn it, Lukyan. I hadn't felt lust in years, and now it was overtaking me at the worst of times.

Sighing, I asked, "Do you plan on standing there all night?"

The way he lifted his shoulders and tilted his face in smug detachment didn't help my dilemma any.

I glanced back again, focusing my ears on Triston's room, making sure his breathing was still even and steady. I knew what I was about to do could be a great mistake, but I couldn't stop myself. Maybe it was because the drama of the day had ended and wasn't carrying the same malice I held earlier. More than likely, it was the racing questions of his talk with Triston that triggered this...

Most likely, it was the bond between us, still tethered between us, causing me to follow through with thoughts I normally wouldn't even entertain.

With only a moment of hesitation, I asked in a quiet murmur,

"Instead of standing out here all night, would you like to come in?"

Chapter 31

Dreams

Seeing Lukyan in my home was surreal. His imposing frame looked gigantic compared to my tiny apartment. His room in the princes' wing of the palace was larger than my entire home. With remnants of the disaster the warrior had made still visible in many places, I felt self-conscious watching Lukyan looking around my meager home, taking it all in.

"Um, why don't we go in here so we can speak without waking Triston," I whispered, ushering Lukyan towards my room.

He lifted a brow questioningly, and it wasn't until he walked past me into my tiny bedroom that I realized I'd just invited my mate into the most intimate setting imaginable. Considering what had happened the last time we were left in a room alone, I'm sure he thought I was mad.

Maybe I was mad. Normally, I would never have considered inviting Lukyan in, but here he was, wandering around the few feet of free space around my bed. My bed, which was less than half of the one we used to share.

"So, this is where you've lived." He ran his fingers over a picture on my wall. It was one Triston had drawn in school of the two of us. His topaz eyes held such intensity while staring at the crude lines.

"He drew that two years ago," I whispered, a warm smile forming on my lips. "He was upset that he couldn't find a brown color for our hair. He mixed black and yellow, thinking it might turn brown and it turned green instead."

Lukyan laughed softly. "He treasures his mother."

Emotions burned behind my eyes suddenly. Maybe because I never thought I'd be telling Triston's father anything about him. It felt like a relief seeing the pride on Lukyan's face. "He's my greatest love."

He turned to look at me, his topaz eyes shining like mine. A sad smile set on his handsome features. "I'm glad."

The small room suddenly felt smaller in the still pause between us. The air was thick, causing me to feel warm. He held my stare for another few moments, then looked around at the other pictures and trinkets I had saved from Triston over the years.

When his eyes landed on a vase of dried flowers by my bed, they narrowed ever so slightly.

"Those flowers…"

"Were picked by Triston," I quickly said. Lukyan's expression quickly relaxed. "Nic helped him gather them and I dried them. I wanted to save them forever."

Lukyan's stoic expression made my heart quicken; even more so when he sat on the edge of my bed.

"Has the Alpha ever given you flowers?"

I hesitated for only a second before shaking my head. "No. The only thing he'd ever given me was that dress." I pointed to the garment hanging on a rack in the corner; the one from that first dinner.

His eyes darkened, which was the only visible sign of his displeasure. If I hadn't known Lukyan, I would have missed it.

"I still have all the dresses and gowns I'd gifted you," he said. "I still have everything."

"Why would you do that?"

"Because," he whispered, his tone deep and heavy. "I'd never given up."

He'd never given up on finding me. That meant more to me than any dresses ever could.

I'd never had a chance to wear any of the elegant outfits Lukyan had his aid deliver to me in the princes' wing. I was a tribute. Roaming the palace freely, like the noble Lycan ladies dressed to impress the highest of nobility, wasn't an option for me. The most if ever done was try them on for Lukyan's satisfaction.

If I returned with the royal inspection, would I be able to wear those dresses at last?

Before I could ask that, I needed to know something else. "What happened between you and Triston?"

His brows pulled down, casting shadows over his face as he looked away. He looked angry, but I knew he wasn't. He was ashamed.

"The boy... He's got the mind of someone many times his age."

An involuntary snort escaped me. "I know. I'm in trouble with him quite often." There was a momentary pause, then I asked, "Was it because of me?"

"Huh." The shadows around his eyes got darker as he looked to the ground. "He's quite protective of you."

"I know," I whispered. Carefully, I sat beside him and took his face in my hand, forcing him to look at me. The sparks of our bond made my voice gentle as I asked, "What is he trying to protect me from?"

The frown lines crinkling the corners of his eyes were evidence of his immense sadness. I could almost feel his pain. "He asked who betrayed. You or Camellia."

That was so like Triston to put the pieces together like that. "What did you tell him?"

His guilt was straining every one of his handsome features. "The truth. That I betrayed you."

My heart contracted at the agony I felt in his voice. Confessing that to Triston.... I couldn't imagine how much worse he felt then, considering Triston's reaction.

"But you didn't. Not like that."

Lukyan shook his head while clasping my hand against his cheek. "But I did. I hid the truth from you, Alesta. I hid everything." He took a deep, shuddering breath. "It was betrayal. I wish it didn't take confessing to my son for me to realize it."

And just like that, I felt the cracking of the walls I'd built between us. His admission was all it took.

"I'm sorry, Alesta," Lukyan whispered roughly. "I truly am."

"I know." The coarse hairs of his short beard tickled my fingers. His topaz eyes were intensely staring into mine with so much remorse, I had no doubts about the sincerity of his words. Not anymore. "I know."

He kissed the inside of my palm as a single tear slipped down his cheek. It was silent for a minute, and then he rasped, "I don't want my son to hate me."

I didn't either. Not after today.

"Come," I whispered, sliding back on the bed. He watched me settle in against the headboard, waiting until I patted the empty spot beside me, just big enough for him to fit if we pressed close. "Don't you want to hear more stories about your son?"

His answering smile told me I made the right choice inviting him in. The bed dipped as he laid beside me, wrapping his arm around my back and pulling me impossibly closer to his side. I nestled in, letting the sparks soothe whatever stress had lingered from the day.

"Thank you," he whispered into my hair before kissing the top of my head.

I smiled at how normal the affection felt.

"Alesta," a full, husky voice groaned desperately in my ear. "You're mine." Topaz eyes shone down at me with intensity. "All mine."

"Yours," I moaned, arching off the bed. "All yours."

"Mine," he growled desperately, sinking deeper.

His rough passion vibrated through my limbs. My racing heart matched his own. As we drowned, our bodies moving in aggressive synchrony, this powerful surge built deep in my core. It suddenly burst through my veins, making my skin and eyes glow.

"Mine," Lukyan moaned deeply. "My Alesta. My queen. My goddess."

Fire erupted in my gums. Fangs elongated as he declared over and over that I was his.

"Mine," a snarl ripped out of me, possessive and domineering.

Squeezing his throat, his eyes shone like fire as I turned his head. His bulging body vibrated atop mine as my teeth scraped across his thick neck.

The explosion of energy that overtook me when my fang pierced through his skin stole the air in my lungs. Every inch of my body, inside and out, felt like it was coming alive for the first time.

"Alesta," Lukyan's husky voice cried. Opening his eyes, a wave of brilliant washed over us, making everything disappear in a blinding glow.

"This is the way it was supposed to be," an ethereal voice echoed in the brilliance. A woman's voice I'd never heard before, but at the same time, sounded so familiar. "It's time, my child. Time to begin...."

∞∞∞

"What are you doing here?" A tiny snarl caused me to jerk awake from the strange dream. "I said stay away from my mama!"

My eyes flew open to see Triston standing at my door, glaring at the space above me. I turned, and that's when I remembered what had happened last night.

I'd fallen asleep telling Lukyan stories about our son, lying on his chest no less. Maybe that was what caused my usual dream of him to morph into something else. Something full of hope. Even if it had a strange ending....

Lukyan, with his bed head and sleep-worn face, looked like a spooked deer. His wide eyes, I'd never known to show fear, looked scared of our six-year-old son at that moment.

"Get out," Triston growled. "Get off my mama!"

Technically, I was on Lukyan. The fearless Lycan king looked lost in what to do. He could push me off, or ignite his son's wrath further. Either option wasn't a real option for the conflicted man.

"Triston, it's okay," I said calmly as I sat up, putting space between Lukyan and me.

"No, it's not! I told you! I said I don't want him to be your mate!" The bed shifted as Lukyan cringed at our son's words. I swear I could feel the blow hurting him as if his pain were my own.

Things couldn't continue like this. It was becoming increasingly clear to me that the Hallowed Moon Pack couldn't be our home for much longer. Not after the events of yesterday. Reaching behind me, I grabbed Lukyan's hand and gave it a gentle, reassuring squeeze. The tingles bloomed and the tension in his grip became less rigid.

"Triston," I said carefully as he glared at where my hand joined his father's. "I think it's time all three of us sat down and had that talk."

Triston

Crossing my arms, I gave stupid Mister King the meanest look I could. Mama made me sit across from him, even though I said I didn't want to look at his stupid sad face.

Why was he sad? He was the wort that was mean to mama. He said it himself. Why is mama letting the wort stay here? Why was he sleeping in her bed?

My chest felt stuffy as I gritted my teeth, and my growl came out again. I should have slept in mama's bed with her. Then he couldn't have.

"Stop glaring," mama scolded me, giving me a stiff look. She set a cup of chocolate milk in front of me, then handed tea to Mister Jerk King. "It's not up to royal standards, but it's all I have."

The jerk smiled at my mama gratefully. His eyes were all sparkles and sunshine, like mama just handed him a gift more precious than tea.

"Thank you." He took a sip, then said, "it's delicious, Alesta."

My chest got stuffier when mom smiled back at him the way she always smiles at me.

"I want tea too," I demanded.

She gave me one of her disapproving looks. "You said you wanted chocolate milk."

"Well, now I want tea."

"I can trade you." Mister Jerk-Wort King set his cup on the table between us and slid it towards me.

I growled, "I don't want your tea. I want my own." I pushed his cup aside, making it spill all over the table.

"Triston!"

My heart skipped like it always did when mama yelled at me. I felt a little sorry, but not enough to admit it.

Mama picked up the cup and started to carry it to the kitchen, but she didn't get far before Mister Jerk-Wort-Stupid King stopped her.

"I got it," Mister Jerk-Wort-Stupid King said softly, getting up and squeezing my mama's arms reassuringly before walking the cup to the kitchen.

Mama turned her mad face back towards me. Wiping her hands down her skirt, she said, "You're acting out ends here. You're being incredibly rude."

"He's rude! I told him to stay away!"

"Triston," she sighed and pinched the space between her eyes. "Baby, this can't go on. It can't. You don't like him because you think he betrayed me. Correct?"

I glared towards the kitchen where Mister Jerk-Wort-Stupid-

Buttface King was looking in drawers for a rag, acting like he wasn't listening. I knew he was. He was opening the same drawer over and over again.

As if the buttface could tell I was looking at him, he turned around to look back at me. Our eyes met, and even though I was mad at the thing he did to my mom, my heart hurt at the same time. I always wanted to know who my dad was, but mom never wanted to tell me. Now I know why. Because he hurt her.

I didn't want him to hurt her again.... Or me.

"Triston?"

My chest got tighter. I had to look away from the Jerk-Wort-Stupid-Buttface King. It was making my heart hurt too much. "Why do you want to be near someone who already hurt you?"

Mama's face tilted to the side. Her smile was a little sad as she said, "Because he's my mate... and your father. And I hurt him too when I left."

My chest felt stuffier, making me uncomfortable, but I tried to keep my anger on my face. "You left because he married that pretty lady." I winced, not meaning to say to mom that Jerk-Wort-Stupid-Buttface King's wife was pretty.

Mom didn't look mad, though. She laughed a little and said, "That pretty lady's name is Camellia."

"I don't care," I muttered, crossing my hands and looking away. "If he had you as a mate, why did he take her for a mate instead?"

"Baby," she murmured, then came around and knelt beside me. "There's a lot more to what happened than you know. Luk-" She paused, smiling sadly. She looked at Jerk-Wort-Stupid-Buttface King, then whispered, "Your father... He made the choices he did for a reason. As did I." Mama then looked back at me with an expression that made my chest stuffy again. I couldn't keep my angry face any more. Not when mama looked at me like that. "Your father is not your enemy, and neither is Camellia. She's really nice, but more importantly, she isn't his mate."

"She's not?" I asked quietly.

"No, baby. She's not."

"She has a mate," Jerk-Wort-Stupid-Buttface King said as he came up to the table with the rag. "She has a mate, and it's not me."

"You're lying," I growled.

Mama touched my face. "No, he's not. She and her mate told me themselves."

The stuffiness in my chest eased up a little bit until I looked over mama's shoulder to Mister King. Then my heart hurt again. All the nights in the past when mama would have nightmares, I'd wondered who she was crying about. I thought she was crying because whoever 'Luk' was had hurt her. Seeing the way they looked at each other now, I wasn't sure that was the case. Mama wouldn't sleep in the same bed as someone who hurt her.

Mama softly cut into my thoughts, "Spend the day with him today, Tris. He's not our enemy. Get to know who your father really is."

Chapter 32

Ostracized

"How's your breakfast?" Mister Buttface King asked me for the third time.

"Gross," I muttered with a mouth full of waffles. They weren't gross. These may be the best waffles I'd ever had. They were made by the Lycan's royal chef. But I wasn't going to admit they were better. Not with Mister Stupid-Buttface King watching me with that hopeful look in his stupid eyes.

He looked like he wanted to ask more, but instead pressed his lips together and knotted his napkin in his grip. I made him nervous. Good.

We were dining in the royals' guest suite instead of the dining hall. I was hopeful when we left home I'd at least get to see my friends after being stuck at home for days, but Mister Stupid-Wort-Buttface King brought me here instead.

I don't know where mama went. She whispered something about tying up loose ends to Buttface, but I don't know what that means. She helps me tie my shoes every morning. Maybe she has to tie the Alpha's shoes, too. She is his secretary. I'm not sure what exactly a secretary does, but she said she helps the Alpha. Tying shoes is helpful. I don't know if I like her doing that for anyone but me.

I wonder if she's tied Mister Stupid-Wort-Jerk-Buttface King's shoes before. He'd probably be jealous if he heard she tied my shoes every morning.

Just as I was about to rub it in his stupid face, another bedroom door opened, and a man with weird eyes and long hair walked out. I'd seen him around the suite a few times yesterday, but this was my first time really looking at him.

His eyes were more than weird. It was like they were moving, swirling in on themselves. I'd never seen eyes like his before.

The man looked startled to see us sitting at the table. "Oh. Why, hello there. I thought you'd spent the night out, my king."

"He did," I growled, glaring at Buttface.

Buttface nodded curtly at the guy. "We're just here for breakfast."

"Ah," the man nodded, like he understood why we were here and not eating with my friends. "I suppose it would be particularly unwise to dine amongst the pack, given the events of yesterday."

Mister Butthead King didn't reply. He just sat back in his chair, looking all gruff while rubbing his hairy chin.

Shoveling another bite into my mouth, I watched the man wave at an attendant, who hurried to bring him a cup of tea. Unlike Mister Buttface King, he actually smiled at the person and said "thank you" to the omega. He then took the seat beside me, staring with that same smile on his face.

He looked nice enough, but his eyes were creepy. They made me feel uncomfortable.

"Good morning, little prince."

"Hi," I murmured before taking another bite.

"Those look quite scrumptious. I've never had chocolate flavored waffles before. Are they good?"

Shrugging my shoulders, I avoided looking at Buttface as I muttered, "They're okay."

"Hmm." He waved the attendant over. "I'll have what the little prince is having."

She smiled humbly at him. "Right away, Sir Ruth." She then hurried out of the room, leaving the three of us alone.

I glanced at Buttface, then quickly looked away when I saw him watching me with a soft smile. I shouldn't have admitted the waffles were good.

"So," the man leaned back in his chair while staring at us with interest. "What are your plans for the day? Anything as exciting as yesterday."

My face got hot and itchy with embarrassment. "I'm not running away again."

"Of course not," the guy, Sir Ruth, replied like that was common sense. "I imagine that was as scarring for you as it was for your parents."

It was scary. Almost as scary as not having control of my body when my bones felt like they were breaking.

"Mama was scared," I said without looking at Buttface. "I don't like when mama is scared."

Sir Ruth laughed softly. "Of course. Being a werewolf, Lady Alesta is probably at a loss about how to help you now that you have the ability to shift."

"What do you mean?"

He lifted his shoulder. "I'm a werewolf as well, and I know from my time with my Lycan mate the differences in our shifts."

"You have a Lycan mate like mama?" I blurted out without thinking.

Sir Ruth chuckled. "I do. I'm in a position a lot like your mother's."

The Buttface was quiet as Sir Ruth said this. His face was hard and a little scary, but he didn't smell scary, or have scary feelings coming out of him like he did yesterday with the rogues.

"You know what?" Sir Ruth asked while I was still studying the butthead's face. His eyes were swirling more than before and his face was excited. "I know a way for you to ease some of your mother's worries."

I sat up straighter. "How?"

Sir Ruth looked at the butthead with a smile that I didn't trust. "You could train, learning from the most powerful Lycan himself."

My answering growl just made Sir Ruth look more excited. "No, thank you."

"Why not?"

"Because he's a butthead."

"A powerful butthead."

My father, I mean, the butthead, growled when Sir Ruth said it. He never growled at me when I called him names. He was giving Sir Ruth a much scarier look than I expected, too. Not that Sir Ruth looked frightened, but I could feel the threat from the butthead in the air.

Sir Ruth just shrugged. "I could ask my mate to aid your training, if that's what you would prefer. Camellia would be eager to assist you, little prince."

My eyes went wide at the name of his mate. "Camellia? Like, the queen?"

"Exactly like the queen," Sir Ruth said with confidence as his swirling eyes danced on his smiling face. "I'd ask her now, but she left earlier this morning to... take care of a few things."

I looked at my father, but his gaze was focused on Sir Ruth. It was like he was assessing him, like Weirdo Zaden would instruct us to do when we're trying to figure out our partner's next move.

He wasn't lying. His *wife* wasn't his mate, since Sir Ruth claimed she was his. As if to prove it, Sir Ruth began to scratch his neck at that moment, making his shirt go down and exposing the mark on his neck. My nose wrinkled, smelling the scent of the pretty woman I saw yesterday.

My father had a mate mark, but it had no scent. That was a big reason I thought he was lying. As I stared at my butthead father's mark, it flickered and then faded away. I gasped, looking back at Sir Ruth, who just winked at me.

Mama was right about the Queen. Maybe... maybe she was right about my father, too. Maybe...

"Fine," I said, staring at my butthead father until he met my gaze. "I'll let you teach me about shifting. Sounds like fun."

***

"This is fun!" I yelled, jumping down from a tree branch into my father's awaiting arms.

He smirked as he set me on the ground. "Don't think you can do it on your own?"

"Channel my Lycan to just my legs? I think I got it."

I closed my eyes, concentrating like my father showed me. When he first showed me how to do a partial shift, he touched my head, then helped flow the heat that would build in my chest down to my legs. It was like he was doing the work for me, even easing the pain, when my bones started to move out of place.

It took me longer than when he helped, but I managed to make the heat all move to just my feet and the bottom part of my legs. He didn't pester me like weirdo Instructor Zaden would. He let me do it on my own.

As my feet took the shape of a Lycan's, I did what I had done every time before and coiled my new muscles to the point that started to throb, then I crouched down and jumped, just as he showed me. I cleared the first several branches of the tall oak tree and grabbed hold of one towards the top.

As I dangled there, I concentrated the heat back to my chest, then breathed calmly until it completely went away and my body was back to normal.

"I did it!" I cheered, swinging my legs to the branch. "I did it all by myself!"

"You did well, Triston," my father called up to me. "That's the highest yet."

"I know! Watch this!" I yelled right before pushing my legs off the branch. I twirled in the air twice before he caught me like the times before.

My laughter and his mixed with the sound of two others. I turned around in his arms to see Uncle Nic and Uncle Casimir coming into the clearing where we were training.

"Uncle Nic! Uncle Nic!" I squirmed until my feet were back on the ground. "Did you see me? My feet shifted! My feet shifted!" I jumped high, and he caught me, then swung me around and around while laughing.

"I saw. You're going to be jumping over the trees soon."

"Yeah!" I looked at Uncled Casimir. "Can *you* jump over the trees?"

"Ah, sadly, I've never tried to jump over a tree before."

"You should try it. It's fun!"

My father walked closer, his face back to looking scary, but his feelings leaking out of him felt happy.

Uncle Nic put me on the ground and bowed. "My King."

"Where's Alesta?" my father asked curtly.

Uncle Nic and Uncle Casimir exchanged a look. I tilted my face to the side, trying to figure out what that look meant.

"Oh, uh… She's going to be a little while longer." Uncle Nic looked worried.

Uncle Casimir didn't look worried at all as he waved his hand through the air. "She's indulging in her own physical excursions at the moment. Nothing terribly exciting, I'm afraid."

Uncle Casimir's eyes glowed a little bit, and when I looked back at my father, his eyes were glowing too.

"Are you two mind linking?"

My father put his hands on my shoulder as the glow faded away. His scary face changed as he smiled. "We were."

"You caught us," Uncle Casimir sighed. "Here I was thinking we could surprise you."

"Surprise me? Surprise me with what?" I looked at my father for an answer, but he was busy staring at Unce Casimir.

"Why, with your own horse, of course. Every young prince needs his own steed for training."

"A steed? Like a horse?" I wrinkled my nose. "Why would I need a horse? I can jump over a tree." Not yet, but I bet I could soon.

All three of them chuckled, then Uncle Casimir said, "But your legs will grow weary from overuse quickly if you were to jump about all day. Plus," he lifted his chin, "you're royalty. It's your privilege to look down upon others."

"Hmm, that doesn't sound right." I shook my head. "Mama says not to look down on anyone. That's we're all loved by the same goddess above."

I felt my father cringe and his hands got a little tight on my shoulders.

Uncle Casimir laughed in a dark way that made me think he wasn't really laughing. He was just making the sound. "If only that were true, my dear nephew. If only...." His gaze moved behind me, and his face looked a little dark. I didn't understand why.

I looked back to see what my father looked like, but he had the same scary face he usually wore. That is, until he noticed I was staring. Then he smiled a little, so he didn't look so scary anymore.

"It's about lunchtime. Why don't we table the talk of horses for after we eat?"

"Oh! Can we eat in the dining hall? Please? I miss my friends." I started to jump on my feet, really eager to see everyone after being locked up with weirdo instructor Zaden for so many days.

"Tris," Uncle Nic said carefully. "I don't think that's such a good idea."

"Why not?" I stomped my foot. "I wanna see my friends."

"Oh, come now." Uncle Casimir slapped Uncle Nic's back. "Let the boy intermingle with his friends."

Uncle Nic sighed, then glanced at my father nervously. "It's not my decision."

I quickly turned and jumped up and down again. "Please? Please? I really want to," I begged with my hands together. "Please.... Please, father?..."

His eyes went wide and his mouth opened a little, like he was surprised. Then he covered his mouth entirely with his hand, and his eyes got all shiny.

"Please, dad?" I asked one last time, doing my best to give him the face that always made mama cave in.

He nodded, then said with his hand still covering his mouth. "Okay. Lead the way."

"Yes!" I cheered, then grabbed his hands and dragged him

behind me.

"What a sucker," I heard Uncle Casimir murmur to Uncle Nic.

I thought my father would growl like he did when Sir Ruth called him a butthead, but he didn't. He had his lips pressed together tightly and his eyes were still shining as he looked down at me.

I just smiled and focused on getting him to the dining hall. This would be my first time having my friends meet my father, and he was the king! I bet Elliot would be so jealous.

When we got to the dining hall, it was loud with everyone just beginning to get lunch. It was a little weird walking through the pack house with my dad, since everyone seemed to avoid him, or got really quiet when we walked by, but the dining hall was still loud.

I saw my friends right away, at the same table they were always at on the weekends when there wasn't a school. I got excited and left my father and uncles behind as I ran over, wanting to tell my friends all about what happened yesterday, and about my training to jump over trees, and have them meet my father. When I was about halfway to their table, the room got super quiet. My excitement died a little when Leroy's mom grabbed him and sprinted away from the table before I could even tell him hi. Then Jeremy's dad did the same while giving me a mean look. Then Elliot got up on his own and cried before running the opposite way, right to his wort mother who was looking at me more angry than she usually was.

I stopped, then looked all around me. Everyone was looking at me like the wort was. Like I was something horrible that would infect them with diseases if I got close.

My eyes burned, and my chest got really hot. Why was everyone looking at me like that? Why did all my friends run away?

Chapter 33

Candor

Two gentle hands held my shoulders from behind, and a cool feeling made the heat go away in my chest. My father was holding me, and for once, the feeling coming out of him felt as scary as his face. Maybe scarier. But not to me. His touch made me feel better, but made me want to cry at the same time.

"W-what did I do wrong?" I whispered to him, trying not to cry. "Why is everyone mad at me?"

"I don't know," he said loudly, his voice feeling like one of the giant stones the warriors train with. Not the small stones, but the boulders. "Would someone like to tell me what *my son* did to earn such a greeting from *his pack*?"

No one would meet his eyes. A lot of people were cringing, like the boulder of my father's voice was crushing them.

"I believe your king asked you a question," Uncle Casimir said, his tone almost as hard as my father's.

I stared at the ground, not wanting to see any of their scared or mean faces. I didn't understand what was happening. Why were they being so mean? Sometimes one or two people would say mean stuff about mama, like the wort did, but this was everyone. Even Maggie, who was always so nice, I caught glaring at me like I'd kicked her cat.

Suddenly, the back doors burst open, and in ran Gamma Kender and Beta Carlston. Gamma looked worried at me, and

Beta had a hard expression as he looked around the room. His eyebrows pulled down into a mean frown the more he looked at everyone.

"Ah, the cavalry has arrived." Uncle Casimir clapped his hands together once. "Maybe you could answer my dear nephew's question." He paused, his half-smile fading away to a look that was a lot like my father's. "What, in the goddess's name, would an entire pack find so untoward in a six-year-old boy to elicit this treatment?"

I bit my lip hard, feeling it twitch when Uncle Casimir said that. I didn't understand. My friends... They were my friends... Maybe Elliot, I could understand being mean now, but not the others.

When Beta and Gamma didn't answer, I asked quietly, "Is it because I'm a Lycan?"

Elliot's wort mother snorted loudly, sounding like a dying pig. "More like a monster. It's about time others finally see what I've known all along."

Beta snarled loudly, taking a step forward. "That's enough, Prissly Orval! Alpha said you- Ah!" He stopped mid-sentence, cringing and taking a step back.

Everyone around the room was acting weird suddenly, like they were all hurting at the same time. Many were moaning, while some were biting their teeth together so hard I thought they would break. All the other kids were crying like Elliot, some falling to the ground and holding their heads.

Then I felt it. Before I looked back, I knew it was because of my father. I felt his feelings aimed at every other person in this room. Uncle Casimir and Uncle Nic seemed to be the only other ones not hurting. I felt it brushing around me, but it didn't fall down on me like it did everyone else. Like when mama boils tea, I could feel the heat coming from the pot, but it didn't hurt me unless I touched it or put my hand over the steam.

My father's killer steam was blasting over the entire room. His eyes glowed and his hairy jaw was flexing, so I could see the squiggly veins popping out on his throat. Mom threatens to kill people when they make her angry or mess with me. It happened sometimes and her face would get scary. My father's scary expression wasn't a threat. It was a promise.

His hands were holding me tight. My shoulders felt warm from him. The room felt icy, but my father was warm.

"This pack," father's words were low but still made me shiver. "You've failed. You have failed in so many ways."

Beta Carlston groaned with his teeth gnashed together. He struggled for a second, then said, "T-this is a misunderstanding. Nothing more, your m-majesty. Alpha will-"

"Your Alpha is your greatest failure," father spat, his tone so dark. He turned his killer eyes towards Elliot's wort mother. "You. I showed mercy once. I will not again."

All of a sudden, two Lycan guards in black and gold marched into the room, heading straight for Elliot and his mother. Elliot's wort mom screamed, falling to the ground in tears while squeezing my former friend against her chest. I watched with wide eyes and my mouth opened just a little as the Lycans easily tore Elliot away from her, then each grabbed one of her crazy arms and dragged her screaming body from the dining hall. I tried to close my mouth or look away, feeling bad for Elliot, but I couldn't force myself to.

Then, as she was dragged right past us, she shrieked wildly with her eyes all crazy looking at me. She spat and it landed on my shoe. The small part of me that felt bad went away, and I felt my chest growling. I took the shoe off and threw it at her face, making her scream louder than before.

My father let me go, and the guard came to a halt, their hold on the wort just getting tighter as she fought. I watched as my father went around me with his killer steam feelings. The room felt so dark now. His body was so big and scary, it was making scary shadows wash over everything.

Uncle Nic took my hand, pulling me against him with a nervous energy. I knew something bad was about to happen.

The wort finally went quiet as father's dark shadow hovered

over her. Her eyes were big and her skin was so pale it looked gray. She looked scared enough to pee her pants.

"I... I-I'm...." she stammered.

"Shhh..." Father crouched down, so he was almost level with her. He reached out and ran the back of his hands down her face. "I know. You're sorry now, but it's far too late."

Screams sounded around us as Uncle Nic's hand quickly covered my eyes. Not before I saw my father swiftly grab the wort woman's jaw and tear it out of place. The noise it made was gross, like a popping snap.

Then I heard my father say, "Rip her tongue out. Burn the wound so she can't bleed to death before my arrival."

I pulled at Uncle Nic's hand until I could see through his fingers.

"Your majesty," the guards bowed, then continued dragging the wort out of the room. Her jaw hung at a strange angle from the rest of her face. Tears were making her face even uglier.

Father stood up slowly, his killer steam only easing a little after the wort woman was gone. Then he turned back to look at me. He seemed worried, so I nodded to him and said, Good job. Now she can't spit on you, too."

He surprised me by smiling, then came to pick me up from the ground. He reached for my foot with my shoe still on, then took that one off too, tossing it beside the one with spit on it.

"Are you alright, Triston?"

I nodded, frowning at my shoes. "Mama just got those for me."

"I'll get you plenty more," he said softly. Then, in a much meaner tone, he asked Uncle Nic, "Where's Alesta?"

Alesta

Sitting in Beta Carlston's office in the warrior center, I stared open-mouthed at Camellia, who was sitting behind his desk with an angelic grin. Ruth was staring down at her with an enchanting gleam in his hypnotic eyes.

Camellia had Beta call for me earlier, right before breakfast. I had expected to be walking her through another inspection, since that was the excuse Beta Carlston had given me. As we walked the training grounds, talking about the variety of different things our pack trained for, that excuse became more and more plausible.

It wasn't until Sir Ruth came to join us later that the meeting seemed to change.

"You...you want to challenge me?" I repeated what Camellia had just declared back to her, forming it as a question. "Why?"

"Isn't it obvious? You're stealing my husband. A challenge was the imminent deduction."

Her matter-of-fact tone elicited a growl of annoyance from me. "You're not serious. You want me dead for something you've given me your blessing for?"

Her eyes widened in surprise. "Who said anything about you dying?"

"You! You just said-"

"My lady," Ruth interrupted. "I think you're misunderstanding something. It isn't you we need to perish." My perturbed expression caused him to continue. "It's Camellia."

Too stunned to conjure up a cognitive response, all I could do was gawk as I tried to make sense of it all in my head. They waited patiently, their expression never faltering from their normal bliss.

When I could finally find my train of thought again, I exclaimed, "No! I'm not *killing* my queen."

"Why not?" Camellia pouted. "I've been waiting for this day for so long."

"You've been waiting for the day I'll kill you?"

Her answering giggle made me think I may actually be capable of such an act. She was infuriating me with her nonsensical responses.

"Your teasing may actually endanger your life, my love," Ruth purred in her ear.

"Oh, all right," Camellia said in the tone of a sulking child who had just had their fun ruined. "I'll tell you everything, but before that, let me ask you something."

"What?" My unease heightened now that her expression was turning serious.

Her eyes hardened, and chin lifted with resolve. "Do you still love your mate?"

My lips pressed together. It only took a few seconds of thought, replaying the events of yesterday and all the revelations that came of it through my mind for me to come up with an honest answer.

"Yes. How could I not?"

She nodded as if she expected as much. "Is that love significant enough to carry the burdens of becoming his mate?"

That question took much longer to think through. I did still love Lachlan. He gave me my child. How could I not love him for that fact alone? But becoming his mate.... It wasn't just considering those burdens for myself, but I had my son to consider as well.

Ruth, studying me with those stirring eyes of his, cocked his head to the side, then asked, "Does your love for him not extend far enough to take the burden of becoming his queen?"

"It's the burden it would put on me I have to consider," I answered honestly.

Ruth titled his head back. "Ah. I see. The love of a mother is great." His smile was kind as he added, "It can far outweigh that of any other. So, let me ask you this instead. How great is your love for your son?"

I growled and said, "Endless. I'd do anything for him."

He smiled and asked, "Is your love for Triston great enough to want to change this kingdom to make it a better place for his sake?"

"I'd do anything for the sake of my child."

Camellia raised a brow and asked with a sphinx grin,

"Including killing me?"

I snarled at her nonsense. "You're testing my restraint as it is."

Ruth and Camellia chuckled together, exchanging a knowing gaze with one another. As their laughter died down, Ruth's eyes gleamed and Camellia nodded.

Ruth turned those shimmering eyes on me. "Allow me to explain in full candor what she means, then you can make a decision for yourself."

∞∞∞

My heart was heavy as we left the isolated office. There was a nagging ache in my chest. I didn't know what I was expecting to hear from them, or what crazy explanation Camellia had for wanting to challenge me to her death, but even in my windless imagination, I could have never come up with *that*.

"You're doing the right thing," Camellia patted my shoulder.

"Don't touch me," I growled.

"Oh. Don't be like that."

There was that annoying ache building inside of me. It was likely from the revelations from our talk just now, but some part of me also was concerned it was something more. After Ruth laid out his part in all this, I told them I needed air. The ache was becoming too great to sit calmly during such a serious discussion.

"Give her some time to process, love," Ruth whispered in her ear. "It wasn't easy so me either to hear the truth of the Lycans, and I was much more involved already than she currently is."

"Oh, alright," she groaned, but I could tell she wanted to say more by the sideways glance she gave me.

I felt a whole new level of deception, but one that conflicted me. I couldn't refuse her now, even if I wanted to. Not after what they told me.

It wasn't like we could easily stay here in this pack, anyway. I know Triston didn't want to leave, but after yesterday and the pack's reaction to his first shift, the hostility was too much for my six-year-old son to bear. Hopefully, leaving him with Lukyan wasn't a bad idea, and they were actually bonding.

Ruth and Camellia were having a whispered conversation, discussing the dynamics of their plans in cryptic speech. I didn't want any part in their discussion. My mind was still reeling from before, and that nagging part in me wanted to check on my son. I felt something was wrong.

I was so deep in thought that I wasn't paying as close attention to where I was going as I should have been. As we were about to pass the door leading to the underground dungeon, it suddenly flew open and narrowly missed hitting my face.

"Incompetent morons," Alpha Mikken growled to himself as he emerged from the other side. "I should have known better than to leave his sister unbothered..." His voice trailed off as he noticed me standing disgruntled from the near impact. "Alesta! What are you doing here?" He cast an anxious glance behind him before swiftly closing the door.

My eyes moved from the door to him in confusion. "Uh, I was guiding Queen Camellia on her final inspection of the grounds," I murmured, knowing better than to reveal why we were actually here. "Beta Carlston called for me to help. But uh... Have you been here the whole time?"

Before he could answer, fervent screams echoed from outside. They were paired with the unmistakable pleas of a young child, one I had heard before. My feet carried me hurriedly towards the doors.

Alpha Mikken called after me. I even felt the pressure of a command in his tone. "Alesta! Alesta, stop!"

The command bounced right off me. I wasn't stopping for him or anyone. Not when my heart was telling me to find my son.

Chapter 34

Challenge

The sunlight was blinding as I burst through the doors to the outside. I held my hand over my head, trying to block out the light.

The scream didn't cease, though they were now garbled like the source was being gagged. No, not gagged. Her tongue was being held.

I gasped, looking on in horror as two Lycan guards had Prissly pressed against a wooden pole in the center of the training grounds. While one Lycan guard restrained her hands behind her back, the other held her tongue with one hand and a sharp blade that glinted in the sun in his other.

As the guard lifted the blade to Prissly's tongue, his intentions clear, my overwhelming shock caused me to cry out, "Stop!"

Everyone stilled. Even the birds in the sky ceased their chirping at my outburst. I took a deep breath, feeling drained suddenly.

"A-Alesta," Camellia whispered with a tone full of concern.

She was staring at me with wide eyes. Alpha Mikken was gaping in surprise. His expression was almost comical. Ruth didn't seem half as shocked as the others, but there was a look of amazement on his face that made me feel awkward under his scrutiny.

Looking back at the Lycan guards restraining Prissly, they were completely still, frozen in place. Even Prissly was silent, only her eyes moving frantically side to side. The guard's hand with the knife hovered in the air, touching her taut tongue lightly. The faintest tinge of blood was spotting the blade, rolling down the gleaming steel.

Anger surged inside of me. Maybe it was the revelation Ruth had given me, or maybe it was the building ache in my chest. Maybe it was the fact that Elliot Orval was about to watch on in horror as his mother was permanently maimed that overwhelmed me suddenly. After everything yesterday and the ostracization we were already going through, were the Lycans trying to make it worse for my son?

"What is going on here?" I exclaimed, marching towards them. Their eyes followed me, and the guard straining Prissly's hands behind her back even turned his head through much effort. They looked as disturbed as I felt. "I asked, what the hell are you doing?"

Elliot's shuddering sobs heightened my fury. He was lying on the ground at their feet, face and hands muddy from crying in the dirt.

That same surging rage made me bellow out like before, "Answer me!"

The guards both jerked, cringing at my voice. Then the one with the knife said hesitantly, "We... We're following orders. King Lukyan said-"

"Lukyan told you to cut off a mother's tongue in front of her child?"

"Well, uh... no. Not specifically. But he-"

"What did she even do to warrant her tongue being cut out of her mouth?"

He glanced worriedly at the other guard, then back at me. His mouth opened and closed a few times, but it seemed he was at a loss for words.

"Mama!" Triston's voice rang out from a distance.

I turned to see him and Lukyan coming down to the training grounds, Casimir and Niccola following close behind them. Triston looked like he had been crying, his eyes red-rimmed and his nose dripping with snot. He wiggled and jerked until Lukyan set him on the ground.

After aggressively taking the knife from the guard's hand and tossing it to the treeline, I jogged towards Triston as he ran for me. I knelt down and caught him in a tight hug, then leaned him back so I could study his tear-streaked face.

"What happened, baby? Why are you crying?" I then glared at Lukyan. "And you. Why are they cutting a woman's tongue from her mouth right in front of her child?"

Lukyan's brows pulled down, darkening his face. I felt it then. His indignation. The ache in my chest was coming from him. His fury matched my irritation.

Triston had to tap on my face to get my attention. "Mama," he hiccuped, tears glistening in his eyes. "T-they... they were mean. Th-they were... they don't like me anymore."

"Who?"

His eyes darkened, looking so much like Lukyan's expression only with tears as he looked at Prissly and Elliot Orval. "Everyone. Th-the wort... she said everyone knew I was a monster now. She... she was..." His lip quivered uncontrollably, then he fell forward in my arms, his body shaking as the tears flowed.

"Alesta," Niccola said in a muted tone, stepping up as I stood with Triston in my arms. "I'm sorry. I should have checked the dining hall before letting him go there. I didn't know it would be like that after," he glanced at Alpha Mikken, "after last night."

"What happened?" I asked, as I tried to comfort my son.

I asked Niccola, but my eyes ended up connecting with a topaz pair instead while waiting for an answer.

"They were cruel," Niccola whispered darkly. "Beyond cruel. No child should have to face the level of ostracism he felt today."

"All the poor boy wanted to do was eat lunch with his friends," Casimir spoke up right as Beta Carlston and Gamma Kender entered the field. Dozens more warriors were following closely behind. "The viciousness of a horde is quite astounding, in the worst of ways."

My eyes met Lukyan's again, and I finally understood. His child was wronged right in front of him. Having Prissly's tongue cut out was his mercy. He would have killed her on the spot if this had been the capital.

Still, we couldn't kill everyone or cut out their tongues for opposing our being here. After my discussion with Ruth and Camellia, I knew if this order of Lukyan's was carried out, it would only make things worse.

"If you cut out her tongue, there will forever be nothing but militancy in this pack against the capital; against you. Are you sure this is the right choice?"

He lifted his chin, a glint of stubbornness in his topaz eyes. "What else would you have me do? She insulted our son."

I'd love nothing more than to kill the bitch right now, but seeing her son weeping for her, I knew that wasn't the answer.

"I can handle this," Alpha Mikken said loudly. "I'll punish her."

"Like you're punishing half your warriors already?" Niccola spoke up, rubbing his hand on Triston's back. Nic solemnly shook his head. "You can't lock everyone who hates Lycans in the dungeons, Alpha. You'll end up with a mutiny of your own."

So that was what he was doing in the basement. I thought the training grounds looked a little sparse today.

I finally noticed Alpha Mikken's features. His stony expression looked more severe with circles under his eyes. He was wearing the same clothes as yesterday, too. He was exhausting himself and disturbing pack rapport trying to put out the fires caused by my being here. It was time for all of this to end.

There was only one solution. It was one I had already agreed to earlier.

"Take him," I whispered to Niccola, passing my son to him.

Triston was heartbroken. I could see it on his teary face. I could feel it in my mother's heart. This place was like a poison now that he wasn't the innocent little pup he once was before yesterday. He was a Lycan, and there would always be that divide in the Hallowed Moon Pack.

"Gamma Kender. Take Elliot and his mom back to their home. Don't let them out again until we're gone, for their own safety." I glared back at the bitch. "Because if I ever cross paths with her again, I won't cut out her tongue. I'll kill her by ripping her rotten heart from her chest."

There was a weight to my words. An authority that had never shown itself before was taking root in my chest and blooming as I gazed around the field to all those looking on at the chaotic scene.

"Gone?" Alpha asked in alarm.

My eyes rested on Alpha Mikken. "The same for the warriors you've locked away."

His eyes widened. "B-but they... they insulted their-"

"They insulted a fellow warrior," I finished for him before he could call me anything else. I was never going to be his Luna, but there was a greater title for me to become. "Call it mercy. My leniency ends today."

Topaz eyes met mine. I'd just defied his command to his guards, but he showed no sign of anger. There was a sense of pride in his gaze instead. The ache in my chest settled at the realization of what I was about to do.

Turning swiftly, before I could second-guess myself, I called to Camellia who was standing with an awestruck expression next to the observant Ruth, "Queen Camellia Amara Nova, I, Alesta Raine, warrior of the Hallowed Moon Pack, challenge you." The weight of my words pressed into me. There was no going back. "I challenge you for the position beside my mate. I challenge you for the title of queen."

Her look of surprise lasted for a fraction of a second, then a sinister grin transformed her lovely face. Her chin lifted, an air of arrogance painting her features. "I accept."

A round of gasps broke through the silence. I locked eyes with Camellia, her gaze fierce and determined.

"Alesta," Alpha Mikken's voice was low and raspy. "You... you can't be serious."

"Oh, I'm serious." A burst of tingles shot through my spine as a large hand splayed on the small of my back. My resolve deepened.

Alpha Mikken looked beyond shocked. His widened eyes and fallen face seemed almost pleading. "Alesta..."

"There's no place for us here anymore," I whispered. I tore my gaze from Camellia to smile gently at Alpha Mikken. "I'm grateful to you, Alpha. In many ways. But this pack is no longer a sanctuary for my son."

Gamma Kender walked passed right then with Prissly, who shot dangers at my son. Gamma had to hiss darkly for her to face forward in the form of a command for her to turn her nasty face away.

Alpha saw the whole thing. A reluctant look of understanding caused his shoulders to fall. Then he swept a hand down his face and nodded, seeming to concede defeat, though he didn't fully agree.

"Alright.... Alright..." He opened his mouth to say something more, but then his eyes locked on something, or *someone,* behind me and his expression turned hard. Then his teeth clenched together and he let out a low growl before walking away.

As I stood there, a rush of emotions passed over me, feeling the weight of the decision I'd just made.

Then, without a moment to let doubt work its way in, a pair of muscular arms lifted me from the ground. Camellia let out a giggle as I flailed over Lukyan's back. She waved her fingers, then winked, like she was wishing me luck.

"W-... Lukyan?" I gasped as he tossed me over his thick shoulder. "Put me down."

He growled, "After that display, be grateful I'm not....hmm." He let his words train off, then after a few more steps, yelled at Casimir, "Make sure our son-"

"We'll take care of our dear nephew," Casimir said before Lukyan could finish. As Lukyan stormed past, I could see the impish smirk playing on Casimir's lips. Like Camellia had done, Casimir gave me a little wave of his fingers, then said to Triston, "While mommy and daddy have a bit of fun, why don't we do the same? Want to go meet your new mare?"

Triston's face emerged from Nic's shoulder, the hint of a smile on his teary face. "Really? I really get a horse?"

"A horse?" I hissed. "Why on earth would he need a horse?"

"Every prince needs a horse." Lukyan's tone came in a deep rumble, "As every king needs his queen."

I scoffed. "Is that why you're mad? Because I challenged your *mate*? Or because I defined my *king* and didn't allow a mother to be tortured in front of her child?"

"You think I'm mad right now?" Lukyan's voice carried obscured humor. He darkly chuckled, "Oh, little wolf. You have no idea what you've just done to me."

I thought Lukyan was heading to the pack house, but he surprised me by running right past it to the woods. My worries multiplied. Was he dragging me off to punish me like I'd half-heartedly accused him of moments ago?

I didn't want to fight in the woods. An argument should be had in the confines of a room.

"Where the hell are you taking me?" I started beating on his back.

"Keep still, Alesta."

"Or you could just put me down and use your words!"

"I did. I told you to keep still."

"But you didn't answer my question." I twisted my body to see his face. His expression was fierce, deepening my concern that he was dragging me out here to punish me.

"I'll give you five seconds to put me down."

"Quiet."

"One...."

He kept walking, heading off the trail towards a secluded space thick with trees.

"Two... Three..."

He didn't even spare me a glance. He seemed completely

unconcerned.

"Four…"

Still no reaction, and now we were far from where someone could find us, due to my slow count.

"Five." He asked for it.

I jerked my knee forcefully into his chin, causing him to snarl. His arm flexed into my skin as he struggled to get both my legs under his control. Then I started aiming my fists at the most painful places I could reach.

"Stop it," he growled. "Alesta!"

"I warned you. Let me go!"

I knew how to land a punch under much more strenuous conditions than being carried like a sack of potatoes. He should have known better, having seen me defend myself plenty when I was a tribute in training. A well-placed punch to his side gave me the outcome I'd hoped for. Even with his back rigid and tense, he couldn't avoid the pain of a blow to his kidneys.

"Fuck!" He felt forward, his hold on my legs loosening enough for me to flip out of his arm and land a swift kick at the side of his head in the process.

"You should have listened," I muttered darkly, straightening my clothing in an unbothered manner as he clutched his side with one hand and his head in his other. "Feel free to try again when you gain the ability to use your words."

As I calmly began walking back in the direction we came from, he turned to grab for me again. I slapped his hand away and kicked him. This time in the stomach. He flexed, so I had the unsatisfying response of a mere grunt. I swung my fist towards his face once, then again with my other, but he grabbed both my hands and pressed them tightly to his chest.

He towered above me. His heart was hammering beneath my finger. His heat combined with the sparks of our bond were making my skin feel like fire. How could someone so infuriating be so handsome? It was quite annoying.

I jerked my hands, trying to hit him again, but his hold was too strong.

"Quit hitting me."

"Quit handling me like an object and speak then!"

His nostrils flared, as did mine. His lips twitched, but he made no motions to say another word. He stared intently at my mouth, which I was sure was twisted into a deep frown.

As the silence stretched, I laughed darkly under my breath and shook my head. "Has anyone ever told you how bad you are with communication?"

He let out a sarcastic snort. "I prefer actions."

Without another second to think, his lips closed on mine, and the heat that had bloomed over my skin took root in the deepest part of me.

Chapter 35

In Due Time

Lukyan's heat seeped into mine. All the pent up aggression from the last half hour released itself in carnal desire. He swallowed my feral growls with an unkept hunger of his own. Our lips battled for dominance. I remained unrelenting even as he lifted me from the ground.

"Fuck," he snarled, skating his teeth along my jaw. They nibbled across my neck before his wet breath fanned over my sensitive ear. He sucked the fatty flesh between his lips. The tingles shot shivers through my core.

"You couldn't do this inside?" I rasped, throwing my head back to give him better leverage. "I thought you were taking me somewhere to punish me."

A throaty chuckle vibrated against my skin, making me whimper. "I would never punish my mate. Not after she just claimed me so magnificently."

"I didn't claim you," I murmured in weak stubbornness. My head was murky with his lips resting against my nape.

His dark chuckle made my legs clench around his waist. His firmness pressed against my center, providing that delicious ache of teasing pleasure.

If there was ever a time I'd been grateful for the overgrowth of weeds and shrubs, it was now. It felt as if we were in our own little world, secluded from everything else. My body was bowing against him, searching for more of that delicious friction. His mouth was leaving a trail of open, wet kisses all across my neck.

When my back pressed against a tree, pinning me in place, I couldn't take it anymore. I started clawing at his shirt, tearing away the thin barrier between us. His muscles were larger than I remembered. The passing of time did him justice. Or maybe this was the result of becoming a king. I was sure as my fingers traced his rigid plains that there would never be another man as desirable as him.

"Alesta," he husked, his voice caressing my flaming desire.

"This," I growled, scraping my nails down his tense abdomen and pulling on the waist of his pants.

"Fuck." He gathered my skirts, lifting them to my waist. Balancing my weight between the tree and his arm, he reached between us and extended a claw, slicing through the tiny fabric covering me.

Exposed, I groaned impatiently as he unclasped the front of his pants. Using my heels, I pushed against them until they fell to his knees. My mouth watered seeing his hardened length for the first time in so long.

My eagerness must have shown, for Lukyan's low laughter displayed his sizzling amusement. His topaz eyes blazed while watching me.

"How long has it been, little wolf?" His sultry tone made my belly clench. His nose nuzzled beneath my ear. "How long has it been since you've taken a man?"

"Seven years…. It's been too fucking long, Lukyan."

That was it. With a possessive growl, he sank into me. I threw my head back with an airy cry. My eyes clenched together from the pain, which was quickly replaced with pleasure as I adjusted to him.

"Good," he snarled between clenched teeth, keeping perfectly still while watching the expression change on my face. "I don't want to upset my queen. She seems determined to keep even the least deserving in this pack safe."

"So, if I had slept with someone else…"

A threatening growl left him. "Not even you would be able to stop me," he whispered in a gravelly tone. "This," he pulled out of me and slowly sank back in, "is *mine. My* pussy to devour as I wish."

I groaned, struggling to keep my wits about me as the bond overcame me. "What about you?" I fought past the pleasure I felt to scowl into his handsome, lusty face. "How long?"

"Ah, I've been a starving man, little wolf. For seven years, I've hungered for this." He thrust upward, making my eyes roll to the back of my head. "I didn't want our first union to be rushed amongst the trees of that bastard's pack, but I couldn't suppress this urge any longer. Not after hearing you claim me like that."

"I didn't claim you," I said again, much more weakly than before.

As he did the first time I said it, he only laughed, then took me with the force of a starved man devouring a meal for the first time.

Lukyan

"Yes! Oh, fuck, yes…. Lukyan!" Alesta screamed into the night air. Her breath left puffs of warm air lingering in the cool sky.

Hearing my name like a prayer on her kiss-swollen lips made me ravenous. I couldn't get enough. Hours had gone by since I took her away, and I still craved more. By the sounds escaping my little mate, I knew she wasn't either.

On a bed of our discarded clothes, I dipped my face between her thighs, moaning into her delicious cunt as her legs locked around my neck. Her back lifted from the ground as she leveraged her body on mine, grinding herself against my willing tongue.

The endless pleasure was wrecking us both. Her juices mixed with mine in an intoxicating cocktail. Grabbing her waist, I lifted her the rest of the way and spun so my back was on the ground. She continued to grate her pussy against my tongue. I drank her in, high on the sight of her losing herself to me.

The bond was pressing in. It was like we were both in heat. The need to mark her was growing by the second. I was playing a dangerous game. I knew marking her now wouldn't be wise before her challenge, but every fiber of my being wanted to say fuck it and sink my teeth into her sweet-tasting skin, anyway.

She stared down at me with a wanton eyes. One hand on my head like she was holding the reins, the other supporting her from behind. The moon shining above her head was like a halo, giving her an ethereal glow. She was my goddess, commanding me in every way.

As she spilled her pleasure over me again, I marveled like a fiend caught under her spell. She was gloriously undone, showering her favor over my lips. I could worship her like this forever, and I would if she'd let me.

She collapsed in a heap beside me. Her legs twitched as fresh nectar seeped from her lips.

"One more, little wolf," I whispered in her ear. I was rewarded with a garbled attempt of my name.

My little mate reacted beautifully as I lifted her leg to rest on my shoulder, opening her pussy for me once more. She cried out when I slipped between her swollen folds. Tingles traveled up my legs and spine. How could she still be so tight?

"Luk…" Her vixen gaze thrilled me more. This woman was my everything. I felt as if my world returned to me the second she challenged Camellia for the right to stand by my side.

I'd have given up anything and everything to bring her back to my side. For her to profess me as her mate, I felt more like a king than ever before.

I love her. Fully and truly. She was the mother of my child, and the goddess of my soul. Even when she fought against me, I felt immense love for the warrior she truly was. She was created to be my queen. I knew it as I watched her take command over everyone.

Leaning over her small frame, I stared into her beautiful eyes and proclaimed with all my heart, "My queen; you are my queen, Alesta."

"Lukyan…" she whimpered, her walls pulsing around me.

After we both found our final ending, I kissed her senseless, swallowing every one of her cries and moans. Holding her face in my hands, I knew she felt this connection between us. It was indescribable, like the first time we made love.

This was our new beginning. There was no turning back. Alesta would finally be mine in every way. It was only a matter of time.

Mikken

"It's all clean now, Alpha." The omega bowed to me awkwardly before retreating from my sight.

Throwing my head back, I stared up at the ceiling, still not ready to enter my office again after discovering the gift left for me all over my desk. My office had been wrecked, but it wasn't until the scents hit me I realized what the king had done.

It was like I was living a nightmare. In just two days, everything had changed and my head was having a hard time catching up.

She was his mate. The weight of that seemed like nothing before, but now it was crushing me to no end.

Carlston came from my office and murmured carefully, "No more smell. I think it's safe."

"Safe," I scoffed. "There is nothing safe about the current state of our pack."

"Hey, it's not that bad. I think we're doing pretty well, all things considered."

The hell we were. At this rate, they'd put us back under the tribute system we'd been free from for decades. On top of that, I had just imprisoned a large portion of my warriors in defense of the king's son and a woman that would never be my Luna. How I was going to justify that action now would depend on the outcome of the challenge she put forth to become queen.

"If she fails to defeat Queen Camellia...." I couldn't voice the rest of that thought. The dread was too immense. I'd have a raging Lycan king without his mate, exacting his vengeance on those that led his mate to make such a rash decision. Forget my warriors who would feel wronged being incarcerated for their behavior towards little Triston and his mother. A mutiny would be the least of my worries with all of us dead.

Carlston sighed, dropping in the chair beside me. "Yeah. I know. She seemed confident, though. Maybe it will end up okay."

"Okay? She's going against a noble Lycan, Carl. Even if it's Alesta, she doesn't stand a chance."

"You don't know that. You've seen her train. She was a tribute too."

"A former tribute going against a Lycan queen. What a close match that will be." I muttered sarcastically. "I should go and challenge the king for his title, too, while we're at it."

"Why not? I'd cheer you on."

"To my death," I huffed, feeling defeated. "At least I wouldn't have to deal with the issue of our warriors."

Yesterday evening, I had Carlston round up all those who opposed Alesta and had treated Triston poorly. I'd smoked them rigorously through the night without a moment's rest.

Then Niccola returned with Gunther. After a grueling training session that went on all night, I locked them all up in the early hours of the morning while I dealt with Gunther personally.

Gunther had returned showing no genuine remorse for his part in what happened to Triston. He had only complaints and brash talk of revenge against Alesta and her son. The other warriors had to listen to his cries for hours.

The fog of rage I'd felt eventually lifted, and just when I was considering releasing the others, I'd gotten word of what was happening in the dining hall. My action to contain the hate shown towards little Triston failed.

Then I ran into Alesta. I'd known she was considering leaving after what had happened with the rogues and the warrior's reaction to Triston, but I had still held hope I could get her to stay. Even after seeing her perched upon King Lukyan's lap. But... there was already something different about her. I didn't know what until it was too late.

Before I could get a handle on anything, she had already commanded the Lycan guards to stop. It was a command; truly and fully. Not a request, but an unavoidable command, more powerful than even my own.

Then she made her challenge. Fear for her life was still terrorizing my mind. I wanted to plead with her, begging her to reconsider and stay by my side. I'd do anything to make this pack a haven for her again. Even if she didn't take me as her mate, as long as she lived....

What little hope I had died when my eyes met with *his.* The arrogance of triumph in his gaze and her declaration to make him her mate shredded my heart to pieces.

Coming here and seeing the state of my office was it for me. I lost her.... But I'd never truly had her in the first place.

"The warriors? You're still worried about that?" Carlston shook his head with a smirk, unaware of the pain raging inside me. "Alpha. What you did was totally justified."

"They won't think so. If it was the mistreatment of their Luna and her child that led to their discipline, maybe. If she becomes queen, then so be it. But if she dies...." I shook my head, my heart clenching in my chest.

Carl rested his hand on my shoulder, squeezing it in support. "This isn't about the warriors. You know it's not."

With a heavy sigh, I dragged my hand down my exhausted face. "No. It's not."

"We told you to act sooner, Ken. I'm sorry, but…" His gaze filled with sympathy. "It's time to move on."

They had told me many times to approach Alesta with my heart on my sleeve. I thought I had all the time in the world. Now, I had no time at all.

Staring back up at the ceiling, I shook my head again. "I love her. How can I move on when I never got to tell her how I truly feel?"

Before I could figure out the answer, there was a knock at the door. We both turned to look at Sir Ruth as he walked in.

He looked far too happy, considering what had happened. It heightened my fear for Alesta. If he was worried that his lover, the current queen, had any chance of losing, he wouldn't be walking around with the same confident air he usually carried.

"Hello, gentleman. Am I interrupting?"

As I scowled, Carlston stood to greet him. "No, Sir Ruth. What can we do for you?"

"Oh, I've just come to discuss the matter of Miss Alesta Raine's challenge to become queen. Preparations need to be made."

My eyes narrowed on the eccentric representative to the royals. "You seem unbothered by the issue."

"Issue?" His smile widened. "What issue would there be?"

I scoffed, shaking my head in irritation. "Considering our discussion yesterday, I thought you would show more concern."

"Our discussion is exactly why I lack concern." His eyes shone with excitement.

I couldn't help the animated scoff that left me at his words. "Is this just a game to your nobles? One of them will die. Either Alesta or your *queen you serve* so devoutly."

His unnerving stare pricked my skin. There was something about his eyes….

"Rest easy, Alpha. The goddess prevails and her will shall be done. This challenge is only the beginning."

"The beginning? What do you mean by that?"

He chuckled low under his breath. "In due time, Alpha. In due time."

Chapter 36

My Mate

Alesta

"Can you reach her yet?"

"*Almost,*" *a soothing feminine voice whispered as I felt a gentle caress against my cheek.* "*Not much longer and she should awaken.*"

"*We've waited long enough,*" *the male voice groaned impatiently.* "*We never should have-*"

"*Shh, shh,*" *the woman hushed his panic. Warm fingers glided over my eyes in a feather-like touch.* "*The time for regrets is over. She's finally on the path she belongs.*"

The man grumbled, "*My trust in you is far too great.*"

"*Oh, I think your trust isn't the issue. It's your impatience wearing you down,*" *she chuckled. Then I felt her touch on my eyes once more.* "*It's time, my child. It's time....*"

My eyes fluttered open, the hint of déjà vu weighing me down. My mind was clinging to a dream, but there was no recollection of what. Just a banding pressure around my head that extended to my limbs. Or maybe it was the stiffness in my limbs making me feel so disoriented.

Something had woken me up. I knew it, but I couldn't recall what. More than likely another nightmare, though it didn't feel as such. There was a looming feeling, but not one of heartache like in the past. This feeling was one of hope.

The fog of sleep began to lift, and I realized I wasn't alone. My pillow was a hard plane of muscle that rose and fell with deep breaths. The pressure I felt banding around me must have been the heavy limbs holding me close.

A thick thigh pressing between my naked legs brought my focus to my throbbing center, swollen and slick. Everything from the evening before came back to me in a rush. As I lifted my head, I was met with Lukyan's handsome face, relaxed in sleep.

Lukyan and I were lying in his guest room inside the pack house. He must have brought us here sometime last night.

He looked completely at peace. It was never an expression I'd seen on him before. The more I watched, the more mesmerized I was.

The fine lines that were always present around his eyes, evidence of his constant scowl, were completely gone. He looked so much like Triston I couldn't help myself but to run my fingers over the flush of his cheeks. He was truly a handsome man, and I was grateful our son gained that from him.

As my fingers brushed over the coarse hairs of his beard, his lips twitched, and his eyes cracked just enough for his topaz irises to shine through.

"Good morning," I whispered, enjoying the sparks beneath my fingers.

He turned his head and puckered his lips to my exploratory touch. He mumbled in a delicious voice, "Morning, little wolf." My body buzzed as he squeezed me close. "How did you sleep?"

"I don't even remember falling to sleep," I admitted with a grin, resting my head on his chest. "You did a number on me last night, my liege."

He chuckled darkly. "Seven years of pent up longing will do that to a man." His face lifted with a smirk. "You didn't seem to have any objections."

"Not a single one," I laughed with him.

"Ah," he sighed, rolling to his side and bringing me with him. "I missed this. I missed us."

After a brief silence and a moment of vulnerability, I admitted, "Me too."

His lips pressed to my head, then he breathed me in deep. We laid there, our naked bodies tangled together. Contentment wrapped around me warmly, making it so I could truly relax for the first time in a long time. Everything felt right. All the worries of yesterday were all but forgotten.

He scoffed lightly after some time. "You thought I was going to punish you."

My face grew hot, pressing deeper into his chest. "In a way, you kinda did."

"That was a punishment for you?" He lifted his face to catch my expression.

"My body sure is sore."

He chuckled, the gravelly sound doing things to me. His hands massaged up my back. "Good sore, or bad sore?"

I suppressed my smile. "I'm not telling."

"Hmm, then I already know." Tingling kisses traveled from my temple to just above my ear. "I'd like to *punish* you again now."

Biting my lip, I tightened my legs around his thigh. The slickness multiplied as my body got unbearably hot. He smoothly ground his firmness against my belly, then nibbled on my ear.

It felt like the morning after our first night all over again. The same sense of new love lit a fire inside me. In the back of my mind, I knew we had too many other priorities to indulge in one another again, but at the same time, separating myself from him was an unbearable thought.

Just days ago, I was avoiding him like the plague. Now I am drowning in his touch, his scent, and his taste....

"Alesta," he husked against my lips. His tongue teased my own, then he devoured me. My mouth matched his intensity. Needy moans left me as he moved above me. My arms wrapped around his neck when his body pressed down on mine. His hand on my throat anchored me to him. "My mate."

"Yes," I breathed with him. The mate bond was impossible to ignore.

His face lifted and his hooded eyes shone down on me in a way that left me breathless. They traced down to where his hand connected with my neck, then his fingers dragged down my nape. They rested on the spot where my neck and shoulder met.

"Soon, everyone will know you are mine." He brushed against the most sensitive area, making a shiver move down my spine. "Mine."

My gums throbbed at the thought of what he was insinuating. I truly couldn't wait either, though I knew we had to.

He was still married, and he was the king.

Instead of using words, I pulled him close once again, letting my fevered mouth crash to his. His hard length was grinding into me, making me lose my mind even more. Just as things were beginning to go past the point of no return, a sharp pounding shook the bedroom door.

"Mama! Mama! Are you in there?"

Lukyan stopped his aggressive movements and rested his head on my chest. I giggled to myself, watching as he tried to calm himself down. The new door was shaking with persistent knocking, but went still for a moment before the knocking got more aggressive.

"Mama! I can hear you!" The doorknob rattled.

"Triston," Nic hissed. "I told you to leave them alone."

"But it's past breakfast time, and she didn't eat. Mama says we can't skip breakfast."

"They can eat later," Nic said. Their voices faded as they walked away.

I combed my fingers through Lukyan's hair, waiting patiently as he regained his composure. "Welcome to the life of a parent," I chuckled. "Privacy will become a thing of the past."

"I see that. I'm glad I locked the door."

"That only stopped him because Niccola was there."

He groaned, throwing his head back on the bed.

I snuggled into the crook of his arm, giving him a moment to let his *excitement* fade away. When he seemed ready, I whispered, "We should probably get up."

He nodded, his intense eyes meeting mine. "You're right. You have a challenge today."

∞∞∞

The return to reality hit me hard after our night out in the woods. The challenge was nearing sooner than I would have liked. All the preparations had been made. The only thing left was the actual fight. The fight to the death.

Camellia and Ruth were set to leave the royal suite first. As she was still the queen in name, the unassuming royal guards had to escort her to the field so she could take her place among them as the mother of the kingdom one last time.

Ruth gave me one of his knowing smirks, then said, "Remember what we discussed."

I nodded. I remembered. Everything. The knowledge felt heavy.

Camellia pulled me into a hug. "Good luck, my darling Alesta." She giggled, then whispered in my ear, "See you in the afterlife."

I growled, not enjoying her teasing today any more than I had yesterday. This wasn't a light matter to me. She may look forward to *dying*, but I wasn't looking forward to what came after.

Soon after they left, Lukyan had to go too. His position as King commanded he officiate, not openly showing favor for me over his wife. It may be a little too late to fool the few guards and omegas residing in the pack house to care for the royals, but the majority of the Lycan guards and the rest of the inspection party were another matter. For official statements, and for the documentation that would be delivered to the council upon our return to the capital, Lukyan had to uphold tradition. Even if all of the Hallowed Moon Pack and those working closest to Lukyan already knew that he favored me.

"I'll be waiting," Lukyan whispered to me, tenderly holding my face while staring down at me with so much affection in his topaz eyes. "The title of queen… Take it back, little wolf. That place was always yours."

His last kiss before leaving for the match grounds was so sweet. He'd been waiting for this day for so long. The anxiety I'd felt disintegrated with the sparks of the bond.

His eagerness motivated me. This wasn't just something I had to do. I *wanted* it. I wanted to finally take my place beside him.

"Ready?" Casimir, my official accompaniment to the fight, was the only one left with Triston and me.

"I'm ready." Ready to start anew.

As we walked to the grounds, Triston chattered blissfully of his adventures with his uncles yesterday. He didn't seem bothered by my absence at all.

"Mama! Mama! Look!" Triston pointed towards the stables. Several royal horses were grazing in the pen beside it. "See that black one with the big red spot? That's mine! That's mine!"

"That huge one?" I almost gasped. "That's… I thought you were getting a young one?"

"No, no. Uncle Casimir said I needed a warrior horse so I can fight dragons like the Prince in my book." He jumped in front of me, flexing his arms. "See? See? I'm a warrior!"

"Yeah…" I glared back at Casimir. "That's what every mother wants to hear from their six-year-old."

Casimir had a smug expression. "I'll be gifting my little nephew a proper sword next."

"You most certainly will not," I growled. "Not unless you want me to stick you with it."

"Oh, how kinky. I thought you'd have enough of sticking and poking last night."

My face flamed, and my backhand flew to his chest. Casimir laughed unbothered.

"What?" Triston pulled on my sleeve. "Mama, did you do sword fighting without me? No fair! I wanna use a sword too!"

Casimir chuckled lightly. "Oh, I've no doubt you will one day. Once you come of age, I'll show you the perfect place at the back of the palace grounds to do all the sword fighting you desire."

"Casimir. I swear I'm going to lock you in that shack and burn you in it if you *ever* take my son there."

"A shack?" Triston looked at Casimir, confused. "You can't sword fight inside. Instructor Zaden said so."

Casimir feigned hurt. "You would trust your *weird* instructor over your own uncle?"

"He should," I growled. "Because his *uncle* is a total pervert."

I instantly regretted saying that out loud. Triston wrinkled his nose, then asked, "What's a pervert?"

"Oh, goddess," I pinched the bridge of my nose.

Casimir looked thoroughly amused. His delight shone in his eyes. "Well, my little inquisitive nephew. A *pervert* is someone who enjoys themselves to the fullest at all times, in all circumstances. I, for one, am proud to be called as such."

"Wow! I want to be a pervert too!"

"That's it," I growled, pulling Triston ahead. "I think you've spent enough time with your uncle for now."

"Ah, mama. But Uncle Casimir is fun. I want him to teach me to be a pervert."

Casimir was choking on his laughter.

With a growl, I turned back to shout, "I hope you're pleased with yourself!"

"Thrilled! Simply ecstatic. I'll teach you all my ways, little Triston. Our nephew-uncle dates are the highlight of my days."

"Your next date is going to be with a match atop a pillar of wood." I walked faster, so fast Triston was practically running to keep up. Casimir still stayed just a few paces behind us, though he didn't seem to struggle to do so.

My son tilted his face up at me, that always curious glint in his eyes. "Who's '*Ahmatch*', mama? Is that one of the warrior she-wolves that chases Uncle Nic around?"

"Yep," I lied, not wanting to explain further.

The mirth in Casimir's laugh turned cold before he said, "Oh, I'd *love* to have a moment of time with *any* of the she-wolves chasing Niccola's tail."

Triston giggled. "There's a lot of them. Uncle Nic said they like to steal his clothes."

"Do they?" By Casimir's tone, I was suddenly nervous for any female that showed Niccola an ounce of interest. "Well... That's quite unfortunate, isn't it? For all parties."

I could see the field roped off up ahead. Royal Lycan guards stood evenly spaced around the perimeter, and spectators were already lining up to watch. Off to the side, where Beta Carlston was organizing the pack's warriors into formations, probably to control the crowd, stood Niccola. He wasn't alone.

Four warrior she-wolves were crowding around him, all with a similar flirtatious expression on their faces. Niccola looked as awkward as he usually was, his eyes shifting for an escape while smiling politely back at them. Wearing nothing but his trousers, it was clear he'd just gotten back from a guard shift. Warriors rarely took more than the bare minimum to put on after a shift.

One she-wolf was in the process of running her fingers down Niccola's bare arm, lingering on his bicep for an uncomfortable amount of time. Nic jerked his arm away, then turned to stare in our direction right when Casimir made an aggressive noise in the back of his throat. Even at this distance, I knew that worrying look. It seemed the pervert would be having a battle of his own very soon.

Feeling another gaze, I looked to find Lukyan, perked on a viewing platform at the head of the field. My heart sped when his lips turned up on one side, breaking his usual stoic demeanor. His dark clothing and tanned skin made his eyes shine even brighter in the dimming sunlight.

Alpha Mikken was seated beside him, along with Ruth and Camellia. Lukyan's eminence outshined them all. Even Camellia's beauty paled compared to his.

That spot would soon be mine. I craved it more than before. I could only hope that I didn't drown in his shadow when that position he'd always promised me was finally mine.

Chapter 37

Coming To An End

T he crowd tripled by the time we reached the field. Everyone from the pack, warriors, omegas, even children were present for the fight.

An eagerness roared amongst them, leaving a tension suspended in the air. Were they cheering for their queen's defeat.... or mine?

It was an unsettling thought.

"Mama?" Triston pulled on my sleeve as we walked to the center of the field. Anxious confusion knotted his little brows as he looked around. "Why is everyone yelling like that?"

Forcing a smile, I combed my fingers through his hair. "They're just excited, baby. It's okay."

Casimir snorted. "They call Lycans bloodthirsty monsters. This is ferocious behavior."

I was in full agreement, but when Triston tensed up again, wrapping both his arms around my middle, I whispered, "Careful," to the provoking Prince.

Casimir glanced at Triston, then sighed. His eyes glazed with the obvious sign of a mind link. Then my chest suddenly tensed.

Looking over towards the podium, I saw Lukyan's expression as stoic as ever, but his eyes shone in the shadow of his brow, and his hands were clenched tightly onto the arm of his chair. Those were the only signs of his anger.

Two Lycan guards then approached us from the perimeter of the field. "Dame Alesta," they both bowed respectfully.

I recognized them from the incident with Prissly yesterday. They were part of the small group attending to the royals in the packhouse. Squeezing Triston's shoulder, I tried to anticipate what they could want.

"Yes?"

One of them, the one who held the knife to Prissly's tongue, smiled gently at Triston. "Young prince." He held his hand over his chest as they both bowed to him.

Triston, never one to be shy, gave them a stare that would rival his father's. He clutched my hand, standing tall and looking proud.

Both Lycans grinned with amusement at Triston. Then the knife-wielding one looked back at me. "King Lukyan requests his son join him, if you have no objections."

So that was what Casimir was doing.

"I wanna stay with mama," Triston growled, his eyes roaming the heated crowd.

His worries matched my own. Which was why I knew keeping him at Lukyan's side was the safest thing to do.

Crouching down, I smiled softly at the stubborn set of Triston's jaw. He was so much like Lukyan. So, so much.

"I would love for you to stay with me, baby. I really would, but I think you should join your father."

"No." He crossed his arms and turned his head. "I'm staying."

"But you'd have a better view up there." I pointed to the platform. "And, look. Alpha Mikken is there too."

"I don't care. I'm not leaving you by yourself."

"Hey." Casimir nudged his shoulder. "What do you think I'm here for?"

Triston narrowed his eyes at his uncle. "*You're* going to stay with mama?"

"Of course I am," he scoffed, looking offended. "I'm your mother's escort. I'll be escorting her until the end."

Whose end, he didn't say, but I knew from the look the guards exchanged, they were more informed than I had assumed. Lukyan trusted the men. I trusted Lukyan.

"See. Prince Casimir will be with me." I cradled his cheek, revealing a flicker of vulnerability in my son's features. "You don't have to be scared."

Triston didn't seem convinced. "I'm not scared," he grumbled. He looked around at the crowd again, then back at Casimir. "You won't leave mama? Not for a second?"

Casimir chuckled, ruffling his hair. "No, little prince. I give you my word."

I watched the guards walk with Triston all the way to the platform. Their chatter seemed friendly, and by the time they reached the stairs, Triston seemed in better spirits.

"Oh, goddess," Casimir murmured, saddling up beside me. "It seems my little nephew is an incurable mama's boy."

"You're one to talk," I scoffed.

He smiled brightly. "You're right. Aw," he hummed. "My nephew can be a perverted mama's boy, just like his favorite uncle."

My elbow flew back, right into his stomach. He groaned, buckling over while waving away the alert guards with one hand and clutching his gut with his other.

"I'm about finished with your rampant mouth," I sneered.

"Apologies," he groaned. Still recovering, a mischievous smirk lifted his features as his eyes flickered to the platform. "Oh, my."

"What?"

I looked up in time to see Camellia hugging Triston tight. She whispered something to him, making him laugh and smile shyly. Lukyan's face, once stoic, now held a look of pride.

Alpha Mikken looked appalled by whatever was said, first staring open-mouthed at my rival then glaring at my mate.

"The game has begun."

"What game? What did she say?"

He chuckled. "Your sister wife just informed the young prince she will love him like her own after the conclusion of this match."

With another glance, I saw the other expressions of the officials nearby. The Lycan guards and council aids not privy to the pack house quarters had a similar smugness about them. The statement may seem innocent and caring to my young son, but to them, it was a declaration that she expected to win. The three looked like the perfect noble Lycan family. The only ones among them that didn't hold the same arrogant air were Alpha Mikken and the two guards who escorted my son.

I was painfully aware of the farce Lukyan and Camellia had to uphold for the past seven years. From afar, they seemed like a true married couple, but I knew the truth. I also knew the game Casimir spoke of. This was the stage of their last act as husband and wife. The final game of deceit was being set in motion.

Camellia's eyes lifted, meeting mine as a prideful grin graced her lovely face. Then she winked, hugging Triston once more before rising from her seat.

As the two guards who had escorted Triston led Camellia off the platform, two other guards approached me.

"Prince Casimir," they bowed respectfully to him, then gave me an imperious glance. "Dame Alesta. It's time. Please approach the center of the field."

Despite addressing me in the more honorable title Ruth had insisted on for the records of this match, these guards clearly didn't think much of me. Not that I expected anything different, but it was a bit irritating. It reminded me greatly of my time as a tribute. That was unsettling in and of itself.

Ruth was already in place, waiting for us both along with an elderly Lycan I could only assume was someone serving the council back at the capital.

No wonder Camellia was so eager for this deathmatch. This game of deceit was her ticket to freedom from the much harsher game she played as queen. That role would soon fall upon me.

This was it. My life hidden from the Lycan world was fully coming to an end.

"Commence with the integral examination!" Ruth announced loudly.

Both Camellia and I were to be searched by the council representative for any hidden weapons or items that could be used to give us an advantage during the match. It was a necessary precaution carried out before any match.

The elderly Lycan started with me, showing no regard for my comfort as he roughly patted me down. I couldn't help the few snarls that parted my lips when his hands wandered too freely over my corset and center.

"Know your place, mongrel," he hissed in warning. "If you had, you could have maybe warmed a noble's bed once or twice instead of dooming yourself here today."

My chest tightened. Without even glancing his way, I knew Lukyan was enraged.

The old Lycan's hands clenched like he was going to continue his invasive search, but then his eyes met mine. He stilled as I poured every bit of my hatred into my glare. I didn't say a word or move a muscle, but I didn't have to. I felt a raging spark in the blood flowing through my body. I'm sure he could sense it. Even the four guards looked at me warily in that moment, no longer snickering at the creepy rep's comment.

The old man averted his gaze, muttering nervous curses under his breath before moving to Camellia. He didn't look my way again.

"You alright, Alesta?" Casimir whispered in my ear, trying to remain discreet.

"Just peachy."

"Ah, you're fine. Use that spunk in your match. Maybe we should have you searched again to finish this quicker."

"I would rather use it on you later," I growled.

"Oh, look who's the pervert now," he chuckled.

Camellia's inspection was done much more quickly, and in a far more respectful manner. He even made a point of apologizing before telling her he expected her victory. Camellia simply responded with a tight smile before dismissing him to the spectators' platform.

I watched him climb the stairs, only to be sharply ordered down by Lukyan to watch with the *mongrels* below. I felt the smallest hint of satisfaction before looking away.

The two guards who had escorted Camellia bowed to her, one even taking her hand and resting his head on the back of it. It was the ultimate show of respect for his queen. Seeing her benevolent response, a lovely smile as she touched his head like a mother would, I almost felt bad for the Lycan guard.

Both guards who led me to the center of the field didn't even spare me a glance. They bowed again to Casimir, then to Camellia with the same earnest expression as their comrades before walking back to the perimeter. Even Ruth, who carried an official title despite being a werewolf, didn't receive any acknowledgement.

All the reasons I hated the capital came rushing back to me. I was a werewolf. The small amount of pity I just felt vanished seeing them walk away.

"I see they're excited for a new queen," I muttered under my breath. "Assholes."

Casimir snickered, "Don't pout, dear Alesta. It's unfitting."

"I'm not pouting. And the only thing *unfitting* will be my foot in your ass later if you don't shut that void in your face."

"Ah!" His mouth dropped open. "How horribly rude of you."

Camellia barely stifled her giggle as we took our places at either end of the marked circle. I simply shrugged, my face remaining passive. I was done with this. Done with all of this, and was just ready for the match to begin.

"Shoes off now, ladies," Ruth said calmly. "Prepare to shift." He may have sounded calm, but looking up, I noticed there was a hint of excitement in his eyes.

Camellia gracefully stepped out of her low slip-on shoes; dainty little heels befitting of a noblewoman. She was prepared to get rid of them quickly, whereas I had on my high-laced boots. They were one of three sets of footwear I owned. I couldn't very well wear my fabric house-shoes or the elegant dress heels Alpha Mikken had gifted me. So, I crouched to the ground, taking my time to unlace my boots like I would any other time, ignoring the impatient stares from all around.

The packed earth of the field smelled of fresh paint from the boundary lines laid out this morning. I focused on that, working to clear my head of any distractions. I tossed one boot outside the circle, and then the other. My short stockings joined them after. I took a few extra seconds to feel the dirt clinging to my bare toes before straightening up again.

With my head in the right space, I met my opponent's waiting gaze.

Camellia's lips curled tauntingly. "Are you finished? Or would you like for us to wait as you clear the lint between your toes as well?"

The Lycan spectators rumbled with low laughter.

"I'll give you that honor, *my queen*. I'll have you cowering at my feet soon enough."

The previous laughter faded to menacing growls. Casimir, who had taken his place beside Ruth as my escort, gasped loudly.

"How dare you!" He placed his hand over his heart in an aggregated look of appall. "I've never witnessed such disrespect."

"Yeah?" I scoffed. Then, I leaned my head back, building the flem in my throat as loudly as I could. With perfect aim, I spat at Camellia's bare feet, just hitting her pinky toe.

She cried out in disgust, jumping back and looking at me with malice on her face.

"Wench!" Casimir stomped towards me. He seemed to me like a child acting his part in a play, but the surrounding silence was telling. The onlookers were completely engrossed by the scene. As Casimir marched on in exaggerated anger, Ruth went to Camellia, kneeling before her to wipe my spit away with a handkerchief he produced from his jacket. Casimir started to berate me, while Ruth kept the appearance of a concerned subject attending to his distraught queen. Only I seemed to catch the glint of the bottle between his palm and his now soiled cloth.

Camellia took the handkerchief from Ruth, discreetly taking the glass vile too as she pretended to scrub more fervently on her feet. While wiping her hands down her front in exasperation, she slipped the vial into one of her satchel pockets; a satchel that was designed to stretch and stay on her body, even during a shift.

"*As we discussed, Alesta,*" Ruth's voice suddenly flitted through my head. His eyes sparkled more brightly than was normal. I could almost taste his magic on my tongue with the invasion of the mind link. "*Now it is all up to you.*"

Casimir was still yelling in my face, but it was just background noise as I locked eyes with first Ruth, and then Camellia, nodding subtly that I understood.

The board was set. Almost everything was in place.

"If this were not a challenge, I'd have you flogged right here!" Casimir continued on. "The audacity of someone like you to-"

"Are you finished?" I interrupted.

He scoffed, sputtering on his words while looking around in exaggerated movements. Once his eyes swept over Camellia a few times, he turned back to me.

"You better pray to the moon goddess above that you don't survive this, because if you do, you will meet a fate far worse than the charitable death your queen would grant you."

I leaned in close, but carried my voice loud enough for the ears of every adult being watching. "No, *you* better start praying to the moon goddess above that I don't survive this. Because if I do, it means your *noble queen*, the highest ranked creature in the kingdom, save the king, has fallen to me. Imagine what I would be capable of doing to someone like you."

The anticipation was at its height. The murmurings had ceased from all around.

Moving my sneer to Camellia, I growled, "Are you finished? Or would you like us to continue waiting as you clear the spit between your toes?"

She lifted her chin indignantly. After a long few seconds, she turned towards Lukyan, as did everyone else. Ruth may be officiating, but he couldn't mark the start of the match. The king was the last piece of this game that needed to be set.

Triston was an exact model of his father upon the podium. His face was stoic, staring down at us with only the smallest wrinkles in the corners of his eyes to show his anger. When Lukyan stood, Triston did too, his hand firmly planted in his father's.

Lukyan's gaze was heavy as he said, "Let it be known to all. The outcome of this match is irreversible. It can not be undone. Whoever holds victory by the end will reign as queen."

The following silence weighed over the crowd. Not a soul questioned his decree. Not even the council representative.

I felt his words as he added more loudly in a command, a command that glided over me, "The victor will be my mate forevermore. NO ONE shall disrespect my mate and my queen. Ever. Again."

He then looked down at Triston, a moment passing between the two, before Triston subtly nodded his head. Then Triston took a step forward. Lifting his free hand in the air, he roared in his sweet, but confident voice, "Let the match begin!"

Chapter 38

Never A Doubt

The crowd erupted at the drop of Triston's little fist. The roaring sent chills down my spine.

"Well, *little wolf*." Camellia's eyes glinted as she called me as Lukyan would. "Don't hold back."

My lip curled venomously. "Oh, I won't."

Ruth exchanged a look with his mate. They did well in their act, but from where I stood, there was no mistaking the affection in their stare.

Then Ruth looked at me. After a subtle nod, he retreated to the line where he would watch. Only Casimir remained between Camellia and me.

Casimir's expression was as arrogant as ever and his eyes sparkled with mirth. With a cheshire grin, he opened his arms to either side of him. Spinning in a slow circle, he swooped them upward repeatedly, hyping the crowd to a thunderous chorus.

Then, he raised his arms high above his head, shouting loudly, "SHIFT!"

The dirt vibrated beneath me. A sickening snapping noise joined the bloodthirsty chorus. The scent of flesh filled the air. Before Casimir was out of the way, Camellia had ripped through her elegant dress as her beast emerged. There could be nothing graceful about a Lycan's shift. It was a brutal vision, even for one as lovely as Camellia.

Her snarl was vicious, so unlike the usual kindness and giggle that spilled from her lips. There wasn't a trace of her delicate nature left.

As she circled me, still in human form, I followed her with my eyes but gazed past to see the reactions of the crowd. The Lycans were the only ones still cheering loudly. The werewolves of the pack grew quiet, looking terrified. Most had never seen a shifted Lycan. None had seen one up against a werewolf.

We were the farthest pack from the capital. The royal and Lycans had no presence here…. Until now.

My eyes caught those of every person I'd grown close to over the years. Every person who nurtured my love for the pack. Every one of them, even those that had acted cold to my son, looked terrified for me.

When I caught sight of Alpha Mullen, it sent a chill through me. Fear didn't begin to describe the look in his unfocused eyes. There was a hopelessness in his expression, like he was seeing his worst nightmare played out before his eyes.

Another earth-quaking roar erupted from Camellia. My focus returned to her. Steam clung to the discharge which was dripping from her fangs. Her eyes were pits of darkness. If not for my time as a tribute, I may have feared her too.

My gaze dropped to the small satchel still clung around her waist. It hugged her center, a bit higher than it should have naturally.

She reared back, bellowing to the sky before launching her monstrous form towards me. With my bare toes clenched into the earth, I took my stance, ready for her.

"Shift!" Maggie from the kitchen yelled above the crowd. "Shift, Alesta!"

A chorus of others joined her pleas, telling me to shift. I tuned them all out, focusing on the oncoming threat. Right before her massive form barrelled into me, I ducked, twisting my body, and slid across the ground. Crouched low a few feet away, my head jerked up, my eyes finding the strap of the satchel on her back.

With a snarl, she skidded to a stop, circling back to glare down at me with those feral eyes.

"What are you doing, Alesta?!" Gamma Kender bellowed from beneath the viewing platform. "Fucking shift!"

"Shift!" Beta Carlston yelled in a tone reserved for the biggest fuck-ups during training. He then turned to stare up at the platform. "Alpha! Command her!"

Alpha Mikken still looked lost in a nightmare. He didn't acknowledge his Beta as he stared vacantly ahead.

Beta Carlston looked expectantly at Lukyan instead. Lukyan's stony face didn't change. Even when Triston looked up at him, his expression stayed the same. His lips moved, and Triston nodded before looking back at the field with the same stoic stance as before.

"Damn it!" Beta Carlston screamed, putting all his strength into his last attempt at a command, "SHIFT!"

Camellia charged. The world around me suddenly grew silent as our eyes locked together. Her aim was high, just enough so that only I could see her true intentions. Ninety seconds. I would have ninety seconds from the time we collided.

Ninety seconds. That was it.

When she was but a breath away, I rolled forward, narrowly missing her dripping fangs. Straightening to my feet, my muscles in my legs coiled, then sprang up, flipping and twisting myself backward. Landing on her back, I grabbed the strap of the satchel, the leather cord so thin, I was sure no one else had noticed it was still on her body until I grabbed it and pulled upwards.

She roared, clawing back at me, her arms up and at the right angle for me to yank the strap the last few inches to lodge the satchel in her mouth. Her jaw clamped down on it, tearing the leather to shreds, while also shattering the glass vial from inside.

That was it. Ninety seconds. That was all we had left.

Leaping after from her, I shifted mid-air, causing the pack to break out into rejoiceful cheers.

"Finally!" Beta Carlston yelled. "Fucking hell, Alesta!"

"Focus!" Gamma Kender was toeing the line of the field, like he wanted to cross and help me. "She's coming! Watch out!"

Camellia had thrown back her head, shaking it back and forth. As the leather fell from her snout, a shimmering liquid glistened on her blackened lips. Her tongue raked over it, then a roar left her as she charged for me again.

In my wolf form, I felt invincible. As Camellia and I danced around one another, I didn't feel like a lesser being. Fighting in this form came as naturally to me as breathing. All the time I spent sparring with the Lycan tributes back at the capital came back to me. I felt more confidence in our plan than before.

Camellia's large body was much slower than my lithe wolf. Before she could get her arms around me, I'd split through her advances and sink my teeth into her flesh, tearing through her skin before skirting away. This pattern continued four times before she roared into the sky, seemingly frustrated.

It was the signal. What I had been counting down for in my head since the vial was broken.

Running full on towards Camellia, she braced herself for my attack. My teeth sank into one of her legs. I made it look like I was trying to take her to the ground by taking out her tendon, but instead, I was finally caught by her claws. A helpless yelp left me before I intentionally went completely limp. She slammed me to the ground, making the whole field quake.

Then she lunged. The Lycans cheered, and the werewolves gasped. Some started wailing and others screamed for me to get up. Even Niccola and Casimir were yelling at me from the sidelines. Or maybe they were yelling at one another. It was difficult to tell.

The only ones that kept silent were Ruth, Lukyan, and Triston. They watched steadily at what appeared to be my inevitable demise.

Right before Camellia's teeth could sink into my neck, I heard Ruth's voice in my head. "*Now.*"

My chest burned, a sign that Ruth was searing away the magic on my mate. That pain came out in a vicious growl as I twisted my body away just so Camellia's jaws could close on empty air. My mouth opened wide, locking over the place on Camellia's Lycan neck that held her mate's mark. The potion in her veins burned against my tongue.

"*I'm sorry,*" I whispered in my head, then tore away Camellia's flesh, spitting it to the muddy ground before the potion could affect me.

Then the glamor began.

Lukyan

My neck began to burn. The place that always held the illusion of a mate mark was being sizzled away to nothing. A primed canvas for a little werewolf's fresh imprints.

"She did it! She did it!" Triston leaped from my lap, throwing both fists into the air.

"Shh," I pulled him back down, then whispered in his ear, "Remember what Sir Ruth said?"

He gasped, his little eyes going wide, realizing he had just showed his authentic emotions. It took all that was in me not to chuckle at his enthusiastic expression. His acting had been flawless. This was the first time he had shown his favor for his mother. It didn't matter as much now. All eyes were on the fighting. None of the spies of the council were looking our way. Triston was insistent on being here for this match. He wouldn't take no for an answer, so precautions were taken.

"*You have a role to play as well, young Prince,*" Ruth had said to Triston this morning. "*We have to give the impression that this was a fair fight. You know your mother will win, but no one else can know. If you want to be there, you have to play along. Do you think you can do that, my prince?"*

He's been doing remarkably, given the circumstances. Even when that snake-like cretin from the council tried to join our viewing party, Triston kept quiet. I felt his anger. It matched my own after watching the man's examination of my mate. I was the one who snapped. Triston kept his eyes ahead, though he did snarl a little under his breath.

My six-year-old son was doing far better than others in attendance. Particularly one Alpha sitting just a few feet away. I almost felt pity for the man, knowing this likely brought back horrid memories of the last royal facing off with a werewolf in this pack. Ruth had kept our secrets from the Hallowed Moon leaders. They were panicking for Alesta this entire time.

They must have never seen her true skills. Battling a Lycan was nothing new for my little mate. She had proven her ability time and time again as a momentary tribute to the capital. Her Lycan adversaries were ruthless then, and she always managed to put them in their place. Even if this was a true challenge, I'd have full faith in Alesta.

One of the council appointed guards watching to the side whispered under his breath, "Did she just tear away the queen's mate mark?"

Another, sounding just as shocked, said, "I... I don't know. I didn't think that was possible. For a werewolf to-"

"SHH!" the council elder hissed. "Our queen shall prevail. Watch, you capricious fools. She's simply toying with the werewolf wench."

Camellia roared loudly towards the sky, blood trickling down her neck. The coppery stench burned my nose. She dropped her heavy hands to the ground, coming at Alesta's little wolf on all fours.

"See!" the elder scoffed. "That girl doesn't stand a chance against any Lycan, much less the mother of our-"

His words hung in the air as a sickening crunch split across the field. Everyone had gone quiet. No one in the crowd uttered a single sound.

Ruth's glamour was taking effect, creating the most disturbing of scenes.

Camellia was lying beneath Alesta, seemingly having her throat ripped out. The garbled screams died into bubbling heaves as blood poured from Camellia's lips. Life was fading from her dark eyes. By the time Alesta had finished mangling her to the point of no return, Camellia had begun to shift back to her human form.

The potion she drank would give the impression of a dead woman, when in reality she would be in a momentary slumber. Her body had likely already healed, but the glamour created the illusion of a woman maimed beyond recognition.

Alesta pranced around her, blood dripping from her pretty little snout. When she was sure she was dead in appearance, Camellia's eyes glazed over and void of life, she stood over Camellia's broken body, angling her head up and howled at the sky. With the sun setting behind the trees, it cast an otherworldly glow over the scene. Alesta looked like an avenging angel sent by the goddess herself. Her beauty mesmerized me.

"Yeah," Triston said triumphantly under his breath.

I chuckled low, running a hand over his head. "You can be happy for her now. She won. This can all be over now."

"Yeah!" He leaped up, both little arms thrust up to the sky. "Mama! Mama, you won!"

As if on Triston's cue, the rest of the werewolf pack followed my son's cheers, breaking into a union of rejoicing chants.

This was what we intended. When I had arrived, seeing the bloodlust of the crowd had given me doubts. Those doubts were all but gone.

The pack was truly happy with the outcome of the match. Not only were they rejoicing, there was a hope befallen upon them. If Alesta, a werewolf that they knew and had lived among them for years, could defeat the Queen of this kingdom, the monstrous beasts of the capital may be defeated by any among them.

That hope... that was what we needed. That would be the driving force of what's to come.

"She did it!" Triston skipped around the stage. "Alpha!" He stopped in front of Alpha Mikken, placing both of his hands on his knees excitedly hopping up and down. "She did it! Did you see? She did it!"

Alpha Mikken was frozen in shock. "She... she won? Alesta won?"

"Yeah! Look!" Triston pointed to the field.

Ruth was checking Camellia's form, his eyes swirling with unidentifiable emotion. Then he said something to Alesta's wolf, causing her to shift.

Blood covered Alesta's naked human body. I'd never seen a more enthralling sight. Ruth took her hand, raising it high into the air.

"We have our Victor! Alesta Raine of the Hallowed Moon Pack!"

The crowd was already cheering loudly, but they went utterly mad after this. The Gamma and Beta of the pack, louder than most, rushed the field. Ruth barely managed to lift Camellia's limp body into his arms and carry her out of the way before others broke through the perimeter of stunned Lycan guards.

The werewolves were all rejoicing, but the Lycans were still in shock. Save my two closest soldiers who were informed beforehand, the others had no idea this was all a farce. They believed they had truly just seen their beloved queen's death.

She may not have been my true queen, but she had been a queen, nonetheless. To our people, she was the mother of the kingdom. Most probably couldn't even fathom she would fall to a werewolf.

The Gamma lifted Alesta into the air, yelling her name proudly. My hands clenched seeing his on her bare skin.

As if she could feel my anger, her head jerked to the side, searching for me. Our eyes met, and my rage diminished by what I saw in hers. Pride. Relief. A deep affection that could conquer anything.

She won more than just the title of queen. She won the place that was already hers. No one could go against us now. She was my mate. It was time she had the markings to prove it.

"Let's go, Triston." I held my hand out for him as she danced in victory. "It's time I finally made your mother my queen."

"Did you hear that, Alpha? Mama's a queen!" Triston yelled as he jogged over to grab my hand.

Alpha Mikken stared ahead, his eyes finally gaining their focus. "She won. She really won."

I scoffed, then murmured in a low breath, "Never did I doubt she wouldn't."

Chapter 39

Meant To Be

Alesta

"**Y**ou did! My goddess, you fucking did it!" Gamma Kender was the first to reach me as I stood in a pool of blood at the center of the field. "Hell, yeah! Ah-lest-ah! Ah-lest-ah!" He started a roaring chant before lifting me into the air, setting me upon his shoulder.

I was slick with Camellia's blood. The glamour worked to give the appearance of fatal injuries, but the blood had to be real. I managed her shoulder pretty badly, waited seconds for it to heal a bit, then started the process over again until I created an undeniable mess all over the ground and me.

Looking back, I caught sight of Ruth darting away from the boisterous crowd, carrying his sleeping mate in his arms. As if he could feel my eyes, he glanced my way, then winked once before continuing on. He had to hurry with the final step of his plan before the council rep demanded to confirm her death.

We pulled this off. I couldn't believe it. The relief I felt was making me feel intoxicated.

As Gamma Kender continued to parade me around, hyping the crowd up more, I searched for the only person I wanted to celebrate with.

Lukyan. He was staring at me with such ferocity. My

satisfaction could touch the sky knowing I'd earned the place beside him. No one had given it to me. I'd fought for it. The battle may have been a stage, but the fight was very much real. Every Lycan in attendance would replay today's battle over and over again, until every corner of the kingdom knew a werewolf had won the title of queen.

That promise that once lay empty was now fulfilled. Not by Lukyan's doing, but by the careful work of Camellia and me.

Everything felt so right. The anxieties I had felt coming into this match seemed nonexistent with all those I care about exulting my victory. I truly did love this pack. I knew we couldn't stay, but leaving like this will give me peace with my decision to take my son and follow Lukyan back to the capital.

"Make way! Make way for the king!"

The crowd split as Lukyan approached with our son at his side. His expression was as hard as ever, but I felt a sense of pride in him. His topaz eyes were shining with it. I wanted to just drown in those jewels forever.

Triston's excitement could not be contained. He was pulling at Lukyan's hand, trying to speed him up. While Triston's over-anxious nature might have flustered others, Lukyan stood firm, carrying the air of a king as he drew near.

"Guess I should put you down," Gamma Kender muttered under his breath.

"Probably so," I smirked, knowing good and well that Lukyan would not approve, given my lack of attire.

The pack's cheers had died instantly, replaced by bated murmurings. All eyes followed their king's every step.

Lukyan wasn't the only royal closing in. Casimir reached me first, with Niccola at his side. Nic had a look of pride I had seen many times before. Triston and I were not the only lives that would change after this. He would be coming to the capital too. I wasn't the only one with a royal mate, though I was not sure how much longer their arrangement would last. Casimir wouldn't need a spy to watch over me and Triston any longer.

"Here, your highness," Casimir bowed to me briefly while

holding out a silk robe.

By the time I had gotten both arms through, Lukyan and my son were upon me. We stood frozen, just staring at one another for several long seconds. Then he grabbed the ties to the robe hanging at my side, yanking me forward.

With only a few inches between us, his scent overwhelmed all others, even the blood drying on my skin. His stoic stare sent a shiver down my center as he slowly tied the string of the robe together.

"Mama can tie her own ties," Triston said in a disgruntled tone, looking up at Lukyan with irritation. He tried to push Lukyan aside, but Lukyan stayed firmly in place. It was like watching a hare push against a tree.

Niccola stooped down and lifted Triston from the ground. Triston tried to protest, but Casimir pressed a finger to his lips. "Give them a moment, little prince." His eyes shimmered mischievously as he looked our way. "The king has one final duty to perform."

The

Once my robe was tied snuggly around me, Lukyan stood straight, looming over me. I held his gaze, not backing down.

Then the corner of his lips curled upward. He carefully tucked my blood-damp hair behind my ear, then grabbed my jaw to angle my head to the side.

Silence wrapped around us, creating a cocoon of heated intimacy. If I closed my eyes, I'd imagine we were the only two standing here in this bloody field.

I couldn't close my eyes, though. I didn't want to look away from the man, sending sparks over my skin.

His expression became fierce and his eyes burned as he said, "Alesta Raine. You've defeated my mate and my queen. As the victor, proclaim once more for all here to bear witness what it is you desire."

His fingers brushed over the place most sensitive to our bond. "You," escaped my parted lips. "I desire you."

The darkest, sexiest half-grin lifted his stoic features. "Then it is me you shall have."

He turned my head completely, opening my nape to be fully exposed. My breath hitched, knowing what he was about to do.

"I, King Lukyan Johann Achlyselene, declare Alesta Raine, victor of the challenge against Camellia Amara Nova, my mate," his voice deepened as he said, "and my queen. Forevermore."

Casimir, along with Niccola and the two guards who had accompanied my son, were the first to drop to their knees. Slowly, every werewolf followed. The Lycans were the last to bend the knee.

The old fart from the council was dead last. He had a mixture of shock and anger in his aged eyes. If Casimir hadn't sent him a pointed stare, I had my doubts the old man would have submitted at all.

Lukyan, focused only on me, slowly dipped his head. The warmth of his breath made my eyes close involuntarily.

"Mine," he growled possessively as I felt the brush of his fangs. Then they slowly sank into me.

A pleasurable fire surged under the surface of my skin. I whimpered, holding Lukyan's head in place. There were no reservations left inside me. This man was mine, gifted to me by the goddess herself. He was finally claiming me as his. That revelation burned hot in my soul as the bond fully formed between us.

But then another searing sensation began to overcome the intensity of the bond sewing us together. The fire in my veins grew hotter than before. So hot, it felt like some part of me was being burned away.

My eyes flew open, only for my vision to blur before a blinding brightness took it away completely. Not just my vision. Every sensation faded. The last thing I felt before being thrust into an eternal brilliance was Lukyan's fangs retracting from my nape. I tried to yell. I tried to scream. I couldn't even hear my own voice. The sensation of screaming was filtered through a groggy fog. It was like an out-of-body experience, but I could see my body to even determine if it was still there.

There was absolutely nothing.... Until there was suddenly *something* that broke through the blinding light.

"*Hello, my child.*" A voice like a dream chuckled around me. "*You have no idea how long I have waited for this moment. It's finally time now, Alesta. Time to awaken who you were always meant to be.*"

Triston

"Mama," I whispered, my throat hurting too badly to speak too loud. "Mama," a tear fell down my cheek. "Please. Please wake up."

Mama has been asleep for days. Too many days. Ever since she won the challenge, she's been lying in my father's bed, not opening her eyes or saying a word.

This wasn't what Ruth said would happen. When he told me mama would win and my father could finally make her a queen, he said nothing about her passing out the moment father would mark her.

That's what happened. After my father bit into mama's neck, she looked sleepy until her eyes went wide and she passed out. But not before she screamed; screamed like she had never been more frightened in her life.

Mama then turned into jelly, like she fell asleep standing up. Father looked so scared as he held mama and begged her to open her eyes. He's been begging her endlessly ever since.

Uncle Casimir came and got my father this morning. Uncle Nic said Uncle Casimir has been doing father's remaining duties for the inspection of the pack. Whatever that means.

The pack and everyone else thinks mama and father are doing the gross stuff new mates do after marking each other. Like, the kissing and stuff. Uncle Nic said to my father that they made the excuse that mama passed out from being really really tired after the fight. Exhaustion was the word he used.

I asked what exhaustion meant, and he said it meant someone was really really tired. Well, I'm exhausted right now. I'm exhausted and just want my mama to wake up.

"Triston," Uncle Nic said as he leaned into the room from the open door. "Your meal is here. You need to come eat."

"I'm not hungry," I muttered, curling up beside my mama on the bed.

"The kitchen brought you chocolate waffles."

"Don't want 'em." If mama can't eat, I don't want to eat either.

Uncle Nic let out a heavy sigh, then walked over to sit in the chair father uses next to the bed. "I know you're worried about your mom, Tris, but you gotta eat."

"No, I don't. Not until she does."

He hung his head in his hands, scraping his fingers into his hair back and forth, like he was trying to squeeze something out of there. "Triston, please. I don't have the energy to argue with you. Please, just eat."

"No." I wrapped my arms around mama's body, burying my face into her side. "I'm not hungry."

"Fine," he groaned, leaning back and looking away in defeat. "If you want to starve yourself, go right ahead."

"I will," I grumbled.

He shook his head. "Damn it, I need a nap. I don't have the energy for this." He pushed himself up from the chair, heading towards the door. "Your waffles will be rotting on the table when you decide to eat them."

"I won't!"

"You will. You always do. Your dad's not here to have them reheated for you, and I'm not doing it."

"Fine," I snapped, turning away. But then curiosity made me peek through the crack beneath my arms. "Where is dad anyway?"

Uncle Nic paused before he could close the door, hesitating

before he said, "Preparing Queen Camellia's body to transport back to the capital. Only he and Casimir have the rights to handle a fallen royal."

I wrinkled my nose. "But... that's not-"

"I know, Triston. I know, but we still have to..." Uncle Nic paused, pinching the space between his eyes. He then blinked at the ceiling, looked *exhausted* as he said, "Please, just eat." Then he walked away, closing the door behind him.

Uncle Nic was never that annoyed with me. It made me mad, but sad at the same time. I suddenly missed the weirdo that was always nice to me, no matter how *exhausted* he was.

I started repeating the word '*exhausted*' in my head, over and over again, letting the sounds of the letters run into one another until the word didn't sound like a real word any more. My fingers were tracing over patterns on mama's blanket when a sudden bright light made me wince.

I looked up, thinking someone had come in, ready to argue if it was Uncle Nic again, but the door was still closed. The light was coming from the other side of me.

Turning over, I gasped loudly; the sound scraping against my throat, when I saw mama's eyes wide open. There was a light glowing so brightly from them, it was hard to look at. It scared me until I realized mama's eyes were open. They were actually open!

"Mama!" I sat up, leaning over her, squinting through the brightness to catch her attention. Her eyes were open, but I couldn't see them. There was only a bright light, stronger than anything I had seen before. Looking into her eyes felt like looking into the sun.

"Mama!"

She didn't move. Lifting her hand into the air, I dropped it only to watch it fall on the bed. Her body was still asleep. Just her eyes were open.

Then her lips moved. "*Luna surget, et nox erit. Luna surget, et nox erit. Luna surget, et nox erit...*"

What? What was she saying?

"*Luna surget, et nox erit. Benedictiones avaritiae furtivae ad puerum et matrem revertentur.*"

"Mama!" I tried shaking her again.

"*Luna surget, et nox erit. Luna surget, et nox erit. Luna surget, et nox erit...*"

"Mama!"

Just as suddenly as she opened her eyes and spoke, the light went out and she went silent again.

"Mama!" I cried, shaking her shoulders.

Her eyes were closed again. She looked the same as before. Mama was awake. She had woken up! Why did she close her eyes again?

"Mama, please," I whimpered. "Please. I don't know what that means."

My throat burned like my eyes. I was about to cry when Sir Ruth startled me.

"The Moon shall rise and the night will fall," he said, leaning against the door.

"Huh?" I wiped the back of my hand across my cheeks.

"What it means; The Moon shall rise and the night shall fall. That's what your mother was saying." He smiled, his eyes doing that weird thing they always do. "*The Moon shall rise and the night will fall. Blessings stolen in greed will return to the child and mother.*"

His voice sounded different, like someone else was speaking through him. His eyes shone while he spoke, but not like mama's had. Mama's eyes were like the sun, while Sir Ruth's were like the moon.

"What does that even mean? Why isn't she waking up?"

Sir Ruth let out a low chuckle. "All in time, young prince. She's almost ready. Your mother shall wake before you reach the capital."

The capital? How can we leave for the capital if she's still like this?

"As for what it means…." Ruth's smile made me feel uneasy. "I suppose you will have to ask your mother once she wakes up."

Epilogue

Mikken

"**N**O! MOM, No!" I gasped, my tiny arms extended desperately towards the nightmare unfolding before me.

My nanny held my waist, tears streaming from her eyes as she fused me to her side. Her hand covered my face, but I could still see through the cracks of her shaking fingers.

With tear blurred vision, I watched the grotesque creature looming over my mother. My father was convulsing on the pack house steps. His gaze was violent. One command and my fearless father was rendered useless, all because a Lycan. Father helplessly watched with angry tears coating his face as the Lycan king tortured my mother.

She held firm on her resolve until the end. Not even at the start of this violence, when she still had time to reverse her rejection, did she take back those words. I screamed, as did my father, begging her to choose life.

"Life without you isn't living at all."

Those were her last words to father before the king took her in his claws and began unleashing his wrath.

First her arm, then a heap of hair still attached to a piece of her scalp. Every time the beast grabbed and tossed her in his madness, another piece of the woman I loved more than my own life was taken from me.

When she was no more than a mangled mess, he clenched her by the neck, venom dripping from his fangs as he drew her broken body closer. He sniffed her bloody face, the life drain from her eyes. At her last heaving breaths, his horrendously vicious gaze fell, as if rational just returned to him.

He looked around, horror changing his beastly features when he took in this violence. The torn pieces of her were coating the bloodied ground. He slowly shifted back, his claws retracting from her bruised flesh.

"No," the king gasped. "No. No, no, no."

He tried to shake her to life, but she was already gone.

"What have I done?"

"You killed her!" I screamed violently. "You killed her! Mom! Mom...." My throat was like sand as my voice cracked into senseless sobs.

The king clung to her, wrapping his agony while father and I had to mourn from afar. Father turned red, his teeth cracking from clenching them so hard, trying to free himself from the command.

Suddenly, a chorus of heart wrenching howls filled the sky. The mournful roars grew louder and louder until it became deafening. The king lifted his head, roaring impossibly louder than the rest. Only father was left helplessly silent, unable to break free from his invisible constraints.

The ground shook at the loss of the greatest woman in this world. All because of the greed of a Lycan king.

As if the king lost all his strength, his hold on my mother loosened until she fell limply on his lap. With shaking hands, he swept the last locks of her crimson-stained hair from her dead expression. But it wasn't my mother's face behind the bloody hair.

It was Alesta.

Alesta was lying there instead of my mother. The former king's weeping face faded to the face of his son. King Lukyan was staring down at Alesta with such anguish, my pain didn't compare.

"They killed her," he hissed brokenly.

"No," I shook my head. "You did."

∞ ∞ ∞

I gasped, a voice in my head startling me awake.

"Alpha? They're gone, Alpha. The inspection caravan just crossed the outskirts of our border."

I'd fallen asleep. I've barely slept in days, so it was no surprise I'd dozed off in my office, but instead of feeling more rested, I felt restless. My dreams exhausted me more than staying awake.

I sighed heavily, not even lifting my head up from my arm as I mind linked the border patrol back. *"Alright. Thank you for letting me know."*

The worry was palpable through the link. My mood has been affecting everyone. I cut it off before the guilt could hit me again.

"Damn it." My fingers scraped against my scalp. Alesta was gone. I didn't get to tell her goodbye. Now.... I'll probably never see her again. I should have gone to her one last time while I still had the chance.

The shock of the match between her and Queen Camellia was too much for me to move from the viewing stand. By the time I'd managed to force myself to my feet, she'd already been claimed and fainted from exhaustion.

That bastard. He'd confined Alesta to his bedroom the second he could. No one could get past his guards to wish her well, even as they prepared to leave. Even little Triston I only caught a glimpse of from afar.

My head was wallowing in self pity when another mind link came in.

"Alpha," Rachel, the office clerk, said to me. *"I, uh, have two people here to see you."*

"I'm not taking visitors today. Carl is on the training grounds. Send them there."

Rachel sounded hesitant. *"I told them that, sir, but they're insistent."*

Fucking hell, I just want to be alone right now.

"They're going to have to be insistent another day. I want-"

KNOCK KNOCK KNOCK

My office door opened before I could finish my thought or refuse. Two robed individuals with their hoods pulled over their heads stood on the other side of the threshold as Rachel fluttered about worriedly from behind. The shadows cast by their garments made it hard to see their faces.

"I'm sorry, Alpha. They wouldn't listen. I-"

"It's okay, Rachel." I glared at the two mysterious visitors.

A cheshire grin appeared below one hood as the person turned to look back. "Some tea, Miss Rachel, if you don't mind." My body froze, recognizing the voice right away. "We have much to discuss with your Alpha."

Rachel looked anxiously at me. I gave her a stiff nod, then waited for her to leave for the kitchen before speaking.

"Sir Ruth. I just received word that your party had departed for the capital. Is there a reason you've returned?"

He chuckled, pushing the hood of his cloak back to reveal his face. "Why, of course. I couldn't very well leave my *mate* behind."

He lifted a hand toward his companion. Dainty fingers appeared from behind the cloak and rested upon his. Then her hood fell back, and I stumbled from my chair, gasping loudly.

"Queen Camellia?"

There was no way the fallen queen was standing before me. I'd been present during the confirmation of her death. I had watched as her body was lovingly placed into the funeral carriage as her former Lycan subjects cried for her in grief.

She died. Everyone witnessed Alesta killing her in their challenge. How was she standing here now?

She and Sir Ruth exchanged a glance, a secretive smile igniting their eyes.

"I'm no longer a queen, Alpha Mikken. And Ruth is no longer a representative of the capital." She lifted her chin indignantly, a resolve making her graceful features harden like I would have never expected. "That life died days ago."

She pulled at the ties of her cloak, revealing her neck. There was a ghastly scar set into her flesh in the perfect shape of a wolf's jaws.

In the center, untouched by the grotesque disfigurement around it, was a preserved mate mark. It seemed untouched since its creation.

With wide eyes, I asked, "How? I... I saw her..."

Sir Ruth's telling laughter made me rethink about what I had seen that day. I had been stuck in a nightmare of my past, but I remembered certain moments. Sir Ruth, through all the preparations, and even during the actual fight, showed no concern for Queen Camellia. Why wouldn't he be worried, given his intimate relationship with the queen?

Blinded by my own nightmarish grief, I'd never thought it odd. Prince Casimir and King Lukyan himself showed no signs of grief either.

"How?" I asked again, realizing we'd all been deceived, but not knowing how.

Sir Ruth looked at the former queen Camellia, warm affection passing between the two in the form of a smile. He gave her hand a gentle squeeze, then released it, taking a step forward with his hand palm up before him.

Then his hand burst into an explosion of colorful sparks, the air growing sweet with the scent of magic.

"You're.... You're a witch..." I could hardly believe it. I'd heard of witches, as much as anyone else, but I'd never met one face to face. A werewolf and witch hybrid was unheard of.

"Bravo, Alpha Mikken," Sir Ruth chuckled. "I thought I would have to spell it out for you."

"I've never heard of a werewolf witch before," I murmured, too much in shock to take offense at his words.

The former queen gave him such a loving look as she said, "He is truly one of a kind."

"Aw. As are you, my love." Sir Ruth snapped his fingers, making a heart-shaped flume of smoke appear, lifting into the air before resting upon her head.

Her soft giggles filled the room as I tried to make sense of everything in my head.

They faked her death. But.... Why?

Sir Ruth blithely glanced my way from the corner of his eyes. "I can see the questions spinning in your head." His eyes sparkled, a sheen of magic giving them the impression of a stormy night sky.

"Why?" was all I managed to say.

Camellia grinned, stepping forward until she stood on the other side of my desk. She leaned forward, then said in a muted voice, "Vengeance, my doleful Alpha. Retribution is my purpose now."

My throat swelled with unease. "Vengeance against who?"

She chuckled darkly, and her eyes sparkled with delight. Then she took me even more by surprise as she asked, "Alpha Mikken. How would you like to help me build the greatest werewolf army this world has ever seen?"

Look For Book Two!

Splintered Moon
COMING SOON

About The Author

C. Hazlewood

Chelsie is an author based out of the southern United States. She lives with her two awesome teenagers that refer to her as "bro", her very supportive husband, and enough animals to start a small zoo. She loves the sand and surf. Her passions outside of writing include traveling, fitness and enjoying nature.

To find out more about the author and her other works, visit www.chazlewoodauthor.com

www.ingramcontent.com/pod-product-compliance
Lightning Source LLC
Chambersburg PA
CBHW030634020726
47493CB00006B/1714